CHICKS, MAN

J.D. HOLLYFIELD

For anyone who needs to hear this. You're worth it.
This one's for you.

Falling in love was the easy part.

Being secretly in love with my brother's best friend is where it got tricky.

Levi Dent was off-limits. Which was probably for the best, since he barely knew I existed.

Until one night I saw an opportunity I couldn't resist.

The problem was, I got caught.

She tricked me.

I knew there was something so familiar about her, but I just couldn't resist.

Hannah Matthews was nothing more than my best friend's little sister. Except she wasn't so little anymore.

I need to forget all about her.

If only it were that easy...

The tongue has no bones but is strong
enough to break a heart.
—Proverbs 15:1

CHAPTER ONE

Levi
Kipley and Stacey's Wedding Day

"Hell, look at all those chicks, man. It's like a flock of fucking flamingos begging for some action." Chase, one of my best friends and fellow groomsman, points out, refusing to take his eyes off the group of giggling bridesmaids huddled in the corner of the church. I pull on the bowtie strangling me and bring my eyes to the ridiculous amount of bridesmaids Stacey, Kip's bride, chose.

"Who the fuck *didn't* Stacey ask to stand up? Jesus." Ben groans, trying to count the small colony of girls, all puffed out in Pepto Bismol pink.

I give up on my tie and scrape my hands down my face. "Dude, I have no idea. I was less worried about the headcount and more like what the hell was Kip thinking when he allowed his bride to pick *pink?*"

Dammit! I tug at my bowtie again. Either my neck grew a solid inch in circumference, or Stacey ordered all our shit a size too small.

Seven months ago, our best friend since grade school, Kipley Matthews, took the plunge and asked his girl to marry him, despite Chase arguing that tying himself down would ruin our bro-power.

The four of us all grew up in the same neighborhood in small town, USA. All the same age. Kipley was always the smartest. Stuck to the books while Chase stuck to chasing girls and getting the younger classmen to help him cheat. Ben and I focused mainly on football and the occasional double dates Chase would force us to go on—he always had a new girl, and she always had a friend. Now, years of friendship later, we're all standing in Saint James Catholic Church, waiting for our boy to walk down the aisle.

"With that lineup, there's no way we can't pull an old-school *Seven Minutes in Heaven*. Just look at all those tits. It's like a buffet of nipples. I mean, ten girls, *really?*" Chase grabs for his dick, and I punch him, shaking my head. Stacey is two years younger. Was top of her class and very popular. I'm actually shocked she only has ten. There are a few familiar faces from high school. Kendall Brice, a former cheerleader, now married with kids. Kristen Mills, girl voted most likely to end up at a strip club. Rebecca Fritz, the world's biggest bitch.

As soon as the thought flashes in my mind, Rebecca hip-bumps the girl next to her. *Always has been and always will be a bitch.* I glower at Rebecca, realizing it's little Hannah Matthews, Kip's younger sister, as she catches herself before tripping over her too-long, pink puff-of-a-disaster. Hannah brushes her over-curled chestnut hair away from her face and tucks it behind her ear, her doe eyes frustrated and plump lips pouty. My curiosity piques, taking note of her missing braces and little girl features before my eyes wander shamelessly to her chest. Her tits sure have made their appearance since the last time I saw her. Wow, when did little Hannah Banana grow up? My dick twitches, and I close my eyes, raking my hands back down my face. What the hell has gotten into me?

"Kristen still looks like a fuckin' stripper. I bet she would meet me in the closet for seven minutes. Ride me like she used to in high school." I smack Chase. We're in a damn church, and god forbid Kip or Stacey's family overhears our conversation.

"What? You know you're thinking the same thing. Weddings are meant for people to get laid. And it's happening. Just like old times. Who are you targeting? Didn't you use to have a thing for Kendall? I bet she would suck you off—"

This time, I punch him in the side. "She's fucking married with two kids. Seriously, grow up," I huff in frustration. The last thing on my mind is getting laid. Not since Teresa broke up with me—*after* finding someone to take my place.

Ben steps forward, placing his hand on my shoulder. "Man, don't even think about that cheating ex of yours. She didn't deserve you." She most definitely didn't. All that bull crap about women wanting a nice guy is just that. When they get one, they never fail to take advantage. I offer Ben an appreciative nod. Unlike Chase, who comprehends nothing about having a relationship longer than twenty-four hours, Ben's like me. I was able to confide in him when shit hit the fan and I caught Teresa with another guy in *our* bed. I almost let her convince me what she did was a mistake and she loved me. Fortunately, I wised up—then I kicked her cheating ass out.

"Okay, fine. Geez, you don't need to be a pussy about it. Might as well go for little Hannah Banana Matthews. Just as plain as she used to be, but damn, did she grow some tits." Chase laughs, and my brows draw together, my frustration building. I'm not sure why I care. I never had before when he'd poke fun at Kip's little sister. "Oh, what? Have I upset you? Do you *want* to hit little Matthews, Dent?" Both Ben and Chase gape at me, and I have no idea why it takes me so long to respond. God no, I don't want to do anything with Hannah Matthews—the little runt with braces who used to bug the shit out of us when we were kids. I pull my eyes away, making the mistake of landing them back on Hannah.

She's standing behind the group of girls, trying to squeeze into a photo. Rebecca is making it impossible, and Stacey is too far away to assist. I glower once again at Rebecca.

"You *are* looking at little Hannah Matthews. That's bad. We need to get you laid tonight, bro." Before I can retaliate, Agnes, Kip's grandmother, walks up.

"It's time, boys."

CHAPTER TWO

Hannah

"Oh em gee, because we're chicks, man. How else are we going to get their attention? It's obvious they're into at least one of us. Look at Chase Steinberg. Remember that guy? Huge slut in high school, but holy hell could he fuck," Kristen, one of Stacey's close girlfriends, blurts out at another girl I don't remember.

I gasp at her vulgar choice of words, tossing my hair out of my face to get a good view of Chase, one of my brother's best friends. I haven't seen any of these guys in years. Probably since they all left for college. By the time they all graduated, it was my turn to test out the big leagues University, and our paths never crossed again. Chase looks the same. Typical playboy. Sandy hair whisked back. He appears more toned than he had in high school, and his eyes still scream he'll do anything with a heartbeat.

I recognize Ben, one of Kipley's nicer friends. Still buff in an athletic sort of way. Chestnut hair, short crewcut, and eyes you can get lost in. There are a few I don't recognize. College friends, I assume. When my eyes land on Levi Dent, my breath stalls. *Levi Dent.* Former football legend. And it's not because he was the number one pick for every college across the state…or that he won the title for First League Division three years in a row. It's because, on top of being the best athletic star to ever attend Breckinridge High School, he was also the nicest. The town sweetheart.

Levi Dent always had a girlfriend. He never slept around, un-like the rest of Kipley's friends, and he never spoke an ill word to me. He may have never really spoken a word to me *period*, but it was better than the teasing the rest of his friends did. *Hannah Banana Matthews*. The stupid nickname Chase Steinberg be-stowed on me when I was young. The stupid name that stuck with me all through high school. Thankfully, by the time I left for col-lege, I lost the braces, grew some curves—*kind of*—and lost my baby face. *Mostly*.

I stop trying to eavesdrop on the girls' conversation and sit down at the head of the table where Stacey reserved me a spot next to her. I lay my purse down and squat just in time for the chair to be stolen out from underneath me.

"What in the…?" I cock my head to see Rebecca, the devil witch, behind me.

"I don't think so, honey. Your seat is all the way at the end. I get to sit next to my girl." I want to tell her she's wrong. I mean, even the nametag on the table says this is my seat. My tiny palm itches to smack her fat fake lips right off her ugly over-Botoxed face, but I chicken out.

Because I am what they call me: timid little Hannah.

"Sure, you can sit here," I reply, grabbing my purse. I shift my body toward Stacey to tell her I'm moving, but she's talking to a relative, and I don't want to disturb her. I barely take two steps before Rebecca is pushing *my* chair back in its place. It doesn't fail, with my luck, the chair catches the bottom of my dress as I walk away. A loud tear ripples through the air, severing the back of my gown.

Dread fills my stomach. I gaze behind me, my cheeks heating with embarrassment. A cool breeze instantly assaults my back-side. I stare at the back of my dress. The rip is all the way up to my butt, exposing my white lace underwear.

Kristen gasps as Rebecca investigates her handywork, laugh-ing and pointing. "Oh my god! I thought only old people wore full underwear!" Her comment riles the rest of the wedding party. Peels of laughter sound out at my wardrobe malfunction.

I'm frozen in place, the humiliation paralyzing my legs. I should be used to being treated so poorly by this group. Stacey's friends were always so horrible to me. Kip's friends weren't any better. A stupid part of me thought time and distance would allow them to finally see me as a human being, not Kip's annoying little sister. My lower lip starts to quiver, and I fight with everything I have not to cry.

"Oh, Hannah, let me help you." Stacey jumps into action, snapping me out of my horror trance. Grabbing my dress, she holds the material together. "There's an emergency sewing kit in the ladies' room. Let's get you all fixed up."

Stacey guides me past the head of the table where each one of her stupid friends laughs and hollers. She throws a few glares their way, but it doesn't hinder the sounds of jokes and clapping echoing down the hall. Once inside, she drops my dress and reaches for the basket sitting on the sink. "Here it is." She adjusts herself, bending down to observe the tear.

Guilt washes over me at seeing her kneeling in her wedding gown. "Oh, Stacey, you don't have to do this. I can fix it. Please, this is your wedding. Go back to the table."

She smiles up at me, her eyes filled with love. "Not a chance. You're my sister now. We stick together." Her comment makes me lose my battle. My eyes fill with tears as I barely choke out a thank you, allowing her to pin up the back. Once she's done, she stands, nodding in approval. "There. Good as new…kind of." Her silly smile makes me break out of my sullen mood, offering a small laugh in return.

"Thanks, Stacey."

"No need to thank me. We're family." I can't hold back the tears that start to fall. "Hey, none of that." She grabs a Kleenex and hands it to me. "Han, please. Don't let them get to you. You're amazing and beautiful. Sometimes people who have their own insecurities pick on people they feel threatened by."

That gets a cynical laugh out of me. "And what exactly do *I* have that they don't?" This should be a good one.

Stacey places her hands on my shoulders. "You have a natural beauty so many girls would sell their soul for. You have a heart of gold. And one day, you're going to use that smart mind of yours to do so many great things."

Stacey squeals when I wrap my arms around her and squeeze, catching her off guard. "Thank you," I whisper, needing her words more than she'll ever realize. Her arms lift, and she accepts my embrace. We stay like that for a few seconds, until I feel more composed, then pull away.

"You should get back out there."

"I'll wait with you—"

"No. It's your wedding. Enjoy. I just want to freshen up. Plus, I'm sure they're ready to start the speeches. I'm totally fine now. I'll be right out. Promise." She eyes me warily, but accepts my words and heads back to the hall. I totally had my fingers crossed. I don't plan on going back out there anytime soon.

I've been hiding in the bathroom for over an hour. My stomach growls because I missed dinner. I was also a no-show for the speeches, but there was no way I was standing up to face everyone now. I couldn't stop the anger and embarrassment. I should have told Stacey how I truly felt. How her friends are bullies. How they've picked on me since I was little. But I said I was *fine*. I'm far from it.

How can someone be so cruel?

Easy.

High school is something I've tried to block out. I wasn't pretty. I didn't have boobs. I was lightyears away from being on anyone's popularity radar. I was the butt of everyone's joke. I got teased, made fun of, bullied. I was a complete nobody. If there had ever been a life or death situation and someone asked what my name was, we'd all be in big trouble. Even my teachers referred to me as Kipley Matthews' little sister. Awesome, right?

Not.

Eventually, I went to college, which turned out to be the best thing that happened to me. Everyone finds themselves in college, and I was no exception. I found a new style, boobs, Sephora, and friends. I actually found a few boyfriends, and believe it or not, at one point, lost my virginity. Can't say it was anything great. My boyfriend at the time was drunk. Thirty seconds in, he finished and passed out. But I got the experience and finally got to say I wasn't a virgin anymore.

After so many years, I hoped when I came home things would be different. I wouldn't feel the sharpness of their nastiness. Maybe they would all grow out of their bitch phase. Clearly, I was wrong.

I bang my heeled foot against the bathroom stall, still angry at the way Rebecca treated me. I wasn't that measly little girl who let people pick on her like in high school. I grew a backbone—*some-what…*—and I wasn't going to take shit from these mean girls who thought it was okay to push me to the side. I huff, swiping a tear off my cheek, even more upset I'm allowing them to get to me. I wipe another tear as the bathroom door opens and a flock of giggling girls walk in.

"Oh my god, did you see the way they were practically licking their lips! They want us. I am so in." *Rebecca.*

"I say you take Chase up on his offer. Why the hell not? To get laid by Levi Dent…man, can you even imagine? It's like getting your high school wish finally granted!" *Kristen.* My ears perk at the mention of Levi's name. As quietly as possible, I climb on top of the toilet seat so they don't see me.

"I'm totally doing it. I'll meet Levi in any closet for an old school game of Seven Minutes in Heaven," Rebecca says, her over-glossed lips smacking together. I peek through the tiny slit in the stall door, my curiosity in full affect. *Seven Minutes in Heaven? With Levi?*

"Okay, so tell me exactly what he said. I was too busy giving Ben *let's fuck* eyes," Kristen says, smearing tacky red lipstick over her lips.

Rebecca primps her hair, puckering her lips some more, and says, "Chase said Levi is feeling down and needs to get laid. Apparently, his girl cheated on him. Simply asked me if I was up for the challenge. If so, meet him in the supply closet three doors down from the left in twenty minutes. He would be waiting for me—and bam! I take Levi Dent for the ride of his life." She giggles, the sound like nails on a chalkboard. I'm disgusted at how his friend can set him up like that. Levi is not like them. He's kind and friendly, polite and actually has manners—unlike everyone else Kipley associates himself with.

"Wow, girl. So jelly. I've always heard rumors Levi is as good in bed as he is at football." All the girls moan, including me—a silent groan of appreciation for my childhood secret crush. Is now a good time to confess it was a *huge* crush? Possibly borderline unhealthy? Not that I was the only one. I had to step in line with every single other girl in his high school class when it came to Levi Dent. He's the perfect guy. Dark hair, green eyes, muscles on top of muscles. And it's not only his appearance—it's all of him. I'm just as guilty of having those fantasies and wishes. The blushed cheeks I couldn't hide for the life of me whenever he came over, always fantasizing about him doing something extremely naughty to me.

I bite on my hand to stop myself from giving myself away. Each one tosses their lipstick-blotched Kleenexes into the trash, and a gust of music flows into the bathroom as one of the girls opens the door.

"Don't worry, I'll be the first to report. When I meet him in the supply closet in exactly twenty minutes, I'll make sure to snap a pic of his prize-winning cock." The flock of giggles exit, and the bathroom once again becomes silent.

Dropping to my feet, I open the door and take a good look

at myself. "God, no wonder people make fun of me. I resemble goddamn Curly Sue." I groan, pulling on my stupid hair Mom insisted I get curled. I run my fingers through it to help loosen the mess, then grab some pins from the emergency basket and fix it, along with the makeup my tears ruined. A pathetic part of me wishes it was me meeting Levi in the supply room. Of course, he would never willingly choose someone like me.

Unless he didn't know.

I arch my shoulders, an insane plan starting to form in my *insane* head. If I got caught, I would be toast. But if I didn't… What do I have to lose?

An *I'm out of my mind* giggle travels up my throat, and I cover my mouth.

One of us would be getting their wish granted tonight.

And I would be doing Levi a favor.

Kind of…

CHAPTER THREE

Levi

I trip into the bar, and Kip grabs at my bicep. "Whoa, you good, man? You've been drinking a little heavy tonight." A worried expression mixes into Kip's drunk gaze. He shouldn't be worried. I haven't felt this loose in ages. After Teresa left me, I couldn't sleep, eat, and my work started suffering. I just needed to find an outlet to release all the pent-up anger I've been harboring. I thought I loved her. God, was I wrong. That wasn't love. It was desperation.

"I'm fine. Just enjoying myself." I slap my hand on the bar to steady myself and empty the rest of my gin and tonic. I peer around in hopes of spotting someone who will take my mind off my ex. Mid-sweep of the room, my eyes land on little Hannah Matthews scurrying across the dancefloor like a girl on a mission. Her cheeks are flushed, as they always are, her full chest bouncing up and down. *I bet she has nice nipples.* The perfect sized breasts. I bet when a man makes her come, she squeals that little timid sound she always made when she was younger and got excited about things her brother would tell her. *What the fuck am I doing?*

I swipe my hands over my face, trying to snap out of it. God, I must need to get laid if I'm standing here wondering how good little Hannah Banana Matthews would squeeze my dick if I made her come. I rotate, requesting a refill from the bartender, when a large hand lands on my shoulder.

"I've got a surprise for you," Chase says from behind me. I loop back around to see him smiling like a fucking idiot—which is never a good thing.

"No thanks, whatever it is," I reply, giving my attention back to the bar.

"No way, dude. You'll want this surprise. *Trust me.*" I turn back. His eyes gleam with trouble. I don't even want to fathom what he's set me up for. Just as I'm about to decline again, Ben walks up.

"Yo, change of plans." We all stare at Ben, me more out of curiosity.

"Change of *what* plans?" My eyes narrow on my two best friends who seem guilty as fuck.

"Bro, you are going to thank us. We just set you up with a hot chick. She's not going to ask you to hold hands, meet her parents, and snuggle. She's going to fuck you like you need, then she's going to leave. No attachments. Simply a place to get your dick wet." Chase smiles, and I instantly want to object. I am not that guy. I'm not a person who can just have sex with a girl. I appreciate those hand holding moments, the closeness of a good snuggle, the scent of a woman you want to have in your arms. God, I *am* a fucking pussy.

"Just say yes. This chick? She's going to make all your problems disappear." Ben's about to burst out laughing. "Chicks, man. Think about how much your sad, lonely dick wants to be inside one," Chase pokes.

And fuck, he's right. My dick does want to be in someone.

"*Do it, do it...*" both Chase and Ben begin to chant. Kipley laughs...until everyone shuts up and Stacey walks toward us.

"Hello, boys, what's so funny?" She smiles, wrapping her dainty arms around Kip.

Chase steps forward. "Oh nothing, just trying to fix Levi up with a nice girl."

Stacey's warm smile spreads across her face. "That's sweet.

Anyone would be grateful to have you, Levi." Her kindness sobers me some. It's that kindness, my *own* kindness, that got me into this position. God, with every single girlfriend I've ever had. "Well, hope you boys don't mind, but I'm going to steal my husband for a quick dance." Kip bends down, sweeping his wife off her feet, and we all watch as he carries her to the center of the dancefloor.

Fuck being the nice guy.

I face the bar, slamming the drink the cute bartender refilled for me, then face Chase. "Fuck it. I'll do it."

Chase howls, and Ben slaps me on the shoulder. "You're gonna love this. Go to the left and meet her in the supply closet, third door down—"

"Change of plans. Opposite direction. Go *right*, three doors down," Ben cuts in.

Chase looks at Ben, confused, and Ben shrugs. "That's what Hannah Banana just told me. Other room was locked or some shit."

"*Hannah* told you this? Since when does she—you know what? Whatever. *Right*, three doors down. She'll already be in there and ready. Enjoy, buddy. And make sure to wrap it up!" Chase laughs, pushing me away from the bar.

I stumble away from the bar, but manage to swing around and give them both the middle finger. I walk out of the banquet room into the large foyer. So, little Hannah Matthews is in on this, huh? I wonder if she thinks I'm a pig. She probably wishes it was her I was coming for. I always noticed the way she looked at me. Her constant flushed cheeks. Her gawking. God, I bet she definitely wishes this was her. Fuck, I probably wouldn't say no if I found her little self waiting for me in the supply room. But then I remember she's still Kip's little sister and he would kill me. She's also still little Hannah Matthews.

I begin to repeat the directions out loud so my drunk brain understands. I can't believe I'm actually going through with this, but maybe I've been doing things wrong the whole time. No attachments, no feelings—just physical.

I knock softly on the door, letting this chick know I'm here. I wait under five seconds before opening the door and closing it behind me, leaving me in pitch-black.

"Hello?" The low sound of measured breaths confirms I'm not alone. "You going to come here, or do I have to come to you?" I start unbuttoning my shirt, fumbling with my buttons. Two small hands startle me as they wrap around mine, assisting me with my shirt. The delicate scent of flowers and vanilla permeates around me. It's girly and light, and damn if it doesn't make my dick spring to action.

"God, you have soft hands. And you smell good." My words throw me off guard. I didn't mean for my thoughts to be spoken out loud. I'm not here to praise this girl. Only fuck. *Stick to the plan, Levi.* I release my grip and allow her to take control. Having her so close, I become anxious, my hands greedy to learn the curve of her waist. I grip at her hips, my palms touching bare flesh. She's already partially undressed. Her skin is warm and inviting, I use my thumb to caress right below her navel, causing her body to shiver.

"Are you nervous, baby?" I whisper, dipping my head down, filling my lungs with her scent. I place my lips to the lobe of her ear. Her fingers stall on my shirt, her quick intake of breath answering for her. The booze is making my tongue loose, so I push her more. "Or are you just as eager as I am to fuck?"

The voice is me, but those words aren't. This is supposed to be mindless. The Levi who spends too much time doting on a woman only to get shit on in return is gone. *Get what you want from her, get out, then drink until the night becomes a blur.*

The chick doesn't reply. She doesn't slap me either for being so crude. She remains silent, her hands working faster on my shirt. When the last of my buttons are undone, she goes for my pants. The way her small hands graze down my chest, the feel of her fingers working the button…I'm hard as fuck and need to explore more of her.

I'd normally be patient and enjoy letting a woman undress me, but the liquor is starting to call the shots and I'm suddenly in no mood to take our time. Unsure of the space factor, I step forward, picking her up. She squeals softly at my unexpected move, and I silence her with my mouth. I press my lips to hers. They're soft and full and taste like cherry and champagne. The silkiness over mine is perfect. I part her lips, linking my tongue with hers. She's hesitant at first, then kisses just as intensely.

"Fuck, you taste sweet. Do you fuck just as sweet?" God, what is up with my vulgar mouth? I break away and bring my lips to her neck. Her skin is velvety smooth. In just a few seconds, I've become an addict, craving a taste of every single part of her. Her breathing is heavy, giving away how aroused she already is. I bring us to a stop as her back hits a shelf and her legs wrap around my waist. I lick and suck on the flesh above her shoulder blade when a small moan filters through the room and my dick fucking jolts. God, that sound. It's like fucking heaven.

"You enjoying this, sweetheart?" Because I am. Way too much. I trail my hand down her taut stomach, wrapping my fingers around her cotton panties, and dip inside. I groan when I find her wet as fuck. Bypassing any pretense of being a gentleman, I slide in one thick finger. Her moans are messing with me, so sweet and needy. Her body trembles in my arms, her warm cunt squeezing around my finger. "Greedy little thing, aren't you?" I say, even though I'm the greedy one. The urge ignites inside me to throw the lights on so I can stare into her eyes, needing to know if they're a mysterious brown or emerald green. Light shade of sky blue or dark as night. I bet she's as beautiful as she feels.

I pump in and out, then take her mouth again, shoving my tongue inside. She returns my kiss with fervor, her legs squeezing tighter around me, her tongue dancing around mine. God, this chick is intoxicating. I pull my lips away and kiss a trail to the center of her tits. Plump and perfect. I suck her nipple through her lace bra, and her hands dive into my hair, gripping against my scalp. The pressure, along with her hard nipple, is the perfect combination. I thrust harder inside her. With each little whimper, my dick throbs, and I increase my speed.

I moan, lifting my mouth from her nipple. "Fuck, you're tight—and so wet," I rasp before capturing the other. Her sexy as fuck moans tell me she's close. Her pussy hugs my finger in a death grip and I pick up the pace, thrusting another inside her. I feel her clench, then her body quakes in my arms. She throws her head back, hitting the shelf, and I smash my lips against hers as she rides out her orgasm.

Her scent fills the room, and I fight not to bring my fingers and my mouth to taste her. My mind is spinning. I'm not sure I can go through with this anymore. One-night stands aren't me. I don't feel right having sex with this chick in a supply closet without even catching her name.

I slowly let her legs fall until her feet touch the ground. What I wouldn't give to get a look at her. My hand reaches out in search of her face, finding her cheek warm to the touch. She surprises me by leaning into my palm. "We don't have to do this. We can just—"

She shocks me for a second time by pushing my hand away and slamming her lips against mine. I take what she's giving, basking in the feel of her. My hands become urgent, pulling her body into mine. I kneel, sliding her panties down her legs and run my nose along her seam, inhaling her scent. Just as I thought. Sweet. I stand, pushing my own pants down, but not before grabbing the condom Chase slipped in my back pocket. I slide the condom down my cock, wishing I could see her face—if lust blazes in her eyes.

"Last chance to back out, sweetheart. Otherwise, you're all

mine until I'm done with you." My voice is laced with desire. I don't think I could back away from her even if she told me no.

Her warm hands lift and wrap around my neck, her breasts pressing against my abs as she stretches. I lift her into my arms again, and her legs wrap around my waist. She brings her soft lips back to mine. I'm not sure if it's the alcohol creating this animalistic compulsiveness in me, but I want—no, *need*—to consume this chick. I increase the pressure of our kiss, pressing her body tighter to mine, no longer able to hold off.

I work my hand around my cock, placing myself at her entrance, waiting for final approval. She thrusts her hips into me, and the final string of control snaps and I drive into her. Our moans mingle as one as I push deep. I pull out, and slam back in, craving the deepness of her. Her needy cunt wraps around me, and I lose control. I thrust into her over and over, her sexy pants adding gasoline to my burning desire.

Everything about this mystery chick has me so worked up. The anticipation of finding out who she is. Learning everything about her. Fuck, typical me, already thinking about asking her out after this. The more I pump into her, riding the high of her, the more I want—no *need*. I can't have this girl once and be done. My eager dick won't allow it.

"Fuck, you're squeezing me tight," I growl, anticipating her pending orgasm. Her moans become louder, her breathing unsteady. When she begins to clench around me, I maneuver my finger to her clit and press down. It's then she loses her fight and comes undone around me.

"Oh, Levi!" Her soft, desperate cry filters through the room, and I pound once, twice, three times before coming like a goddamn rocket inside her.

My chest heaves, trying to catch my breath, my mind still foggy as I come down from the best sex I've had in a long time. I release my grip on her and pull out, allowing her legs to fall. She stands, and I pull the condom off, knot it, and toss it in a corner.

"I get this was a one-time thing, but you're amazing. I'm not normally like this. Maybe we can exchange—"

She doesn't allow me to finish and pushes me to the side, searching for something. The sound of shuffling material is her only response. She's slipping her dress back on.

I begin to dress as well. "I know this was a casual thing. I don't normally do this…" She continues to hurriedly dress, tripping over the long material. I reach forward to steady her. "Maybe just a name?"

The only response I get is the sound of the commotion as she tries to get herself back into her dress. My brows knit at how unaffected she's acting. I'm not a jerk, so I step forward, offering her my assistance. "Fine. Let me at least find the light and help you into your dress—"

"No!" Her voice booms throughout the supply closet.

I freeze. So does she. Panic fills the small room as she continues to fumble.

"What—who are you?" I ask, my tone suddenly serious. I recognize that voice, but in the heat of the moment, I can't pinpoint who. I reach for the light again, and she makes another wrong move.

"Levi, no!"

No fucking way.

Shock. Anger. Denial. It all hits me at once. They wouldn't do this to me. Set me up like this.

She doesn't say another word. She knows she's caught.

I shuffle to find the light switch as she tries to scurry past me. "I don't think so," I tell her. Not before I get that light on. My stomach drops as my fingers scrape against the wall, searching for the damn switch. My heart is pounding for a whole other reason. "Fuck," I growl, impatient. My mind races. Images of us as kids. Her running rampant, annoying us. The summer I stayed with them. "Fuck!" If I flip on that light and see—

That's when she kicks me.

"Ouch!" I yelp as I grab for my shin. The door opens, light blasting through, causing my vision to strain, but I only need the sliver of light to recognize the tiny girl, her curls in disarray. I grunt as I race toward the door, shielding my sensitive eyes. Just as she veers the corner, I recognize her.

Hannah fucking Matthews.

CHAPTER FOUR

Hannah
Three weeks later…

"Are you sure I can't convince you to stay? A person with your smarts and ambition…I would pay triple what your father's offering."

I laugh at Professor Fischer, my mentor and former colleague. Double majoring in international business and business law wasn't the easiest, but Mr. Fischer's been there for me since day one. I came to college with the ambition to study business law. My goal from the start was to come back home and work for Matthews and Associates, my dad's law firm.

"If I'd majored in Criminal Justice, I would love to. Since I didn't and I've been wanting to work at my dad's firm since I was, like, five, I have to sadly turn you down." I pat him on the shoulder. "But thank you. It means a lot that you would fight the education system to pay me three times more than I'm worth to keep me around." We both laugh as I gather up my sample testimonials from the internship course. After graduation I stayed working under Mr. Fischer as his aide. My dad would have taken me under his wing instantly, but I wanted to be ready. I wanted to make him proud.

"Well, know the offer always stands. We'll miss you around here. You're destined to be somebody great. There's no doubt about that." My eyes begin to shine with unshed tears. This has been my home for the last four and a half years. This building. This classroom. I blossomed here. Gained my wealth of knowledge. I aspired to be a *leader* here. And in less than three hours, I'll be headed back home and my life here will be a thing of the past.

I jump at Mr. Fischer and hug him tightly. "Thank you," I reply, hiding the tears that have escaped.

"Now, now, don't get all soft on me. Be the Hannah Matthews I watch in the classroom. The fierce, determined young lady who, when she's in her element, scares me."

I laugh. "I'm anything but fierce."

"I'm only speaking the truth. Make sure to bring out that fierceness more often. Now…" we break apart, "if you don't get out of here, you're going to be late for your celebration barbeque."

I nod. My parents are throwing me a welcome home/graduation party, and if I don't get on the road soon, I'll hit traffic and miss it.

I say no more, grab my things, exit the law building, and get in my car. I brought most of my things home three weeks ago when I went home for Kipley's wedding, so whatever was still lingering in my apartment is now stuffed inside my tiny Honda Civic. I toss my computer bag in my passenger seat and climb in. I suck in a deep breath, fighting back the tears as I pull away, the law building soon in my rear-view mirror. Over four years of my life is about to become my past as I indulge in an exciting future at Matthews and Associates. All gassed up and ready to dive into the unknown of the real world, I crank up my music, my favorite chick band blaring from my speakers, and cruise down the highway toward home.

The past three weeks have been a whirlwind. Between keeping myself busy with my final weeks of my internship and making sure I close this chapter of my life, it's also been a fighting battle not to replay the memories of my brother's wedding. Specifically, the night in the supply closet with *him*.

Levi Dent.

The second the door opens, I bolt. I shouldn't have said any-thing—should have kept the silent act going. But then, what was going to happen once we left that room? How was he not going to acknowl-edge it was me? I didn't think that far ahead when I put this whole plan in motion.

I make it down the hallway, catching a glimpse of a silhouette standing outside the supply closet before whipping around the corner and slamming into someone. Kipley wraps his arms around my shoul-ders, catching me before I go down.

"Hey, slow down, little sister. Where you off to in such a hurry?" I look up to see my brother smiling, his cheeks flushed and eyes confirm-ing he's been a bit overserved.

"Uh…nothing. I…uh, I need to pee. Really bad." I try wiggling out of his grip, my panic rising.

"You're going the wrong way. The bathroom is this way." He at-tempts to twirl me back to where I just came from. Fear rises in my throat. If I don't free myself from Kipley's grip, I'm done for. I can't let Levi catch up to me.

"Geez, kiddo. Why so feisty? Hey, Levi, can you show my sister—"

I kick my brother as hard as I can in the shin.

"Ouch! Shit, what the hell did you do that for?"

I don't answer because I'm already running past him into the banquet room. I get lost on the dance floor and pop out on the opposite side. I weave through family and strangers, thankfully exiting out the side door. My heart races so fast, I worry it's going to jump out of my chest. I run down the hallway to the stairwell, not bothering with the elevator. I climb up five flights before my lungs finally give out and I collapse against the cement wall.

Bringing my hands up, I run them through my hair, wiping the thin layer of sweat building on my forehead. My hands shake as I attempt to pull my hair into a ponytail, not caring it'll mess up my ridiculous hairstyle, then place my palms over my beating heart.

"Holy cow," I pant, trying to catch my breath.

I did it.

"Holy flipping cow!" I begin to laugh at myself. I just had sex with Levi Dent. I shake my head, my laughter transforming into more of a cackle. The sound of a door opening a few flights below me has me throwing my hands over my mouth, holding my breath. The clanking of heels hitting the concrete stairs, and I continue to hold my breath while they make it to the floor below me and exit to the floor.

I slide down the wall, taking in a deep breath. My legs are still shaking. I close my eyes, the blackness a reminder of the supply closet. I wrap my arms around my stomach, brushing against my tender breasts. I bring my knees up to my chest, the soreness between my legs prominent. I can still feel his strong hands all over my body, raking over my skin. With every touch, squeeze, pinch, he brought me to places I've never been. His seductive words set my skin on fire. His lips were so soft and greedy as he kissed, sucked, bit. The feel of him inside me, his moans, his praises…it was more than I could ever fantasize. Better.

I didn't want it to end. I could have stayed in that closet forever.

But then, he had to bring reality to its head. He asked for more. I was right when I said I didn't think past getting Levi in that room. I didn't think how I would get out of the room without exposing myself. But I knew once those words left his lips, I was already caught. He wasn't going to allow me to slip through without being identified.

God, I wish I could have told him it was me without judgement.

But that was just a fantasy.

So I ran.

The doors open again, and laughter echoes throughout the stairwell. I jump to my feet and run two more flights before I exit onto the seventh floor and run to my room.

The drive home is quick. I got on the road in time to miss the mid-afternoon traffic. Downloading an audiobook the night before kept my attention. Pulling into my childhood neighborhood, I take a left onto Clinton Street and wave at Mr. Johansson, our old science teacher from high school. The sun is out, and the trees are in full bloom. Growing up in an older neighborhood, the trees are thick and overgrown, creating a beautiful tunnel of greenery. Taking a right onto Fairview, my house comes into view and I groan at the cars lined up down the street. "Small family party my butt," I mutter.

I park my car in the driveway and spot Stacey's car and my brother's Tahoe first. I haven't talked to him since the wedding. To be on the safe side, I was up early and gone before anyone saw me. I texted Mom telling her I had to get back to school and skip the champagne brunch. My brother called a few times before he left for his honeymoon, but I declined each one. I couldn't bear to answer any questions or have him yell at me for what I did.

But his messages were always kind. And no mention of Levi. He didn't know. Levi didn't tell. But why?

As much as it ate at me wondering, there was no way I was going to dig into the whys. I needed to leave it alone. Avoid. Deny. Ignore.

I grab for my computer bag and jump out of my car. I trek up the driveway, enjoying Mom's hibiscuses blooming gorgeously. Opening the front door, my mom spots me instantly.

"My baby is home!" she yells, scurrying toward me and pulling me into her motherly hug. "Congrats, baby. I'm so proud of you."

I wiggle out of her hold. "Thanks, Mom. I thought you said family only," I mutter low. There are way more people than expected.

She lifts her arm to wave off the crowd. "Everyone is family. And here to celebrate you. You're right on time. Dad just put the burgers on. Come." She wraps her arm around my waist, dragging me through the house to the backyard. The moment my dad sees me, he starts hollering.

"The graduate returns!" He laughs, bringing me in for his big dad bear hug. He kisses me on my head. "Welcome back, baby girl. Mom and I couldn't be prouder of you." I wrap my arms around him and close my eyes, trying to ward off the tears. I love my dad. He's been my mentor for as far back as I can remember. I've wanted to follow in his footsteps since I understood what lawyer meant.

And to imagine I'll be working at the company he built from the ground up makes me shine with pride.

"Thanks, Daddy." He offers me one more kiss to my temple and releases me.

"Perfect timing. Burgers are almost done. Get a drink, say hello to your grandmother and Aunt Getty." He goes back to tend to the grill as I reach for the cooler on the patio and grab a cold beer.

I spend the next ten minutes listening to my grandma complain about her arthritis, and then Aunt Getty who felt it necessary to tell me she's been constipated for three whole days now. Kipley thankfully saves me by snatching me away and pulling me into his chest, messing up my hair. I try to swat him off, but since I'm like a little mouse compared to him, it's useless.

"Look who's home. Congrats, little sis." He smiles, lifting me up and spinning me.

"Kip, put me down," I whine, hating that he always has to treat me like a little kid. He does as I ask, but goes back to messing up my hair. "Kip, stop," I groan again. I don't have the perfect hair genes like Kip and everyone else. I was blessed with Grandma's wild genes, and my hair is always a frizzy disaster. My school schedule had been so hectic, I never had a chance to do anything but wrap it up in a messy bun, but today, I took the time to flat iron it. I would prefer my brother not turn my head into a beehive before I say hello to all our guests.

"Sorry. I forget you're not so little anymore. My baby sister is all grown up." I pull away and catch his happy grin. Marriage definitely looks good on him. I'm glad he's happy. It makes me feel guilty for not saying goodbye after his wedding. He may not care, but I owe Stacey an apology. Kip lets me go when an old neighbor starts up a conversation with him. I tell him I'm going to go find Stacey and head back toward the house as the back-screen door opens—and my jaw drops to the ground.

Levi Dent.

Shoot.

CHAPTER FIVE

Levi

Three goddamn weeks. That's how long the night in the supply closet has been playing through my mind. The anger hasn't dimmed. The confusion is still in full-force. The memory of what happened is so fresh, I can still smell her.

My anger erupted when I connected that once familiar voice to a name, feeling the kick straight to my gut and balls. I'd been tricked. The fury of what my friends tricked me into caused a murderous fog inside my head. I was going to kill them. I was also going to kill Hannah for going along with it. Before I had the chance to drag her back and scream bloody murder, she kicked me. Fucking *kicked* me and ran off. I took off after her, stumbling a few times over my own damn two feet. The realization of what had happened sobered me up real fast, and the second I saw Kip holding his sister, I knew I was in deep shit. Chase and Ben might have thought this was a great joke, but Kip wouldn't. He was going to kill me. My friend since before puberty, and in a matter of seconds, he was going to find out what I did and kill me.

But she didn't say a word. She seemed to have a thing for kicking and did the same injustice to her brother, then took off running. When I made it to Kip, he swung his arm over my shoulder and gave me the drunk "best bud" speech. From over his shoulder, I watched Rebecca storm out of a room down the hallway toward us. The second Kip released me, she slapped me, shouting how much of an asshole I was for standing her up and making her wait. How dare I send her to a room to wait for no reason. Murderous rage gleamed in her eyes, but I was confused. I stood *her* up?

Then it clicked.

I stared past her, in the direction *she* ran off to, putting it all together.

Ben's comment.

Change of plans, three doors to the right, not left.

Hannah Matthews.

She lied and set me up.

My expression shifted, matching Rebecca's. Her pursed lips smacked together, her voice, like nails on a chalkboard, suggesting we fulfill the deal, which I replied to with a big fuck no. God, if I would have screwed that bitch, I would have been even more furious with my friends. But I can't grasp what was worse: banging bitch Rebecca or Hannah fucking Matthews.

I went back to the bar and drank more, trying to pretend none of it had ever happened, but I couldn't. I couldn't get the taste of her off my mind. It was like I could still smell her sweet perfume, her sweet sex. Hear her sweet moans. Feel her soft, sweet skin. I was so confused how I just had the best sex in I couldn't even fathom how long, and it had been with her. And I fucking loved it. The way her tiny body fit seamlessly around me, her legs, her arms—it all was perfect. I couldn't stop replaying the moment I'd pushed inside her, how tight she was, how warm and wet. Her body succumbed to me, begging for everything I gave her. I couldn't stop drinking, trying to erase what I had done, while wishing never to forget how wonderful it was. Needless to say, in due time, my confusion dimmed. Because I blacked out.

She was in the wind the next day. I heard her mother say she had to get back to school. But that was bullshit. She would never miss out on anything for Kipley. She loved her brother. It had to do with her little scheme.

I had been torn on what to do. When the guys asked me how Rebecca was, I told them I'd backed out, choosing not to mention the Hannah incident. I couldn't work it out, so I definitely didn't need them to fuck with me about it. Let alone have it slip out to Kip and sign my death warrant. So I kept it to myself.

The problem was, as the days passed, I couldn't keep it to myself. I needed answers. I needed to understand why in the hell she set me up. I dreamed about finding her and strangling her. Then I fantasized about taking her roughly again and again, sucking on those plump lips, pinching those perfect nipples. I found myself beating off more than I wanted to admit to the memory. Then getting angrier after the fact. I was going to have it out with Hannah Matthews. It was just a waiting game. She was coming home soon. And I would get answers.

Today, the Matthews' are throwing their youngest child a welcome home and graduation party. Kip mentioned it would be family and some friends, lowkey, but I insisted on coming to show my support for his little sis. I wouldn't miss it for the world.

As I walk through the back door, it's no surprise she's the first person I spot. What catches me off guard is the way lust clouds into my anger. Losing my focus, I stop in my tracks, intrigued by the panic prominent in her eyes. Her lips part as she takes me in, and she almost drops her beer. Fumbling with the bottle, she surveys the yard in search of an escape I'm sure.

Her eyes come back to mine. I take one step into the Matthews' backyard, and she takes off, speed-walking to the other side. I fight not to go after her. I won't leave until she gives me the answers I want, but I don't want to attract attention, so I let her run and hide.

"Hey, you made it." I follow that familiar voice, seeing Kip with Stacey on his arm. I offer him a smile and reach in for our man-hug.

"Yeah, wouldn't miss it. Hey, Stacey. You look amazing as always." I lean in and place a gentle kiss to her cheek.

"Oh, stop. I look fat already. Married life doesn't lie when they say *eat*, drink, and be merry."

Kip laughs, bringing his lips to his wife's head. "You're gorgeous. So, how's work? I hear you're going above and beyond the expectations. Congrats, man."

I shrug off Kip's compliment. "Thanks. I think I'm holding my own. The workload's been heavy, which I enjoy, and the hours late, but it's the only way I'm going to get ahead." I wouldn't lie and say work has been easy. The law firm has been insanely consuming since coming on board six months ago, but I wouldn't expect anything less. I also embrace the distraction. My focus is work. As it should be.

"Well, all power to you. I hear the boss is a total ball-buster." We both laugh, and another old family friend catches Kip's attention. I wave them off, letting them know I'll catch up with them later. I say hello to Grandma May Matthews and a few more familiar faces, luckily avoiding Kip's Aunt Getty. The last family party I attended, she caught me in a forty-five-minute conversation rant about her bladder infection and exactly how she thought she got it.

I'm two beers in when I catch sight of her again. Dressed in a plain white summer dress exposing her tan legs, she's hugging a neighbor while scanning the backyard. She doesn't see me, since I'm blocked by a group of family friends. Thinking she's in the clear, I watch her excuse herself and walk into the house, and I follow.

Just as I step through and close the door, I reach for her. Her squeal is loud, but cute. This time, she does drop her beer. Stepping over it, I pull her down the small hallway off the kitchen and stop once we hit the laundry room. I push her back against the wall, meeting her wide-as-fuck eyes.

"Hello, Hannah," I say, my voice low. Her face instantly pales. Good. She better be scared of me. Her chest rises and falls in quick pants. Her lips part, and I find myself staring at her mouth, wondering if her lips taste like cherries and beer. But then I remember her deceit, and my anger kicks back in. "Have anything to say to me?" I ask in a cool tone.

Her head begins to shake. "Um…no…I—no. Why would I?"

"No apology for *tricking* me?"

Her color returns as her cheeks flush. "What? I…um, I don't know what you're talking about."

I place each hand on the wall, caging her in. Leaning forward, the smell of flowers and vanilla assaults me. For a quick moment, my anger dissipates, reminding me of her addictive scent. My closeness is making her extremely uncomfortable. Her cheeks flare and her body trembles. "You know exactly what I'm talking about, and I want an answer on why the *fuck* you tricked me."

My words come out harsh, but dammit, I'm pissed. No— I'm *angry*. Her mouth opens, then closes, her words stuck in her throat. There's no way out of this, and she's coming to realize it.

"I'm not sure what you're talking about. Did Kip tell you this was going to be some other kind of party? Yeah, so boring. Family and all. But please, stay for the burgers. My dad is great with the grill—"

I slap my hand against the wall, silencing her rambling. She jumps, and I almost bring her tiny body to mine. "You know damn well what I'm talking about, Hannah. The supply closet. You and me. How'd you do it? Switch the plan with Ben so you could be the one to be in that room? Did you plan that all along? Set me up so you can get me to fuck you? What was it, Hannah? Did you get what you wanted? My hands, my tongue, my—"

"Ah, there you are!" Both our heads whip to the right to see Mr. Matthews standing at the end of the hallway. I causally step away from Hannah, trying not to set off any fatherly alarms. "Hello, Mr. Matthews. I was just asking Hannah how the rest of the internship went. Smart girl, your daughter." I smile kindly, sticking out my hand. He makes his way to us, and I shake his hand as he slaps his free hand to my back.

"She sure is, Levi, and I can't wait to see what storm she creates at the office. Luckily for you, you'll get to witness my little baby at work."

Hannah gasps. "Wait—what? Why would he see me at work?"

I enjoy watching her mouth fall open, staring down her father. She hasn't been told.

"Levi is our newest top resident lawyer. I've been trying to snatch him since he passed the bar, but he wanted to make sure he earned his position. He came on board about six months ago. Doing a stellar job. Couldn't be happier with his performance." Her dad smiles, and she turns back to a shade of white.

"Wh-What?" she barely whispers, her eyes tracing over to me. I offer her a grin, the satisfaction of her shock pleasing me. I knew she was coming home to work with her father—and she'd be starting as my paralegal. Little Hannah Matthews wanted to follow in her father's footsteps, but to do so, she needed to start from the bottom. Learn all the tedious stuff before she worked her way to the bigger jobs. That's where I stepped in. Her father came to me a few weeks back asking if I would allow his daughter to shadow me. Help her learn the ropes. Teach her. Mentor her. Little did Mr. Matthews know, I had already taught his daughter a few things. I more than happily accepted the challenge.

"That's right. And come Monday, I get the pleasure of being your mentor and teaching you all my tricks."

The poor girl looks almost sick. I worry she might barf on my brand-new shoes, but she's too polite for such a blatant act.

"It'll be a great pairing. You've both known each other since you were little. It will be easy working together. I actually look forward to it." Mr. Matthews offers another fatherly pat to my back and steps away. "Burgers are done. Baby girl, your mom wants to say a speech before we eat. When you two kids are done chatting, make your way outside, okay?" She nods, and we both stare at her father's back as he retreats. Once he disappears outside, I aim my searing eyes back to her just as she ducks and tries to escape.

"Not so fast, sweetheart." I grip her bicep, pulling her back to me. "You were about to tell me something?" Her eyes resemble those of a scared kitten. I'm ashamed to admit I'm turned on by her timidity. Her doe eyes, bright with embarrassment. I'm tempted to talk dirty just to watch her cheeks explode in flames of discomfort.

"I have nothing to say to you." She sticks her chin out, but can't hide how badly she's trembling. I take a step toward her, forcing her back against the wall. Leaning in, I speak low. "We had sex, Hannah. Against my will. I would have never fucked you if I knew it was you." My words turn sour as they leave my mouth. I didn't mean them the way they came out, but the damage is already done. The hurt washes over her gentle features. Her bottom lip begins to quiver. Fuck.

"That came out wrong. You know what—"

I don't get to finish because she lifts her foot and kicks me in the shin. Dammit with that move. "*Ouch!* What the hell, Hannah?"

She pushes past me, but not before stopping to face me. "I'm not sure what you're referring to, but if I did, I would also regret doing anything with someone as cruel as you. You're definitely not the person I held in such high regard years ago, but I only have my horrible judge of character to blame."

With that, she flees down the hallway and out to the backyard.

CHAPTER SIX

Hannah

Five in the morning is here before I'm ready, and my alarm starts to blare. I slap the snooze button and throw my blanket over my head. I've barely blinked by the time the alarm goes off again. *There's no way that was nine minutes.* I hit the snooze once more, flipping onto my back, trying to pry my eyes open. *Big day. First day. Huge day.* So huge, I manage to fall back asleep because my alarm wakes me up once again. "Ugh, the devil's device," I groan and flop to my side, shutting it off.

"Time to get up, baby girl," Mom sings as she opens my door. I pop up, confused at why I was sleeping in the first place, and glance at my clock.

Shoot! "I'm awake!" I jump up and spring out of bed ten minutes behind schedule. How did I fall back asleep! I practically had one foot hanging out of my covers. Ugh. I race through the shower and quickly blow-dry my hair. I wanted to straighten it so it looked perfect for my first day, but my "I need more sleep" illness took that option away from me. I twist it into a neat-as-I-can bun and pin it tightly to my scalp. I laid out my outfit last night—well, I laid out my entire week, but I wanted to be prepared, and look professional. This is the day I have been dreaming about. I'm starting at Matthews and Associates.

Grabbing for my computer bag, I throw the strap over my shoulder and race downstairs, where my mom is pouring a cup of coffee for my dad.

"There she is. Ready for your big day, baby girl?" Dad chirps, folding his paper and setting it on the kitchen table.

"Yes, extremely." I sit down as my mom sets a plate of eggs in front of me. I thank her and wait for my dad to take a sip of his coffee before I bring up the speech I practiced all night long. The speech where I ask, without sounding like I'm begging—which I am—to be mentored by someone other than Levi.

I was shocked—no, I was *floored*—when my dad said Levi works at his firm. Not that I keep track of him...okay, I have a Google notification on his name, but still! My dad's firm? How was I not informed? I followed Levi from afar as he went to college on a full scholarship, when he turned down his opportunity to go pro, and then went off to law school. When the notifications stopped coming through, I assumed, once he was out of the sports spotlight, his name became irrelevant, hence the lack of notifications. It was then I started to lose track of him, which wasn't the worst thing, since my obsession was a bit out of control. I needed to grow up and put my time and heart into someone who *wasn't* my brother's best friend. When I did what I did, I thought that'd be it. Our paths, with the exception of Kip's wedding, hadn't crossed in years, pretty much since he fell off the grid, why would it start now? I know I was naive in thinking I wouldn't see him at one of Kip's get-togethers or a family function now that I was home, but never *this* soon. And at my dad's firm. *My* firm. And to top it off, he's my mentor!

This is a disaster.

I've worked my butt off to land a job after college at Matthews and Associates, and it's not because my dad owns the company. It's been my dream since I was little to follow in his footsteps, apply to law school and work side by side, making him proud. But now... This... *Him!* Not going to happen. And to imagine working with *him?* Naive isn't even the best word to describe how I've been about Levi. I couldn't believe what a jerk he turned out to be. Putting him on a pedestal like he was this great guy all girls dreamed about. He was just another jerk with a well-seasoned act—and he proved it with his cold remark.

A part of me couldn't blame him. I had deceived him. Set him up. But I was truly doing him a favor. Sleeping with Rebecca Fritz would have been way worse. At least I thought. But to insult me and say he would have never had sex with me hurt. Then again, why was I shocked? I was no one special—nowhere even close on the radar of girls Levi Dent dated. They are all beautiful, popular. I am a plain Jane, short and mousy. My hair is a hot mess on a good day. My eyes are too big for my face. I'm not on Levi Dent's radar—pfft, or anyone's, for that matter.

"Um…Daddy? I want to talk to you about Levi," I start off, then jam some eggs into my mouth. I don't want to appear nervous, which I certainly am.

"Ah, yes. Good ol' Levi. What a pair you two will make. He'll take good care of you," he replies, taking another sip of his coffee and flipping the page of his newspaper.

"I'm sure he would, but I was wondering if there was anyone else who would be able to let me shadow them?" I ask, stuffing my mouth some more.

My dad drops his paper and glances at me. "And why would you want that? Levi is the best for the job. He's becoming well respected at the firm, and being a longtime friend of Kip's and close to this family, I thought he would be a great choice for you." God, he is making Levi into a saint. Seems like my dad has his naive blinders on too. "Plus, there are a lot of eager men at Matthews and Associates. I don't want anyone trying to take advantage of you. You're a pretty girl. I have faith Levi will protect you and keep all those boys away from my baby." He smiles, then his attention is back on his paper while I try not to choke on my eggs.

My dad offers to give me a ride to the office, but I don't want to show up pegging myself as the boss's daughter. I mean, I *am* the boss's daughter, but I want to stand on my own two feet. So, I drive behind him. Because there's really only one feasible route to his office. I check in with the front desk, letting them recognize who I am, and Vanessa, the receptionist, walks me back to HR. I meet with Melanie, the head of human resources, who has me sign all my papers and gets my picture and badge. By mid-morning, I am officially a real employee at Dad's firm, and Melanie is walking me over to my new desk and wishing me well.

"But...wait, what do I do now?" I ask her back as she leaves me at my bare desk.

"You wait for me to tell you what to do."

I whip around to see Levi standing in the doorway of the office right behind my desk. *You have got to be kidding me.* I narrow my eyes as he stands there, his arms crossed over his chest, looking absolutely stunning in a fitted black suit.

"Please tell me you're visiting someone else's office," I say in a not-so-friendly way.

Levi shakes his head, not bothering to offer me any kind gesture in return. "Can't do that since this office belongs to me." He pushes off the doorframe and eliminates the space between us. I take a hefty step back, hitting the corner of my desk. "Jesus, Hannah, I'm not going to bite you," he snaps as he brushes past me, placing a manila folder on my desk, then whips around to face me. "Listen, I'm not happy about this either. But this is what your father wants. I'm sure we can manage to work together without any *scheming*. Before long, you'll be on your own and out of my hair."

I can't fight the gasp that escapes my parted lips or the hurt in my eyes. He catches it, and it makes me even more upset to give him an ounce of satisfaction that he's gotten to me. I clench my hands into fists, trying to control my building anger. "You know what—"

"No, *you* know what..." He bends down, his face too close to mine, "you had no right to do what you did. Do you even comprehend what kind of trouble I can get in if Kip finds out? Your father?" His warm breath hits my face as fury pours from his words. He's angry. And I get why. I didn't think past myself. But it doesn't excuse his harsh treatment.

"I thought—"

"Hey, Levi." We both cock our heads to see a woman, blond and flawless, standing next to us, smiling all sweetly at Levi. He pulls away from me, replacing his snarl with a casual smile. "Hello, Becca. How was your weekend?" he asks as polite as can be.

Becca giggles and flips her hair over her shoulder. "Oh, it was the same. Boring. Would have been more exciting if you had joined us on Saturday. The party was a huge success." She licks her over-glossed lips, taking her eyes off him to scan me over, then moves her attention back to him.

"Sorry I had to miss it. Becca, this is Hannah Matthews, Jim's daughter. She's starting with us today as my paralegal. Hannah, this is Becca. She works in records." Becca turns to me, and with minimal effort, waves in my general direction. "Hey," she says lamely, then brings her attention back to Levi. "Well, it was good seeing you. Definitely have to lock you in for next time." And then she's off.

We both stand there in silence, unsure what to say. When I open my mouth to make an attempt at defending what I did, he brings his hand up. "Don't. Let's give you the tour." He starts to walk away, and I wrap my fingers around his thick bicep.

"Wait." The moment my fingers touch him, he freezes. I panic and pull back. He whips around, his eyes on fire. "I'm…I'm sorry. I didn't mean to touch you. It's just that…I already learned the building. I don't need a tour," I reply, pulling my eyes away, looking anywhere but at him. I fidget with my hands, and I can't stop pulling at my pencil skirt that suddenly seems too short for an office environment. Levi's eyes follow my hands, but continue to travel down my bare legs, slowly making their way back up. The moment he lands back on my eyes, he slams his lids shut, raking his palms down his face.

If I wasn't mistaken, Levi Dent just got caught checking me out.

I think.

Because I'm not technically sure what a guy looks like checking me out.

"You may know the building, but you don't know the people. The routines. Schedules. It's important to grasp that. What happens when there's an emergency and you don't have time to take the elevator? If you need a signature notarized and the one you need is not around, who is their back up notary? That kind of stuff. Now, let's go." He changes his course, and without waiting for me, heads toward the elevators.

As if no deceiving supply closet sex had happened between us, Levi, the gentleman, kindly escorts me through each department, introducing me to the people I need to get familiar with. John in accounting, Frank in IT, Rachel in legal administration—which will be my biggest asset since I'll be working with her once I'm out from under Levi's shadow. There's Sue, the legal secretary, and her daughter, Heather, who works as the law librarian, and Braydon, first-year associate. Braydon is super friendly with a nice smile. He started only a few months ago and is quickly moving his way up. He hands me his card, offering his services anytime I need them, and I thank him. Before I even finish our conversation, Levi pulls me away. I try snapping at him, telling him how rude it is, but he just says, "You're not here to land a date, Ms. Matthews," and continues to introduce me to more staff.

Matthews and Associates is filled with employees. Marketing, paralegals, technical assistants, I can go on. By lunchtime, my head is spinning trying to remember everyone's name, their titles, and how, when, and why I'll need them. I can't even hide the stress covering my face at how much information was just fed to me.

"Relax, you don't need to master everything on the first day," Levi states as we make it back to my desk.

"Sure I do. I want to succeed. I need to know—need to remember." I grab for my bag in search of a pad and pen. I need to get these names and titles down before I forget. I get out my notebook, but Levi shuts my bag and pulls my arm away. I frown, my brows drawing together as I ping him with a quizzically stare. "What are you doing?"

"Relax," he says, slow and calm. His voice soothes my overworking mind. I stop in my tracks and stare down at his hand still wrapped around my arm. He catches what has my attention and quickly lets go. "Listen, I want to start over. I'm not this person I keep showing you. I'm not normally such an ass."

I stare at him, wondering about the change in him. I nod, letting him understand I get it. I normally don't go around tricking guys into sleeping with me either.

"It's fine," I say, wanting to brush it off. If we never had to bring up the whole supply closet again, I would be just—

"But I need answers, Hannah."

And there goes that hopeful theory.

"What happened…it was fucked up. I've known you since you were practically out of diapers. Your brother has been my best friend since we were kids. It shouldn't have happened."

I go to open my mouth, but I'm not sure what to say. He's right. It shouldn't have. Even though it's been the only thing I think about—the only thing that settles in my mind when I lay in bed at night. It's a movie on repeat behind my eyelids every time I close them. It may have been the best thing to ever happen to me, and it shouldn't have happened.

"Say something."

It wasn't a mistake. "I know. It was a mistake. I shouldn't have done it, but I did it because I—"

"There you two are." My dad's voice interrupts, and I jump, dropping my pen. "Nothing!" I spit out, whipping around to my dad, who's smiling, his brow arched in confusion at my outburst.

"Nothing what, baby girl?"

Levi steps forward. "She meant she has nothing for lunch. We were just discussing what to eat. We've had a busy morning. She was able to conquer the entire first two floors of departments. I think she and Rachel really hit it off." Levi's smile matches my dad's, and I take a deep breath, offering him my silent thanks.

"That's fantastic to hear! Lunch is at Savino's. Both of you, my treat."

CHAPTER SEVEN

Levi

Walking back to my office from a long litigation meeting, I want nothing more than to lock myself in my office and take a few swigs of the top-notch bourbon I keep stashed in my bottom drawer for high-profile clients. Hannah is not at her desk, but I can smell her lingering scent of flowers and sweet vanilla. I push past the urge to grab the pale pink cardigan hanging over her chair and press it to my nose. Making it into my office, I shut the door behind me, startled when I notice movement toward my desk. Hannah is sitting in my chair.

"What are you doing in here?" My voice comes out hoarse. I don't like that she's in here. Sitting in my chair. Her hands fondle a pearl necklace hanging low along her collarbone, her silk shirt unbuttoned lower than it should be for a work setting or my wandering mind.

"I was waiting for you, Levi. I can't deny us. I need you inside me again." Her words stroke me, as if her soft hands are wrapped around my hardening cock. I wipe the beaded sweat off my brow and pull away from the door. I walk closer to her, needing to get her out of here.

"There is no us. You need to leave." My statement holds no truth. I don't want her to leave. I want her to stay and allow me to unbutton each button on her blouse until her perfect breasts are in view and my mouth is around her hard nipples. I walk over to her, ready to lift her and drag her out if need be. She stands to meet me, and I go to grab for her hands when she reaches out and her blouse falls open. Her white lace bra peeks through, her breasts on full display.

"Touch me, Levi. I need to feel you on me again."

God, she tempts me. But I can't. I need to deny her. Stay away from her. "No." My voice is barely a whisper. And though I say the word, my hands push her blouse off her shoulders, and my feet move without permission. I'm so close to her, the heat from her small, taunt body warms me. "We can't do this," I say one last time before dipping down and putting my mouth to hers. I want to be gentle, but I can't. I need her. Bad. I lift her up, placing her on the top of my desk. My lips haven't left hers as I finesse her mouth, parting her full lips with my tongue. Her hands work my belt and zipper, finding their way inside my pants. I groan as her fingers wrap around my hard cock and stroke me. God, her touch is amazing. I moan into her mouth, lifting my hands up her ribs toward her perky breasts. She squeezes my cock as she works me faster. I can't help it, but I buck forward, thrusting my hips, fucking her hand. As I lift my hands to her breasts, she stops. "Hands to yourself, Levi." Her words confuse me, but I stop and she brings her attention back to my dick. This is complete heaven. Her other hand dips in, grabs my balls, and softly squeezes.

"Fuck," I moan, bringing my hands down and grabbing her sultry smooth thighs. I need to see how wet she is. But when I slide my hands up her thighs, she stops. "Hands to yourself, Levi," she says again. Shit. I need to touch her. Suck on her. Fuck her. She strokes me again, harder and faster. I'm so close. I need... need...

"Let me touch you, baby. Let me show you how much I want you," I plead, taking her mouth and roughly kissing her. Small pants leave her lips, and I come undone. I release her lips, my eyes moving to her breasts and the way they bounce as her hand works me. Fuck, I don't care what she says, I need my hands on her. Inside her. As I'm about to blow, I shove my fingers up her skirt without invitation, reaching for her wet sex. Before I make it to her cunt, her words echo in my ear, "Hands to yourself, Levi…"

I shoot up in bed, the tightness in my stomach almost painful. Trying to catch my breath, I survey my surroundings. I'm in my room. My bed. Alone. I wipe the sweat off my face and notice I have a boner harder than a cement fucking brick.

"Fuck," I groan, raking my hands down my face. What the *fuck* was that? I take in the time. It's almost four in the morning. I throw myself back onto my mattress and stare at the ceiling. I have to be broken. I can't keep doing this. Fucking fantasizing about Hannah. I throw the covers off my waist and get up in search of my running gear, aware sleep is a thing of the past.

Three miles later, and the dream of her still hasn't waned. Maybe agreeing to be her mentor was a bad idea. I wanted answers, maybe a bit of revenge, but all it seems to be doing is blowing up in my face. Having her so close, for so long, it's torment. Even when she's not around, she's still affecting me.

My mind goes back to yesterday. Lunch at Savino's panned out to be a great time. A family staple for the Matthews' and the best damn pizza around. Jim and Hannah went back and forth sharing stories, and I sat back, enjoying their father/daughter banter. There's no doubt how much Jim loves his daughter, how much she idolizes him. I found myself more relaxed than I've been in a while, listening to their stories, watching Hannah devour a slice of pizza, taking bites way bigger than her slender month could chew. Even after some time, I found myself chiming in with old memories of when we were all kids and went camping together.

One in particular came to mind. Kip and I were sixteen, and Hannah was going on eight. The Matthews' went on camping trips all the time to the same small town of Kettersville. The summer had been hotter than normal, and we were lucky to find a camping spot that had a lake.

We're all in our suits, ready to jump into the lake, when Hannah walks out in a bright yellow swimsuit. It barely fits her since she's so tiny. Chase being Chase, his eyes light up, seeing the opportunity to pick on her.

"Geez, what is that, a walking banana? Can we peel you too, Hannah?" Chase laughs, smacking Ben in the stomach to play along.

"I didn't know bananas liked to swim," Ben jokes, adding to Chase's banter.

Hannah simply walks past us all, ignoring everyone's jokes. She drops her yellow towel on the dock and begins spreading it out.

"Hey, Hannah Banana, be careful, you might be mistaken and eaten by a wild animal."

That gets her. Her eyes widen, and she turns to face us, dread swimming in her eyes. "You lie. Your nose is growing, Chase Stinkberg." Ben and I burst out laughing at her rebuke, but it only frustrates Chase more.

"Not lying, Hannah Banana. Don't you know there are tons of bears in the wild? Don't get me started on the fish and hungry water creatures living in the lake. Once they set their eyes on you, you're a goner." Chase laughs harder as her eyes fill with fear. It's not as funny as it was when it was simple banter. I actually feel bad for her.

"Liar!" she yells at Chase, bending down to pick up her towel. She whips around, sticking her chin up in defiance to stop her tears from falling. She walks past us all, and Chase reaches out, trying to snatch her towel.

"Hands to yourself, Chase. You might find your fingers missing from a hungry banana biting them off." Chase lets go of her towel, shocked at her bold statement. We watch Hannah pick up the pace before she begins a full sprint back to the camp, passing Kip along the way.

I take a cold shower and dress for work. It's not a bad thing to get in early since I have a lot of briefs to read through for the Miller lawsuit, one of the biggest cases I've landed since starting at the law firm. If I nail this one, it can mean a big promotion in the company, therefore, I've invested all my time and energy into it. Not that the case doesn't deserve it. Some asshole construction company scammed their way into building on land unsuitable for construction, resulting in the deaths of too many innocent people without taking any responsibility. It's messed up what kind of people are out there, and it's all just another reason why I chose to become a lawyer—to help stop every one of them.

Since lunch had gone longer than planned, a shit ton of work piled up. Even though it had been with the *boss*, it didn't eliminate everything that still needed to be done.

Aside from my own workload, I never got to finish all the tasks I had planned for Hannah. By the time we got back to the office, it was past work hours and we were both wiped. Not to mention, I needed to get away from her. She wasn't hiding the fact that she wanted nothing more to do with me, so when the time came, we went our separate ways, and that was that. I came home, drank more than I should have for a Monday night, and concentrated on watching football until I passed out.

Now, Tuesday, I step off the elevator onto the quiet office, thankful no one's here. These are the best times to get shit done and really focus. Some days I work, others I spend wondering how I got here. Deciding to become a lawyer had never been my plan. Football had always been my first choice. But the deeper I got into my football career, the more I questioned the sport. Would my future truly be about the love of the game or the perks and highlife? As I prepared for the career move of my life, I watched so many of my fellow teammates get hurt, the injuries completely taking their career right out from under them. Not that that should have swayed me; that was the risk of the game. A high intensity contact sport, you're bound to get injured at some point. As friends got drafted into the NFL, I sat back with envy, waiting patiently for my turn. There was no doubt it was coming. I didn't need to toot my own horn to know I was the best.

My skepticism grew with every player who lost himself to the lifestyle. It was easy to let the spotlight get to you. The money, the fame. For so many, they lost sight of the game, and I hated that for them—and myself. The fear I would end up like that—drugs, women, reckless decisions leading to ruining my season and career—overwhelmed me. Then, one night, I got a call that a close friend and old teammate who'd recently been drafted was found dead from an overdose in a Miami hotel room, and I finally made up my mind.

I wanted to play football. It's what got me up every day. But I also wanted to stay true to myself. I was afraid to put all my eggs in one basket, scared I would get hurt and that would be that. So, when my agent approached me with a contract inviting me to play for a major NFL team, I turned it down. I stayed at college and finished out my football career there while majoring in political science. I wanted to make something of myself. And if it wasn't going to be in football, it was going to be something greater. So, during my senior year, I applied for law school—something I'll always be indebted to Jim Matthews for.

Hannah wasn't the only one who looked up to her father. Growing up, I loved listening while he spoke about his cases. It was like being in the theater, watching him put on a show with so much passion for each story he told. No case was too mediocre. They ranged anywhere from copyright infringement to spousal abuse, but he put so much emotion into each one. When his firm was first getting started, he did it all. But the more prominent his business became, the less he took on general cases and focused more on corporate law, while creating departments that handled other specific cases, like human rights, juridical, tax—you name it.

Jim Matthews was the one person I chose to confide in when I'd been stuck at that fork in the road of my life and needed advice on how to handle my career. He dealt with small sports law cases and was able to break down all possible scenarios for me—if I got hurt, if I went pro, if I got traded. I would've still been able to go back and finish college, but at that rate, would I have wanted to?

Getting a taste of the big league is hard to come back from. That's when he asked me if I ever thought about becoming a lawyer. And in that moment, I said yes.

I turn the corner and head toward my office when I hear soft mumbling. My steps slow as I make one more turn, finding Hannah, wrapped up in her jacket, already at her desk, flipping through notecards, muttering names and titles. You've got to be kidding me. "Tell me you haven't been here all night playing memory with the company org chart." Hannah lifts her head and barely registers my presence before sticking her nose back into her cards.

"I'm prepping."

"For what, the name game?" I make it to her desk and look over her shoulder. Indeed, she has notecards with names, titles, contact info, and purpose for contact. I chuckle at how ridiculous that is, worrying she actually has been here all night with the amount of coffee cups already lined up on her desk.

"It's important to gauge the people you're working with. Knowledge is power." I laugh out loud. She's seriously one of a kind. "See? Look. Braydon Connor." She smiles, waving his personal notecard. "He already left me a message asking me if I need any advice on any new cases. Offered to sit with me and show me some of his litigation cases."

The mention of Braydon blackens my mood. That little shit has no business reaching out to Hannah. His litigation cases have nothing to do with what she'll be handling. I snatch the card out of her hands and toss it in her trash. "Enough playtime. I need you in my office to help me prepare the Miller case for this morning's meeting." I walk past her, not bothering to acknowledge the anger building in her eyes. Entering my office, I throw my bag onto my couch, place my coffee on my desk, and settle into my chair. A small memory of this chair from my dream filters through my mind, and I quickly shake it off.

"You didn't have to do that, you know," she says as she walks in dressed in a gray suit dress. Her hair is pulled back into a tight bun, and I wonder why she doesn't let it down like she used to in high school. She places her pad of paper down on my desk and takes a seat in the lounge chair opposite me. As I pull out my laptop and get set up, she looks around my office, taking in some photo frames, certificates, and my law degree.

She stalls on my football trophy.

"You ready to go over the Miller litigation files for today's meeting?" I try pulling her attention away. She takes a few more seconds to stare at a college trophy before drawing her eyes back to mine. "Yeah, of course." She opens her notebook, clicking her pen. "Can I ask you a question?" And here it goes. It was only a matter of time before she asked. "What happened with football? I swore you would have gone pro. The way you were with that ball, it was like no other. I mean, no one else stood a chance against you. You owned the field, the game, the whole school…"

I lean to the side of my open laptop with a raised brow, smiling at her rambling.

"Oh…well, um…I meant to just say you were really good. I guess I didn't need to…uh, go all—"

"It's fine, Hannah." I grin, and her cheeks flush. "So, you thought I was good, huh?" I poke, watching her cheeks redden even more.

"No. I mean…yes. I mean…"

I burst out laughing. "I'm messing with you. I was good. But thank you for feeding my ego. It's been a long time since someone gave me any football praise. To answer your question, I was drafted, but I turned it down."

Her shocked gasp makes me laugh again. "Why in heavens would you do that? You were the best!"

I shut my laptop to offer her my full attention. "Because I wanted to have a future. A future in football isn't always guaranteed. I chose to secure mine by getting a degree. I still got to play in college. Broke some records. But it ended when I graduated." Her eyes become sad. "What's wrong?" I worry I've upset her. I didn't mean to make fun of her response. I push my laptop aside and lean forward, grabbing for her hand resting on the desk. "Hey, what did I say? I'm sorry. I didn't mean to upset you."

"No. It's just…you loved football. It was your dream. The way you used to talk about it. It makes me sad you had to choose to let it go." My lips twitch at her confession. My worry dissipates, and a smirk creeps along my features. "What? What's so funny?" she asks.

I squeeze her hand. "So, you used to listen to me, huh?"

Busted.

I laugh harder while she tries to hide the fact that she just gave her own secret away. I continue to stare at her, enjoying the way she squirms in her chair. Her hand fidgets under my palm, her eyes bright.

"I'm flattered. Good to know I had at least one fan out there." She pulls her hand out and slaps mine. "Levi Dent, you had the entire school as your fan club, and you know it." My chest rumbles, and I sigh in satisfaction. "What can I say, small towns and their love for football." Her lips curl into the most tantalizing grin, and her smile becomes my new favorite thing. There's serenity behind her laughing eyes.

A few seconds pass, a fleeting moment being shared between us. It stirs something inside me. A need for this connection. She has this way of drawing me in, and I refuse to drop her gaze. Everything about her becomes more prominent. Her dimples that pop out. Her tempting mouth as she gracefully extends her tongue to wet her lower lip.

I never paid much attention to Hannah when we were kids. Sadly, no one did. She was timid, scrawny, and annoying. Mouth full of braces. Squeaky, high-pitched voice. I stab at my memory for the last time I saw her before Kip's wedding. It had to have been right before she left for college and I left for my internship, prepping myself for my future at Matthews and Associates.

When did Hannah Matthews grow up?

CHAPTER EIGHT

Hannah

"Steve Waters, technician for computer occupations. Christine Beeker, litigation assistant. Bridget Simms, first year lawyer, handles all general practice. Justin West, senior associate." I grin as Levi makes it to the end of my notecard pile and I take a bite of my sandwich, doing a little booty dance in my chair.

"Congratulations, you've memorized the entire Matthews and Associates staff." Levi smiles, dropping the cards and taking a hefty bite of his own sandwich. It's been a full week since we shared that bizarre moment in his office. Levi switched gears quickly, going into work mode, but not before exposing something in his eyes—something I refuse or want to acknowledge. It all led to the same result: this couldn't happen. And I had to accept it. Not that I thought about the what ifs *if* it did.

Pfft.

Liar.

I swiftly jumped into working with my team on litigation proceedings, helping with small stuff. And by small, I mean *small*. Copying reports, getting coffee, taking notes. I was everyone's runner. I knew I had to start from the bottom, but I didn't realize the bottom meant the *bottom*. It's like I was fair game for anyone. Even when I thought someone was way out of line with their request, I chose to keep my mouth shut. I didn't want any favors or leniency because the boss was my daddy.

Braydon has been awesome, though. Levi hasn't always been able to assist me, so when he's gone for full days or in meetings, I head down to Braydon's desk, and he gives me insight on notes I took while sitting in on the Miller lawsuit meetings. We seem to have some things in common, and the more time I spend with him, the more I come to terms with the fact that Levi Dent is *definitely* out of my league. I just needed to get over it.

"So, what now? Ready to run Kellan Styles out of VP? Take over the company?" Levi grins, taking a sip of his soda. A smirk fights through my lips, and I chuck a chip at him.

"Not yet. Need to learn a little bit more before I start claiming my board member seat."

We laugh as a knock sounds at his office door. I cock my head to see Braydon standing in the doorway.

"Hey there," I chirp.

"Hey…uh, sorry, I didn't mean to disturb you, but, Hannah, I was just checking to see if you've eaten. If you haven't, do you want to go up to Vince's Deli? I have some cases I'd thought you'd enjoy going over with me." I return his cheerful smile and put down my sandwich.

"We're busy—"

"I'm actually done eating," I cut Levi off, wrapping up the other half and stuffing it in the paper bag.

"What are you doing? You haven't even finished your lunch," Levi barks, as I veer around him, noticing his demeanor has suddenly changed.

"Oh, I'm full. I had a big breakfast," I reply, taking the bag and tossing it in his garbage.

"You had half a muffin. I watched you." He frowns at me, and I offer him my *what's your problem* scowl. Standing, I brush off my skirt and scoop up my cards. "Thank you again for lunch and helping me. I do appreciate everything. I'm sure you're relieved to know you won't have to spend your lunches with me anymore. Thanks again." I wave and give Levi my back, offering Braydon my attention.

"I'll tag along while you grab something, then we can review your cases and maybe you can quiz me on them. See if I have what it takes to be a lawyer." There's a flash of joy in his eyes, sending a spark of anticipation to mine. I'm glad he enjoys my company as much as I do his.

Looking forward to our time together, I leave Levi's office without another word. Braydon and I make small talk while he picks up a sub sandwich from the food cart outside the building and we settle at his desk. When I pull out my notes, our eyes graze and we're both sporting goofy grins.

"Okay, what do ya feel like learning today?" he asks. While he unwraps his turkey sub, I pull out my notepad and flip through. I sneak a peek at Braydon as he takes another bite, then bring my eyes down, hiding my giggle at a piece of lettuce hanging from his mouth.

"I must look like a savage trying to get this sandwich down," he mumbles, his mouth full. I catch myself staring at his lips longer than necessary, and when he notices, he brings his fingers up, wiping some mayonnaise off. I flush with embarrassment at getting caught checking him out and throw my attention back to my notes.

"No, you...um, look fine."

"Just fine?" he asks.

I raise my eyes. "What does that mean?"

"Well, I was hoping I looked more than just fine. Like handsome. Or hot. I'd even take cute, though guys hate being called cute." I can't believe he's being so blunt. Calling out the attraction I think we've both been noticing this past week. I shake my head, smiling even more. He's definitely attractive. And funny. I can see something more happening outside of our work flirtation.

"I'm not sure about all that, but I find you somewhat...fun." I smirk, trying to hide my building laughter. His mouth drops, a theatric gasp leaving his lips.

"Fun? That sounds horrible! It's like when you ask someone

if the person is good looking and their response is they are super nice. Ouch." He brings his hands to his chest, as if I wounded him. "That hurts. I was hoping I've impressed you enough with my stellar knowledge, you'd be obliged to maybe go out with me when I finally got the courage to ask you."

It's my turn to gasp, and he shoots me a silly grin. "You want to go out with me?" I ask, shocked.

"Of course. I think you're amazing. Smart, kind, and if it matters, I think you're more than fun. I think you are absolutely stunning." It's been a long time—okay, maybe never—since anyone has said something so nice to me. I'm beyond flattered and conclude I would have a great time going out with Braydon.

"Well, I guess maybe we should go out sometime," I return.

His eyes widen in excitement. "Really?"

"Unless you were just messing with me." I panic. Guys don't normally ask me out—scratch that, they *never* ask me out. Shoot! Maybe he *is* just messing with—

"I would love to take you out. And sooner rather than later, in case you change your mind." I giggle at his good-natured charm. He's not as tall as Levi or as built, but he's got a nice smile. His eyes are hazel with this beautiful green speckle that make him that much better looking. Whereas Levi's hair is dark brown, Braydon's is a dirty shade of blond. *And why am I comparing him to Levi?* I shut that down real fast. I need to get over that long-lost fantasy. Levi hasn't made any sort of pass at me—not that he ever has—but he's been kind and considerate. Like a friend. And I get it. Sadly, I do.

"*Yes!*" Shoot, did that come out too eager? He probably thinks I'm desperate. But the sooner I banish Levi out of my thoughts, the better. "I mean, yes. Sooner is better. How about tonight? I have nothing planned." Because I don't ever have plans. Geez, can I make myself look any more pathetic?

Braydon nods and opens his planner. "Tonight. Hmmm... special date with Hannah Matthews." He scribbles in his planner.

"There, it's set. You can't back out now." A subtle blush spreads across my cheeks, and I find myself smiling at the thought of what can come out of this…us.

"Agreed. No backing out." A bashful giggle flees my lips. His goofy grin matches mine and we sit there, enjoying the silent flirtation, until someone walks by and breaks the moment. His hands disappear under his desk and he begins nervously slaps his thigh. "We should probably get to work so we can finish up and focus on that date. I have *the best* pizza place in mind." *Right. Work.*

"Of course, I'm probably keeping you from your busy workload. What was the one case you said you were swamped with?" Confusion forms around his eyes. "The one you were just telling me about?"

"Oh yeah! The…um…child services case. Christine actually asked to assist on that one, so I threw her a bone. Can't have all the cases to myself." He winks causing me to giggle. "Speaking of cases, fill me in on the newest case they have you sitting in on? The Miller case, right?"

"Yeah! Sure, unless you need to get going."

He leans forward, speaking in a medieval fashion. "My ears are at your service, my lady."

When I'm done yapping his ear off, we say our goodbyes and I head back upstairs to my desk. When I turn the corner, knowing he can't see my face, my lips breach into a wide grin. I, Hannah Matthews, have a date tonight.

I'm nervous.

Not as nervous as if I was conjuring up a plan to trick a specific someone into sleeping with me, but there's a jitter in my belly. A good jitter? Guilty jitter? *Why would I feel guilty?* How about it's simply because it's been a million years since I've been on a date. I'll stick to that.

I walk out of my bedroom, passing my parents on the couch watching their nightly news. I pick up the pace, hoping to get out without a billion questions. After pacing for a solid thirty minutes, I decide to withhold my real plans. Explaining I'm going on a date with a guy from work, which will set off a round of questions, sounds like an unneeded headache. Plus, question overkill is my parents' favorite game.

"Bye, guys…I'm going to…uh, get pizza with some high school friends." *Go. Go. Go…*

My parents, both seated closely together, bump heads when they cock their necks back, eyeing me curiously. My mom is wearing her one glass of chardonnay smile. "Okay, honey."

"Where you headed to, kiddo?" Dad questions.

Darn it. Nosy parents.

Have I ever mentioned I'm a horrible liar? Make-believe friends are a hard fable to master.

"Yeah, um…Bill's Pizza—"

"*Bill's?*" Dad's voice hikes, and his nose crinkles in disgust. My mom's lips thin.

Great.

Here we go.

Bill's Pizza Pub—the only restaurant on my family's do-not-eat-ever list. We're a Savino's pizza family. We stick together when it comes to our slice of pie. So, when Braydon texted me with his *perfect* place, I theatrically groaned at my phone. I know there are people out there who believe pizza is all created equal. Not the Matthews. It must have the perfect amount of ingredients and true love for it to come out just right. One night, the weather had been so bad, it knocked out the power at Savino's and they had to close. Desperate for pizza, we ordered from Bill's. A house full of food poisoning later, we swore never again. A year passed, and when no one still cringed at the memory of the fights of who got to barf in the toilet and who barfed in the laundry sink, we tried it again. Same. Damn. Thing. Every time we attempted, shit hit the fan, literally. We all agreed that place was cursed, and no Matthews was to ever eat there again.

"Bill's? We hate Bill's."

"*Everyone* hates Bill's," Dad gripes. "They should have shut that place down by now!"

"Honey, you remember that one time you had such bad poops, we had to get those wipes—"

Gah! Don't remind me! "I didn't pick—"

"Why aren't you guys going to Savino's? It's your favorite."

"And it's closer," my mom chimes in.

"Who are these friends you're meeting? Everyone around here knows Savino's is the best. You're going to get sick. I can't allow my daughter to eat their poison pizza."

"Dad, it wasn't my pick—"

"Honey, you should really consider cancelling. Linda from Bunko just ate there and she said her bowels—"

"Okay...well, bye!" I shut them down and practically run out of the house. I certainly don't need anyone reminding me of how I convinced myself I had deposited my intestines into the toilet after attempting their meat lovers.

It will be fine.

I'll just order a salad.

Plain, dry salad.

Pulling up to Bill's, lucky me, I find a close parking spot in front of the restaurant. Probably because everyone knows to stay clear of this place. My stomach starts to churn seeing the neon sign, but I push away the convulsions and force my legs out of my car.

"Hannah!" I hear my name, and I spin around to see Braydon walking up as I shut my car door. "You made it." He smiles, leaning in for a hug. I'm caught off guard by his friendliness, unable to make a move before he captures me in his arms and cocoons me to his chest. "So glad you came." We stand there for a few short seconds, until he offers me one more tight squeeze, my breasts pressing against him before he releases me.

"Yeah, me too!" I reply, regaining my composure. I smile, pushing away the stupidity at the place he chose and remember why I said yes. Because I want to get to know him better. Not lose five pounds fast. He's changed out of his suit attire into a pair of bootcut jeans and a forest green polo. He appears younger in casual clothes.

"Let's go in. I bet you're starving. This is the perfect place." Without another word, I allow him to take my hand and escort me inside. The lighting is dim, the air thick with Italian spices. We're quickly seated in a corner booth, and our drink orders taken. "I have to say, Hannah, I didn't expect you. As in…you as a whole. I knew you were starting, but never did I imagine you being so…this…well, special." Braydon stares at me from across the table, his eyes confident as they peer into mine.

A timid blush cascades across my cheeks. His compliment comes out of left field, surprising me. As I allow his words to sink in, I realize how blind I've been. I've been acting so childish about Levi, I didn't appreciate the great guy I had right in front of me. As if something snaps inside me, a true smile breaches, and I allow my walls to fall, ready and willing to enjoy my date.

"Thanks. I didn't expect you either."

We share a silent moment, until our Cheshire grins win and we laugh at our silliness. "Wow, that was corny, wasn't it?"

"Maybe a little," I chuckle, then take a sip of my water. "But I enjoyed it."

He nods in approval as the waitress returns with our drinks. "You two ready to order?" she asks.

"Yes. We're going to share the meat lovers. Extra cheese please." He turns to me. "Trust me. You're going to love it."

CHAPTER NINE

Hannah

I finish typing up a testimony for Gale in legal and click print, saving the file to my computer in hopes to get them to her before she leaves for lunch. The office has been quiet all morning with meetings in place, which has also left me with time to analyze my date last night, breaking down all the good and bad. For one, the off-the-starting-line spark. His compliment gave me the confidence I needed to let loose and truly allow him to get to know me. He was nice, funny…

I slump in my chair, remembering the bad. I had such great expectations.

Further into the date, I started to discover, besides the basics, we barely had anything in common. That short-lived spark I tried to keep lit, fizzled out. I spent the whole dinner convincing myself it was my nerves while he coerced me into eating the pizza of death. How was I supposed to focus on his charm and wittiness when I was too worried about my stomach lining? It had to be that. I convinced myself of it so much, I accepted another date offer for Friday.

But those missing fireworks…

He's nice. Charming. Funny. Repeat. He's nice. Charming. Funny—

"Gah!" It's fine. Focus on the good parts. Again, nice, charming—

"Working hard? You look in deep thought about something." Levi's voice catches my attention, and I glance up as he drops a handful of manila envelopes on my desk. I choose to keep the reasoning for my deep thinking to myself and focus on the contents in front of me: witness testimonies for the Miller case. Clara Hill's name on the front of the folder, a large confidential stamp below it.

"Are you going to answer me?" My eyes finally meet his. His usual steely gaze is missing, exhaustion in its place. This case is taking all his focus, and it's apparent he's running on empty. Even in his state, I can't help but admire how handsome he is in his black fitted suit, always lacking a tie, and giving the world a tease of his muscled chest with his top button left unlatched. *Stop drooling over him! You just went on a date with someone else! And you accepted another one for Friday. Levi is bad news. Braydon is good news.*

"No deep thinking. Just thinking about how wonderful my date was last night." I pick up the confidential folder, but Levi slaps it closed.

"Wait what? With who—?"

"Oh, fantastic, you're both here." We both cock our heads at my dad's sudden appearance. Levi pulls his hand away from the folder, replacing his snarly growl with a smile.

"Mr. Matthews," Levi greets, but my dad waves him off.

"Honestly, son, you have been part of our family since Hannah here was practically in diapers, call me Jim. Hi, baby girl." My dad leans down, placing a kiss on my cheek. "I just spoke with Kip. He brought up a fantastic idea. Ketterville."

We both stare at my dad, waiting for him to elaborate. "The campground?" Levi asks, his brows furrowed in confusion.

"You bet'cha. This weekend. We're all going. It's been ages since we've all done a camping trip up there, and what better time to get the gang back together? Kipley and Stacey are all for it. She mentioned bringing a friend along. Levi, you'll join us. Bring a guest as well. I won't take no for an answer." *Oh god, I am* not *going back to Ketterville.* The horrid memories of being taunted by Chase Steinberg and the birth of Hannah Banana. No flippin' way.

"Daddy, I can't. I actually have plans this weekend." My dad's brows shoot up in shock as if I just told him the sky wasn't blue.

Gee, thanks, Dad.

"More plans? What kind of plans, honey?"

I peer from Levi, who seems too interested in my answer, back to my dad. "Well, I have a date. A second one, actually… with…um…Braydon Connor. He works here, down in litigation." My dad will handle this information in one of two ways. He will tell me absolutely not and try to fire Braydon for even thinking about engaging in anything less than a professional relationship with his daughter, or he'll simply say absolutely not.

"Well, bring him along. Nice kid. But separate tents, or I'll kill him and hide the body." My brows shoot up to the moon. Totally didn't see *that* coming.

"Daddy!" I slap his shoulder as he laughs, facing Levi. "I look forward to it, kids." And with that, he disappears down the hallway toward his office.

"You went on a date with *Braydon Connor?*" Levi growls, startling me. I turn to him, taking in his dark scowl. Realizing he's showing his cards, he cools his features. "You understand your father will have him fired for this."

This gets my attention. "He would not," I argue. "He just invited him to Ketterville. Why would he fire him?" I ask, praying he won't.

"Because when he thinks about it more, he'll see some newbie geek hitting on his little girl when he should be doing his damn job." I thrust my hands to my hips, ready to stand my ground. "Maybe a little whispering in daddy's ear would—"

"I am *not* little. And you wouldn't dare."

"I would. You're not going on another date with him."

I transform into Puff the Magic Dragon as steam blows through my nostrils. "He wouldn't believe you."

My dad is protective of me, but he wouldn't simply fire someone who's exceptional at their job because they asked out his daughter. Or would he? Shoot. My battle smile wavers.

"Yeah, that's what I thought. See ya, Brady." He walks away, leaving my mouth hanging open, and disappears into his office.

I snap out of my shock and storm after him. "It's *Braydon*, and my dad wouldn't do that to me. Not if he sees I finally found someone who makes me happy." If I wasn't staring so intently at his back, I'd almost miss the falter in his step. He doesn't respond to my reply, but simply sits at his desk and begins typing on his laptop.

Feeling dismissed, I whip around and walk out of his office. I don't care what Levi Dent says, I'm going to ask Braydon to go camping. Give us the whole weekend to find that spark. If my dad gave me the green light, he's okay with it.

It's settled.

I throw myself back into my chair, ready to take on the rest of the day, when an evil growl erupts from my stomach.

"You've *got* to be kidding me."

"Oh, okay…no, I understand. Honestly, it's fine. It's just a family trip. You would have hated it anyway—been weirded out and never spoken to me again." I sigh into the phone, trying to hide my disappointment. We are literally seventeen minutes from leaving for Ketterville, and Braydon just called to cancel. Apparently, there's a case that needs special attention, and he was asked to stay and work through the weekend. He said he'd try to get out of it, but what does that say about me if I hold him back from getting ahead at work?

Am I mad? No.

Disappointed? Yes.

Everyone will have someone, and it will be just me. Not that I'm not used to being a one-woman band, but still. And then there will be Levi, who will throw it in my face. I tell Braydon for the millionth time it's fine, and we make plans to reschedule for when I get back. I drag my feet out of the kitchen and step out onto the front porch. My brother is at the end of the driveway helping Stacey put her bag and tent into the back of his SUV. I catch movement coming from the street. "You have got to be *kidding* me," I groan watching Rebecca sashay up our driveway.

"Eeeek! This is going to be so much fun!" she squeals to Stacey as they hug and bounce up and down. What a joke. Rebecca? Camping? I doubt she's ever been inside a tent or on a campground in her life. I roll my eyes as I step off the porch, walking toward my brother's SUV.

Stacey sees me and releases her friend. "Hey, honey! Excited?" She wraps me up in a hug. I return her embrace with warmth. I love Stacey and don't think my brother could have gotten any luckier.

"I am. Should be fun." I pull back, and like the polite person I am, I try to say hello to Rebecca, but she flips her hair and offers me her back. Not in the mood for her attitude, I move on. It's like they say, once a bitch, always a bitch.

"Hey, Kipley, where's Dad? He should be here already," I ask as Kip throws another cooler into the back.

"Oh, didn't you hear? He's going to be running behind. He's got a case that won't wrap up. He's hoping to meet us by tomorrow."

I lift my shoulders and let out another huge sigh. This trip is going downhill fast. With each passing minute, it's sounding better and better to stay home.

"Finally! There you are," Kipley says, and I cock my head to see who he's talking to.

Great. I was praying he'd come down with leprosy or something and cancel.

"Traffic was a bitch, sorry," Levi says, regarding me with a nonchalant smile. "Hannah." Without meaning to, I roll my eyes.

"Geez, little sis, that was rude. What's up with you?" Ugh.

"Sorry. It's nothing. Just…Braydon called and cancelled on me. Work came up. And now Dad. I'm just not sure I'm up for going anymore." I understand Dad had good intentions of getting us all together, but this is far from a family trip. Just glimpsing the amount of suitcases Rebecca brought is a clear indication of it.

"I'm sorry, Han, but you can't back out. It'll be fun. I promise. Plus, your tent and bag were the first to go in. It would take me an hour to rearrange." He winks at me and brings me in for his infamous brotherly hug. He squeezes tight and places a kiss to the top of my head.

"Don't worry. Levi can keep you company. His date seemed to back out last minute as well." I pull away to get an eyeful of Levi. He shrugs at me, his hands in his pockets. I assumed after seeing Rebecca they were trying to pair those two up—again.

"Oh," I manage to say, trying to sound uncaring. "Well—"

"There you are! I heard you were coming. We get to spend all weekend catching up since we weren't able to do it at the wedding, yay!" Rebecca's smile resembles a dying rat. I don't get what anyone saw in her in high school, and even more so now. Aging has done her no favors, nor has the tanning bed and Botox.

"Yeah…um, great." Levi doesn't take the bait and offers his back to her. "So, where should I put my stuff?" he asks Kip, holding a small backpack, his tent strapped to the back.

"I'll take that, man. We're almost ready. Grab shotgun, yeah?" Kipley says, tossing Levi's things in the car.

The car ride is going exactly how I imagined it would. Absolutely horribly. With Levi riding shotgun and the two girls in the backseat, I was left to the third row by myself. As in, all the way in the back where no one can hear you when you talk or truly pay attention to you. Anything I try to say, Rebecca, the evil witch, talks over me. Stacey has given me a few apologetic smiles, but at this point, I just give up. I sit back and stuff my earbuds in my ears and listen to an audiobook while watching the scenery pass by.

We're only an hour into our five-hour drive when Rebecca starts whining about having to pee. Matthews' number one rule: you go before we get on the road and again when we hit our destination. Even Stacey knows that. But if anyone has to hear Rebecca's nails-on-a-chalkboard voice any longer, we might all jump out the window.

Kipley stops at a rest stop off the highway. Being as the weather is starting to get chillier the closer north we go, I get out and pop the hatch in search of my bag.

"Need help?" I cock my head to see Levi standing beside me, leaning against the Tahoe.

"No, I got it," I lie. I can't get my bag out for the life of me. I have no muscles and trying to lift one of Rebecca's many suitcases is impossible.

"Here, let me help you."

"Seriously, I don't need any—" He doesn't listen and cuts me off as he moves me to the side and leans in, grabbing for my bag. His arms flex, his gigantic bicep in clear view. A screaming voice inside my head yells at me to turn away, but it's like watching a train wreck. I watch as he maneuvers bags and coolers and reaches far back, his t-shirt lifting up for a sneak peek of his toned obliques. Jesus, it's like Christmas in summer getting an eyeful of his yummy—

"Here you go." He pulls back, and I completely forget why I was even standing here in the first place. "This is yours, right?" Bag. Oh yeah! Bag! Mine. Sweater. Weird, because now I suddenly feel on fire.

"Uh…yeah, thanks," I mumble and grab for my backpack. During the exchange, our fingers touch ever so slightly, and I can't deny the spark flowing through my hand as his skin skims against mine. I fight not to raise my head, but I have no control. Our eyes lock, and there is no doubt he felt it too. Seconds feel like an eternity as we stare at one another, unwilling to break contact. I want to say something, but my throat is suddenly drier than the Sahara.

"I…uh…"

"You're really quiet back there. Not your normal self."

I didn't realize he'd been paying any attention to me. He and Kip have been locked in a conversation since we pulled out of our driveway, even brushing off Rebecca any time she pathetically attempted to intervene.

"I was just—"

"Hey, Levi!" I'm interrupted, our connection lost, as we both rotate to face Rebecca. "I got us some snacks. Anything you like?" She sticks her hands out to display her array of strange picks. We're both quiet as we observe her choices of roasted soy nuts, turkey jerky, vegan protein bars, and Big Red bubble gum. Levi's eyebrows rise as I fight the smirk growing on my face. If Rebecca knew anything about Levi, she would know he's allergic to nuts. Not to mention, he thinks anything cinnamon is the devil, remembering his rough night in high school with some Aftershock, scarring him for life. "The gum's my favorite. Always leaves my mouth tingly. You should try it sometime."

That's it.

I did my best, but my laughter slips up my throat. I try sticking my head in my bag to mask it, but Rebecca clearly hears me.

"And what are *you* laughing at?" she snarls.

I pop my head up, trying to practice my breathing techniques so I don't lose it again. I sense Levi's grin without even looking at him, which makes it harder to keep my cool. He knows what I'm thinking about, since I was the one who found him in our backyard passed out behind our shed with a puddle of red vomit around him. I also remember him swearing to do horrible things to the next person to ever offer him anything cinnamon again. I'm hoping the threat still stands.

"Who, me? Uh...I was just...uh, remembering a joke. I was going to tell you guys later...at the campsite..." Wow, that sounded super lame. Levi chuckles, catching Rebecca's attention. "Anywho...I'm gonna go change." I unsnap my tent from my back-pack, dropping it into the back of the car, and with my bag over my shoulder, excuse myself, feeling both sets of eyes on me as I walk up to the convenient store.

"Hey, Hannah?" Levi calls out, and I halt in my step, turning back. Rebecca's sneering eyes shoot daggers at me, but I let her nastiness roll off and move my focus to Levi.

"Yeah?"

"Can you check to see if they have any Aftershock in there?"

My lips break into a mischievous grin that mirrors his own. I nod, offering a small chuckle, and without giving Rebecca another thought, I give them my back and practically skip into the general store.

CHAPTER TEN

Levi

My mood is a lot lighter the rest of the drive. It could have something to do with the image of Hannah and that cute fucking smile of hers floating in my mind. I turn my head to reply to something Kip says, seeing her in the rearview mirror, and force that image away. *Ain't gonna happen, bro.* I must be losing my marbles to even consider anything between us. I shake my head and stare out the window. How the fuck did I find myself even considering that? I tell myself I wasn't. But I was. Watching her face light up did something to me. Made me happy to make her smile. Put some color in her cheeks as she blushed, sharing an inside joke. And shit, I remember that night. I thought I'd thrown up my liver. I barely remember passing out, but I do remember small hands wiping a wet towel over my mouth and holding my chin to get water down my throat. Ashamed, I also remember taking her down when she tried to get me to stand and go into the house. I remember passing back out and waking up on top of her. Scared the shit out of me, wondering why the fuck little Hannah Matthews was under me. Funny thing was, it was *her* trying to reassure *me*. She wasn't trying to pull anything on me. She was only trying to get me inside before her parents found me. It was while I stumbled inside, my arm wrapped around her tiny shoulders, that I swore if I ever drank Aftershock again, it would be the end of the person who gave it to me.

The next morning was hell. I woke up feeling like death, but at least I was in the guest room instead of behind the shed. I never said anything to Hannah, and she never mentioned it. I steal another glance through the rearview mirror, able to catch a silhouette of her all the way in the backseat. Her head is leaning against the window, and she appears to be lost in thought, her emotions unhidden by the crease of her brow and down curve of her lips. I wonder what she's thinking about. Gone is the baby face, braces, and childish grin. In its place, a woman all grown up. She has a beauty someone like Rebecca wished for. Natural. Soft. Enigmatic. Robust. I wish I could see her eyes. Get lost in the beauty of her soul. Feed off the passion radiating from within that makes her irresistible.

Shit, what's wrong with me?

It doesn't help that I can't pull my eyes away from her pouty lips, reminding me of when my mouth was on hers, savoring the smoothness, the sweet taste. It's a shame any time I get lost in the memory, the anger of how she got to me resurfaces, putting me back in my foul mood. What the fuck was she even thinking? The trouble she could have gotten me in. The lifelong friendship she could have ruined. It takes a lot for me to get mad, and Hannah Matthews went straight for the jugular. That breaks the hold she has on me and I rip my eyes away from her to get a quick glimpse of Kip. He's still going on about a time when we came up to Ketterville with kegs and almost got busted, having to roll three full barrels down the side of the dunes so we didn't get arrested for underage drinking.

"But shit, remember that? Took all seven of us to roll those kegs back up the hill."

"We're here!" Stacey chirps from the backseat as we all spot the *Welcome to Ketterville* sign. Everyone, minus a few garbles from Rebecca, admires the scenery as we drive through the quaint, historical town. The place has made a few changes, but it still has that small-town feel. We pass the bait shop, the bakery, the diner, and the small antique store, before hanging a left onto the dirt road leading to the campground.

We pull up to the familiar spot that's been the Matthews' stomping ground since day one, a patch of land surrounded by a thick forest aged beyond our lifetime. Hidden behind the greenery lies the most peaceful natural lake, which backs up to the wide rivers, perfect for kayaking. Kip pulls to the right to park, and everyone begins to shuffle out. Kip helps Stacey, and when Rebecca gets out, I watch her shut the door before allowing Hannah to exit. I shake my head, then open the door, lifting the seat up to give Hannah space to get out. I grab her hand, making sure she doesn't slip, but it doesn't stop her feet from tripping when they hit the ground. She falls into me, her body carved perfectly to fit against me. The beating of her heart and jagged breaths has me transfixed on her full lips.

Rebecca clears her throat, and I snap out of my haze. I quickly release her, not needing any more contact than necessary.

"Thanks." Her voice is soft as she adjusts her hair and tugs at her oversized hoodie. If I wasn't still fighting to hold onto my anger, I'd confess she doesn't need to hide herself, because under those thick clothes, she's beautiful.

"Yeah, whatever," I reply like a dick, then walk away from her, unable to miss the wave of sudden hurt settling in her eyes. If I stick around, she will see the confusion flooding in mine. Possibly a little bit of Dr. Jekyll and Mr. Hyde, because what the fuck is wrong with me? One minute, I'm trying to earn her trust and friendship, and the next, I'm giving her the cold treatment. *Figure your shit out, man.* What I need to do is keep my distance. Let this little infatuation brewing die out. Because there's no way I'm actually interested in Hannah Matthews.

I head toward the rear of the car as Kip throws the back open.

"All right. Everyone grab your shit." Kip starts lifting coolers and placing them outside the Tahoe. I grab for my bag and walk right past Hannah, not bothering to acknowledge her. When I pass by Rebecca, she sways into me, purposely causing our bodies to graze against one another.

"Levi Dent, be careful now," she teases, tossing her hair back and sashaying to the back to get her ridiculous amount of luggage.

I start setting up my tent when I hear Hannah's voice rise amongst the group.

"But I *did* bring it. I had it at the gas station."

"Are you sure?" Kip asks his sister. I head back to see Kip and Hannah still standing by his SUV.

"Kipley, I'm not dumb. I brought it." Hannah blinks rapidly, on the verge of tears, while Kip gives her the once-over, confused. Stacey walks up to Hannah and rubs her back, telling her it's going to be okay, while I take a peek at Rebecca, who looks guilty as fuck.

"What's going on?" I ask. What the fuck is Rebecca up to now?

"We can't find Hannah's tent."

"What do you mean you can't find it?" I ask again. There's no doubt Hannah brought her tent. I saw it myself.

"It's not in here. But I brought it," she snaps, bringing her eyes straight to Rebecca.

Kip bends forward into the back of his Tahoe in one last attempt to find it and climbs back out. "I'm sorry, Han. It's not here."

"That's because *she* probably threw it out back at the gas station! She was the last one by the car!"

Rebecca theatrically brings her fingers to her chest. "*Me?* I wouldn't do such a thing."

Bullshit. My focus is on Hannah, her hands formed into tight fists, her eyes shooting off daggers at Rebecca. She's pissed as fuck, and I'm about to be the same.

Kipley tries to console his sister. "Listen, no need to blame anyone. It could have accidently fallen out while we had the back open. We can call Dad and have him bring one up tomorrow. For tonight, I'm sure we can figure something out—"

"She can sleep in my tent." *What. The. Fuck?* Did that just come out of my mouth? Hannah's head flies in my direction, her posture becoming rigid. Her almond eyes shine with shock as my offer sinks in. A heavy feeling settles into my stomach, realizing my mistake. What did I just do?

Rebecca's audible gasp breaks our strange moment, her mouth dropping and practically crashing to the ground. "You have to be kidding me," she whines, stomping her foot on the ground.

"That's a great idea. Thanks, Levi," Kip says, patting his sister on the shoulder. "No different than sleeping in our tent."

Hannah's still in shock. Rebecca reins in her tantrum and speaks up. "Wait, I mean, isn't that weird? Can't she, like, sleep in the Tahoe or something?"

"Levi and Hannah have known each other since we were kids. It's like sleeping with her brother. They'll be fine," Kip says nonchalantly, brushing it off. He sees no problem with us sharing a tent while the red flags are flying all around me, bashing me in the goddamn face. Hannah must feel the same way, because she's suddenly turning pale as shit.

"See, Han, it'll be fine." Kip walks past me, slapping me on the shoulder. "Thanks, man." And he's off with Stacey to set up their tent.

What the fuck did I just do?

I can't figure out whether to aim my anger at Rebecca for being so conniving or Kip for thinking this is a good idea. Maybe I should be angry at Hannah for putting me in this position. For making me care. Because she should *not* be my problem. *Then why the hell did I get myself involved?* She would have been just fine sleeping in the Tahoe. Shit, she can *have* my tent, I'll sleep in the fucking car. There's no way I can sleep in the same small, cramped space as her. Not without tempting myself.

Have I mentioned what a horrible idea this trip was? I take another hefty swig of my beer. Sixth, to be exact, while I watch with narrowed eyes as Kip, Stacey, and Hannah all participate in what seems to be the funniest conversation ever.

I, on the other hand, am stuck on the other side of the fire, trapped by the one and only bitch stalker. When I originally sat down, I made it so Hannah would have a spot by me. But Hannah felt it necessary to create her own makeshift seat, nearly sitting on her damn brother's lap. That left the seat wide open for yappy trap to get her sharp claws into me and talk my goddamn ear off. Hence the sixth beer.

I slam the rest of my beer and toss it into the fire along with another log. The flames ignite, sending a soft glow into the night. Hannah's face appears a bit flushed, probably from the two beers she drank and all the laughing. I've done a great job tuning out Rebecca for the last hour or so, but that could be because I'm too focused on staring at Hannah and thinking about how I want to take her over my thigh and spank the shit out of her for fucking up the seating arrangements. If she would have just sat next to me, I wouldn't have been forced to listen to this nonsense next to me. I imagine her small little body cradled over my knee, her summer dress hiked over her perky little ass. I picture my palm spanking her porcelain skin, each slap leaving my handprint on her flesh.

"Fuck," I groan, swiping my hands down my face. *Get ahold of yourself, Dent.*

"Fuck is right. I mean, how can someone just pick the same color polish as me when I was totally about to grab it? I told that little high school brat to get her own color. Ugh." I twist in my seat toward Rebecca, fighting the urge to knock her off her chair. The way she ogles me makes me want to push her into the fire. "You know, the way you're looking at me, I would think you wanted to take a tour of my tent."

I laugh, loud and boisterous, unable to hold back at how

dumb this chick is. I lift my hand to correct her when I decide pissing her off is not in my best interest.

"No, I'm good, but if you wanted to fetch me a beer, that'd be great." She smiles like I just offered her a marriage proposal and pops up, skipping over to the cooler. I debate on getting up and moving my chair. Or just going to bed so I don't have to be tortured anymore. Or simply going over and pulling Hannah off the damn ground and placing her little ass in the seat I set out for her.

I do none of it. Rebecca is back before I can execute any of my plans. I go to grab for the beer, but she lifts her tank, revealing her stomach, and uses it to twist off the cap, then takes the first swig before slowly handing it over to me. *Remind me to burn my lips off after drinking this.* I thank her and direct my attention back to the fire. Or at least what's happening on the other side of it.

One, two, three, four gulps, I take from my bottle as my eyes lock on her. I should stop staring. I know Stacey caught me eyeing her sister-in-law. I should stop. But I can't. The way her face lights up at anything her brother says. The way she moans, placing her s'more into her mouth, the marshmallow slightly burnt, just how she likes it. I watch her fingers brush against her chin as she wipes away some excess chocolate from her sweet bite. The way her lower lip—

"Levi, did you want a s'more? You look like you're salivating over there," Stacey busts me. I blink, trying to recall what she just said.

I feel Hannah watching me. I fight to keep my eyes off her. "Nah, I'm good." I shake my head, finishing off my beer. I toss it in the fire, and take the time out needed to piss and get a new beer.

The remainder of my night is pretty much the same. I drink too fast and take every opportunity to imagine doing something extremely fucking dirty to Hannah. When she gets up to go to the bathroom, I imagine finding her in the dark woods and pounding her against a tree until she explodes around my cock. When she takes a sip of her beer, I imagine her sucking me off. Every time she bends over to stoke the fire, I imagine myself behind her, fucking her into oblivion.

It's not until she finally says she's tired and going to bed that I feel some relief, needing her out of my sight...then she disappears into my tent and the agony in my pants gets worse.

She is sleeping in my goddamn tent.

Therefore, I drink more.

And more.

Until I'm the only one awake. And unless I plan to sleep on the ground, it's time to face the music.

I stumble through the dark campground, taking a piss, then putting out the fire. I stand outside the tent entrance for god knows how long, debating on what I'm going to find. A part of me prays it's her naked and awake, waiting for me, while the sane part begs for her to be in a damn snow suit huddled in the corner.

I sway, hauling the zipper down, and trip as I step over the flap of the tent. My eyes try to adjust to the darkness, curious where she is. I use my phone flashlight and find her cuddled up at the far end of the air mattress. She has a small blanket covering her bare legs, but it appears she's changed into a pair of pajama shorts and tank top. My eyes fixate on the pink lace bra strap hanging out of her bag and my mind goes back to the supply closet and the way her plump breasts fit perfectly in my palms.

"Don't go there, Dent," I mumble to myself. Hannah sighs, stretching her leg down the mattress, and I slam my eyes shut, refusing to steal a peek. I wobble, forgetting I need my eyes to see, and open one to maneuver through the tent. "Eyes to yourself, buddy," I chant, stumbling over to the other side of the tent where my bag sits. I debate sleeping in my clothes, then decide fuck it. I toss my shirt off and drop my pants, then grab for a pair of gym shorts. Without throwing Hannah off the mattress, I crawl onto the bed as gently as possible. It's tough since I weigh three times as much as she does. The second I lay down, the mattress causes her to slide toward the center of the bed and roll into me.

"Fuck me." *Don't touch her. Don't touch her.* I'm too drunk for this shit. I need to get up and sleep this off on the ground outside. I attempt to sit up when her hand moves, brushing against my side. She tucks her hand under her face, but not before leaving a trail of vanilla in its wake.

I try covering my nose, waiting for the smell to disappear. Once it's gone, I'm out of here.

A few more seconds, then I'm getting up.

Two more…

CHAPTER ELEVEN

Hannah

I'm dreaming.

I'm in my bed, consumed by the warmth of the person enveloping me in his arms. His solid chest warms my back while his arms wrap around my body, keeping me close. His fingers graze around my navel, and with each breath, they lower to my sensual place that aches for him.

My center pulsates for him to touch me in the most shameful way, and only in a dream would I find myself acting so brazen at his subtle touch. I use my hand to cup his, pushing his thick fingers past my pajama shorts, through my soaked folds.

I'm rewarded with an elusive groan, and his hand takes over, working me. His fingers graze up and down my center, spreading me as one slips inside. My head tosses back at the too real sensation. His warm breath caresses my shoulder as his lips consume the skin above my collarbone. *God yes, this is what I've been wanting. Needing.*

Small whimpers of pleasure fall off my lips, rewarding me with a second finger. His hardness thrusts against my backside as I work my hips into his hand. *Yes, yes...this is what I crave.* I beg my conscious to never wake up.

I'm getting close. So close. His hand speeds up, moving more aggressively in and out of me, giving me exactly what I want. Small, short pants fall from my lips. My walls start to squeeze around him. My hand lowers inside my panties, my fingers barely covering the top of his hand as I ride his motions.

"Fuck, you're so wet and tight," a familiar voice moans into my ear.

The vibrations of his words seem so real.

Almost too real.

"That's it, baby. Rock your pussy against my hand."

God, his voice. It's always his voice when I have these fantasies. I don't want to open my eyes and kill my dream. It's right there...

"Ahhh..." I moan, breathlessly, as my orgasm explodes, clenching around his thick fingers.

My eyes open suddenly, my dream feeling way too realistic. I've never had such a powerful sex dream before. I shift from my pillow, realizing I'm not in my bed.

I'm not even at home.

Camping.

Levi's tent.

Levi.

I scream and throw myself off the air mattress, tossing Levi off me. He must have been in a deep sleep, because while I fly off one end, he flies to the other side and flips off.

"Fuck...fuck...what happened?" He shoots up, and I jump up and fall into the side of the tent, practically taking the whole thing down.

"Oh my god. I wasn't dreaming." My voice shakes. I'm going to throw up. His gaze, still clouded by sleep, darts around. His hands scrape down his face, over his frown, and when they land on me, horror threatens to take me out by the knees. He was also dreaming. Does he know? What we just...

His hand stalls over his mouth, and lines begin to form between his eyebrows. His mouth opens and closes, attempting to form words, but nothing comes out. But there's no need for words. Realization is sparking him awake when he registers the scent of me on his fingers.

"Shit, what the—?"

The scent of me lingers against his lip, and I jump headfirst into panic mode.

Oh god! I need to get out of here!

"Oh shit, Hannah! I...*shit*, wait, I thought I was—"

"Gah! Don't say another word!" I grab for my shoes and throw down the zipper to the tent. It snags on the fabric, getting stuck. Because of course it does. I yank and pull as a lifetime of awkward seconds pass. As soon as it frees, I stage-dive out of the tent. What in the ever loving—?

"Hey, are you okay? I heard you scream."

I scream again, nearly coming out of my skin. Stacey jolts with a start at my reaction. "Oh, Jesus all mighty, I'm sorry. I didn't expect you to be out here."

"I was trying to get some breakfast started. You okay?"

Absolutely not. "Yeah, fine. I saw a spider. Freaked out. Probably gonna have to take the whole tent down." Stacey peers over my shoulder at the tent, then back to me. There is no doubt my face is flushed. I mean, I *did* just have an orgasm. GAH!

"Yeah, sure. Okay. Is Levi up?"

Oh, he's up. "Yeah, could be. Not really sure. I wasn't paying attention..."

Just then, his head peeks through the opening of the tent, followed by the rest of his body. I throw my eyes everywhere but in his direction.

"Hey, Levi. Hear you have a spider. We have spray if you need it." My mind suddenly forms this image of myself spraying repellent all over Levi, hoping he stays away...or maybe should I spray myself? *Who even initiated that?* I'm getting flustered all over again just thinking about it. I need space. Tons of space.

"I'm gonna go to the bathroom."

"I'm just gonna go take a leak."

We both whip our heads in each other's direction.

"Oh, you go then."

"No, it's fine. You go."

"Well, someone go. Geez." Stacey steps in, breaking up the battle of who's going to run and hide. Since I can't imagine having to stick back and deal with Stacey's curious inquiries, I volunteer and take off into the woods.

Slipping on my flip flops, I grab my towel, tanning lotion, and sunglasses. As soon as I step out of the tent, the sun almost blinds me, so I drop my shades from the top of my head and peer over to my right where everyone seems to be huddling.

"All right, everyone, double check you have your life jackets. You don't want to kayak without 'em." Kipley instructs everyone on the rules of the lake while I head to the Tahoe to grab my kindle and headphones. I close the door—and jump fifty feet backwards, practically denting Kipley's SUV.

"Jesus, Levi!"

"Sorry. I thought you saw me."

"I didn't." I push off the Tahoe and start walking back toward the camp. Kipley is snapping Stacey's life jacket on, while Rebecca attempts to put hers on backwards. I shake my head. What an idiot.

"We're getting ready to leave. If you don't change your shoes, we're going to miss the kayak excursion."

"I'm not going on the excursion." At that, Levi stops, but I don't. I keep walking until I get to my brother and hand him his keys.

"And why exactly aren't you going?" he continues to dig.

"Who, Hannah?" Kipley laughs. "She hasn't gone near the river since Chase knocked her out of her kayak that one year."

Levi's eyes shift back to me in question, but I ignore them. I slide my glasses up my nose and throw my backpack over my shoulder. Leaning in, I give my brother a kiss on the cheek and tell him and Stacey to have fun. I don't bother wishing Rebecca well since I hope she floats off a waterfall...not that there are any.

I continue my walk through the pathed woods, which eventually lead to the open lake. When I make it to the clearing, the sun shines beautifully over the water. The old deck in need of a slight makeover makes me smile. The memories that have been made throughout the years. Good and bad. The place where I got my stupid Hannah Banana nickname, to our family competitions of who could hold their breath the longest under water. It makes me wish my mom had been able to join us for this trip, but with her donating her free time to the local flower shop, she sadly had to decline Dad's offer.

I lay my towel on the deck, feeling the heat below my feet from the hot sun, then place my earbuds in my ears. The upbeat sounds of my favorite artist play in my ears as I lay my head down—

"Room for two on this deck?"

My eyes fly open, the sun blocked by a tall, built, gorgeous problem. "What are you doing here, Levi? I thought you were kayaking?" I sit up, the annoyance in my voice evident.

"I was. But I didn't feel well. So, I came back."

"Then why are you *here*?"

He shrugs, dropping his towel next to mine. "Thought some sun and relaxation would do me good." Ugh, he is *not* planning on staying here with me all day! "Unless you'd rather be alone." He stands there waiting for a reply. I want to say yes, I would *love* to be alone. Spending the day with him says no relaxing will be had. My nerves are already going bonkers, and my body is tense simply from him standing here. And god forbid if he dares attempt to bring up this morning.

He's surveying me with those deep emerald eyes. Nothing says he's here to bust my chops. Maybe it's just me all worked up and overthinking. Maybe we can pretend this morning didn't happen.

What morning?

Exactly.

"No, it's fine. Have at it." I scoot my towel a little to the right so he can fit his on the deck. He nods and smiles, adjusting his towel. We don't speak for some time while he sits and stares off across the lake. I would ask him what's got his attention, but I get it. The view is breathtaking. It's when I place my earbuds back in and lay back down that he breaks the silence.

"What happened with Chase and why you won't go kayaking?" I remove my earbuds and sit back up. "You don't have to tell me. I'm just curious."

"I almost drowned."

He pulls his eyes away from the lake to connect with mine. There's an intensity in his stare pleading for me to explain.

"It was when I was eleven. We all went on the kayak trip like we did every year. The whole family, and of course, that year, Kipley had his whole gang with him, minus you. I think you may have had a game that weekend. Anyway, we were all on the water and Chase thought it would be funny to flip me. We were in a low current so it wasn't like I couldn't stand if I wanted to. He rocked my boat, the usual Chase taunt. I wasn't afraid to flip, but when I did, I became stuck. My foot had been caught on the beach bag I jammed in the front of my boat."

"Jesus Christ, Hannah." I shrug away his distress. It was a long time ago. "Tell me. What happened?"

"I tried to free my foot, but it wasn't budging. I banged on the boat, but you know Chase, he probably got a bigger laugh at the fact. Either way, time passed, and thankfully, right when I ran out of air, they figured it out. Ben came under and grabbed me, pulled me out, and gave me the ol' mouth to mouth." I pause, embarrassed at having to admit that.

"Hannah, Jesus, I'm so sorry."

"Pfft. Don't be, it wasn't a big deal." But in reality, it was. There was more to the story I chose to keep to myself. The fear that consumed me thinking I was going to drown. The anger at how someone could be so cruel. Chase didn't seem guilty in the least bit. He laughed it off, claiming I was probably faking to get attention. Poked harder by saying it was my way of getting Ben to kiss me. The humiliation on top of the fear that took over my wellbeing…I'd never been able to put myself back in that boat. I loved kayaking, and after that day, I hated it.

"Either way, it's in the past. Water under the boat." I wink, trying to make light of the situation, but his hard stare says he finds this anything but humorous. "Not funny?" I smile at my super lame pun.

"No, not funny."

"Oh well. I was never headed for a career in comedy." He studies me for a quick moment, then lays down on his own towel, closing his eyes. I can't help but admire how handsome he is with the sun basking on his skin. Birds flock over the calm lake, the chorus of chirping blowing in the small breeze, a sweet smell in the air from the wildflowers growing along the water's edge. He seems so peaceful here, like he always did when we were kids. My emotions start to take me back to a time when my world revolved around him. My silly, magical world of dreams that carrousel around the fairytale of my version of a happily ever after. Silent laughter seeps from my eyes as I gaze down at him, curious if my feelings were ever visible to him. Would he laugh away my crazy childhood fantasy? I pull my eyes away, forcing myself to leave those long-buried emotions at rest.

Picking up a leaf that's blown into my lap, I tear it in two. "Your turn. Care to enlighten me on how you became teacher's pet to my dad?" I ask, changing the direction of my thoughts. I smile down at him, a tightness in my heart at the way his lips form into a smirk. I should have stayed quiet. Allowed myself the time to push down the old feelings that have been resurfacing since the night of the wedding. I peer down at him needing another quick hit to feed my childhood addiction. When I steal a quick peek, his eyes are already on me. Busted. He holds my gaze, locking me into his emerald embrace. After a few seconds, I shift my head, pretending to be fascinated with the scenery in front of me.

"He's been more of a father figure to me than my own dad, and ever since I could remember, I wanted to be just like him." He breaks the silence with his sobering words, bringing me back in his line of sight. My mind searches for any memories of his family, his dad specifically, but none really come to mind. I think his dad is still alive, unless...

"Is your dad—?"

"Dead? I wish. No, sadly." I stare at him, blinking away the shock at how he can speak so bluntly about his parent. His words catch me off guard, and my reaction doesn't go unnoticed. "No need to look so surprised. My father was a drunk. He loved his booze more than he did his family and that never changed. And once I was about to go big, he loved the possibility of my money even more. He didn't attend a single game, ceremony, or sponsorship camp. He was never a true father to me. But your dad was. He was the one who showed up to all my games, dinners, and went with me to all my scout trainings."

"*My* dad? How come I never knew this?"

He shrugs, throwing his hands behind his head. "It's not like it was a secret. But for some reason, we both chose to keep our time together private. Jim…your dad, came to my house one day, wanting to speak to my father about tagging along on a scout trip. He didn't want to overstep so he thought to get my father's approval first—not having a clue what he was walking into. My father, drunk off his ass, took a swing at me right in front of him. He tried to break it up, but it only made it worse. My mom had just left us. She'd had enough, got smart, and took off. Shitty thing is, she didn't think to take me with and save *me* from him. But your dad stepped in and took me in. That's why I stayed with you guys that whole summer."

I remember that. I mean, who wouldn't? The lead football star living in the room next to me for three whole months. I remember putting a cup to the wall almost every night trying to eavesdrop on anything he was doing.

"From there on, he just stuck by me. Stepped in as my father figure and helped me make the right decisions along the way."

"And what happened to your dad?"

"He showed back up years later when scouts were calling. I'd been in my second year of college. They'd gotten his phone number somehow and started sweet talking him with money and boats and fame—all the shit that would come my way if I signed with a certain team. Of course, my father ate it up. Made commitments behind my back. Thought he was going to get a piece of my hard-earned pie."

He pauses, and I raise a brow, eager for him to continue. "And?"

He laughs. "Your dad, once again, stepped in. Gave me the advice I needed, and I took it. I knew my dad would always be there trying to rob me somehow. And a small part of me felt I was robbing myself by not taking the road less traveled. So, with your dad's help, I chose to complete my education. With no money piling in, my dad, once again, was in the wind, along with my NFL career." My somber expression doesn't go unnoticed when his eyes peek back open. "Don't give me that pity look. I chose this path, and I don't regret it. Not for a single second. Being the teacher's pet was the best thing to ever happen to me."

I want to sit here and dwell on how hard his life had been, and how he felt the need to keep it a secret. I would have never thought Levi Dent had it any way but good. I want to tell him how sorry I am for the hardships he faced and hug my dad for being such a great figure for him.

"So, you going to enjoy the sun or block mine all day?" His smile, the most beautiful thing I've ever seen, extends to his eyes, burying any dwindling emotion I was beginning to harbor. I decide it's best to drop the topic and refrain from saying any more. I lay down, pressing my back against my sun-heated towel and close my eyes, allowing the warmth of the sun to relax my mind.

The rest of the day pans out to be quite lovely, a constant chatter fluttering between us. We stay away from any deep topics and avoid the I-thought-I-was-having-a-sex-dream catastrophe. He shares funny college stories about some of his old teammates, while I try to counter-share, failing miserably since my college experience was less exciting. We eat the snacks I brought while he listens to my playlist. He laughs at my Kindle library, wanting a detailed summary of each book. Of course, he picks out only the ones with the smutty covers. We enjoy the day, the sun, a place where we both spent most of our childhood.

It's late afternoon when I sit up, pressing my fingers against my skin.

"You're getting burnt. Give me the sunblock." Levi sits up with me and reaches for the bottle of lotion, nodding for me to give him my back, though I'm not sure having his hands on me is the best idea. We've had such a great day, I don't want to ruin it by things getting weird. He seems at ease with the situation, so I hand over the bottle and pivot.

The second his hands touch my sunned skin, I shiver. "Oh, that's cold. But it feels fantastic. I may have waited too long to reapply," I say, closing my eyes. His strong hands work me slowly, gently, reaching the top of my neck to my lower spine. I feel guilty for enjoying it as much as I do, but lean into him anyway.

"You're probably going to need some aloe later," he says, his voice sounding a bit off. I wonder if he senses the same electricity between us. Or is it just me and my wishful mind?

His palms wrap around my hips, his thumbs dipping just below my bathing suit bottoms, continuing to work in the lotion. If I were honest, I'd admit the lotion soaked into my skin ages ago, but I wonder where his hands will go next. Will they move up my back, possibly to my front…touch me below my waist?

Before I have a chance to wonder any further, his hands are

gone. Levi clears his throat. "You should be all set." He pulls back and stands, facing away from me.

"Did you…uh, want me to get your back—?"

"No! No, I'm good. It's actually really hot. I'm just gonna dive right in."

And with that, he jumps headfirst into the lake.

CHAPTER TWELVE

Levi

The rush of the cold water smacks onto my hard-on, causing me to groan as I go under. It was either bruise my dick or risk Hannah seeing what she did to me.

I break through the surface, whipping my hair back out of my face. I wipe the water dripping down my face and catch Hannah standing at the edge of the dock. It's a damn good thing my lower half is under water. My dick is a resilient motherfucker and hasn't gone down.

Hannah's pink and white bathing suit is modest on top, covering her full chest, but leaves nothing to the imagination with her bare legs. The sun offers her skin a nice glow, and her cheeks are flushed from the heat. She is absolutely stunning. While I still battle with what she did—and why—there's something about Hannah Matthews that intrigues me. Makes me want to get to learn everything about her, inside and out. There's no doubt I want her. My dick pops up to salute her every time she's near, and I finger-fucked her in my sleep for Christ's sake.

I freaked the fuck out when I fully woke up, realizing what had happened. I was having the best dream ever—until I realized it wasn't a dream. My fingers were deep in her warm cunt, stroking her, listening to her soft moans. When she screamed and jumped off the mattress, I panicked, scared I assaulted her, possibly still drunk and forced myself on her. I felt like a huge asshole, fearing

Hannah was going to rat me out the second I heard Stacey's voice outside the tent. I threw my hands over my face, waiting for the wrath. That's when I smelled her, brought my finger to my nose and inhaled. I'm a sick fuck, but it was heaven. Would it make me even worse if I tasted her off my finger next? She was doing things to me I couldn't explain. I want to be so mad at her, but I can't.

Because I want something from Hannah Matthews in a deep way. I'm just afraid to admit to myself what that is.

"You gonna come in?" I ask, needing to get her body out of full view and into this water so there's less for me to see.

"Debating. I hear there are monsters that eat people in there," she teases, reminding me of the time we were all up here and Chase really laid into her.

"Are you chicken? Too scared to find out?" I start making clucking noises, egging her on. My dick perks at her glowing smile, and now I'm rethinking her joining me.

"What if I get sucked under? It's going to be all your fault."

"I'll tell everyone you put up a good fight before you went down." I waggle my brows, waiting for her to make her move. She backs up, catching me off guard. Getting a running start, she cannonballs into the lake.

The large splash causes me to lose focus on where she lands. I wipe the water from my face and spin around, waiting for her to pop up and scare me. She was always a little ninja when she was younger, coming out of nowhere when we would be doing something we shouldn't have been.

A few more seconds pass, and I do another spin. Where the fuck is she? "Hannah?" I call her name, spinning again. I stare at the water, searching for air bubbles, but nothing. No riff whatsoever.

"Okay. You win. You can come up now," I say, my nerves coming through in my voice. "Hannah, for real, this isn't funny." I dip my head under, trying to open my eyes, but it's too murky to see. I pull my head back up to take a large breath and scan the water around me to see if she's come up, panic gripping my chest. Maybe she hit something when she went down. Caught her foot on something. Fuck, she could be stuck, freaking out—

A break in the water causes a huge splash and Hannah pops up. She laughs, wiping at her face, and I grab her, pulling her body into mine.

"What the fuck, Hannah? I thought you hurt yourself." I'm suddenly angry. Frazzled at the thought of something happening to her. Being so close, she has no choice but to wrap her hands around my neck.

"Sorry, I was just playing."

"You were under forever. I thought you drowned. How was that even possible?"

"Years of practice holding my breath. I guess when you're kind of a loner and have nothing else to do, you teach yourself how to stay under water the longest."

I watch her eyes soften, the sad truth in her voice ruining me. All those years we picked on her, made her feel alone...she *felt* alone. I want to kick myself for how I treated her. Not that I took part, but I never stopped it. I stood by and watched Chase dig at her every chance he got. Ben wasn't any better. I want to tell her she isn't alone anymore. I want to kiss the sadness off her lips and tell her I'm so fucking sorry for never being there before.

Our bodies are pressed tightly to one another, but her closeness isn't enough. The protector in me aches to build a steel wall around her to protect her. Slay anyone who ever dares steal that sparkle out of her doe eyes. I'm fixated on her damn lips, full and wet from the water. My heartbeat picks up, and I wonder if she can sense the change in me. My muscles press against her as I pull her closer. The way her lips part, she senses the hardness growing in my swim trunks. Fuck, I want to kiss her right now. Her hooded gaze tells me she wants to kiss me too. This is wrong. I need to rip myself away from her and do the right thing. But there's a pain in my chest at the thought of denying myself this moment. Her wet, full lips against mine. Fuck, I can't stop it. I'll deal with the consequences later. But I need her mouth.

I lean forward, gauging her reaction, watching for any hesitation on her part. Her eyes become heavy with lust, her cheeks flushed, breaths coming faster. Her eyes meet mine, lids half-mast, and the way she looks at me...

I move to press my lips against hers, to take what I crave, when Kipley's voice echoes across the lake.

"Hannah! Where are you at!"

My heart shoots out of my chest, and my stomach drops to my ass in panic. Before I can think better of it, I dunk Hannah into the water.

"Hannah...? Oh, Levi, s'up man? Hannah with you?"

Yeah, she's under the water, probably floating right next to my hard-on.

"She was here somewhere, you know her, all over the place." I try to hide my shock when Hannah pops up almost at the other end of the lake. *Jesus, how does she do that?* She lifts her head, waves to Kip, and begins her swim back to shore.

"Hey, how was kayaking?" she asks, climbing up the deck ladder.

"Fun, minus all of Rebecca's whining." Kip turns to me. "You really screwed us by pulling out. She complained the whole time about wanting to come back. Unless that's what you wanted?" Kip wiggles his eyebrows, and it instantly pisses me off.

"Trust me, not my plan, man." I swim up to the dock and climb up. Hannah wraps herself in her towel, refusing to make eye contact with me.

"Speak of the devil. Beware, she's on the prowl."

We all turn to see Stacey and Rebecca walking down the hill.

"There you are! I went to your tent to see how you were feeling but you weren't there." Rebecca comes right up to me, not bothering to read my body language that says *don't you dare fucking do it*, and places her hand on my chest. "I was so worried about you." She talks to me in a tart baby voice, and I want to throw her in the lake. Out of the corner of my eye, Hannah grabs her things, cramming her towel in her backpack. I want to tell Hannah she has the wrong idea—really wrong idea—but there's no way to do that without Kip hearing me and throwing my dead body in the lake after he kills me.

"I'm fine. You don't have to worry. I was just hanging out with Hannah." I try to include her, hoping to show her I'm happy to have spent the day with her. Rebecca does not take lightly to the new information.

She aims her bitchiness at Hannah. "Wow, Hannah. What are you wearing?" She cynically laughs. "Is that a sports bra? Girl, it's a new age. You can wear a bathing suit nowadays," she jokes.

Hannah frowns, peering down at her suit. "This *is* a bathing suit. What's wrong with it?"

Rebecca lifts her arms, tossing off her cover up. "See, girl? *This* is a bathing suit. I guess if you don't have anything to flaunt, you wear something like that. Little Hannah Matthews, still the little tomboy," she taunts, pointing to her chest.

"Rebecca," Stacey warns.

I keep my eyes on Hannah, watching the sparkle slowly fade from her eyes.

"What?" Rebecca grins, looking at me. "Don't you agree, Levi? You would much rather look at something like this, wouldn't you?" She steps closer, lifting her hair over her chest to expose her too obvious fake tits. Anger sears through me at her cruelty. I search out Hannah, her eyes flickering with fury and unshed tears. Withdrawing, she bends down, snatching up her bag and throwing it over her shoulder. Without another word, she pushes past me and Kip, thrusting her shoulder hard into mine, and storms away.

"Hannah! Where are you going? She's just joking." Kip tries to grab for her, but she throws his arm off her shoulder and treks quickly up the hill. "Hannah! Come on." He makes one last attempt, but lets her go.

"Gosh, what's *her* problem? I was only trying to help her out. Poor girl needs some fashion advice."

"And *you* need to get some fucking manners," I bark, pushing her away from me and sprinting up the hill after Hannah.

I'll give Hannah one thing, she sure is fast. I make it into the woods, but she's already clear across the way. "Hannah, wait!" I call for her, but she's not stopping. I pick up the pace, practically in a jog before I finally catch up to her. "Hannah, fuck, slow down, I'm trying to catch up—"

She swings around, her cheeks soaked with tears. "What? Go back to the fun. You're missing out on all the jokes." She turns again and starts walking.

"I don't want to go back there. Just stop for a second." I speed up and grab for her. "Hannah, stop." She whips around and surprises me when she lifts her hands and shoves me away from her.

"No, you stop! You all stop! I'm not eight anymore. I'm not eleven, thirteen, sixteen. I'm not the little Hannah Matthews you all got your kicks making fun of. I won't take it anymore!" Her eyes are on fire. She's breathing in quick pants, quivering with fury. The hurt radiating from her wounded eyes guts me.

"Hannah, I don't think that."

"Right," she laughs cynically. "Go back, Levi, and leave me alone."

"I said no. God, will you fucking listen to me?" I snap.

"Listen to you? Why? You think because you're not the one throwing the insults that you're any better? Why didn't you stick up for me? Why didn't you ever stick up for me?" Her tears begin to fall again, crushing me. I take a step toward her, but her hands go up defensively. "No, I'm done. I'm done taking shit from you and your group—people needing to pick on the less fortunate to get off. I get it. I'm a loser. Always will be."

"I never fucking said that."

"You don't need to. I made a huge mistake with you. I thought you were different. But you're not. I may have tricked you that night, but I was the one who was truly fooled. Leave me alone."

She turns to run, but I'm on her. I grab her shoulders, whipping her around to face me. Her eyes are wide with hurt and shock. I waste no time bending down and slamming my lips to hers. I kiss her aggressively, showing no mercy as I take her mouth hard. At first, she tries to push me away, denying the kiss, but it's no sooner she allows me access, her mouth widening as my tongue wraps around hers. I push her taut little body up against the nearest tree and grab for her hips, grinding into her, needing her to understand exactly what she does to me.

"Levi," she moans my name, and my dick doubles in size. I love the way my name sounds off her lips. I grind into her again, deepening our kiss. I want to kiss her forever, take everything from her and when she has nothing left, take some more.

"You're not done with me," I growl, demanding she understand. She woke something inside me that day in the closet and is crazy if she thinks I'm just going to walk away from it. I kick her legs open with my knee and shove my hand down her suit bottoms, finding the tight warmth I've been fucking dying to feel again. I slide two fingers inside her slick sex and swallow each moan with my kisses as I work her hard and fast.

"This is not something you quit, Hannah. What you started, it's nowhere near done." I take my fingers and push up, going as deep as I can, until a small whimper escapes her lips.

"Levi." My name off her lips is like music to my ears.

"That's it, baby, let go." I fuck her with my fingers, feeling the exact moment her orgasm takes over. Her walls clench around me, her lips breaking from mine as she leans back against the tree.

God, she is fucking beautiful when she comes. I work her slowly, until the sensitivity of her post-orgasm causes her to squirm. I pull out and put her bottoms back in place, taking in her flushed cheeks and glazed-over eyes. It puts a cocky grin on my face appreciating I brought her to that place.

"Oh my god." She lifts her head, trying to hide her face. "I can't believe we just did that."

"Again, you mean?" I push, testing her comfort level. She groans, and I laugh.

"I was hoping you were too asleep to remember," she mumbles into my shirt.

"I fucking sucked on my fingers after you left. I'm pretty sure there was no way that was a dream." She lifts her head, her eyes shy but curious.

"Oh god, what are we doing here?"

That's a damn good question. And I have no idea how to answer it. Never in a million years had I imagined I'd have my mind wrapped around Kipley Matthews' little sister. But dammit, I'm fucking glad it is.

"I have no idea, but I'm nowhere near done finding out." I waste no more time. I scoop her up in my arms and start hustling her back toward the campsite. Her little squeal turns me on and makes me walk faster. If I wasn't worried about tripping over a branch and launching her out of my arms, I'd start sprinting. Now that the barrier between us is finally down, I have one mission and one mission only.

CHAPTER THIRTEEN

Hannah

I cannot believe what's happening right now. I saw my day going to crap as I hurried back, ready to hitchhike home. But then Levi came for me. And before I knew it, *I* was coming for *him*.

Oh god!

I giggle as he essentially runs while carrying me back to the campsite. I want to ask him why he's in such a hurry, but every time I open my mouth, he trips, and I yelp, scared I'm going to go flying.

When we make it back, Levi goes straight for his tent, unlatching the zipper and throwing it down. He carries me inside and lays me on the air mattress, wasting no time in covering me with his strong body, his mouth over mine.

I still can't believe this is happening. Levi, in all his glory, kissing me. *Me!* And this time, I can't say it's because of trickery or sleep. My body is intuitively sensitive to the way his molds to mine, the way his lips consume me. He stimulates every sensual fiber in me as my tongue does a perfect waltz around his.

I wrap my arms behind his neck, bringing him closer, silently showing him I want this too. All the years I pined over this man, it almost doesn't feel real. I never felt worthy of Levi. Never imagined he'd give me the time of day. Doubt sours my stomach, afraid I might be looking too far into this. But how could I not? I'm so far out of his league, it *does* seem too good to be true. The doubt grows heavier as I think about how we got here: my scheme, a typical man's need for sex. That's all this could be. He was right when he said this was wrong. The trouble he would face from my brother if he ever found out. His job. The disappointment from my father.

"Oh god." I start to pull away.

"What? What's wrong?" His eyes cast over me with concern.

"I just…I'm not sure this is right. You have a lot to lose, and I'm not worth it. I know I tricked—"

Levi's finger presses against my lips. "Stop. I know what you're doing. You're doubting this. Stop."

"But you're right, we—"

More pressure to my mouth. "Yes, this is a crazy fucking idea, and if anyone finds out, I'm dead. But don't get it in that pretty little head of yours that you're not worth it. Because you are."

I suck in my lower lip and bite down to stop the emotions from overcoming me. No one has ever said that to me. My whole life, I've struggled to fit in, be noticed, be someone, and in one sentence, Levi has made me feel all those things.

"Thank you." It's barely a whisper, but he hears it. His tender smile touches my heart, and he bends down, replacing his fingers with his soft lips. He kisses me gently, taking it slower.

All too soon, he's pulling his lips from mine. "It's the truth, Hannah. I may have never seen you before, but I see you now. I have no idea what we're doing. Not a fucking clue. But I want this. I know you do too. Let me show you just how much."

His lips are back on mine as his hands roam over my body, the tips of his fingers inciting sparks from every single nerve ending. He unsnaps my bathing suit top, skimming the straps down my arms, then moves to my bottoms. His fingers run along my hips, gripping the fabric, then rolling it down my legs. I kick them off, and he pulls at his, throwing them on top of mine. His shirt is up and over his head, leaving us both completely bare and vulnerable. His mouth drops down to my chin, kisses trailing down my neck, past my collarbone, between my breasts.

I arch my back as he cups my breast, massaging my hard and perked nipple between his fingers. It's impossible to keep silent as he sucks it into his warm mouth, using his teeth to scrape at my flesh. The amount of buildup sparking from his assault has my body in flames. My skin is overheated, my sex pulsating on overdrive.

My hands work their way into Levi's thick hair, unsure if I should pull him closer or push him away. I've never been so consumed with need for someone as I am for him, and I'm not sure if it's a good thing. His painstaking slowness has me on edge and in dire need…of what, I'm not sure.

"Levi…" I beg him to give me the answers I'm desperate for.

He releases my breast, working his way back to my lips. "Jesus, Hannah, you're shaking."

"I'm nervous," I confess. "I feel…I feel…"

"I know exactly how you feel. I can tell by your flushed skin, the way your hands grip my hair so tight. I bet if I put my mouth on your clit, it would throb against my tongue."

His brash words cause my legs to squeeze, and he grins, adjusting himself so his hard length rests between my legs. "Tell me what you want, Hannah." He bends down, placing a wet, open-mouth kiss to my neck. "Tell me so I can give you exactly what you crave."

His words have me in a trance. My body is begging for him. "I want you inside me," I respond fearlessly. I've never been so bold with my words. But he doesn't judge me, laugh, or pull away. He centers himself where I want him, and with one last connection of our eyes, pushes inside me.

Sheer bliss channels through me as he fills me. I spread my legs wider offering him all of me, and he pulls back to enter me with more force.

"Fuck, I want to go slow with you. But you feel so damn good." Another thrust, and I can't agree more. I thread my fingers through his hair and wrap my legs around his waist, lifting my hips slightly, giving him deeper access. He shifts, his movements becoming faster, more punishing, aggressive, amazing. My vision blurs as I fall down Levi's rabbit hole, basking in his wonderful, orgasmic ways. The world around me fades away, and Levi slams into me once more before pulling out and soaking my belly with his own orgasm.

We're both at war with our pounding chests, fighting to get our breathing under control. "Holy hell, that was…"

"Hannah? Kip? Anyone here?"

Time stops. We both freeze, hearts pounding for a whole new reason.

"Oh, fuck." I have never seen true fear in someone's eyes until this moment. As my dad's voice travels through the campsite, we both lose our fresh, post-sex flush.

"*Shit.*" Levi jumps up, grabbing his t-shirt and throwing it at me. I hurry and wipe at my stomach, frantically searching for my clothes. "Here," Levi whispers, tossing me my tank top. Next, my shorts are thrown at me, while he hobbles on one leg, trying to get his foot through his board shorts.

"Hello?"

"Oh my god, he's right there!" I'm dead. Levi's dead. My dad is going to kill us both.

"Seriously, calm down. He's not gonna know. He has to know we shared a tent. We were taking a nap. You didn't feel good." I nod furiously, trying to calm down, which is impossible. "I'm going to go out first. Come out in like five minutes." He unzips the tent and hops out, closing it back behind him.

What in the hell were we thinking? If it wasn't my dad, it could have been my brother, or Stacey, or…ugh Rebecca. I wouldn't mind *her* catching us.

"Hey, Mr. Matthews. Glad you made it."

"Stop. It's Jim. Where is everyone? Did I miss the party?"

"No. Hannah didn't feel well, so she's taking a nap."

Oh god, I *know* my dad. He's going to want to check on me

and it probably smells like fresh sex in here. I panic and bust out of the tent.

"Daddy! You made it!" I boast, saving Levi from answering the question we both knew was coming.

"Hey, princess. How're you feeling? Where's the rest of the gang?" The moment my dad starts walking toward me, something hits me. What if *I* smell like fresh sex? I panic some more and step away from him, heading toward the fire.

"They're at the docks swimming. I wasn't feeling well. Too much sun. Levi walked me back up here. Did you bring me a tent?" I ask, lifting a charred piece of wood, purposely rubbing ashes on me. Levi begins staring at me strangely, but I don't care. Shit, I should probably get him over here to do the same.

"Honey, you're getting yourself all dirty."

"It's fine. Keeps the mosquitos away." To make matters worse, I start spreading the ash all up and down my arms. Levi shakes his head, staring at me like I've lost my mind. I'm not sure why, though. He should be following suit. A father's instinct is very strong. If he wants to live, he would be smart and start rolling in the dirt or something.

"Whatever you say, baby. So, Levi, I can't thank you enough. Your recommendation to have Braydon stay back and assist on the Clifton case was a lifesaver. Fine job that young man did."

Hold the phone—what? My brow furrows, and I turn to my dad. "What did you just say?"

Levi steps in. "It wasn't a recommendation, just offering some names."

"Son, you personally guided me to the best shot we had. Recommending Braydon for the job saved us. Great work."

My mouth drops, and my wide eyes find Levi, who refuses to make contact with me. "You *told* my father to put Braydon on the case?"

Levi turns to me, his eyes seeping guilt. That *asshole*. "I didn't tell him—"

"After you knew he was coming, you picked him out of everyone, knowing he was my date for the weekend?"

"Oh, come on now, it wasn't like that. He didn't need to be here anyway. He's not family."

My eyes squint, my lips pressing into a hard line. Family? Is he insane right now?

"Baby, Levi's right. These are family trips. He would have felt out of place." My head snaps toward my dad.

"Oh, is *Rebecca* family now?"

"Honey, Rebecca's one of Stacey's closest friends, Braydon is just an acquaintance of yours. It wouldn't have been right for him to come."

Everyone has lost their marbles. I face Levi, shooting daggers at him with my glare. They are aimed and firing right at him.

"You had no right to mess with my plans."

"Oh, and you still wish he was here? That he came?"

I'm so mad, I can strangle him. He had no right to decide what was best for me. He had no right to choose who I spent my time with. My anger fuels my response. "Even more so now." I drop the stupid piece of wood and turn to my dad, not caring he just witnessed our argument.

"I'm sorry. I'm not feeling well. Can I just take your car home? You can ride back with Kipley." Levi's eyes dart my way, but I ignore him and anything he wants to say. I also know he won't in front of my dad.

"Are you sure, honey? It's a long drive."

"I'm sure. This was a mistake coming here. I just want to go home."

My dad's eyes soften. "All right, honey. I bet your mom will be happy to have some time with you."

I don't waste another second before going to grab my bag, sensing some relief Levi won't dare follow me. Luckily, my dad traps him with work talk, allowing me the space I need to pack my things. Once I'm done, I exit the tent and take the long way around the fire so I can hug my dad without giving Levi anything but my back.

"Drive safe, baby girl. Call me when you get home."

"Will do, Dad." I offer him a kiss on the cheek, and before Levi can think of a clever way to get my attention without being obvious, I hightail it to my dad's car and out of Ketterville.

CHAPTER FOURTEEN

Hannah

"Seriously, don't worry about it." I smile across the desk at Braydon as we sip our morning coffee. I sigh into my cup, the first taste of French vanilla gracing my taste buds. "I'm glad you were able to help. My dad praised how you came through. Great job!" My mind wanders from the present to the weekend, and I lose myself in thought.

I drove straight home Saturday, making it home by nine. My mom was super happy to see me, and it allowed us to cuddle on the couch and catch up on some of our girly shows.

I texted Dad I got home safe and placed my phone on mute. I half expected Levi to make an effort to call me, text me at the least, to explain himself, but those messages never came. For a second, I made an excuse, trying to convince myself he didn't have my phone number, but we work together. He has all my information.

As the night progressed, I received a few texts from Kip telling me he was sad I left and everyone missed me. I laughed. I couldn't help it. What a lie. Then, when Kip sent a snapshot of them all by the fire, Rebecca's claws all over Levi, I shut my phone off.

My brain and heart were at war. What was I really doing with Levi? Playing with fire? Probably. Setting myself up for major heartache? No brainer. I don't get who I think I am trying to play on the same field as Levi. I still can't understand what he truly sees in me. Then again, people say so many things in the heat of the moment.

As *Golden Girls* played, I wondered how it would have been if I'd never tricked Levi into meeting me in the closet. If we only worked together, would he have ever seen me as more than Kipley's younger sister. Or would he have grown to see what he claims to see now? Would my smarts and dorky personality have won him over?

I slumped into the couch, using my mom as a comfort blanket to coddle my wounded heart and feeling defeated. I already knew the answer. And it was a big, fat no. And that's what made this whole situation even worse. I finally got what I've always dreamed of, but it was at the hands of a lie.

I was playing so far out of my league. I had to stick with what I knew. And that was someone like Braydon Connor.

Braydon's voice brings me back to the present. "I know, but I still feel horrible. I got you this." I shake off my thoughts and focus my attention on Braydon as he bends to the side of his desk, surprising me with a single red rose.

"Oh, Braydon! You didn't have to do that." I accept the flower, bringing it to my nose.

"It's the least I could do. And hopefully you'll allow me to take you to lunch today. Help cure my guilt with food and great company."

I offer him an easy smile, faltering slightly in my enthusiasm. My mind wants to go back to *him*. Wish it was him working for my attention. But he's all wrong.

This is right.

It's for the best.

"Absolutely."

"Great! I have just the place. If you want, you can stay down here for a bit, keep me updated on your current workload. Learn any new juicy details on the Miller case while in the woods?"

"The Miller case? No, why?"

There's a pregnant pause between my questions and his response. "Just curious. That's a huge case to be on, especially one to start on board with. Kind of want to live vicariously through you."

"Me? I don't think I've done anything too exciting. I'm just a paralegal. Entering all the testimonies and babysitting all the confidential files."

"Now you're just showing off." He laughs.

"What do you mean?"

"Tons of people died. Huge conspiracy. Who are the bad guys and good guys? I'm curious what information they have to win. I'd cut my left arm off to get on that case."

This is the case everyone is talking about. And lucky me, I guess I did come on board at the right time. The firm has been working diligently on this the past year. But it wasn't until a few months ago a witness came forward to testify, offering them new evidence that would land them a win.

Miller Industries, a pretentious construction company, was originally founded in New York, but has since expanded all over the states. A heavy-hitter in the building industry, they have their name on half the construction in the Midwest. They pushed their way into town after town, the latest being the off-the-map town of Crete, and convinced—more like coerced—the quiet town to allow them to expand and build a new state of the art business center. They broke ground a year ago, doing everything possible to push through all the ordinances to get the project under way. An eleven-month timeframe was going to be done in under six. This was going to be the first and only business center in the small town of Crete, creating an abundance of new jobs. The only problem was the blueprints were approved under what seemed to be the duress of the city council. The owner of Miller Industries, Benjamin Miller, was what you called a man who didn't play by the rules. From all the testimonies I read, he had so many people in his back pocket, I couldn't grasp how he kept his pants from falling off.

The project began as scheduled, and the development was underway. Everything was running smoothly—until it wasn't. Per the reports, they started having issues with the foundation, a matter that was addressed by the city planning commission but shoved under the rug. It seems, when they discovered thermogenic methane, natural gas that forms deep underneath the Earth's surface, it deemed the land unhabitable. Mr. Benjamin Miller felt otherwise.

Our case proves the company hid the findings and demanded they continue with construction. Even after the crew went on a small strike, they were paid hush money and told to get back to work. Four days later, a steel beam slid off one of the terrain cranes, smashing into the bottom of the foundation. It hit just right, causing friction to the soil and disrupting the buried organic material. One tiny spark. That's all it needed. Within five minutes, the entire structure exploded. Thirty-five people died, and twelve endured injuries and will never work again.

Benjamin Miller claimed zero fault. He quickly turned around and tried to sue the city, pointing the blame on the man who signed off on the land. Problem was, two weeks after the accident, that man committed suicide.

His wife, Clara Hill, claims murder. There was no way her husband would have taken his own life. He was ready to fight Miller Industries, no matter the consequences. Problem with that? No one can prove that theory.

About a year ago, some families got together and reached out to Matthews and Associates. They weren't going to bow down and wanted to see justice for their lost loved ones. Being a huge family man, it was no shocker my dad took the case immediately. Hearing all the stories about children who lost their fathers, wives who lost their husbands and sons, families who lost everyone…it was gut wrenching to even fathom.

I only just learned about the case, and I've already memorized every single person's name, who they lost, how old their kids were.

These were real people. They deserved to be heard. To understand their loss wasn't for nothing. Anything I touched, I read twice, studied, checked to see if there was anything I could offer advice on. I was only a college graduate, but with a set of fresh eyes and dedication, I could be of use.

There was no doubt the firm would win the case, granting each family a large sum of money—not that money will replace their loved ones. But these people took away not only their family, but the main source of income. It's only right they pay for what they've done.

Even thinking about all I've learned gets me heated. "Man, don't get me started on this one. Whoever this Miller guy is should rot in jail for life."

The morning flies by, and before we realize it, we've chatted in depth about the Miller case all the way to lunchtime. I probably shouldn't be so loose-lipped about the case, but Bradyon is so easy to talk to. He actually succeeded in putting a genuine smile on my face and giving a few much needed belly-laughs along the way. There's definitely something missing in the spark department, but sometimes that takes time. Getting to know him better can fix that.

I place the small rose to my nose again, inhaling the floral scent. I journey back to my desk and grab my purse to head back down for lunch when Levi's door flies open.

Darn it.

"Where've you been?"

I whirl around to face him, unable to stop the intake of breath when I become acutely aware of his alluring appearance. Gray fitted suit, no tie, one open button. He leans against his office door, his translucent green eyes boring into mine. I almost cower at his intensity, but just as quickly, I fight out of his trance, my brow crinkling at his tone. If he thinks he can get away with talking to me like that, he's wrong.

"I was downstairs."

"Why exactly?"

What a jerk. He knows why. He just wants me to say it. "I was going over some notes with Braydon, if you care so much." I give him my back and drop my pad of paper, ducking down to my lowest drawer to pull out my water bottle to use as a vase.

"There's no reason why he still needs to coach you. You know everything you need to know. Plus, you can come to me." As if. I don't plan to come to him for anything. "And what the hell is that?" he barks as I stick the stem into the bottle.

"It's exactly what it looks like, Levi—a flower. Braydon gave it to me because he felt so horrible for having to bail on me this weekend. You know, because YOU put him on the assignment." I don't hold back, offering him the same snarl he's giving off. It only seems to anger him more. Grabbing my forearm, he grits out, "Get in here. I need to speak to you in private."

I tug at my arm, but he's already dragging me into his office and slamming the door. "What the fuck, Hannah? What are you trying to pull here?"

"*Me!* What do you mean what am *I* trying to pull? You're the liar."

Levi laughs. "Oh, that's rich coming from you."

What a *jerk*! "You know what, this is ridiculous. I have a lunch date, so unless you need something *work-related*, we're done here."

That sets a whole new fire in his eyes. "A lunch date? Are you kidding me? With who? Your little boy toy downstairs?" I hate that he can even call him that. Yeah, he's not big and macho and strong and perfect, but he's kind and nice and not a liar.

"For your information, yes. And I plan to enjoy myself immensely!"

"You're not going."

Ugh, he is so frustrating! "Yes, I am."

"No, you're *not*."

How dare he! "You can't tell me what to do or who to have

lunch with!" He steps into my personal space, almost knocking me over with his heaving chest.

"You're not going because you're going to have lunch with me. We're going to talk about what happened on Saturday, and you're going to get over whatever issues you seem to have."

My biggest issue *right now* is the way he's trying to control me. I stick my chin out and straighten my shoulders. I will not let him boss me around. "Not gonna happen."

I wouldn't be lying if I said I may have seen flames shooting out of his nostrils.

"*Excuse* me?" he breathes, his voice low and dangerous.

"You heard me. Not gonna happen. Now, if you don't need anything else..."

He has me backed up against the wall, his hand threading into my hair, his mouth a hairsbreadth from mine, his warm breath caressing my face. "You're not going. I mean it, Han."

God, the way he uses my shortened name sends a flutter down to my belly. "Yes, I am," I continue to challenge him. My cheeks feel flushed. Knowing I'm poking the bear creates a buzzing sensation between my thighs.

He leans in closer, his lips touching mine. I tell myself to pull away, but my body has a different idea. I allow his lips to skate against mine. His strong palm reaches for my hip, roaming up my ribcage and stopping just below my breast. "If you go on that lunch date, I'll be forced to handle the situation in my own way." He takes my lower lip in between his teeth. "And my recommendation to your father would be to terminate the employee who seems to be getting too friendly with his only daughter."

Oh, that rat...

I raise my hands and push him off me. He stumbles back, and I stab my index finger in his direction. "If you think you can threaten me to stay away from Braydon, you're wrong."

"Watch me. We have something here, Hannah. If you choose that kid, I'll put a stop to it."

"You...you're unbelievable!" I huff, stomping my feet.

"I might be, but I'm simply playing your game. Next move is yours. What's it gonna be?" I stare at him in complete shock. He's blackmailing me. Too bad for him my dad has always taught me never to stand down from a fight.

"Well, Mr. Dent." I walk toward him, placing my palms on his rock-hard chest. I graze my fingers up and down, pushing gently so he begins to walk backwards. His eyes light up with triumph when the backs of his legs hit the chair. "Looks like you have yourself a challenge." His eyes go from glory to confusion. "I'll think about you while I enjoy my nice lunch." With a shove, I push him, causing him to fall backwards into the seat. Turning around, I walk out, grab my purse, and strut—okay, maybe partially run so he doesn't chase after me—to the elevator to meet Braydon.

"Still with me?"

I catch myself staring out the window of the quant sandwich shop Braydon took us to, my mind far from whatever he's going on about. "Oh yeah, sorry. That's great!"

"Yeah, and if I stick with the reports, I have a chance at being promoted. Pretty pumped." My spurious smile is perfectly in place as I sip my soda.

"Do you not like your sandwich? You can have the other half of mine if you want."

"Oh no, it's really tasty. I'm just..." Hungry for something else. *Someone* else. Even though I chose to spend my lunch with Braydon, my mind hasn't left Levi's office. I watch Braydon's lips move, but I hear nothing he says. My thoughts are stuck on replay, Levi's threat to have me or else.

"You sure?"

"Yeah. Just ate a big breakfast." Which is a lie. I'm starved, but it's not for food. Or Braydon's company, sadly. I pull out my phone and take in the time. "We should probably get back. I have a lot of stuff to take care of before I leave."

"Sure. Levi is pretty hard on you, huh?"

You don't even know the half of it. Hard on me, against me, inside me. Jesus. I swipe the back of my hand along my forehead.

"Uh-oh, not feeling well?"

How does one explain their entire body is out of sorts over a man who's been in my dreams for half my life? "Yeah, we should get going. I don't want Levi to get mad if I'm late." Braydon guides me out of the sandwich shop, grabbing my hand. It's strange, and I'm not sure I enjoy it, but I don't ask him to let it go.

"Maybe you could talk to your dad. Tell him Levi's not doing his job. Maybe he can move you. Or shit, fire his ass. He seems like a hothead."

He has no idea. But I could never do that. What's going on between Levi and I has nothing to do with his ability to move mountains at Daddy's firm. "It's fine. I can handle Levi." *I hope.* Or else it's going to be me who moves—preferably across the state where my heart is safe.

CHAPTER FIFTEEN

Levi

"Have you cross-checked all the affidavits?"

"Done and done. The Sworn Oath Statements have been filed. If this deal shows any loose ends, it will be a total surprise to me. We have Benjamin Miller nailed."

Jim stands, slapping me on the back. "That's why you're my guy, Levi. Smart, eagle eyes—this case wouldn't be where it is without you." He addresses the rest of the boardroom. "Meeting's over. Please submit your notes and file them by day's end. We'll contact the courts to set a date tomorrow. Splendid work, everybody."

Everyone takes their cue and exits the boardroom. I don't understand how I've managed to focus on a damn thing since Hannah left. That mouth of hers has my blood boiling, but my fucking dick hard as stone. The urge to throttle her in my office earlier has my hand shaking again. Why the hell am I letting her get under my skin? *Because you've gotten a taste and now you want more.* Fuck yeah, I want more. But it's not just that. I want to slide into her warmth and stay there forever. Smell her on me always. And fuck if she's going to act like she doesn't want the same.

I'm no fool. I was well aware little Hannah Mathews had the googly eyes for me when we were growing up. I can also sadly admit I never gave her a second glance. Back then, she was thin as a rail. Her hair was always wild from getting into shit she wasn't supposed to. Her mouth...well, that's the same. She still has to have the last word. But throughout the years, I never paid attention to her. We left for school, and when we returned, she was gone. Our paths never crossed. And now, having her back in my life, like this little tornado causing havoc in my head, my heart, my fucking pants, I can't comprehend what it is I feel for her. But it's something I need to pursue.

My phone rings, and I glance down. Kip. Fuck. I ignore his call. There's a guilt that weighs heavy on my shoulders realizing what I'm doing is wrong. If…or when, he finds out, it's not going to be good. Even looking at Jim, he respects me. Loves me like his own son, but I wouldn't doubt he would help Kip bury my body if he found out the things I want to do—am going to do—to his daughter. Because no matter what bullshit Hannah is pulling right now, we're not done.

"Hey, baby girl." Jim breaks my thoughts as he takes a call. "Oh no, are you sick? Oh, okay. Well, don't forget tonight is poker night. Kipley and Stacey will be there. Sure, baby, bring whoever you want. Okay. Love you." He ends the call with a smile on his face and slides his phone into his jacket pocket. The love for his daughter is limitless—another reason this may not end well.

"Everything all right?" I ask, needing a gauge on what's wrong with Hannah.

"Oh, yeah. Hannah isn't feeling well. She's going to take the rest of the day off."

Not feeling well, huh? More like avoiding me. I don't picture Hannah bowing down to a little stomachache when it comes to conquering the work empire. "That's too bad. Maybe I'll go check on her on my way home. Make sure she doesn't need anything." *Or bust her.*

Jim pats me on the back. "Kind man. That's what I admire about you, Levi. She said she'll be okay. Still gonna make it to family poker night. You're coming, right? Hannah is bringing a friend as well."

I wasn't planning on it, but now I sure as fuck will be. "Wouldn't miss it for the world, Jim."

I'm sipping on a bottle of beer when Hannah finally walks in. My mood darkens when that punk Braydon steps in behind her. He seems boring, dweebish. I can't understand what she even sees in him. My grip tightens around the bottle when he presses his hand to her lower back. If he wasn't standing so close to Cheryl, Hannah's mother, I'd throw my bottle at his funny shaped head.

"Hannah, honey, you're not feeling well?" Cheryl brings Hannah in for a hug, not missing her eyes when they land on me.

"Fine, must have been something I ate."

"Bad lunch?" I say, unable to pass up the opportunity to add to her discomfort. Her eyes find mine, that little fire causing my lips to curl into a smile. I sit up straighter and stand. Annoyingly, so does Jim, going to greet the punk.

"Braydon! Welcome to our home. Hope you know how to play some poker. We take no prisoners over here." Jim shakes Braydon's hand, and I slam my beer as I watch Hannah smile at their friendly connection. Jim thinks he's this perfect employee, but I went over some of the litigation reports he's handling and found errors. If I wanted to be a prick, I could have brought it to Jim's attention, but it's not my job to tattle. It's my job to find errors and keep clients.

Watching Braydon's chest puff out at Jim's approval makes me wish I had. Something about him irks me. That he thinks he has a chance with Hannah for one. But it's something else. That's when he grabs my attention. With a bright smile, he nods at me. *You can take that nod and shove it up your ass.*

Jim claps his hands, getting the room's attention. "Looks like everyone's here. Let's play some poker!"

I'm going to take his head and rip it off his skinny little neck.

"Wow, another full house! Braydon, you sly guy! It's normally Levi over here taking my money. Looks like my daughter found a keeper!" Jim chimes, sipping his whiskey neat. The shit-brick smiles at Hannah, his hand disappearing under the table on her thigh. My knuckles grip my cards, and I catch myself crumpling them in my hand. I drop them on the table and get up for another beer. I make it to the kitchen when a hand grabs my shoulder.

"What up, man? You seem uptight. Work going well? Need a lady friend to cozy up to?" I knock Kip's hand off, throwing open the fridge.

"Nice try, man. Work's fine. Just got some shit on my mind."

"And the other? You know Rebecca won't stop talking about you. A little phone call and I bet—"

"Dude, I'd rather saw my dick off."

Kip laughs and accepts the beer I hand him. "Damn, that's brutal. I didn't think she was that bad."

"Bad? She snuck into my tent and hid her thong inside my pillowcase in hopes her smell would lead me to her!"

Kip buckles over laughing, and my stomach churns at the memory. After having a taste of Hannah, I about vomited when I found them and threw them in the fire.

"She wants a piece of that Dent dick, bro."

"Never gonna happen." I take a swig of my beer. "Speaking of, what do you think of Hannah's boy toy?"

Kip shrugs, chugging the rest of his beer to grab another one. "Seems okay. Kinda dorky, but I think she likes that style. Who knows? I can't say I've ever seen her with a guy. If he's good to her, then I couldn't give a shit." I want to tell him he's a fucking shrimp and to scare him off. But that would open a shit-ton more questions on why I give a shit. *Because I'm secretly banging your sister and want to continue banging her, so I need her little fan freak to beat it.* "Why? You don't like him?"

I fucking want to pummel him. "Nah, no sweat off my back. Hannah's like a little sister to me." God, I'm going to hell. "Just looking out for her." And possibly my own interest.

"True that. Need eyes on her. She sure grew up in college.

Gonna have dudes all over her. We need to make sure no asshole tries to screw her over." That includes me. "Here." He hands me a bottle of fancy tequila Jim brought home from a client. "Bottoms up. Hurry, before Stacey comes in and stops me."

The joys of married life. I grab the bottle, and with a hefty pull, let the liquor slide down my throat, hoping to drown the idea of pummeling Hannah's nerd toy.

Thirty minutes pass before Kip and I stumble out of the kitchen. We lost track of time, catching up on work and bullshit. Since he got married, his priorities have shifted. Not that it's a bad thing. I love Stacey, and she deserves all his attention, but our guys' nights have been put on hold. Not that I've been any better. He informed me Ben was on some Safari donating his time to the poor, and Chase was in Mexico on another solo vacation probably picking up gonorrhea.

When we head back into the living room, we find Stacey with Cheryl and Jim, while Braydon and Hannah appear comfy sitting together on the loveseat. She laughs at something he says, and I fight not to aim my bottle at his crooked nose. Her eyes find mine, and her demeanor quickly changes.

"Excuse me. I'm going to go to the bathroom." She gets up, but doesn't miss the opportunity to scowl at me as she saunters down the hallway. Knowing this house like the back of my hand, I excuse myself back into the kitchen and take the other hallway that wraps around to the second door leading into the same place Hannah disappeared to. Just as she begins to shut the door, I slide in through the other door, shutting and locking it behind me.

Hannah whips around and jumps back, startled at my presence. "Jesus! Levi, what are you doing?"

"The question is, Hannah, what are *you* doing?" She wants to play dumb, but she knows better. She sees I'm not fooled by this whole boy toy charade.

"I'm going to the bathroom. What does it look like? Get out."
I do the opposite, taking a few steps closer. She starts to back up,
until her back hits the wall.

"I'm not one for playing games. But maybe this once. Because
it's you, I'll play along."

"What games? I don't know what you're talking about."

I cage her in, resting my forearm against the wall. Leaning
in so my breath caresses her cheek, I say, "You know exactly what
game you're playing. The one where you play hard to get and pretend there's zero urge inside you begging for me to rip this cute
little dress off you and fuck you hard and fast with my mouth." I
watch the fire ignite in her beautiful eyes, so I continue. "Have my
tongue devour you." I raise my other arm so she has nowhere to
go. "Should we pretend you're not wet for *me* right now? Pretend
you're not wanting *me* to spread your silky thighs so I can do what
I want to you." I bring my body up against her, not hiding my erection. "If I tore this strap off your shoulder, exposing your beautiful
tits, would your nipples already be hard and primed for *me*?"

"Levi." My name is a soft plea, and I love it coming off her
tongue.

I can't help but grind slowly into her, the friction causing her
eyes to fall shut. "What if my teeth wrapped around you and I
sucked you hard into my mouth until your perfect little bud
turned a deep plum?" She's jelly in my arms. I bet if I stepped
away, she'd fall to the ground. I'm starting to forget whose game
this really is. If I don't get myself in check, I'm going to fuck her in
her parents' bathroom without a care who hears.

I lower my arm, allowing my fingers to graze the side of
her breast. Licking my lower lip, I bend down so she can feel my
breath skate against her lips. "Or am I just making this all up because *you* have no interest?"

I've rendered my girl speechless.

Her eyes blink open, but her lips aren't forming a single word.
That's right. I've got her exactly where I want her. "That's what I

thought. You think your boy toy knows how to use that thing in his pants?"

If she even answers, she's going to get fucked against this wall, consequences be damned. Why the hell would I even ask that? The thought of that little shit inside her makes me murderous. "Answer me—"

"Hannah, you okay in there?"

Her eyes widen.

"Your little boy toy is beckoning you. Should I tell him you're busy?" I can't help it. I'm a selfish bastard sometimes. I grind into her, stealing the words right out of her.

"Yes," she moans, not loud enough for him to hear.

"What was that?"

Again, I take advantage.

"Yes!" she says louder, her voice strained. This time, I steal her lips and kiss her savagely. She's mere seconds away from falling apart in my arms, and I'm loving it. Before I pound her through the wall, I break away. I keep my composure, even though my heart is beating like a rapid drum.

"I think this game may end up being enjoyable after all."

Before she has a chance to answer, I sneak back out the way I came.

CHAPTER SIXTEEN

Hannah

"Levi Dent's office. I'm sorry, he's in a meeting. Can I take a message? Angela Salem. Dinner confirmation. Will do. Bye-bye." I slam the phone down. Another dinner confirmation? I hate him. *No I don't.* This is just to get a rise out of me and it's not going to work. *Yes it is.* No it's not!

This game he thinks we're playing? Well…it's stupid. And I refuse to give in. I'm not letting him bait me with random women rubbing their dates with him in my face.

I check the time as the conference doors burst open, the team exiting for lunch. My eyes find Levi instantly, his easy-going smile causing a warmth in my belly. Screw him. It's just hunger pains. I skipped breakfast.

"Great work everyone. Take lunch. We'll reconvene in an hour." He shakes hands with Samantha from legal and stalks over to my desk. I swear, if he says anything cocky, I'm going to take my umbrella and stab him in the—

"Morning, Hannah. You look very nice today. Any chance William Sullivan called while I was tied up?"

What? I look *nice*? And *who*? "Uh…no." But a bunch of hussies called, confirming their dick ride later. Ugh! Pull it together. "I forwarded all other messages to your email."

"Perfect. Thanks. Enjoy lunch." And with his easy-going, kind attitude and everyone-loves-me persona—including me— shit—he closes himself in his office.

What in criminy hell was that? I want to bang on his door and scream, I'm *not* playing this silly game. He can stop tormenting me with his stupid laid-back attitude. Because no one is feeling laid back! I grunt, slamming my fists on my desk, followed by another grunt, because that kind of hurt.

If he wants to be immature about this, so be it. I won't fall for his trickery. He won't get me to admit he's winning the game I'm *not* playing, or that I want to disassemble every woman who calls and scream from the rooftops I saw him first. Wait…what?

Shoot…

"Levi Dent's office, how can I assist you? No, he's in meetings all day. Wednesday? Same. I'm not sure what his evening schedule looks like, I only tend to his office hours' schedule. I will. Melissa with two s's. Got it. Bye-bye."

I hate him.

"Levi Dent's office, how can I assist you? His personal line? He doesn't have a personal line. How do I know, because he would have told—I mean—no! This is a business. Not a dating hotline. Get lost!"

I slam the phone down. I really, really hate him.

"Levi Dent's house of whor—oh, hi, Daddy." Oops.

"Hey, baby. How's it going up there? I miss you. We've been in the bullpen really working on this Miller case. Everyone still treating you fair?"

Everyone but Levi.

Not that his laid-back, everything-is-fake normal treatment is bad.

Okay, I take that back. It's *horrible!* I'm on day three of having him give me this…this…blah! How do I even define it? The normal Levi? Gone is that man-handling aggressive side I dream about, the one where his hands dominate me, owning me. In its place is the nice, gentle Levi who asks if I need coffee before he runs out, or tells me to have a nice lunch and my shirt is pretty. Fuck that! Fuck him. I hate him.

"Baby, you still there?"

Mentally, no. "Yeah, Daddy. Sorry. Just busy learning the cases and sitting in on mock trials. I don't want to disappoint you."

"Sugar, you can never disappoint me. You make me proud every day." His kind words have an opposite effect. Doing a commendable job should make me feel great, but I don't feel like I am. At least when it comes to the person I'm working for.

"Hey. Earth to Hannah."

I turn to Braydon as he shoves a gross amount of cheese battered fries into his mouth. "What?"

"I've been talking to you for the past five minutes and you haven't even touched your food." After a long morning of complete bull crap calls, I debated on unplugging my phone. But then I worried it was a job violation since it *is* my job to answer his calls. My mood is as sour as my stomach watching Braydon shovel the greasy food into his mouth. And to make matters worse, Levi sent an email saying he was working remotely today. Not that I wanted to see him, *which* only consists of him zipping back and forth past my desk. But even so, in those short spans, his cologne lingers, which I shamefully inhale, basking in the memory of—

"Well, like I was saying, the gala is tomorrow, and if you don't have a date, I'd love to go with you. I'd go myself, but it's only for the top employees, and well, I wasn't invited. But! I'm headed there. Really been putting in my time. I think your dad sees my efforts. If you ever have the chance, you should put a good word in for me. I can decrypt those accounts just as efficiently as the next guy. Not even sure why what's his name is so loved. Saw he put a plus-one for his extra gala ticket. Can't imagine what train wreck would want to put up with him for a night. I bet I could beat him in a court—"

"Sure."

"Sure, I can go with you?"

"Sure." *As in anything for you to stop talking.* Levi's bringing a date? Having to hear women call confirming dates is one thing. Having to see one on his arm is a whole other ballpark.

That's it.

He wants to play?

It's on.

We pull up in the limo Dad arranged. The valet opens my door to assist me out of the car. My dress, a silver couture gown, spaghetti straps, and silk material, flows to the ground as I step out. The chill hits my open back, and I shiver, wrapping my arms around myself. Braydon climbs out behind me, not taking notice of my coldness, and starts forward.

"Holy cow, this is some fancy shit."

"Yep. Sure is." I shrug off his excitement. Normally, I pass on these things. Growing up, instead of playing with dolls and dress up, I was catching frogs and making dirt castles. Even today, the glitz and glamor isn't my thing. But tonight? I had a war to win. Which meant I finally allowed Mom to play her part and dress me to the hilt.

Remembering his manners, Braydon secures my hand and escorts us down the red carpet inside the lavish hotel until we're met by my parents, Kipley, and Stacey.

"My, my, look at you," Stacey gushes, taking my hands in hers and spinning me. "You're like a true Hollywood star."

"Okay. More like a washed-up, D-list celebrity."

"Shut it. Take the compliment." We go in for a hug, and I

repeat the same embrace with my brother and parents. Dad begins making small talk with Braydon, while my traitorous eyes search the ballroom. I don't see him. Maybe he won't show. Save me the—

"Good evening all."

My shoulders tense, and I can't stop my eyes from squeezing shut. Even his voice ruins me. I open my eyes and inhale a deep breath for strength. I can do this. Whatever hussy he has on his arm won't have any impact on me. It won't—*are you kidding me!*—affect me.

"Well, look who the cat dragged in. Didn't realize *you* knew how to wear a dress." Rebecca laughs, pulling Levi close to her, her arm draped over his. The phony smile I worked so hard on keeping falters.

"Rebecca," Levi warns, taking a step forward. "Hannah, you look lovely tonight."

Breathe in. Breathe out. Breathe in. Breathe out.

"Thanks, Levi. You too." I'm furious at myself for allowing my voice to sound weak. I refuse to let him see he just won. He hurt me with this one. His eyes spear into mine, waiting for something. A white flag? To congratulate him? Forcing myself to reel it in, I search for my date. "Ah, Braydon. Would you be so kind to escort me to the bar?" He doesn't miss a beat, probably because free booze is the best booze, and grabs my hand, leading me away. The tightness in my chest doesn't let up, even with the building space between us. Braydon doesn't waste time and orders multiple shots of tequila. After we consume a second shot, my heart still hasn't stopped racing.

"Got to use the bathroom. Be right back. Don't lose our spot." He bends forward, slapping a quick kiss to my cheek, and takes off toward the restrooms. I signal the bartender for another round, grabbing my phone to scroll through my social media while I wait.

"You should probably slow down on those shots. The night's still young."

His voice at my back is like a million needles taking aim at my heart. I don't even bother to face him when I speak. "I'm sure we won't stay long. Have other plans. Ones that don't consist of staying in this stuffy dress." It was low of me. And a complete lie. I don't even know why I said it.

"That's a shame. The dress fits you like a glove. You should stay in it longer. Allow others to enjoy you in it." I clamp my eyes shut and inhale for strength. My eyes open, and I snag the shot, taking it down. Then I whip around.

"Shouldn't you be over there complimenting Rebecca's dress?" I snap.

"I already did. Now I'm here complimenting you. You really do steal the show tonight, Han."

The nerve. My hands begin to shake. "You're a grade-A asshole."

His relaxed smile falters and his eyes light like a Christmas tree. "Watch it."

"No, *you* watch it!" I raise my voice, causing a few attendees to stare our way. Levi grabs my arm, and without causing a scene, drags me away from the bar down a less busy hallway. "Let go of me!"

"Not a chance." He doesn't stop until he reaches for a door, finding it unlocked, and pushing me inside it. I stumble forward, and when I spin around to give him hell, he's already on me. "Wanna take that asshole comment back?" He leans forward, stealing the space between us.

"No. How could you bring *her* here?"

"How are you pretending *he's* the one you want?"

He's not. "Braydon? Because he's not a liar." I want to say more, but I trip backwards into a chair, grabbing for something to steady my fall, which ends up being Levi's large bicep. "And he doesn't flaunt woman after woman at me—Jesus, stop walking, I'm going to fall!"

"He's a little shit box who has no idea what he has. And I'm not a liar. I made a decision based on what I thought was best for you."

My nostrils flare like a bull. "You have no right to tell me what's best for me!"

He reaches out and latches around my waist, crashing my body firm against his chest. "He had no right to be at the lake. That place is for family. He had no business being there with you when I wanted you there for myself."

My breathing stops. My words escape me.

"Cat got your tongue? I threw him at your father because that way, you'd be all mine. Ever since you tricked me—and yeah, I'm putting it out there, you *tricked* me, I can't stop myself from wanting you. Needing you all for myself. Would I have gone into that closet if I'd known it was you? Fuck no. Am I glad I did? You bet your ass. Because at least I'm adult enough to admit it. Unlike you, who continues to hide behind the truth."

"I'm not—"

"You can't even admit it now. Even after I've admitted how I feel. Jesus. Maybe you do need to grow up, Hannah. Maybe then you'll be able to admit what's happening between us—"

"What do you want me to admit! That I've fantasized about you since I was seven years old? That I've always wondered what you smelled like, felt like…God, moaned like? I tricked you because I saw an opportunity to scratch an itch that would've never been fully satisfied had you known who I really was. I was no one to you. But without actually seeing me? You felt me. And yeah, you're right, I'm hiding from what this is. Because unlike you, it's going to hurt a lot more for me when it doesn't work out. People like you, they don't end up with people like me."

"Says who?" he growls.

"Says reality. Says Rebecca."

He hooks his hand around my neck and smashes his lips to mine. He doesn't allow me to fight him, his strength and determination too overpowering. His tongue breaks the barrier of my lips as he kisses me with fervor, the faint taste of champagne on his tongue. I feel angry, dizzy, needy, confused. My hands fight him, pulling at his hair, urging him closer, pushing him away. I don't know what I want. I'm scared.

"Stop fucking denying this."

"It's what I'm doing to protect myself."

"From what, Hannah? The possibility that this may be something really amazing? Hell, I didn't plan this either. You think having to one day explain to my best friend the things I've done with his sister? Your father? I'm taking a risk too. But at least I'm willing to. At least I'm fighting for it. You're just hiding."

"I'm not hiding."

"Then what are you doing? Tell me, 'cause I need to know what your next move is here."

I struggle with the honesty lingering on the tip of my tongue, but it's the only answer I can give. "I'm scared."

He wraps his arms around me, pulling me into his chest. "I am too. But I want this. You do too. I'm not asking for forever. I'm asking for right now. Let's see right now where this leads. Maybe you realize the infamous Levi Dent is nowhere near the attractive stud you pictured him to be and end this. Maybe I realize what I already know. That you're too good for me, and I cut you loose. But for now, let's try."

I wonder if he notices the saturation of my tears soaking his chest. His words. His affirmations. How do I tell him I've loved him since I was seven years old, and if this ends—which it will— it won't be because I have a change of heart?

"What about Kipley? My dad?"

"For now, we keep this between us. Not that I'm hiding us, because hell, if I could show everyone you're mine, I would. But to keep me alive, we should maybe keep what's going on a secret." As scandalous as it sounds, I do agree. We would be done before we even started if either of them got wind. I nod.

"So, you agree? You're willing to test the waters? See where this goes?"

I am. I want to take a risk. Live. I want to jump headfirst into this crazy idea that Levi Dent and I could actually have a happily ever after. "I do. I do. I—"

His lips crash down on mine, kissing me with such fierceness, my legs buckle. Before I lose my composure, he swoops me up, cradling me in his arms. "Fuck, I've been going mad all week wanting to do this." More kissing, biting, growling. "I wanted to give in, take you into my office, and spank the stubbornness out of you on Tuesday wearing that cute little pink shirt. I almost dragged you in my office on Wednesday with that pale thingy—"

"My dress suit?"

"Fuck, you looked hot." His tongue dives into my mouth, massaging mine. "I was so frustrated with you, I almost beat off in my office watching you bite at your nails through the window. Fuck, you drove me nuts."

"What about all your dinner dates? None of them scratched your itch?" My stomach tightens, fearing his response.

"Fake. Had the receptionist at my gym call you all week in exchange for Chase's number."

I want to punch him for tormenting me. All week long, Googling all the numbers I saved, trying to search out who these girls were. Instead, I kiss him harder.

The door bursts open, and we peel our lips from one another, startled. A janitor sticks his head in. "Oh, come on, this isn't high school prom. I ain't cleanin' up after ya'll."

We both try to mask our laughter. Levi grabs my hand and tugs me toward the door. "Come on. Let's go."

"Where?"

"I got a room. I need you in it and naked right now."

"Wait, what about the gala? My parents will wonder—"

"We'll figure it out later. Right now, I need only you." He takes my hand and guides us through a hallway until we pop out by the elevators. We stand next to one another, waiting for the doors to open. The energy between us is so electric, it's dangerous. We may be standing silent, but the drumming of our hearts is deafening.

The doors open, and he tugs me inside. The second they

close, he pushes me against the mirrored wall and kisses me. His heart hammers against mine, his hands hungry to get to me. "This dress needs to go." He nips at my bottom lip, and I squirm under his hold. He presses his hard erection into my stomach just as the elevator dings, and we rush out. I barely register the rooms we pass, then he's swiping his key against the electronic lock and we stumble inside.

At the sound of the door closing, I spin around to face him. Levi Dent has always been a sight. But tonight, there are no words to describe how he takes my breath away, all handsome in his tuxedo, his hair disheveled from earlier. And those eyes. They've lost the calmness they normally carry. They scream hungry. Needy. Determined.

"Levi."

"Hannah." He takes one predatorial step toward me. My mind races with his intentions. Will he make good on his promise at my parents' house and run his mouth along my center? Use his fingers to send me into oblivion? Will he hold me and allow me to bask in his scent and comfort?

"What are you planning?" My voice is timid. With two long strides, his large frame eats up the last remaining space separating us, and his hand reaches up to cup my cheek. "I bet your mind is running rampant wondering, maybe even hoping, about all the things I plan to do to you. But right now, I want to drown all your worries and insecurities." His lips dip to mine, kissing me softly, then he pulls away. "I want to show you why you're something special. Why I'm thankful you're giving me a chance. Why there is nothing more perfect than this moment." His lips return, stealing my breath, our tongues doing a slow dance. My arms travel around his neck, and he lifts me up, carrying me to the bed.

He lays me down, his lips never leaving mine, his hand caressing the side of my ribcage, a low-pressure squeeze to my hips. He's fighting to go slow, and it's killing me. My dress is too heavy against my skin. I need it off.

"Your body is buzzing for me. Tell me what you want, Hannah?" His voice is low yet demanding in a way that sets my core on fire.

"I want to feel you. All of you. This dress. It's in the way." His lips move down my chin, my neck, stopping at my collarbone. His tongue making circles against my hypersensitive flesh is too much. I lift my hips, needing friction, needing something more. "Levi, please," I beg.

His hands dip lower, pulling at my dress, hiking it up just enough for his fingers to disappear under the silk fabric. The warmth of his palm skates up my thigh, and I bite my tongue when his fingers brush along my folds.

"Always so wet for me. Perfect. Beautiful," he hums against my skin, pushing one finger inside. My head tilts back at the welcomed intrusion. Using his other free hand, he pulls the dress strap off my shoulder, trailing kisses down to my breast. "I dream about these. In my mouth. In my hands. Owning them, sucking them, marking them." He wraps his mouth around my nipple, circling the bud with his tongue. With each measured thrust, he grazes his teeth along my flesh, making me crazy. My hips can't fight his slow torture. They lift, welcoming him deeper.

"Naughty little Hannah, always wanting more." He pulls out and inserts two fingers. I lose my breath on a moan, needing more, and he knows it. There's a crack in the air. A spark threatening to detonate my entire body when a third finger thrusts inside me. With each addition, he's less gentle, more urgent. The brush of his knuckles at my opening has me crying out in pleasure. He takes no pity on me as his teeth clamp down on my nipple.

"Levi, more," I beg. I ride his fingers, unable to hold on any longer. My hips thrust up, and he doesn't hold back, powering inside me, filling me until my orgasm ignites and my walls come crashing around his fingers. He swallows my cry with his mouth, kissing me hard, working me until my spasms subside.

His mouth eases up, and he pulls away. Our eyes connect, and it's impossible to miss the shift in the air. The electricity that surrounds us. "You're beautiful, Hannah Matthews. Inside and out. And I'm going to spend the entire night proving that to you."

I bite my lower lip, fighting back tears. No one has ever spoken such beautiful words to me. Words that hold so much honesty. His eyes stare back at me, shining with sincerity, and I want to break down all these walls I have built so high around me and confess all the love I've held for him all these years. Confess just how perfect I hold him to be. But he doesn't allow it. He climbs off me, and the lack of his warmth disappoints me. There's a low chuckle falling off his lips as he loosens his tie. "Relax, I'm not going anywhere. Just getting rid of these unwanted barriers. I want nothing between us."

Relief settles in my chest, and I relax, my eyes clouding over when he tosses his tie to the ground, working at each button, exposing his firm, tan chest. His bronze skin is smooth and flawless, and I can't help but gawk at how stunning he is. Once his shirt is gone, he undoes his pants, pushing them to the ground, along with his boxer briefs, and I struggle to keep my composure.

He's gorgeous. Any time we've found ourselves in this situation, I've never taken the chance to admire him. Truly view and enjoy. "Seems unfair you get to do all the looking."

I snap out of my haze and sit up, pulling my dress strap off my shoulder. Constricted by my long gown, I'm forced to stand, allowing the silk to fall in waves past my hips, leaving me bare except my white lace thong.

"Jesus," Levi moans, taking in my form.

"I could say the same thing," I reply, getting an eyeful myself.

He takes a step toward me. His lips hit mine, and his arms envelop me, carrying me back onto the bed. Laying my head gently on the pillow, his mouth opens, warming my bare skin with his inviting lips. I lose my fingers in his thick hair, pressing his head closer, needing more. His slowness creates this animalistic urge inside me. My hands become greedy, trailing down his back, my nails scraping against his skin.

"Levi, please." He takes a soft nip at my skin, using his knee to push my legs apart. A strong hand dives into my hair as his other guides himself between my thighs. I realize there's one vital mistake we're making, and it's protection. But I trust him. With everything.

The tip of his cock pushes at my entrance, and it's almost too much. His eyes find mine, waiting for approval. "I don't have anything. I didn't plan this, so I—"

"Nothing between us, right? I trust you. Completely." His steely gaze fills with a mixture of appreciation and arousal. With no further need for approval, he powers into me. The sonorous sound of pleasure fills the room, two voices, piercing with the same guttural need. He offers me a few breaths to adjust, but rears back and fills me once again. One after the other, he consumes me. My mind loses itself in the feel of him, the way his heart slams against mine, our bodies in tune. The tingling of my skin, the beating of his pulse. The sweat and buzzing around us. This isn't just him taking from me, it's him giving to me just as much. And in return, I offer him everything. My heart, my body, my trust. His lips find mine, knowing I'm close to falling, exploding, and losing myself to all things Levi Dent.

"So. Fucking. Beautiful…" he growls, and I let go. The air in my lungs gets trapped by the silent scream of my orgasm blasting through me, my walls breaking down, my heart cracking open. My fingers dig into his skin as I try to hold on, afraid I'll float away. It's only a few more powerful thrusts until his chest rumbles, telling me he's just as far gone. Warmth fills me as his orgasm throws him off his own axis, his mouth slamming down on mine.

"Why'd you bring Rebecca?"

My question stirs him. We've been lying in bed, enjoying our after-explosive-sex high. My head is on his chest as his fingers play with my hair.

"I didn't."

"Then why was she with you? The gala roster said you added a plus one?"

He squeezes me, leaning up and placing a kiss on my head. "Checking up on me, huh?" My fingers find his bare nipple, and I pinch. "Ow! First off, the plus one was because Kip asked for it. When I showed up at his place to catch a ride with them, she was there. I guess she swindled her way into going."

Of course she did. My anger at seeing her on Levi's arm rears its ugly head. "Calm down, tiger. I would never lay a hand on her." Even so, the simple gesture was enough to send me into an ass whooping frenzy. "Speaking of unwanted sidekicks, why Braydon?" Now I wish I never brought it up. Because my answer isn't as innocent as his.

"I invited him to make you jealous."

"Did you now?" He squeezes my breast. "Well, it worked. If he hadn't left you at the bar, I was going to have a waiter tell him his mommy was on the phone to get him away from you." I shamefully laugh, then knock his hand away.

"Stop. He means well."

"He's a little shit."

"He's nice. And helpful."

Levi makes a quick adjustment, and I find myself under him. "He's off. I don't want you talking to him anymore. You're mine. I don't want to share you with anyone—not even Poindexter."

I laugh. He is kind of geeky. "I can't just stop talking to him."

"Yes, you can. And you better. Otherwise, I'll have to find a way to ruin his life so he quits." I know he's joking, but I don't want him making trouble for Braydon. He's done nothing wrong. "Promise me you're done with him."

I don't reply fast enough, and his teeth cover my nipple. "Ouch! Okay, I won't! Levi, stop!" I start to laugh because his attempt at torturing me morphs into pleasure. "Please, stop, I'll behave. When we go to lunch, I'll tell him—*ahhh...*" I arch my back as he sucks so hard, he's sure to leave a mark. "Levi, please," I can't not beg when it comes to him and his mouth, the way he touches me, soothes me, dominates me.

"I need you to be a good girl, Hannah, or else I'm going to have to torture this tight little body of yours." I feel his smile through his lips pressing around my breast. He releases my flesh and moves to my other breast. "You eat lunch with me from now on. In my office, with the door shut. Because my lunch is going to be you, devouring this sweet cunt of yours." I choke on my own laughter as he slides down my stomach, placing his mouth on my mound.

"Now, be a good little paralegal and open wide for me. I need to taste perfection." My hands go limp, and my eyes fall shut as I lose myself into the abyss of Levi and his hungry mouth.

CHAPTER SEVENTEEN

Hannah

I don't understand why people don't enjoy Mondays. It's the start of a new week. Brand new—"*Shoot!*" I trip over my own two feet, stumbling out of the elevator.

"Ms. Matthews, are you okay?" Vanessa pops up from her chair as I pick myself up off the ground. Okay, I take that comment back. Mondays suck! I brush off my scraped knees, feeling the back of my skirt for any tears. Why would I even think Mondays are good? *Maybe because you're sleeping with your boss and you get to see him for the first time since your rendezvous all night Friday into Saturday?* Of course not!

Also, yes.

When we were forced to check out and go our separate ways, I wanted to pout like a baby. So, maybe I did a little bit, but if we aren't careful, we could risk getting caught. Thankfully before the night got too late, Levi had me shoot off a text to my parents, letting them know I'd left early and went to hang out with a friend. You know the make-believe ones I all of a sudden seem to have.

By morning, I had a dozen missed calls from Braydon. I sent him a quick text apologizing, saying I'd gotten sick and went home—praying he didn't go to my house to check on me.

Levi had the same amount of missed calls from Kipley and Rebecca. My pout changed into a frown thinking about him calling her back and easing her worry, but then he made it all better by not responding at all, telling me she wasn't his problem. Point for me.

I wanted nothing more than to spend the rest of the weekend with him, but if we wanted to keep this under wraps, he had to play it cool. I did my own thing, and so did he. On Sunday, while I was laying in the backyard with a face mask on, my hair flying high in the wind to air dry, Mom informed me Kip and Levi were stopping by to pick up Dad for golf. Not thinking I'd see him, especially wearing a bright green mask and my hair resembling Frankenstein, I booked it to my room. Sadly, I wasn't fast enough, and Levi got a sneak peek of me at my best. I could hear his soft chuckle as I took the stairs two at a time, cussing under my breath.

But today, my skin glowing, my hair flat ironed and somewhat tamed, I walk into work, ready to see my man.

Okay. Rewind.

That sounds so weird!

My man. My man. *My man.*

Suddenly, my knees don't hurt anymore and making a fool out of myself in front of the receptionist is no big deal. I wave her off, cheery as can be, and head toward my desk. I wonder if he's in. If he's as excited to see me. His office light is on, and when I peek my head in, I see him at his desk typing away.

"Morning, boss."

His head pops up at my voice. "Well, hello there." His smile makes Monday the best day of the week again. He stands, coming my way. "How was your weekend? I wanted to come by, but—"

"No, I get it. We're undercover—"

"I don't want to be."

"I know, me either." He stops in front of me, unsure what to do with his hands, so he shoves them into his pockets. "God, I want to kiss you right now."

Monday sucks again.

I've wanted his lips back on mine since Saturday. I fiddle with my necklace, turning to the door, wondering if we could get away with shutting and locking it. Technically, it is still early and—

"I know what you're thinking, and trust me, it's already crossed my mind too. But I have a meeting in five minutes with your dad. I don't think closing that door and eating you for breakfast is the best idea."

Go to hell, Monday!

Geez Louise. As Monday rains down and soaks my mood even more, a tap on the door has us turning and directing our attention to my dad.

"Morning, you two. Hannah, proud to see you up and in the office bright and early. Glad you're here too. I wanted to talk to you both." My dad's face is serious, not his normal, carefree self.

Which means...

Holy Toledo! Is this it? Did he find out? *Do both of our faces say we were about to shut the door and do naughty things under this roof?* I knew I shouldn't have pretended I had friends! "Um, what is it, Daddy?" Maybe if I use the sweet five-year-old daddy lingo, he won't ground me for life and kill Levi in front of me.

"I've been watching you two..." *oh crap,* "...and how hard you've been working my daughter." *The end. Bye-bye, Levi.* "I think it's time we bring you fully onboard to help with the Miller case." *Wait, what?* "From what I gather, Levi's had you working on small stuff, but this is the perfect case to get your toes wet. We already have it practically sealed, so Levi, use Hannah as your apprentice on this. I believe she would learn a lot from you and this case."

I didn't realize I was holding my breath until he stops talking.

"Well? What do you say? You both look like I just fed you bad news." *Actually, spectacular news since you don't know our dirty little secret or plan to ship me off and kill my man.*

I giggle on the inside. *My man...*

"Wow, Jim, that's great. I think Hannah would be great for this case. From what I've seen, she's very observant and takes a lot of pride in her work. I have no doubt she'll do fantastic. And I'll make sure to watch her like a hawk."

My dad smiles and hands Levi a huge stack of files. "I knew I could count on you two. Here are the key witness statements. They are not to be shared at this time. Very important we keep these between us."

"Why?" I ask.

"It's to safeguard the client. Without these, the case is dead. It's protocol in huge trials like this. You tend to keep the big stuff to a small staff. These files go missing, so do our chances of winning."

I nod, sensing the importance. "All right, you two, get on with what you were doing. I have an offsite meeting all day." With that, he says his goodbyes and is gone.

We both stand there silent, until the air around us is so electric, anyone who enters is in for quite a zapping. "Well…" Levi faces me, "looks like we should shut that door after all. I have a lot of prepping to do with you."

My panties just melted right off me. "Yes, boss."

And like a good little apprentice, I shut and lock the door.

I'm on my way back from the bathroom, reminiscing how fantastic my Monday morning has been. Catching the clock on the wall, I see it's already past noon. Levi had to leave and meet Dad at another meeting, so this leaves me the afternoon to catch up on filing and data entry. When I turn the corner, I spot someone in my chair.

"Braydon?"

"Hey, you!" Jumping up, he pushes in my keyboard tray and steps away from my desk to give me a hug.

"What are you doing up here?" A lot has changed since last week, especially any attraction I had toward him. Now, it seems awkward and forced.

"I wanted to come say hi. See how you were doing and take you to lunch."

The last thing I want to do is go to lunch, especially knowing Levi would not be happy about it. "Um, thanks, but I'm still not feeling one hundred percent. I'm just gonna work through lunch." My eyes land on the pile of confidential folders on my desk—the ones Dad handed us this morning. The manila folders aren't aligned in the perfect stack I left them in, a few sheets of paper are sticking out from the top folder. I raise a brow. "Were...uh, you looking at my files?"

His eyes land on the stack, then back to mine. "These? No, of course not. I'm sorry. I bumped into them and a few fell. I put them all back in order. I hope I didn't mess anything up."

Geez, what's wrong with me? "Of course not! Sorry, it's been an eventful morning." I think my dad made me on guard about this case now, paranoid everyone is out to get these covert files or something. I shake it off and stuff my purse under my desk. Levi won't be back until late this afternoon, so I don't see any harm with spending my lunch hour chatting with a friend. "How about this, if you don't mind, I'd love to keep you company while you eat. We can find a spot in the lunchroom and go over some of my Miller notes. There are a few things I'd love clarification on."

Braydon offers me his customary smile. "Deal." He pushes in my chair and sticks his hand out, offering me to lead the way. I open my bottom drawer and place the files inside, locking it.

"Okay! Let's go!"

"Right! If you want to claim theft, don't wear the missing jewelry!" I laugh as Braydon and I take the stairs up to my floor for the Tuesday morning staff meeting. He called early this morning asking if I wanted coffee and to help him go over a small claims case for practice.

"Who knows, maybe they'll believe her and grant her the

insurance money. But let's just say it doesn't look promising." He jokes about what we reviewed, a woman who claimed her house was robbed, only to show up to testify on a suspect she pointed out in a lineup while wearing the exact piece of jewelry she claimed he stole.

"Some people." I shake my head, amazed at how some idiots try to scam the system. Braydon pulls out his keycard and swipes it to the door. A red light flashes. "Hmmm...your keycard not working?"

"That's strange. It worked yesterday."

"Here. Use mine." He swipes mine, and we get the green light. We exit the stairwell right outside the conference room, and it's already full. My eyes gravitate toward Levi, who is absolutely delicious in his navy-blue suit. The top few buttons open and absent tie. Yum. He takes me in, his eyes eating me alive. Noticing who's next to me, his brows crinkle. It's clear he doesn't like that I still converse with Braydon, but if he wants to keep this up, I need Braydon as my decoy. Not to mention, I still do enjoy his company on a friend level.

The meeting gets started, and I pull out my notepad. Dad discusses all the new cases and assigns them to teams. When he says my name, my cheeks flush as he announces I'll be joining the Miller case, and to my surprise, so will Braydon. I pat him on the shoulder, congratulating him. An hour goes by, and the meeting wraps up.

"Hannah, hold back." Levi's voice stops me. Braydon and I turn around to see him shaking an associate's hand, then heading our way. "Braydon, you can go. I have no need for you. Just Hannah."

Braydon opens his mouth to say something, but decides against it. "Yeah, sure. I'll see you later, Hannah." And he walks away.

I give Levi my full attention. "That wasn't very nice."

"I'm not worried about being nice to him. You look lovely

today. How does lunch in my office sound? I'm famished and know the perfect meal."

My belly tightens. It's impossible to hide the spark in my eyes. "After you, *boss*."

I'm hammering away on my computer, down to the last two witness testimonies. I pull out the last one: Clara Hill, wife of the city councilman who took his life. It's hard to read her statement. How she found her husband. The typed suicide letter. The conversation they had the night before he died, coming clean about what he was asked to cover up. Her statement will singlehandedly take down Miller Industries.

"Hard at work as always?"

I gaze up to Braydon standing at my desk. "Hey there. Aren't you supposed to be at the meeting with everyone?" I swore I saw his name on the list of attendees, along with my dad and Levi.

"Nah. It was an error. I get to slack off today. Just kidding. What are you working on?"

I peer down, then close the file. "Oh, nothing. Just entering in witness testimonies for the Miller case. Nothing I'm sure you don't already know." I press enter, finishing up and saving the document. Taking the large rubber band, I secure the folders and stand. "Hey, I gotta run downstairs and sign these into records, wanna come with me and tell me more about the theft case?"

"Oh, you bet I do!"

"Great! I just need to run to the bathroom. Give me two minutes, okay?"

He takes his index finger to his watch. "Tick-tock. This amazing story won't wait for just anyone."

I shake my head. "Goof. I'll be right back."

When I return, he's gone. There's a post-it note stuck to my computer screen, telling me he had to run and owes me a raincheck. Suddenly bummed, I check my watch and realize it's way past lunchtime. With Levi missing in action since yesterday due to this case, I have no lunch date. Not that we really eat lunch when I'm in there. But it also triggers another emotion. I miss him. I debate on sitting in his chair and sniffing the leather to feel closer to him, but I'm not a weirdo, or a stalker, or psycho, so, like a normal human with a secret boyfriend, but *not* boyfriend, I walk down to the sub shop and have a lunch date with me, myself, and I.

CHAPTER EIGHTEEN

Levi

"These aren't the files. The testimonies. They're wrong." I've gone over the files a dozen times. Something's missing.

"How could this have happened? We had them all contained. Each statement. Who entered them?" Jim runs his hands down his tie, as confused as I am.

Fuck, I can't tell him, so I put the blame on myself.

"It was me. That's how I know they're wrong. These statements, it's all bullshit." What's bullshit is I was too consumed with getting Hannah alone in my office that by the time we resurfaced, I only had time to skim the documents before entrusting Hannah to do her job and get it all entered correctly. But I can't tell her father that.

"I think you're just burning your candle at both ends. You've been working so hard on this. Head home for the night. Tomorrow, with a clear head, we'll gather the team and research the files. This has to be a mistake. Hopefully a computer error."

He's right. The last hour has been pointless. The documents we're reviewing are shit, but I can't figure out why Hannah would enter false statements. Or not file the information correctly. Something's fucked up. I'm not on my game. Normally, I'm a mastermind when it comes to memorizing things. Names, dates, numbers. The little mole behind Hannah's left butt cheek or the tiniest little birthmark on the back of her neck. *We're a week away from trial. Get your shit together.*

"Still with me?"

I shake my head. "Yeah. Maybe you're right. Some rest will help clear my head. Let's call it a night and reconvene in the morning."

I leave Jim and head down to my office in hopes Hannah's still here. Maybe I can get some answers from her without coming off as accusing. Peering at my watch, I realize it's past seven. Shit. This week's been insane. The only time I've been able to spend with her is during our private lunches where I call her in and she obeys, bringing her little notebook and shutting my door. My pants thicken at each memory, her over my desk, riding me in my chair, fucking her until I'm forced to shove my tie in her mouth so she doesn't alert the entire floor I'm balls deep inside her.

Even though my mood plummets seeing her empty chair, my smile stays intact at how things have progressed since the gala. Hannah Matthews, my little firecracker. The best thing to have ever happened in my life was her deviant little ploy to get to me. She may have once been inexperienced, but her eagerness to learn, experiment…shit. I adjust myself so I don't scare off the cleaning staff or take out the plaque sitting on top of my desk.

I grab my things and shut my light off to head home. I want nothing more than to see Hannah, not that showing up at the Matthews' home would be out of the ordinary since I practically grew up there. But asking to hang out with their daughter doesn't exactly stick to our rule of keeping us a secret. Not that we didn't almost blow it the night of the gala. We weren't smart. Two un-wanted guests started asking questions when we disappeared. Hannah shot a text out to Braydon saying she felt sick and went home. I didn't even bother sending one to Rebecca. I didn't will-ingly bring her, nor was she my problem. After Hannah confessed about the night of Kipley's wedding, I could have strangled my friends. If Hannah hadn't stepped in…the possibility of Rebecca in that closet has me crawling out of my skin.

I run into Jim and the little shit-box at the elevator.

"Great work today, son. What's on your evening agenda?"

Braydon smiles, not missing my snarl aimed right at him. "Thanks, sir. I was actually going to surprise your daughter, if that's okay. I have tickets to see the new Marvel movie. I hear it's really great."

Fucking nerd. I can't help but smirk. Hannah hates super-hero shit. If he knew her at all, he'd notice her quirky obsession with all things documentaries and history. The elevator dings, and I step inside, blocking Braydon's entrance. "Hey, favor, go make sure the fax is on in the copy room, will you?"

"It never gets shut off," he says, confused, trying to bypass me.

"Still. Expecting an important file to be sent through tonight. Need to make sure." He eyes me, but goodie two-shoes won't say no in front of Jim.

"Yeah, sure."

That's what I thought. I press the close button before he even rears back around. Jim continues to chatter about his golf score while I pull my phone out and shoot off a text to Hannah.

Me: Pack a bag. Tell your parents you're sleeping at a friend's house. Meet me outside in twenty minutes.

Hannah: You know, my parents are going to want to know who these amazing friends I have are soon...

Me: Tell them you're going to a nunnery lock-in then. You need to pray all night for your sins and all the naughty things I'm going to do to you.

Three little dots pop up, and I anticipate her response.

Hannah: Anything else, boss?

Shit. Nothing like standing next to the dad of the girl you're growing a boner for. Hannah loves calling me boss in this seductive way right before I plunge into her. That sweet spot, made just for me. And her dirty little mouth drives me absolutely mad. I've never been the rough, dominating type. I like sex just as much as the next guy, but with Hannah, it's different. I don't just want to be inside her, I want to dominate her, own her, mark her. This part of what we're doing scares me. I don't know how to control this beast she's released. As long as Hannah's in my life, there's no controlling him.

Me: Don't bother with any panties, I'll just destroy them.

Hannah: I haven't had any on all day, why would I put some on now?

Fuck me. I rush out of the building, giving Jim a short goodbye, and jump in my car. I step on the gas and take the left faster than I should. Having to miss our lunch date threw my afternoon off. I knew she was waiting for me and the call I had to place telling her I wasn't going to make it back down soured my mood the rest of the day. It didn't help that Jim called Braydon in to assist. The kid gave me bad fucking vibes. The ass kissing galore wasn't even the problem. If Jim enjoyed Braydon's tongue all the way up his ass, so be it. It was something else. The questions. The looks. He was planning something. And the way he scrutinized me, as if he had something I didn't. Twice today, I wanted to put him in his place, confirming he didn't have shit. One being Hannah. I made sure of it. Their little meet-ups were done. Dead in the water. I even attempted to have his keycard revoked to get onto our floor until he complained like a little pussy about needing access to our printers. Of course he went to Jim. And he fucking gave it to him. A part of me wants to tell Jim about us. He may fire me or kill me, but at least he'll stop encouraging that piece of shit to take his daughter out.

I make it to the Matthews' residence in record time. Like a good little girl, Hannah is waiting for me.

"Hey," she says as she climbs in. My shitty day washes away the moment her sweet scent fills my car. I want to lean over and take her mouth, but I need to be smart. Anyone can see.

"You smell delicious." I pull away from her street and take a right before Jim gets home and spots my car.

"You mean you smell Mom's pot roast?" She giggles, putting on her seat belt. I used to love pot roast nights at the Matthews'. When I lived there for the summer, I'd request it all the time.

"Keep talkin' like that and I may have to turn around and

ditch you for your mom's cooking." She slaps me, her smile causing this heavy feeling inside my chest.

"You don't really look like my fake new bestie Becky, and I'd have to explain why I spent so much time with you." I chuckle, bringing my eyes to the road. Fifteen minutes pass, but it seems like forever until we're finally pulling into the underground parking garage of my condo and taking the elevator to the fifteenth floor.

"Wow, this place is nice," she states, looking around. I toss my keys on the counter and head to the fridge.

"Thanks. Want something to drink?"

She faces me, offering me her kind eyes. "Sure, I'll take a beer." I pour myself a hefty glass of whiskey and grab her a cold beer. "For some reason, I always imagined your place being full of sports memorabilia."

"Why's that?" Handing her the beer and taking a much-needed swig of my own, I watch her as she takes in my place. The walls are mostly bare, painted a subtle shade of gray. When I kicked Theresa out, I got rid of everything that reminded me of her. The only thing that stayed was the furniture, some old photos of the guys on the end table, and a large tv on the console in the corner. Aside from that, there's nothing left to admire.

"I don't know. I always thought you loved the game. Imagined it being like Kip's place—full of sports stuff. You know, the stuff Stacey always complains she's going to throw in the garbage when he's at work."

"That part of me kind of died when I turned down the NFL." Fuck. Why'd I say that? Her smile, the one thing I constantly crave, falters.

"I'm sorry. I—"

"No, no. Don't try that sad little Hannah act on me. I didn't mean it in a pity me way. I meant it as I chose to leave it. It's not who I truly was. I was good—"

"You were *amazing*."

I pull her into my arms, loving the way her back molds perfectly against my chest. "Well, aren't you my biggest fan. I loved playing. But I love doing what I do now way more." I kiss the top of her head, inhaling the smell of her cherry shampoo.

"Do you ever miss it?"

"Yes and no. I miss the rush. The smell of the fresh grass mingled with mud and sweat. I miss feeling the wind in my face as I rush down the twenty-yard line. The winning. But I don't miss the politics of it. The deals. The shadiness. People in that business are ruthless. I've seen players go down in freak accidents. Deals fall out. The cheating. Behind the love of the sport is a lot of ugliness. That shit, I don't miss."

She shifts in my arms, raising her chin, and I press my lips against hers.

"I came to every single one of your games."

"You did?" Her cheeks flare a cute rosy shade at her confession. I suddenly feel like an asshole because I don't remember ever seeing her.

"Yeah, I made Kip take me. And when he couldn't, I went with my neighbor, Mrs. Bealson who I think was equally as obsessed with you—the team winning. You truly were amazing on the field." My guilt grows like an unwanted weed. "Remember your last game, junior year. It was raining cats and dogs. You were down three points with seventeen seconds on the clock."

"I tackled Jeremy Ruther, retrieving the ball and won the game. Got us the title." Fuck, that was one of the highlights of my junior year. "You really are my biggest fan, aren't you?" I tease, squeezing her closer to me. "Hannah…" I breathe into her hair, engulfing myself in her scent.

"Yes, boss?" her voice is soft, laced with desire. My naughty little girl wants to play. I squeeze her to me, my teeth grazing her earlobe. "No playing tonight. Tonight, I just want Hannah and Levi." I take her lobe into my mouth. Having her in my arms eases the worry from work. The stress of hiding this from our family. The thorn in my side, Braydon.

"Everything okay?" she asks, her hands gliding up my chest.

"Yep. Just want to enjoy you. It's been a long day. And this is helping." She works her fingers in circular motions over my temples. My eyes close, and I rest my forehead against hers. "Feels amazing."

"I don't have to stay. If you wanted to get some sleep." I'm discarding our drinks and she's up and over my shoulder before she can even finish her nonsense. My hand finds her ass, and I offer her a nice smack, the sound echoing throughout my bare condo.

"Nice try. You're not going anywhere. If you're a good girl, I plan on ordering pizza from Savino's—your favorite. But first, I need some Hannah time."

With one goal in mind, I carry her into my bedroom. Turns out, it's not always a bad thing to have dessert before dinner.

CHAPTER NINETEEN

Hannah

"**S**top!"

"I can't. Plus, we have three more floors to go."

Two. One. And he's off me as fast as he was on me the moment the elevator doors to the office building closed. With barely enough time to adjust myself, the doors open to a busy Matthews and Associates.

"Morning, Mr. Dent. Ms. Matthews," Vanessa greets us as we walk into the office, cool and collected—like we weren't totally making out in the elevator. "Mr. Dent, Mr. Matthews is already set up in the conference room and asked me to inform you when you arrive."

"Thanks, Vanessa." He turns to me. "Hannah, I have a ton of files to go over today. Clear your lunch schedule. We're going to work through it." I nod, biting the inside of my cheek to hide my excitement. He's fighting off his own mischievous grin and nods, heading in the opposite direction of his office to the conference room.

I practically skip to my desk, my cheeks sore from all the smiling and laughing I've done over the past twenty-four hours—shoot, ever since we started this. If my younger self knew she'd be sleeping in Levi Dent's arms, having the most amazing sex ever, she would have fallen over and died! A giggle erupts up my throat, and I cover my mouth.

"Aren't we in a chipper mood today."

My head whips toward my desk to find Braydon sitting in my chair. "Hey...uh, what are you doing up here?" I offer him a half smile, hoping it masks my concern. Levi's probably already in the conference room, but if he were to forget something and see him... I take a quick glance toward the conference room.

"To see you, of course. I called you again last night. Wanted to see if you wanted to go out for Chinese and a movie."

"Oh, yeah, sorry. I had a ton of work to do. This case is wearing on us all." Translation: I had so much sex, my right leg may be out of place.

"No problem. What's on your agenda today? Wanna go to lunch?" Shoot. I feel like a jerk. He's been nothing but nice to me and doesn't deserve the cold shoulder coming his way.

"Um, darn. Not today. I have a huge project Levi has me on and I need to work through lunch. Raincheck?" His smile doesn't match the scrutiny in his eyes. Oh god, don't call me out...

"Sure, raincheck."

Phew!

"Well, have a great day!" I say, signaling it's time for him to get up. Levi might come back for a pen or a file or a notepad. Thankfully, he takes my cue, swivels once in my chair, and gets up.

"You too. Don't be a stranger, okay?" he says before heading toward the stairs.

When I put my bag down, I notice my computer's on again. "Hey, were you on my computer?"

He turns, eyeing my laptop. "Oh, yeah, sorry. I was checking my email while I was waiting for you. Hope that's okay."

Strange. I nod. "Yeah, of course."

"See ya." And he's gone.

The second the clock hits noon, the doors fly open and the entire team hustles out of the conference room. They've been in there for four hours without a break. I spot Levi in a deep discussion with my dad as they walk this way. I straighten my blouse and adjust my hair. Once they're near, I stand.

"Hey, baby girl. How's your morning been?"

"Great. Busy. And yours? You in there finalizing the Miller case?"

There's some strain in my dad's eyes at the mention, but he clears it instantly. "Never a dull day. Hey, Mom said you haven't confirmed if you're going to dinner with us all on Friday? Better say yes. We have reservations at your favorite steakhouse."

I completely forgot about dinner. Kip and Stacey set it up asking to get everyone together.

"Um…yeah, sure, wouldn't miss it."

"Great." He leans in to give me a kiss and waves off Levi. The moment he's out of earshot, Levi speaks.

"I hope you're prepared. This is going to be a really intense lunch. If you can grab what you need and shut the door after you," he says, fighting a smirk, then walks into his office.

Like a kid being handed the keys to the candy shop, I scoop up my notepad and walk as slow as possible into his office, shutting the door behind me.

At the click of the lock, my legs leave the ground and he has me pressed against the bookcase, knocking off a picture frame. "Fuck, I've been thinking about you all morning." His lips fuse to mine in a rough, heated kiss. He's already hard, pressing his erection into me.

"Same," I moan, wrapping my arms around him.

"An hour isn't going to be enough for what I want to do to you." He bites at my lower lip, pushing up my skirt and finding my panties. "Goddammit," he growls at the wetness between my legs. "Always ready for me. Love it." I moan again, allowing my head to hit the bookshelf when a finger breaks past my folds. He pumps in and out, working me up, the quivering of my body telling him it won't take long before I'm exploding all over his fingers. "Levi," I whimper as he thrusts, knocking off a book. We both start to laugh, and he slams his mouth on mine to mask our sounds.

"You were made for me. This cunt. Perf—"

Knock. Knock.

We both freeze. "Levi? Hannah?"

Oh no! "Stacey."

He pulls out, and my feet drop to the ground. We're both fussing with one another to make ourselves appear decent when there's another knock.

"One second," Levi calls out, looking me square in the eyes. "You good?"

"Yes. I'm fine."

"You sure? Because you were just about to come all over my hand. I felt it. We can leave her out there. I can finish—"

I smack his chest. "*Seriously?*"

"Of course."

Oh my god, that smirk. He *is* serious. I shake my head, the laughter unstoppable. Pushing past him, I unlock the door and greet a curious Stacey. "Hey!" Darn it that sounded way too boisterous. "What brings you here?"

She takes notice of me, then Levi, who has his back to her, pretending to organize a pile of already organized papers on his desk. "Well..." She's stalling. Shoot. I run my hands through my hair. Do I have lipstick smudged all over my face? Holy moly. Does Levi? "I wanted to see if you wanted to go to lunch. I have some stuff I want to run past you."

Lunch? *Boo...can't. I already have plans to get railed by my boss.* "Hmmm..."

"You can go. I'll finish up here."

My head whips around. He better not finish up without me. My core is still throbbing, in need of that release. "You sure?"

"Yep. Enjoy. Oh, and hi, Stacey."

"Uh...hi, Levi," she says, her head tilting to the side. Levi, who is still facing his desk, which is probably for the best since he would have to explain to Stacey why he has a hard-on in the middle of the day. "You okay there, Levi?"

Gah!

"Yep. All good. Busy. You two should go. I have this case to get back to."

A few unsettling seconds pass before she thankfully brings her attention back to me. "Well…okay. Wanna try out that bistro a few blocks down?"

"Yep. Sounds great. Let's go." I grab her, dragging her curious eyes out of Levi's office.

"Wow, this sandwich is delish!" I take another bite of my club to avoid confrontation. She hasn't stopped looking at me strangely since we left the office. "What's wrong? Don't like yours?"

"No, it's fine. It's just…what's up with you? You're acting really strange."

Strange? Why would I be acting strange? I mean, you came ridiculously close to catching me and my brother's best friend about to fornicate in his office under my dad's watch. "Hmmm…not sure why you think that." Another bite.

"Hannah, you know I love you like a sister, right?" I nod. Oh god. "Is there something going on between you and Levi?" I choke on another bite. It also doesn't help I still have the other three in my mouth.

"What? Why would you think that?" I muffle through my unchewed food.

"I don't know. I'm sorry if I'm overstepping, but it's just…at the lake you two were different with each other. Like you were fighting. I've never known you two to chat much, let alone have an argument. Then poker night, I caught him scowling at you. Then just now. Why was the door locked?"

'Cause we were forni—"Levi just doesn't like being interrupted when he gets on a roll with work. It's no big deal."

"Okay, but you still didn't answer my question. Is something going on between you two?"

Yes. "No, don't be silly."

She eyes me as though her bullshit meter is dinging in the red zone. "Okay. I'm sorry I mentioned it. My hormones are out of control and my mind is running away with itself."

I reach over to cup her hand. "Oh no, are you not feeling well?" I stare at her with kind, worried eyes, until hers shine with happiness. "Wait…are you?"

"Pregnant."

I scream.

Then choke on my food. I spit it out, getting a few nasty eye-rolls from the table next to us. "Oh my god! I'm going to be an aunt! Does Kipley know?"

She laughs. "Of course. But you're the first person we've told. I wanted you to hear it first." Tears well up in my eyes. My brother is going to have a baby. I scoot my chair out and stand while she does the same. Hugging, we both fail at keeping it together and shed tears of joy.

"I'm so happy for you both. You're going to be amazing parents. And I'm going to spoil him *or* her rotten." I love my brother so much. And Stacey. They couldn't be better for one another. And they deserve the world.

We spend the remainder of lunch chatting about baby stuff. I ask to be part of the baby shower planning, even though she has a million girlfriends to do the job. She tells me the dinner tomorrow night is to tell the whole family, and I can't wait to see Mom and Dad's face when they find out.

"Thanks for lunch. This was nice." She goes in for a hug.

"Agreed. Minus all the choking."

We share a good laugh, and she pulls away. She studies me with unwavering concern. "I bet I'm misreading the situation, but if I'm not, be careful. Levi is one of your brother's oldest and dearest friends. It would hurt him immensely. Be smart about what you're doing. You know he would choose you over him. Just don't put him in that position."

I don't say anything. I can't. I convince myself I don't need to. Because I won't be putting anyone in any positions. Levi and I are adults. And this won't get out. It's fine. We're fine.

Nothing to worry about.

Nope.

CHAPTER TWENTY

Levi

"What the hell kind of play was that!" Kip yells at the screen, a few other patrons along the bar agreeing. "Jesus, who the hell hired this guy?" He throws his hands up. "Catch the damn ball!"

I take a sip of my beer, barely paying attention to the game.

"What's up, cocksuckers!" Chase slaps me on the back and slides onto an open stool next to me. "Been too long. Where the fuck's Ben?" he asks, flagging down the bartender.

"Couldn't make it. He's sick or some shit." Wish I'd thought of that excuse.

"Well, fuck him. Sick or not, you don't miss boys' night. What's on the agenda? Strippers? Molly?" He laughs, winking at the girl on the other side of me giving him the stink eye.

"Sorry, no more strippers for me," Kip says, flashing his wedding ring.

"See, I told you not to go through with it. Women turn crazy and won't let you have any fun anymore. Levi, how about you? Once his curfew hits, you wanna get down on some pussy?"

The girl next to me snatches her drink and leaves. I shake my head. "No, man, I'm good. Weren't you just in Mexico? Your dick didn't fall off while you were there?" Kip laughs, and I take a swig of my beer.

"Fuck no. Plus, the *pharmacia* is basically a free for all. All good, man. Also, when did you turn into a pussy again? What, you datin' someone?"

Kip aims his attention on me. Fuck.

"Just because I don't want to conjure up some strippers doesn't mean I'm dating someone." It means I'm boning Kip's sister and have no interest in strippers.

"Whatever, pussy."

"What *is* up? You've been off the radar the past couple weeks. Work getting to you?"

Another swig. *Yep. Work.* "Yeah. We're working on a huge case. It's a big deal for the firm. We win this, it's huge. We lose… it's bad."

"My pops is the best. And with you helping him, what's the problem? Is it a non-winnable case?"

"No we have it in the bag. Or had it. Somewhere along the way, some files went missing. Information was inaccurately entered. So now, our witness statements claim no foul play. Someone entered in the wrong information or got to the files, but I can't prove it because I can't find the original docs."

"Well, who filed it? Go to them."

That's the thing. Another swig. "Hannah filed it."

"Oh shit."

Yeah, oh shit is right. When I went back to check the logs, Hannah's initials were there. I couldn't believe she would have made such a mistake. The entire stack of testimonies wrong? I asked her about it nonchalantly, and she confirmed, pulling out her safety notebook and stating times of when she documented it. It didn't add up. It wasn't like Hannah to make a mistake. I just couldn't figure out another reason for it.

"So, what happens? Does my pop know?"

"No. I've been trying to resolve it without him getting wind it was Hannah. He trusts me to figure it all out. I'm just running out of time. If I can't, I'm going to have to tell Jim who documented it."

And that will cost her her job. Not to mention, her pride, her confidence, and her career at the firm. Because if we lose this case, I can't fathom where the firm will stand.

"Just ask Hannah straight up. She's resourceful. She may be able to help. If she says she did something, she's normally spot on. You know her. Kind of nerdy when it comes to her smarts. Speaking of Hannah, how's she doing? Pop told me she's still dating that kid from the office."

No, the fuck she isn't.

My fingers clamp around my beer, trying to keep my eyes focused on the game. If he saw my expression right now, he'd see rage. "Who knows. I don't think she's into him. He's a fucking dweeb."

Kip laughs. "Yeah, well, maybe she's into that type. Not that I know. This is the first guy I've seen her date." I want to snap at him that she's not dating him. She's dating—*shit*, we're not dating. *Are we?* I'm so confused at what we're doing. We're together all day. She's in my bed at night. We're having the best sex of my life. And we're getting to know each other. And I love every fucking second of it. "Maybe we should fuck with him and drill him for answers on Friday."

"What's Friday?"

"Family dinner? Hello. I literally *just* told you about it, are you not listening to me?" Oh yeah. Man, I'm a bad friend. He just told me he's having a baby and I'm fantasizing about how I made a sundae off his sister last night.

"Oh…yeah. Sorry. But what does he have to do with dweeb boy?"

"Pop said she's bringing him."

Over my dead body.

I slept like shit.

Probably because I didn't have a warm little body next to me. Or because I drank too much driving myself mad about Hannah and her non-boyfriend. I walk into the office and spot Hannah already sitting at her desk. She's wearing a pale gray skirt with a top that brings out her eyes. "In my office. Now," I snap, walking past her. I'm sure my attitude is a surprise, because it sure is unexpected. But I need to get a few things straight before I lose it.

"What's—?"

"Shut the door."

She does as she's told and waits. I rein in my anger and step around to face her. "What's the deal with you and Braydon? Are you dating him behind my back?"

Her eyes go wide. "Braydon? No! Why would you think that?"

"Because your entire family does." I might as well be her boyfriend. I sound like a jealous one.

"Well, I'm not. And I thought that was a good thing. So they don't pay attention to us. That's what you wanted, remember?" Fuck, it is what I wanted, but is it what I still want?

"What's wrong? Why is this suddenly bothering you? Do you…you want to end this, don't you?" Her eyes blaze with panic. My chest constricts at the thought of us not being an us. I swallow the space between us and wrap her in my arms.

"Fuck no. I'm sorry. That's far from what I want. I just…I don't like the fucking kid. Even if it's a ruse. He's trouble."

She snuggles her head into my chest, and I squeeze her tighter, needing her close. "He's harmless. But if we want to keep us secret, we need him. Stacey was asking questions about us at lunch the other day. She suspects something."

That's not good. If she shares her thoughts with Kip, I'm a dead man. "I don't like that kid. We need to find another way."

"Want me to come out and tell my family I'm a lesbian? That'll take you right off their trail. Not that they'd be all that shocked since I've never even brought home a guy before recently." I chuckle, feeling some relief. I'm glad to hear I'm the one who's giving her all her firsts. Showing her how she should always be treated. Cherished.

Kissing the top of her head, I say, "No, then I'd just be jealous of your fake girlfriend."

She pulls away, and I want to fight to keep her in my arms all day.

"You realize, if you took the job, you wouldn't have to worry about anyone else filling it."

"What job?" I'm back to being on edge, worrying she's going to leave the firm and I won't get to be near her every day.

Becoming nervous, she bites her bottom lip, and I find it sexy as hell. "Boyfriend. But it was a joke. That would be—"

"I'll take it."

"What? Really?"

I pull her back into me, her breasts snuggled up against my chest. "I said I want the job." Her chin lifts, her expression morphing into shock. I laugh. She's so damn cute. "So, *girlfriend*. What do you say we get this god-awful day over and you tell your parents you're sleeping at Becky's? I'll cook you my specialty—delivered pizza—and we'll watch mindless television until we fall asleep."

Her eyes light up. God. Beautiful.

"Sounds perfect. Except we have family dinner tonight."

Fuck, that's right. "Scratch the pizza. Just dessert then. But knowing it will be some time before I get you home, there's something else I need from you."

"What's that?"

"Ditch the dweeb. He's absolutely not coming to dinner tonight. I can't come as your date, but I sure as hell don't want him there. We will have to figure something else out as our decoy. Just to get rid of him, I may take you up on the whole lesbian idea."

She takes too long to agree with me, and I fear having to spank her silly, but then her arms wrap around me, hugging me. "Got it, boss."

Dammit, she knows how to get to me.

"Good. Now, let's make up for some lost time. I haven't eaten breakfast yet, and I have the perfect meal in mind."

CHAPTER TWENTY-ONE

Hannah

We're on our way to the restaurant straight from work, Levi insisting we drive together. No one questioned why I wasn't driving myself, or why I came into work with Levi all week. He told Dad he'd give me a ride after we finished searching for some files Levi said went missing. The windows are down, and the wind is blowing fresh air though the car. Some eighties band is playing on the radio, and my heart skips when Levi holds my hand as he drives. He's holding my hand!

He is my boyfriend. Secret boyfriend, but still. I panicked earlier, afraid he was done with…whatever we were. He shocked me saying he wanted to fill the boyfriend role. I wanted to tell him he had been my boyfriend since I was seven, about all my notepads with Hannah Dent written all over them a million times, the love letters I pretended he wrote me… Boy, he would probably drop me off at the looney bin if he knew how deeply in love I've always been with him.

Which is strange to say now.

And a bit creepy.

Maybe for a good laugh, I'll show him his hoodie I still have from the summer he stayed with us. I'd stolen it from the laundry room, unwashed, and slept with it the entire next year.

"What's got that quirky smile on your face?"

"Oh, I was just remembering when we were kids. The

summer you stayed with us. Remember your football hoodie you lost?"

"Yeah, the one I swear Kip's girlfriend at the time stole because she secretly had a crush on me."

I laugh. "It was me."

He cocks his head, eyeing me. "No."

"Guilty." I laugh. "Right under all your noses. No one suspected sweet little Hannah, but I took it. Still have it too. Maybe if you're nice, I'll give it back. It's a little worn, though."

His laughter seeps through me and tickles my soul. The sound of him happy, relaxed…it's like heaven. Lately, he's been so stressed with this case, and I hate that I haven't been able to do anything about it. I've thought about going to Dad and asking him to lay off, but that would cause more issues.

"Wow. Never knew little Hannah Matthews was a hoodie thief."

I shrug, playing it cool. "If we're being honest, I snagged a few other things from you over the years."

"You didn't. Spill. Now."

I refuse to confess all the things. His toothbrush, a pair of boxers, a letter Lindy Robertson wrote him his freshman year— which I stabbed a hundred times and buried in our backyard. "I went through your phone once."

He throws his head back, and a laugh bellows out. "Why?"

"I wanted to see all the photos you had, hoping for some naked selfies or something I guess." I hadn't found any. Guess he hadn't been into taking dick pics and sending them to girls.

"Sorry, you were probably disappointed. I guess it's a good thing I fixed that by giving you the real thing." My cheeks flare. Shoot. I should have never brought it up. "Hey, I'm kidding. No need to get all shy on me now." He squeezes my hand, his smirk giving me those constant butterflies.

We pull up to the restaurant, and sadly, he releases my hand. "Don't worry. In and out. We get our dessert to go, and I'll eat it off you tonight, deal?" Okay, he's making up for the loss of hand holding.

"Deal."

We walk close, our bodies brushing up against one another as we make our way inside. Like a gentleman, he holds the door open for me. I can't help but brush my hand along the side of his hip as I step inside.

"Watch it, or we're not making it through appetizers." I don't look back. We won't be making it to the table if I catch that predator gaze in his eyes. We're greeted by the hostess, and Levi informs her we're with the Matthews' party. She guides us to the table where I spot Kip and Stacey.

"*You have to be shittin' me,*" Levi hisses, and I slam into him when he stops suddenly.

"What?" I ask, peeking around him to see for myself. Braydon.

"I thought we agreed. What the fuck is he doing here?"

"We did. I have no idea. I avoided him all day."

We stand there staring at the scene going down, my mom and dad flaunting over whatever story Braydon is telling. "Fuck this, we're leaving—"

"About time, you two! We've already ordered drinks. Sit, sit." My dad waves us over as Mom gets up to greet us. Neither of us move.

"We have to," I tell him, realizing we're stuck.

"I'm gonna pummel that shithead," he growls as Mom makes it to us.

"What's got you two looking so sour?" She leans in and gives me a hug, then goes for Levi. His mask quickly in place, his demeanor changes, his carefree smile on point.

"Oh, nothing. Traffic. We're glad to be here in good company. Always lovely to see you, Cheryl."

"Yes! Come, sit down. Hannah, your boyfriend was just telling us about all the cases he's been prepping you on." *Oh, crap.* Did anyone else feel the shift in the air? The ground rattling? Possibly a low octave growl coming from Levi? I decide not to comment or make eye contact with Levi. There's nothing we can do about it now. Following them to the table, we stop in search of seats. Great, one open seat next to Braydon, and one next to…*Rebecca?* Why is she *always* at family events? Because neither of us make a move, Braydon stands, signaling for the open chair by him, right as Rebecca pops up.

"Saved you a seat!"

Saved you a seat. God! I want to rip her hair out.

Left with no other choice, I break away from Levi and walk around the table, right as Braydon goes in for a hug. I consider ducking for any flying objects in our direction. "Hey, I couldn't find you, so I caught a ride with your dad."

I want to ask why, since I have no recollection of inviting him. "Yeah, no problem," I reply, taking my seat instead.

"Now that everyone's here…" Kip starts, standing and holding his drink up. There's a full glass of red wine in front of me, and without asking who it belongs to, I snatch it up and inhale a huge gulp. Unfortunately, the expensive pinot noir does nothing to soothe my nerves. Two more large sips, and I hit the bottom of my glass.

Mom nudges me. "Honey, slow down. He hasn't even told us the news yet."

Stacey's pregnant. Rebecca's a tramp. Braydon needs to beat it. Oh yeah! I'm dating Kip's best friend and having the most amazing sex known to man. Cheers! I'll take the filet.

A huge sigh slips from my lips, and I mumble, "Sorry." Putting my glass down, I tuck my hands in my lap. My butt jumps two feet off my chair, knocking my knees into the table when Braydon's hand touches mine under the table.

"We wanted to start off by saying thanks to everyone for coming tonight. We have the most important people with us to share a very exciting announcement." Kip gazes down at Stacey with such affection, then back to the family. "We're having a baby!"

Everyone goes nuts. My mom starts to cry, and while she's distracted, I grab her wine glass and chug it. My dad stands to congratulate my brother. I wish I was sharing in the enthusiasm, but my eyes are set across the table at a hussy who has her claws in my boyfriend. I vaguely hear Braydon excuse himself to go to the bathroom over Rebecca's squeaky voice.

"So exciting. Isn't it, Levi?" Rebecca places her hands over Levi's, acting as if she even cares about a baby. She slides off her chair, closing in on him, and leans forward to whisper something in his ear. This time, I wonder if *he's* smart enough to duck because my glass is about to bounce off her head. I just don't understand why she doesn't get the hint. *That what? He's secretly dating you and is no longer available?* Correct. *Because I don't see him removing her hand.* Also correct. Darn it. She finishes whatever she's whispering and follows up with a giggle.

"Don't mind me, I'm just gonna use the ladies' room." She winks at Levi, then is up and sashaying toward the restrooms. My eyebrows shoot up, curious what the hell that was about. There's no doubt I'm shooting daggers at Levi. When his eyes meet mine, his burn with the same fury.

"Excuse me," he says and stands, dismissing himself, also making his way toward the restrooms. *What in heavens—?*

"Hannah, baby, isn't this just wonderful?" Dad says as my eyes follow Levi until he hits the hallway and disappears. "Another Matthews. Just wonderful!"

Yeah. Wonderful. Where are they going? He wouldn't be meeting her in the bathroom, would he? My mind is playing evil tricks on me. Rebecca is currently ripping Levi's clothes off as they both laugh at my expense. Oh god. "Waitress! Refill!"

Levi

That's it.

He's done for.

I've had enough with that little turd thinking he has a chance with her. I don't care if this blows our cover, I'm willing to risk the consequences to make sure he stays the hell away from my girl.

I get up, excusing myself, and follow Braydon toward the restrooms. I'm probably not thinking this through, but all I can think about is kicking that shit's ass. I whip around the corner and slam into Rebecca.

"Oh, wow. Just the person I was waiting for. I knew you would take me up on my offer—"

I rip her hands off my shoulders as her lips almost make contact with my neck. "What? What's wrong? No one will miss us. We can sneak away in the bathroom. I've been thinking about—"

"Rebecca, stop. I can't grasp how to express this more than I already have. I'm not interested. At all. Not the slightest bit. I suggest you spend your energy and time on someone else." Her lips form a thin line. Her expression morphs into anger, but I don't give her the chance to lash out. I gently move around her and storm into the bathroom, catching Braydon as he washes his hands.

"Great news, huh? I bet Hannah's excited for her—"

Without further thought, I take him and slam him into the wall. His body buckles under my hold, and a grunt escapes his mouth at the impact. "What the fuck—?"

"I'm going to say this once and only once: stay the hell away from Hannah." I wait for him to react to my threat. Shock to form in his eyes. His body to shake with fear. But none of that comes. Instead, his eyes darken, a wicked smile creeping across his face. His body shakes all right, but it's from laughter. I pull him from the wall, slamming him back against it. "What's so funny?"

"Oh wow. Does someone have a thing for his best friend's little sister?"

"That's none of your damn business," I growl, practically spitting in his face.

"Seems it is, since the big bad Levi Dent is in the bathroom threatening me." His smirk widens, and a disturbing chill skates down my arms. "Newsflash: I'm not gonna do that. I have big plans for Ms. Matthews. Maybe work up to your level and fuck her like a whore in the offi—"

I swing at him before I can think, making contact with his jaw. Blood spurts from his nose, splattering onto my shirt. Braydon doesn't react or show a single ounce of pain or fear. The little fucker laughs harder.

"Did I hit a sore spot? Did you think no one knew about your private lunches? You don't think I couldn't smell the filth on her—"

Another hit, this time to his gut. He buckles, but I don't allow him the chance to coddle his wound or catch his breath. "You better watch it. You say one more thing about her, you're done. You attempt to lay one hand on her—"

"Oh, I plan on more than just one hand. I plan on ruining you. And once you're out of the way, I'm taking your place. Get a taste of the sweet Hannah Matthews. I bet she tastes like innocence." He licks his lips, and I lose it. My fist clenches, and I rear back. "Oh yeah, hit me again. Dig your grave some more."

My fist plows toward his face as the door to the bathroom opens. My hand drops, and Braydon's body slumps against the tiled wall. My breathing is heavy, my chest heaving. A man walks in. His eyes widen in shock, then makes the wise choice and walks back out. I quickly gather myself and step away from him. "Stay away from her."

Braydon's eyes flicker with challenge. He wipes the dripping blood from his nose, steps away from me, and walks toward the door. Before opening it, he veers around, his cold gaze fixated on me. "It was nice working with you." His lips break out into a vile smile, leaving me uneasy as he turns back and exits the bathroom.

My hands shake with anger. My fists clench, needing to chase after him and do more damage. Make sure he heeds my warning. My eyes find my reflection in the mirror, and I stare back at the blood splattered on my shirt. My knuckles are scraped up and swelling. Fuck. A few labored breaths to force myself to calm down, then I wash my hands and do my best to erase any sign of Braydon on my clothes. Once I've gathered myself, I exit the bathroom.

When I return, Hannah is in a conversation with Stacey, and thankfully, Rebecca gives me the cold shoulder. I pull out my phone, my hand killing me, but shoot off a text to her. She grabs her phone and reads my message.

Me: Tell everyone you're not feeling good and ask me to take you home.

Her eyes lift in my direction. Stacey notices her shift in attention. She goes back to her phone.

Hannah: What happened? Where did you go?

I watch her peek over at a snarling Rebecca. It's only time before Rebecca aims and fires her ugly attitude on Hannah.

Me: We'll talk later. Just do it. I need to get out of here.

She makes eye contact with me again and nods. I make the mistake of looking at Stacey, who's staring curiously at me. Hannah's phone dings again, and her expression changes.

"Who's texting you?" Stacey asks.

"Um…it's Braydon." Fuck. He's going to sell me out. I prepare to explain why I just kicked his ass in the bathroom. "He said he's not feeling good and apologized, but he had to leave."

More like his face is busted up.

"Oh, that's too bad," Stacey comments, eyeing me.

"Yeah, ugh…I think whatever he has, I have it too. I'm really not feeling well either all of a sudden." She brings her hands to her stomach. "Oh no. I think…" Her eyes find mine. "Levi, do you think you can take me home?"

That's my girl. I stand.

"Honey, what's wrong? You don't feel good again? Should you see a doctor?" Dad takes note of our small commotion.

Hannah shakes her head, grabbing her purse. "No, Daddy. Sorry. I think I have to go home. I don't want to get sick in the restaurant."

Stacey stands as well. "I can take her."

"*No.* I mean, no, you stay. This is your celebration dinner. Levi can just take me home." She goes in and hugs Stacey, who appears less than convinced, but offers her a hug back. Kip's on cloud nine, thankfully not picking up any red flags. Once we go around and say our goodbyes, we're out of the restaurant and speeding down Jefferson street to my place.

"You going to tell me what that was all about?" Hannah breaks the silence, but I'm too angry to rehash what happened. I need to get her naked and under me and prove to her she's mine— not his. She was never his. Her sudden gasp has me whipping my attention to her, just as she reaches over to gently press her fingers to my hand wrapped around the steering wheel. "Levi, what happened to your hand?"

I wince, but still don't answer her. I can't. I need to ease my insecurities before I give her any answers and accept the well-deserved anger she's going to have.

When we pull into my garage, I throw my car into my reserved spot. We walk in silence up to my condo. The moment the door shuts behind us, I'm on her.

Without question, she kisses me back with the same fervor, until we're forced to come up for air. Her eyes are fogged over, and I love that I do that to her. "What happened back there?" she asks, her voice soft, yet laced with concern.

"Let's just say I had a little run-in with Braydon, and it didn't end well."

"Oh my god, what happened? Please tell me it doesn't have anything to do with your bruised hand."

I take a step back, my hands running down my face. "It's not a big deal. Nothing for you to worry about. Come on. Let's pour a drink, then we can talk." She's compliant and doesn't push, following me into the kitchen. A heavy pour of whiskey for me and a beer for her, and we're seated on my couch, facing one another. With a big pull of my drink, I start. "I think it's time we tell everyone about us."

She chokes on her beer. "What? Why?"

"Why *not*? Do you not want people to know?" My question comes out angrier than I mean it to.

Hannah shakes her head. "No, I do. It's just…I thought we had a plan. What happens if they don't approve?"

I've put so much thought into this, I'm ready to accept the consequences. "Our plan was to see where this goes. And it's developed into more than what I could have ever imagined. I like you, Hannah. Shit, I may…" I shake my head, afraid to admit how deep my feelings for her go. "The thing is, we chose to hide it in case it didn't work out. But now? I can't imagine you not being mine. I'm ready to take the next move. Together."

I watch her lower lip quiver. Shit. What if she doesn't want this? "I…I don't know what to say."

"Say you want this as much as I do. And we'll deal with the repercussions together."

Her eyes swell with tears. "What about Kip? He may hate you. My dad. What if he fires you? Maybe I can leave, then there won't be any—"

"No. You're staying. If Jim fires me, then I'll take it as my sign and branch off on my own. After all the shit I've seen in the sports industry, I've always thought about opening my own firm for sports players who've been taken advantage of by the league."

"But you've always wanted to work at my dad's firm."

"*You've* always wanted to work there. And that won't change. That place deserves you."

She's staring at me, unsure. She doesn't feel the same way. She doesn't want to risk—

"Okay. Let's do it."

"For real?"

Her shoulders raise as her smile broadens. "Why not? How can I say no to a man who's willing to risk his life and career for me?"

I reach for her, not caring that her drink spills, and take her mouth with mine. I kiss her hard. With meaning. With promise. This won't be easy, for either of us, but I'm willing to risk it all for her. My tongue parts her lips, and I deepen our kiss. I pull her to me until she's in my lap, straddling my legs. I quickly get rid of our drinks, because I need both hands for what I have planned for her. There's no need for her shirt, so I tug it up and over her head. Her breasts, perfect and inviting, call to me. I place my mouth around her nipple and suck through her lace bra, loving the way she melts in my arms. "I want everyone to know you're mine." My teeth graze her flesh, biting down, my cock hardening with a fierceness as she squirms on top of me. "You're done with Braydon. I want him nowhere near you. Hear me?"

Her lips barely part, her heavy breathing a sign she's hardly listening to a thing I say. I bite down, and her rasped whimper is music to my ears. My hands become greedy, coddling her ass, hauling her closer, my aching cock brushing between her thighs. "If your dad doesn't kill me on the spot, I'm going to insist he throws him out."

Her small hand slips between us, grabbing at me, and begins to stroke me over my slacks. I throw my hips up, filling her hand, the friction of her movement driving me crazy. "Fuck, that feels good. You're gonna make me call your dad right now just so we don't have to sneak around doing this." Another thrust into her hand.

"Why? Do you plan on us doing this in public with him around?" She squeals when I take my open palm and smack her ass.

"No one gets to see you like this but me." I take her mouth and swallow her giggle, kissing her rough, never hating clothes more than I do in this moment. Not that it will matter since I'm about to tear out of my pants I'm so hard. She's so pliable as I caress her mouth with my tongue. My hands wander, squeezing her ass, rubbing her covered pussy. Her little moans are my driving force.

I suck in her bottom lip, grazing my teeth against her soft flesh. "Bedroom. Now." She doesn't need further explanation and wraps her arms around my neck as I pop up, cradling her legs around me and carrying her down the hall to my room. When we hit the bed, I almost trip, throwing us onto the mattress. My weight doesn't bother her. She only succumbs to me more, her entire body as jittery as mine.

I've never felt this urge before. This need for someone. An emptiness when she's not with me, and a fullness when I have her wrapped in my arms. I never saw my life taking this turn. Not with Hannah Matthews, but fuck, my heart beats only for her. I rip her pants down, doing the same with my own clothes. I'm back laying over her, throbbing and ready to plunge into her and stay there forever.

My eyes find hers, and I'm a goner. Her expression, the way she offers herself to me fully, her trust in me...I want to give her the world. I drop my lips to hers, the buzz around us electric. I can't wait another second and drive myself home.

Waking up to her little sounds is like heaven. Sleeping with her naked little body cuddled next to mine is my utopia. She's still asleep, her mouth parted slightly, tiny moans telling me she's deep in a dream. I tug her closer to me, my morning wood pressing against her ass cheeks. I'm tempted to thrust inside and give her a wake-up surprise, but I have another idea.

Shifting her onto her back, I work my way down her stomach, spreading kisses to her skin, my tongue circling around her belly button. She squirms in her sleep but doesn't fully wake. My mouth dips in between her thighs, and I can't help but swipe my tongue between her folds. This gets her moving. When I begin to suck at her opening, her hands work themselves into my hair. I could wake up like this forever—tasting my girl, pleasuring her. Her hips slowly ride my mouth as I lick and suck. One finger enters her, and she hums.

"Levi." My name from her lips is a gift. I work my mouth harder, taking her faster, inserting a second finger. God, she drives me absolutely mad. I can't imagine my life before her, missing out on the sweetness of her cunt.

"Morning, beautiful," I hum into her warmth.

"Morning, boss—"

"Levi! Where you at, man?" *What the fuck?* I freeze. My grip tightens around Hannah's thigh, needing to confirm I didn't hear what I just thought I heard.

"Oh my word, Levi was that my—?"

"Shhh!"

"I know you're in here. Your car's in the garage! You with a girl in there?"

Holy fuck.

Hannah starts to vibrate under me. "Levi, we said let's tell them, but this is not what I had in mind," she freaks out. Shit, me either. I pop out from under the covers, placing my finger over my mouth. Her eyes are smoldering with panic.

"Don't say anything. I'll get rid of him." I jump off the bed, throwing on a pair of shorts, and exit my room, shutting the door quickly behind me.

I'm barely two steps away from my bedroom door when Kip comes around the corner. "Well, well… I was banging on the door, but you weren't answering. Good thing I still have your key. Go get dressed. We're going golfing."

He keeps walking toward me, and the closer he gets to my room, the more I begin to sweat. I meant it when I said it was time we came forward, but finding his sister naked in my bed is not how I need this to go down. "Dude, not in the mood. Another time." I walk forward, getting him to change routes and head back to the living room.

"Why not? You love golf. Let me borrow a polo. Stacey bought me this, and I didn't have the heart to tell her I hate it—"

"NO." I throw my hand out, stopping him from getting any closer.

"Seriously?" He surveys me with a quirky, confused grin. "Let me just borrow a shirt. I'm not Chase. I won't get the drink cart girls' lipstick all over it and ruin it." He laughs, making another attempt to push past me.

His eyes meet mine, but then they peer mischievously at my bedroom door. Those damn wheels begin to spin, and a bead of sweat starts to form above my brow. "Why are you acting weird?" His vision is going back and forth from me to over my shoulder. Shit. "Wait a minute..." Please no. "You got a girl in there?" He smiles as if he's caught me. "Hello in there!" He takes a step closer. I would never lay a hand on my best friend, but right now, it's the only thing stopping him from murdering me. I throw my hand to his chest and shove him.

"Have Chase go."

"Damn, calm down, bro." He throws his hands up in surrender. "And no on Chase. He always gets us kicked out for being too aggressive with the cart girls. Stacey won't let me golf with him anymore. Plus, my pops sent me to scoop you up. So, let's go. Tell your lady friend it's time to go."

Sure, why don't I tell your sister I have to go golfing with you and her dad. Maybe then I can mention I'm having wild sex with his little girl and watch myself get pummeled by his nine iron.

"Dude, hello? Go get dressed. Want me to keep her company?"

"No!" I snap too quickly.

His eyes light up with more curiosity, which doesn't bode well. Shit. "Man, why so jumpy? Wait...don't tell me that's *Rebecca* in there?" Christ, please don't let Hannah hear that. She'll have my balls. "I'd rather saw my dick off, I told you. Fine, let's just go."

"Sweet."

I push him down the hall, away from my door, and stop at my laundry room to grab a clean pair of shorts and a polo.

"Aren't you gonna say goodbye to your date? And what

about my shirt?" he asks as I snag a pair of golf shoes and my clubs from my front closet.

"No, she'll get a clue and leave on her own. And salmon looks really pretty on you."

Kip laughs, then slaps me on the back. "You dawg, you. Nice to see you finally playing the field."

I push him out of my front door, wishing he's this cheerful when I break the news my field is all things his little sister.

CHAPTER TWENTY-TWO

Hannah

I jump out of the shower, my mood light and *ah-mazing*. I dance around my room, re-enacting the intro scene to Adventures in Babysitting, singing "Then He Kissed Me" into my brush.

Making it home without being stopped and questioned was pure luck. My dad was on the golf course, and Mom was out, already buying out all the baby stores.

On my Uber ride home, I got a text from Stacey inviting me to lunch this afternoon and to do some baby registry shopping. If I wanted a buffer between my brother and I, she's it. Kipley and I never fought as kids, but I have a feeling this may be our first. To be honest, I'm not sure how he'll react. If I was a one-night stand to Levi, it wouldn't go over so well. But we're more than that. And with Stacey's help, if I can get him to listen long enough to understand, then I feel hopeful he won't kill Levi. He may even rally with us when telling Dad.

But first, I *have* to tell Stacey. I accept her lunch invitation, knowing this will be the perfect time to confess.

I haven't heard from Levi outside of a quick *I'm sorry* text, which is okay. It at least tells me he's still alive. It also reminds me to ask him who else has a key, because that could have ended badly. And that's not how I want us to start off. Everyone upset at us. Our intentions aren't to hurt anyone or be deceiving. Keeping us a secret was for the best. But what's best now is honesty.

Slipping on a cute tunic with leggings, I head downtown to the quant French bistro Stacey recommended. I wonder what their baby will look like. If they'll have a boy or girl. How broke I'm going to be spoiling him or her rotten. That's if Mom doesn't buy out everything first. My mind wanders, and I start to think about what *our* baby would look like if Levi and I had one.

"Oh…geez. Stop while you're ahead, Hannah." We just decided we would officially date and tell the world. Let's ease up on marriage and babies. Not that I don't already have a binder from when I was thirteen planning out our entire wedding. I wonder if he would think it was creepy to learn just how deep my childhood obsession ran? *Maybe he'll think it's cute.* Good luck with that, crazy.

With the weather still hot for the middle of summer, the city is crazy. Finding parking is a pain. By the time I locate a spot, I'm almost ten minutes late.

"Hannah!" Stacey calls my name, and I find her seated at a table by the back. She stands as I approach. "Glad you could make it. How was traffic?"

I lean in for a hug. "It was fine. This place is super cute. The smells. I may have to order a ton of food." I take a seat and grab for the menu. Missing out on the breakfast Levi promised me, I'm actually starving.

"You're feeling better then?"

I lift my head. "Huh?"

"You're feeling better? After you left last night…?"

The lie. Us leaving abruptly. "Oh, yeah! Fine. Must have been something I ate." I lift the menu over my face. *Don't lie. This is your chance to come clean.* I inhale deeply and drop the menu. "Okay. I wasn't really sick."

"I didn't think you were. Want to tell me why you lied?"

It's now or never. The faster I tell the truth and get this out in the open, the faster we can all move on. I love Stacey. I trust she'll listen and help me. Not pass judgement before understanding. It's why she's so perfect for my brother. Once she hears how much we mean to one another, she'll be on my side. "I lied because—"

"Shit, can traffic be any more intolerable!" My confession is interrupted as Rebecca nears our table. Of course she would pick the one place we're eating to show up at. Hopefully they say quick hellos so I can get back to confessing. "Oh, how lovely. You're eating with us. Clearly you're not allowed to pick out any baby clothes." She points to my outfit. "Do I need to say any more?"

My eyes shift to Stacey. She offers an apologetic expression, but stands to give Rebecca a hug. "Glad you could make it." *Make it?* As in she was *invited* to this? My mood plummets, shaking the ground beneath us. "Sit, we were just chatting about dinner last night. I was about to tell Hannah what a good meal she missed."

Rebecca rolls her eyes at me and takes a seat, throwing her purse and knocking over my glass of water into my lap. I jump, but not before it soaks my pants. "Oh, gosh. I'm such a klutz," Rebecca says, though her laughter is anything but apologetic. Thankfully, a waiter walks by, offering me a pile of napkins.

"Come on, let's have a nice lunch, okay?" Stacey says, trying to mediate. She should have known from the start this was going to be a bad idea.

"Whatevs. Speaking of dinner last night, what was your problem? Did you finally get your period or something? Had to drag Levi away from me?"

That gets my attention. "Excuse me?"

Her laugh is mocking. "What, you get jealous we were about to hook up and fake sick so he would take you home? Seems to happen that way a lot."

My body shifts, giving her my full attention. There's no hiding the mounting anger in my voice. "I'm not sure what you're getting at, but you better watch it."

"Hannah," Stacey warns.

"Yeah, *Hannah*. It's obvious you have a crush on Levi. But come on, you don't think he would ever go for you, do you?" She laughs even louder. "Just before you played sick, Levi and I were about to get to know each other better in the restaurant bathroom. I couldn't believe he wanted to be so careless. But who was I to say no to Levi Dent?"

She's lying.

He would never.

Not with her.

"Rebecca, enough. Hannah has no interest in Levi. They've known each other since they were kids. They're like brother and sister. Right, Hannah?" She waits for me to confirm what she just stated, and all I want to do is lash out and prove Rebecca wrong. Throw it in her face that someone like me *can* actually get someone like Levi Dent, and I already have. There would be nothing sweeter than putting her in her place.

But this is not how I want Stacey to find out. The words taste sour leaving my mouth. "Right. Friends." Her satisfactory smile makes my stomach churn. I excuse myself to go to the bathroom, and the moment the stall door closes behind me, the tears begin to fall.

I'm upset for allowing Rebecca to get to me, but her words hold some truth. Levi *is* too good for me. He may see an us now, but what about all the pressure we'll face once we come forward? How many other Rebecca's are out there, ready and waiting to tell Levi he can do better? Convince him he's too good for me? How long until the pressure of people's opinions weigh so heavy on us, he starts to agree? I can't wipe my tears away fast enough. They're out of control, flowing like waves of sadness down my cheeks.

I send a text to Stacey saying I must have not been feeling as good as I thought and sneak out the back exit of the bistro.

I'm a total chicken.

I spent the rest of the weekend in hiding. From everyone. Even Levi. I didn't want to let the doubts win over, but they were—in a fierce way. Why wasn't I just talking this out with Levi? Telling him my insecurities? Allowing him the chance to ease my worries, especially about the story Rebecca tried to feed me.

Please refer to my main statement.

I'm a total chicken.

Now, it's Monday morning, and I'm walking into the office unsure of what I'm going to say or how to act with Levi. Do I tell him it's off and save him the future headache and myself the future heartache? Not that the damage isn't already done for me.

Then there's Braydon. No matter how this ends, there isn't and won't be anything between us. As much as I'd like to remain friends, I can't do that to him knowing I've been using him as a decoy.

Yelling erupts from the office the moment the elevator doors open.

Worry shoots through me, recognizing it's coming from Levi's office. I race down the hall and throw open his door.

"It wasn't me, Jim. I would have never done this."

"It has your name on it! How are you denying it? Proof! Here, here, here!" Dad throws the files across Levi's desk as the papers explode in waves to the floor.

"Like I said, I have no idea. I've done nothing but dedicate all my time to this case."

"To sabotage it!" my dad yells back.

I take a step into the office. "What's going on?" They both whip in my direction. My dad's expression angry. Levi's disappointed. "What happened?"

"It seems Levi can't be trusted after all," Dad bites out.

"Oh, give me a break! Why would I do this? What would I have to gain?"

"I've heard what you've been planning," Dad argues. "Setting up your own firm. Blow this lawsuit for mine, and when I start losing clients, you scoop them right out from under me."

What in the heavens is going on?

"That's ridiculous! And you damn well know it!" Levi throws his hand in the air.

"Someone needs to explain to me right now what you two are arguing about," I snap.

"Someone got to Clara Hill," Dad hisses.

"What do you mean got to her? Is she…?"

Levi snatches a letter off his desk, thrusting it at me, and I fumble with it until I unfold the piece of paper, reading the first few lines of the letter. My stomach drops. "A carrier delivered it this morning. Signed by Clara Hill herself. She's retracting her statement. Claiming harassment on the firm. If we pursue this case, she'll sue."

"How on earth?" I finish reading the letter, stating very clearly she's no longer willing to testify. How could she do this? So many people lost their lives. Her own husband and son included. And now, none of those people will see justice. "She has to have been threatened. There's no other explanation." I search out my dad. "We can't let this happen. She has to testify."

His murderous glare pins Levi.

"Dammit, Jim, I had nothing to do with this."

I come to Levi's defense. "Come on Dad, why would Levi go and threaten—"

My dad's voice booms through the office. "Because his name is all over it! Signatures! Logins! I trusted you with this case. And now it's all gone. Months of work. Credibility. Gone."

I've never seen my dad so angry before. I turn to Levi for answers. His muscles strain under his dark fitted suit, his jaw clenched. "Levi, what is he talking about?"

Chills spread down my spine when his eyes glare into mine. Is that anger? Guilt? In an audibly tense tone, he says, "The original testimonies are gone. Someone deleted them from the server and swiped the hard copies from the storage room. We go to trial in twenty-four hours and we have nothing."

My mouth drops open, a stunned gasp falling from my lips. "What? How is that possible?"

"Good question," Dad snaps, addressing Levi. "You knew the importance of those files. Now those people won't see justice. I hope you're happy." My dad pivots on his heel and storms out of the office.

"Levi, what happened? What did you do?" He doesn't answer, but gives me his back as he stares out the window. "Answer me. Why would you do this to my dad? After all he's—"

"Why would *I*?" He storms over to me, stopping mere inches from me, his face red and scrunched in anger. "Why would *you*?"

"*Me*? Why is this my fault?"

His hands swipe through his hair. "Those files went missing under your watch. You were the one who entered them. Wrongly, I might add."

How dare he. "That's impossible. I would never make such a mistake—"

"Well, you did. I've been covering for you since I noticed it. Tried to figure out how it could have happened. But seems little Hannah Matthews isn't as perfect as she claims to be. Those files went missing under your watch."

"You're lying."

"I wish I was. But it gets better. Now the system is showing *I* was the one who entered them." He sighs, once again giving his attention to the outside. "The files were tampered with. Every single document *you* read, filed, submitted, touched, it's all under my login and signature now. Well…was, since the server is showing *I* went in and swiped it all off. Even Clara's original testimony is gone."

The room is starting to spin. Dizziness threatens my vision, and I shake my head in disbelief. I'm struggling to process what he's telling me. There's no way I made a mistake entering those testimonies. Since the moment I stepped foot into this firm, I've been working to make sure everything I touch is treated with the utmost importance. So, if it wasn't me, then who?

"I didn't enter those wrong. I wouldn't have. Someone must have changed it."

Levi whips around. "Oh yeah? And who? Who would want to do that?"

"I don't know! But it wasn't me. There has to be another reason." He stares at me, wanting that reason, but I can't give it. "Do you truly believe I made those errors?" I need to know. Because if he does, then I don't know where we, as a couple, go from here. There's a long pause, and my stomach tightens.

Finally, he speaks. "I don't." The breath I'm holding releases. "I never thought you did. That's why I never came out and asked you. I thought I could figure out what went wrong and fix it. You were so diligent. It seemed off right from the start. But now this. Someone has access to those files and is purposely sabotaging this case—us."

I want to deny that theory because it sounds crazy. But without that, the finger points to one of us. "Has anyone had access to your files? Computer? Keycard?"

"No. No one."

"Braydon?"

I shake my head. "Of course not. Just because you hate him, doesn't mean he—"

"Hannah, we got into a fight in the bathroom at dinner on Friday."

"What? What do you mean a *fight*? You said it wasn't a big deal. Nothing—"

"I lied. I couldn't stand him touching you. I went after him and threatened him to stay away from you. It got physical."

I gasp, anger setting in. *His knuckles.* That's how they got bruised and bloodied. "Levi, you didn't. You can't get—"

"That's not what matters. What matters is he threatened me back. He told me, 'Nice working with you.' The way he said it…it was creepy. Like it had an underlying meaning to it."

"Like he's going to get you fired for assaulting him?"

"No, he told me he was going to take my place. Get rid of me, then slip into my spot. Meaning with you. He knows about us."

There's no way. We've been careful. This is all too insane. I just need to retrace my steps. Backtrack all my notes. Braydon never showed any liking to Levi, but he wouldn't do anything to jeopardize his career—*my* career. "I don't know. I think you're looking at the wrong person. There has to be somebody else."

He's back to pacing his office. He doesn't offer any other solutions, and I don't have any. *Think, Hannah. Think...* It can't be Braydon. Can it? "We need to get the trial postponed."

He finally faces me. "And how do we do that? You don't just call the supreme court judge and tell him you lost all your files *and* your only witness and need a continuance." His words come out harsh, but I try not to take offense.

"Tell him we found a break in the case and need a few extra days to deliberate."

"No."

"Why not? If we can delay the trial, I can backtrack my steps. Search deeper for clues. My criminal law internship taught me a lot about reading between the lines and finding clues normal people would never check for—"

"Stop being so damn naive! This isn't a class project. Don't you think we've tried to get that continuance? We were denied. Don't you think *I* backtracked all your steps? Everything you touched. Witness lists, leads—all wiped out. And now Clara Hill is a ghost. Braydon Connor is behind this. I know it."

Not this again. I sigh, my own tone now laced with annoyance. "I just don't see—"

"Jesus Christ, Hannah! Open your damn eyes! It's him. If you can't see that then..."

"Then what?" I ask, my stomach dropping.

Levi shakes his head, turmoil in his eyes. His palms swipe down his face. His chest rises and falls in heavy pants. *No...* "Listen...I can't do this right now. We need to take a step back.

Us…it's clouding my judgement. If I wasn't so…" He pauses, as if measuring which words will hurt less. "If I was focused on work, this wouldn't have happened."

He may as well have punched me. My gut would have felt the same powerful blow as his words have.

"Levi…don't." My desperate plea falls off my quivering lips. I take a step toward him, but his hand reaches out, stopping me.

"I can't right now. I need to focus on how to fix this."

"And I can help—"

"You've done nothing but the opposite! Stay out of this, Hannah. All of it. For once in your life, just listen." When his dark, solemn eyes find mine, a pain in my heart seizes as my breath fails me. He's not only demanding I stay away from the case…but him as well.

"You're breaking up with me." I'm not sure if I say it as a question or statement. Either way, it's a razor blade through my heart at each word falling off my tongue. My worst fear. He doesn't want me anymore.

He steps toward me, and this time, it's my turn to slap his incoming touch away.

"Hannah—"

"Don't touch me." I'm struggling to breathe, but I refuse to show how bad he's hurting me. I inhale the thick air, hardening my features. "I'm so stupid. I actually believed you. I actually thought we were going to beat all the odds against us. But one little bump, and there goes Levi, running. What about all that trust you spoke of? Where the hell is that now while you point fingers, huh?" I raise my voice, ashamed when it cracks.

"Hannah—"

"I don't know what hurts more: the lies about me being something special, or how easily you lost faith in me." He ignores me when I throw my hand up for him to stay away and gets into my space. "Hannah, stop being like this. You have to—"

I slap him. Hard. The sound echoes throughout his office.

His eyes spark with shock, probably matching my own. His hand lunges out and clutches at my bicep, pulling me into him, his growl setting my core on fire. "Don't you dare ever question what I feel—"

A knock on the door interrupts him.

We both shift our attention to Vanessa. "Um...sorry to interrupt." She stares between us, pretending she didn't witness our altercation.

Levi quickly releases me. "What is it, Vanessa?" he asks.

"I...um...I was sent by Melanie in human resources to, um... she would like to see you in her office." She's extremely fidgety, clicking her pen a thousand clicks a minute.

"About what? I'm busy. Tell her I'll come over when I'm—"

"Yeah, actually, I wasn't supposed to leave your office until you came...with me. I have to escort you to her office...now." Her face pales, and I swear she's about to barf in Levi's doorway.

Levi throws his hands up. "Fine. Let's go." Before he leaves, he turns his attention on me. "We're not done here." He storms out, leaving Vanessa chasing after him.

I'm the one who throws up. I race out of his office and barely make it into the bathroom. I'm not usually one for dramatics, but the severity of the situation hits me hard, the impact flipping my stomach upside down. The case. Accusations. My dad's anger. Levi's withdrawal. Another wave of nausea punches me in the gut. I bend over and puke again. How did all this happen? What went wrong? Was it really me? Did I sabotage this case?

Levi's withdrawal left a bruise on my heart. My stomach aches at the cuts left by his doubt in me. I try to sort through the rubble of his words after our fight, but I'm left even more confused. The twister of emotions cause havoc in my mind, and I bend over, dry heaving. "Pull it together, Hannah." I coach myself, wiping at my chin. This is not me. I've never been one to cower when someone hurts my feelings. Levi was right to accuse me of never listening. But it's always been imbedded in me to fight. Debate. My dad always taught me to never stand down to an argument I can win. And right now, I have to put my emotions on the back burner and focus on the facts.

I did my utmost. I have no doubt in my capabilities. If those files went missing or were tampered with, it was not on my watch. Which means someone else changed the information in the computer. The thought of Braydon being involved crosses my mind. Doubt forms. I'm not sure why I was so quick to defend him against Levi's accusations during our fight. Putting all the facts in place, there were some situations that could raise red flags.

"I was checking my email while I was waiting for you. Hope that's okay."

"Sorry. I bumped into them and a few fell. I put them all back in order. I hope I didn't mess anything up."

"Son of a bitch."

Maybe this *is* my fault. Maybe Braydon's been taking me for a ride this whole time to get close to those files. I had a loose tongue around him when I spoke about the case. The testimonies. When mine and Levi's relationship took an unexpected turn, I too got sidetracked, my thoughts shifting from my *responsibilities* to him.

My fists slam on the counter. "Dammit. How dumb have I been?" Levi is right. I'm the one to blame. I need to spill the beans. Bear the responsibility. Before I rush out of the bathroom, I come to my senses. What would that do? Nothing. My dad's words ring in my head. *"Actions always speak louder than words, princess."* So, I begin to construct a plan in hopes of saving this case.

If Clara Hill won't come to us, I'll go to her.

CHAPTER TWENTY-THREE

Hannah

I'm taking a chance. More like playing with fire. This trip can blow up in my face. I could end up in a jail cell for obstruction of justice, tampering with a witness, trespassing, harassment—"Oh god, please let this work out." There's no hiding my sweaty palms or the nerves fluttering in my stomach. As I drive, I imagine Levi's reaction. Okay...maybe let's not focus on his reaction. There's no doubt he's going to be mad. But there's no way whoever scared Clara off is going to get away with it. I want her to tell me to my face she's giving up, and then I have one shot to change her mind.

Thoughts of Levi take a backseat as I enter the rural town of Crete. Unlike where I'm from, the streets are deceptively quiet. They aren't filled with impatient drivers, sounds of horns honking, pedestrians dodging cars, or do-not-walk signs. It's just...quiet. Also a little eerie. I drive down the ghost town on Main Street. One after another, each storefront displays a closed sign. It's been almost a year since the accident, and the town still hasn't recovered. But how can they after everything they've lost? Crete was an off-the-map, small town, famous for its tucked away paper mill. A good ninety-percent of the community worked there. The other small percent held the storefront jobs. The antique store, the barber, the corner bookstore, the pub. It was your typical hidden place in the world everyone forgot about. Until Miller Industries showed up.

Benjamin Miller offered them a deal. Painted them this beautiful image of what life in the town of Crete could be if they allowed them to build. Growth, jobs, life—he promised it all. They simply had to sign off on a high-rise deal. The town had been divided. More jobs, more future opportunities for their kids, their kid's kids. But also, disruption of their small-town feel. It would bring a wealthy amount of traffic to Crete. Theresa Simmons would no longer lose sleep at night worrying how she was going to make enough sales to keep her antique store open. Jerald Hope needed renovations to his barbershop. With the posh hotel they would build within the high-rise, it would bring an abundance of travelers to his shop. More business equated to extra income. Those repairs would be done within the first year the construction was complete. They even convinced Alba Winters from the bookstore this boost in traffic would bring in the possibility of famous authors to her establishment. Signings and readers from towns over visiting her store. They created the perfect picture, and they knew how to wine and dine each townsperson and business owner.

These people were barely making ends meet. They couldn't afford to have Benjamin Miller come in and plant workers in their town, taking jobs away from the ones who desperately needed them. No need to fear, Miller Industries said. They already had a plan. They would hire from within. Anyone of age to work had a job. By the time Miller Industries was walking out of those meetings, those townspeople had already written their lists of what they would be spending their future influx of money on.

That money never came.

Theresa Simmons was visiting her husband on that construction site the day of the accident. She lost her life in the process, and so did her husband. Jerald Hope's oldest son, Bryce, who had just turned eighteen, lost his life. Alba Winters' husband and two sons were lost. Four months ago, she was found in the back of her store. She'd hung herself. My stomach drops, chills cascading down my arms as I pass the bookstore.

So many lives lost. For nothing. These poor people didn't even have the means to fight what Miller Industries did to them. The entire community was forced to bury their loved ones and spend whatever they had left trying to pick up the pieces. Until one person stepped up: Clara Hill, the only person who still had a sliver of faith in the world. Just as tired as the rest, she used the last of her energy on finding someone who would take pity on their case—aka my dad.

Clara was suffering too. Not only did she lose her husband, but her oldest son had been on the job. It wasn't until later she realized her youngest, Gregory, had been on the site that day as well. He'd wanted to watch his brother work. He had been out of the building when the explosion occurred, but still endured extensive injuries, almost losing both his legs when flying debris smashed into him as he was riding his bike away. So many people are hurting. Some won't ever recover. And if Clara gives up, she gives up for the whole town. She *is* their only fighting chance. And I can't let that happen.

Clara's home is on the far end of town. A small little ranch in desperate need of repairs. I pull into the gravel driveway, my tires crackling over the gritted rocks. A dim light glows from the front room window. Clara's phone was disconnected, so I couldn't call and warn her of my visit. Even though I knew she would have told me not to come. Putting my car in park, I climb out. Walking up the narrow walkway, I peek into the window and see a tiny woman sitting on the sofa watching television. When I ring the bell, she twists to peer out the window. It takes a few moments for her to open the door a smidge, a metal chain stopping it.

"Can I help you?" she asks through the slit in the door.

"Clara Hill?"

"Yes? You are?"

I reach my hand out to shake hers, realizing how silly that is since she can't even fit hers through the small crack in the door. "Um...hi, my name is Hannah Matthews. I'm from Matthew and Assoc—"

"I have nothing to say to you." She slams the door in my face. What the...? I take my fist and pound on the door.

"Mrs. Hill, please hear me out. Someone's gotten to you. I read your testimony. There's no way you decided to stop fighting for justice. For your husband and your son—"

The door flies open, and I stumble back a step. "Don't you tell me I'm not fighting for my family. I'm doing what I need to do to keep the family I have left alive. Now, get off my property or—"

"No!" I yell, slapping my hand on the door so she can't shut me out. "I refuse to sit back and allow a monster to win. To threaten people and continue to hold power over this town. He's guilty. He took your loved ones away from you. He knew what he was doing. You know that. Your husband knew that. Whatever he's threatened you with, we can protect you. Don't turn your back on this—on the other people depending on you."

Clara's eyes blaze with emotion, tears welling and spilling over. "You don't understand." She swipes at her face. "He's—"

"Mrs. Hill, invite me inside. Let me understand. Let me convince you no matter how much Benjamin Miller thinks he owns this town, he's not above the law."

There's so much pain etched into her features. Her eyes are red, indicating she probably hasn't stopped crying since this nightmare began, let alone slept. She wants to fight me, but she's tired. She nods, unhooks the lock, opens the door fully, and allows me to enter her home.

It's small, quaint. The walls are littered with family photos— memories of a life she'll never have again. She waves for me to take a seat, and I accept, making myself comfortable on the loveseat. I look at the tv, and my heart cracks when I realize she's watching a homemade family video.

"Would you like some coffee? Tea?"

"Water would be great, thank you."

She disappears into the kitchen while I bring my attention

back to the television. Two kids laughing as they run around the backyard being chased by their dad. I recognize Clara's laughter as she records her husband and sons.

"Joey, better run. Daddy's gonna get you!"

Joey, who appears to be about five, runs in circles around his dad, squealing, waving a stuffed animal in the air. "Catch me, Daddy! Catch me!"

Paul Hill laughs and shoots up, growling like a lion. He snatches his son into his arms, taking him to the ground and tickling him. Their other son, Gregory, jumps on his dad's back. Clara's laughter rings out behind the lens.

Just as Paul faces the camera, mouthing "I love you" to his wife, Clara walks back into the room, holding a glass of water.

"Joey was four there. He would have been twenty-one next week." She hands me the glass and takes a seat across from me.

"I'm truly sorry for your loss, Mrs. Hill—"

"Please, call me Clara."

I nod. "I'm not married, but I do have a brother. I can't imagine losing him or anyone I love."

She shakes her head, tears flowing down her pale, lean face. "I'm sorry. I can't do this. I shouldn't have let you in. They said... my son...I can't lose anyone else." She covers her face with her shaking hands as a sob breaks free. I'm up and taking the open spot next to her, doing my best to comfort her.

"Clara, they won't hurt you. I promise."

"They will. They've already tried. Gregory...he had a scare at the rehab center. They said it was a glitch, but *he* said it was a threat—retract or I'd pay the ultimate price."

Jesus. What kind of monsters are the Millers? "Clara, you're scared, but giving them what they want won't keep you safe. It won't give you the closure you deserve or the compensation you need. Without the compensation of this lawsuit, how will you pay for Gregory's rehabilitation bills? How will you support the two of you once he's finally ready to come home?"

"I won't be supporting anyone if he's dead. And they made that very clear. If I talk, they'll kill my only living son."

My anger gets the best of me. How does someone think they can control someone's life? Have so much power, they chose who lives or dies? Without thinking, I grab Clara by the shoulders, shaking her until her eyes lock on mine. "I won't let that happen. I promise you."

"The day the news broke of the explosion…" She pauses, as if the reel of that horrific day begins to replay in her head. "That morning…I'd been so busy in the kitchen. Paul and Joey were off to work. And Gregory…I—just thought he was in his room. I didn't even think to check—" She stops, hiding her weeping face in her hands. I give her a moment, until she composes herself enough to continue. "I'd been baking all morning for Alba's baby shower."

"Alba Winters from the bookstore?" She confirms with a single nod. "Wait, she was *pregnant*? It didn't mention that in the report."

"They left out a lot in the news. A pregnant wife, losing her husband and son. Unable to cope, commits suicide. She was so strong. But a moment of weakness, and she was just gone…" I hold her as her body trembles and she cries for her friend, community, and the burden she still bears for being a survivor.

When she pulls herself together once again, she continues. "I'm sorry. This is very hard for me." She wipes at her soaked cheeks, taking a deep breath for strength. "Paul wanted to go to the police the moment he realized what caused the explosion. He told Mr. Miller over and over the land was uninhabitable. Something like this had been inevitable. But Mr. Miller shut him down at every angle. The threats started shortly after, and the scare tactics worked. Showing up at all times of the night. Rocks being thrown through our front window. He even had his son stalking us."

"His son? Why?"

"Mr. Miller claimed innocence the whole time. In his statement, he argued my husband signed off on those contracts willingly. There was no duress involved, and clearly my husband was only trying to cover himself. We'd gone to the police about the threats and stalking, but they didn't do anything. Couldn't. Mr. Miller had an alibi for every situation. Of course he did since his son was doing all his bidding. He would sit at the hospital, find ways into Gregory's room. When we showed up, he'd be there sitting by his side. But he wasn't there as a support system. Every time, he would be standing next to his defibrillator, as if he were seconds from pulling the plug."

"Did you ever go to the police about *him?*" I ask.

"Again, we tried. But they didn't believe us. His son had an outstanding record. No one would believe he was doing his father's dirty work or had any ill intentions."

"The guilt got to Paul. He told me he had to go turn himself in and confess his wrongdoings. It was weighing too heavy on his shoulders. The lost lives of all those people. His own son. He couldn't live with himself. The morning he was set to go to the police station, I found him in the garage—apparent suicide." Her voice cracks, and a guttural sound of agony slices into me. "He was hanging there. Pale. His eyes..."

I fight my own emotions, feeling the muscles in my chin start to tremble. "I'm so sorry, Clara." Because I am.

A few staggered breaths, and she goes on. "The letter was typed. Didn't sound like him at all. That's how I knew."

I rub her back, hoping to offer her any sort of support. "Clara, did anyone see anything that night? That morning? Anything off that could be a clue to help us? Anything you didn't add in your original report?"

"Maribel from across the street said a car woke her up in the middle of the night. She thought it was strange being so late. When she peeked out the window, she saw a young man wearing a hoodie running across the street."

I don't recall this information being in any of the files I studied. "Why didn't you ever mention this?"

"Because by the time Maribel realized what she'd seen, it had spooked her. She packed up and moved to Alabama with her sister. She wouldn't be of help to the case, so it didn't matter."

It all matters. Every single detail. "Do you have any idea who it could have been?"

She pulls her head from her hands, her eyes beaming with confidence as she answers me. "It was Benjamin Miller's son.

By the time I exit Clara's home, the sun is setting. I throw myself into my car, my heart racing. This is it. This can save the case. As I pull back onto Main Street, I shuffle through my purse for my phone. I dial Levi's number, but it instantly goes to voicemail. "Oh, come on!" I impatiently wait for the voice message until the beep sounds. "Levi, I need you to call me back the second you get this." A notification dings on my phone, telling me my battery is low. "Oh, come on!" Go figure I left my charger in Levi's car. I utilize my remaining phone life and dial the one person I can trust to help me: Professor Fischer. He always mentioned his connections with the court system judges, from civil to supreme. It may be a longshot, but at this point, what do I have to lose? Twenty minutes and a three-way call to the supreme court judge later, thanks to Professor Fischer, I'm being granted a continuance on the Miller case.

"Yes. I agree, sir. Fully. Not a second longer. Thank you. You have no idea. Goodbye." I end the call, squealing into my steering wheel, accidently swerving into the other lane. A car honks at me, and I jerk, dropping my phone. "Sorry," I wave, gathering myself. Holy crap. I got it. I really got it. With Clara back on board and the continuance, we can nail this case.

I left Clara in search of finding a photo of Benjamin Miller's son so we can submit him into evidence and subpoena him for trial. I dial Levi's number again, and again, voicemail. Dammit! I need to get home—fast. This changes everything.

Will it change Levi's mind about us? The wounds from his hurtful words slice at my heart all over again. "Stop," I scold myself. As much as my heart bleeds from his distrust, I need to band-aid my emotions and focus on what's important. Levi may have given up on me, but I refuse to give up on him. Unlike my upbringing, he was always surrounded by people who let him down. His mom, his dad, countless girlfriends who took advantage of his kind heart. I won't be another person in his life who does. Whether we have a future, he's always been family. Always will be.

I *need* to get ahold of Levi. I call his office line and get his voicemail. A call to my dad, and I get his voicemail too. Where in the world is everybody! I decide against calling Braydon. My suspicions where he's concerned has my radar dinging in the red zone, and that nagging feeling inside my chest tells me Levi has been right about him all along.

I dial Levi's number one last time. It hurts to consider it, but he may purposely be avoiding my calls. Just as I decide to leave the information on his voicemail, he answers. "Jesus, what? Not a good time, Hannah—"

"I got a continuance," I spit out before he can say another word.

There's a short pause, then he speaks, his voice low and laced with annoyance. "How's that possible? I tried. We were denied."

"It doesn't matter. We now have an additional forty-eight hours until trial begins."

There's shuffling in the background. "What the fuck did you do?" His anger seeps through the phone, rattling my already frayed nerves.

I bite my lower lip, but there's no way of hiding it. "I went to see Clara Hill."

A thunderous boom echoes in the background, and I imagine Levi taking his fists to something hard. "Tell me you didn't."

"I can't. Listen to me. She's back on. I got her testimony. The Miller's did get to her. Threatened her son. I told her we'd protect her. There's someone else—"

"Jesus Christ, Hannah! What were you *thinking?*"

"I was—"

"What you did not only could have jeopardized the company, but you could have been slapped with a lawsuit. Not to mention she's being *threatened!* That puts *you* in fucking danger!" The last of his sentence comes out on a roar. I'm forced to pull the phone away so he doesn't blow out my eardrums.

"Listen, I know I was taking a risk—"

"A *risk?*"

"Yeah, a *risk!* But in the end, it worked out. I got what we needed. I got us a continuance! The case isn't dead. We can win this." He sighs heavily. I know Levi well enough to know his hand is wrestling in his hair, his mind racing. "Where are you? Are you at the office? I'll meet you."

A short pause, and he answers, "I'm at home."

I search the clock on my dash for the time. It's a bit early for him to be off work, considering the extensity of what's going on with the case. "Why are you at home? Shouldn't you still be at work?"

"Have you talked to your brother?"

Why does that matter right now? "No, why? Why are you at home? I'm coming over—"

"No. I won't be here. I have to meet Kip at Jake's soon."

"Fine, I'll meet you there—"

"Hannah, Jesus, no! Something happened at work today. Kip—" His voice cuts out, the line going silent.

"Levi?" I pull my phone away from my face. Dead. "Oh, come on!" Kipley what? Is he hurt? Did something happen? My nerves rattle into a state of electrified panic. I check the time. I'm only twenty-five minutes out. I race with all my might, weaving in and out of cars, breaking a long list of traffic violations, until I'm pulling into the parking lot of Jake's bar.

I get out—or attempt to, forgetting I'm still latched to my seat belt. Of course it's the most inconvenient time to get jammed. "For the love!" I fight with the strap, until it finally releases, and I slip, falling sideways out of my car. I grunt when I stick my hand out to catch my fall, scraping it against the gravel. Gathering myself, I get up and sprint toward the building, getting held up by the doorman requesting my ID.

I frantically scope the bar in search of Levi. That's when I spot a wide-eyed Stacey. She waves me over, and I scurry in her direction. "Hannah, what are you doing here? I don't think this is a good idea." Her face is red with worry. Her eyes wander down to my scraped palm. "What happened?"

"Nothing. It's fine. Have you seen Levi?"

She stares at me, confused. "No, not yet, but you really shouldn't be here. Kip is very angry right now. If he sees you two in the same—"

"What do you mean angry? Why is Kip angry?"

"Hannah." Levi's voice has me spinning around to face him. God, I missed him. I want to throw my arms around him and bask in his comfort. Have him tell me he forgives me and things are going to be okay. "You can't be here. You need to leave." Or not. His voice is dripping with disgust. Anger.

"Why? I told you. Everything's going to be okay. I'll tell my dad—"

He takes a step toward me, latching his hand around my bicep. His grip is hard. "Forget about the fucking case, you need to fucking—"

"You son of a bitch!" We both turn at my brother's voice as he storms toward us. I don't even have time to register as Kipley's fist cocks back and smashes into Levi's face. I scream as his head flies back. His hand jerks as he releases me and I fall backwards into Stacey.

"Kipley!" I scream in horror.

Kipley ignores me and goes barreling into Levi, throwing another punch. "You motherfucker! For real? My fucking *sister*?" He goes for another swing, and I scream while Levi willingly takes the blow.

"Kipley, stop!" I throw myself in between them, but Kip's too enraged to acknowledge me. He goes after Levi again, shoving me out of the way. Stumbling, I lose my balance and land hard on my butt.

"How fucking could you?" Another swing. Another shriek from me. Why the hell isn't Levi fighting back?

"Kip, stop! It's not what you think!" My cry falls on deaf ears as my brother wrestles him to the ground, getting a good shot to Levi's ribs.

"You think I wouldn't find out? You piece of shit, you've been like a brother to me since we were kids. Sexual harassment?" Kip's voice cracks, but he quickly regains his composure. "She's like your sister!" he yells, landing blow after blow. "You sick fuck!"

His words halt me. "What? No, what are you talking about!" I push off the ground and lock my fists around Kipley's shirt, pulling him off Levi. "You're wrong. That's not what's happening." My eyes take in a bloody Levi. "Tell him," I beg. Levi coughs, blood splattering from his lip. "Levi—"

"Hannah, you don't have to cover for him. Dad told me—"

"Told you what?" I snap at my brother. I turn my confused eyes back to Levi. What is he hiding from me?

"You should have come to me. I would have helped you. Taken care of—"

"For what!" I yell. Something's not right. I shift my attention to Levi, a silent plea to please tell me what's going on. This is more than just them finding out about us.

Levi coughs. Bending forward, he grabs his wounded ribs and wipes blood from his nose. "A sexual harassment complaint was filed at work today." My eyes shoot wide open. "It came from you."

My knees threaten to give out. "No...I—I didn't do that." My voice shakes.

Kip finally pushes off Levi and stands, reaching for me. "No, fuck him. Don't take it back because he's here. It's done." His anger directs back to Levi. "Get the fuck out of here. You ever lay a hand on my sister again, I'll kill you myself."

"Kip!" I yell and get in his face, but Levi puts his hand out.

"Hannah, don't."

"*Don't?* It's not true! I would never. Levi, you have to believe me." I reach for him, but Kip uses his body as a barrier between us. "Kip, stop. This isn't true. Levi's done nothing wrong—"

"Just let it go, Hannah." My attention retreats to Levi. "Let it go," he says again, coughing out more blood, his voice stern. His face bruised and beaten, his arm cradling his stomach, he turns and walks out.

I twist around to face my brother. "How could you?" My voice is riddled in anguish. "He's your best friend." He reaches for me, and I slap his hand away.

"What the hell, Hannah?"

"No, what the hell to *you*, Kipley? You are so wrong about what's going on. He never did anything to me I didn't want." His brows crease, his eyes thin with confusion. "I would have never put in that complaint because I'm in love with him."

Stacey gasps as Kipley's posture stiffens. His hand brushes down his face, unable to grasp my confession. "What did you just say?" Stacey takes a step closer, wrapping her arm around him. She tries to soothe him, but he brushes her off, his eyes laced with anger and hurt. "*What* did you just say?"

A heavy feeling settles in my stomach. I knew the day he found out would be hard. For everyone. But I never imagined it would happen like this. I never wanted to hurt my brother over this. But to see Levi so broken down may be worse. My eyes begin to shine with tears, my voice quivering. "I love him. I have my whole life." Kip stands there, his eyes holding mine captive. His disapproving frown and deep-set gaze has a pain radiating inside me. I try to swallow the emotions fighting to erupt inside me, but tears fall unchecked down my cheeks. "I'm sorry," I cry. "I didn't want you to find out this way."

His brows draw together, and he inhales a staggered breath. "Jesus, Hannah, a childhood crush does not give him the right to force himself on you."

What? "No, it's not a childhood crush. We mean something to one another. I love him—"

"Okay, that's enough." He comes at me again, and I shove him away. He glares at me, his sudden onset of anger aimed toward me. "I'm not going to let you take the blame for this. He's wrong—"

"He's not!" I scream. "He's done nothing but show me how it truly feels to be loved. To be wanted and cared for. To be *noticed*." I wipe a tear off my cheek, taking a moment to breathe. "Those accusations are false. And if you were a better friend, you would have come to one of us before letting your fists do the talking. Shame on you." I shove my heel into the ground and race out of the bar in hopes to still catch Levi.

"Hannah, wait," Kip calls out behind me, but I don't.

Once in the parking lot, I search for his car, but it's too dark, I begin to panic. "Levi!" I yell out, praying he's close enough to hear me. Maybe his window's down. Maybe he knows I'd come for him and he's waiting for me. I yell his name again, but nothing. I reach into my back pocket, but remember my phone's in my car. I book it toward my car and jam my key in the lock. Throwing my door open, I snatch my phone up and wait for it to turn on, forgetting my battery is dead.

"Dammit!"

No, no, no...

I spin around, the anxiety that's growing like a disease in my chest starting to suffocate me. *Sexual harassment. Punch after punch. My brother's face of disappointment.* "Levi," I call for him, his name barely above a whisper, my words choked out through my crushing lungs. I can't breathe. My brain replays the images of Levi, bloody and broken on the bar floor. *How is this happening? Who would do this?* I try to suck in a ragged breath, but the air is too thick. I grab at my neck, dizziness fueling my fear. I want to scream for help, but I can't find my voice.

I need to find Levi. I need to tell him I wasn't behind this. Make things right between him and Kip. Oh god, what have I done? Stacey warned me. She warned me, and I didn't listen. I whip around again, gasping for air, my brain seizing to my panic attack. The pit in my stomach is like a grenade detonating, and the havoc I've caused has my heart beating too fast. Too hard. My body starts to convulse with the wracked sobs of regret. "Levi!" His name is a hoarse shriek. I spin around, almost falling to the gravel, but two hands wrap around me.

"Oh, Levi, I knew you would—"

I turn into Braydon, and my eyes expand in shock, then confusion. "Braydon—wha—what are you doing here? It doesn't matter. I need your help—"

My eyes widen when I feel a sudden sting in my neck. "What...?"

Braydon's hand pulls back, a long needle between his fingers. "You should have stayed out of this, Han..."

CHAPTER TWENTY-FOUR

Levi

Banging on my door jerks me awake. I grunt as I jolt forward, my bruised ribs causing a wave of pain to shoot through my body. "Fuck," I grunt, holding my stomach as I slip off my couch. I stumble over a layer of beer bottles and trip over a bottle of whiskey before falling and landing on my side. "*Fuck!*" Shit, that hurt. Seems drinking myself into oblivion doesn't erase the wounded pride or injuries from getting your ass handed to you.

Whoever's at the door can fuck off. I'm not sure I can get off the floor. My eyes shut, and I doze off before banging startles me back awake. "Jesus, fuck off!" I roll onto my back, and my sour stomach turns, threatening to vomit the overindulgence of booze I took part in. My head is hurting, not to mention my nose, lip, and dignity.

In the matter of a day, I lost my job, respect from a man who's been a father to me almost my whole life, and my best friend. Not to mention I probably lost the girl too. Which is well deserved. I knew this could happen. And I chose to go against what was right. I should have come out from the beginning. Instead, I chose to lie to someone who's been a brother to me...a family who's done nothing but stand by me when my own wouldn't even acknowledge me.

The disappointment in Jim's eyes with the case. The shock followed by rage when he got the call from HR. If we hadn't been in his office surrounded by other staff, I'm sure he would have done what Kipley got the pleasure to do, but worse.

How the fuck did everything go so wrong, so fast?

Another wave of nausea has me rolling back to my side, ready to yack all over my floor. "Ughhh…" I groan, pulling myself up.

The banging starts again, like drumsticks beating on my brain. "Go away!" I yell, dragging my sore body to the kitchen. I grab a bottle of beer, still half full, and chug it. "Hair of the dog," I grumble, throwing the empty bottle into the sink, hearing it shatter.

Bang, bang, bang. "I know you're in there. Open the fucking door, Dent!"

Fuck.

Kipley.

I'm not sure I'm in the best shape to take another beating. Even though I deserve more than what he dished out last night. I snag a beer from the fridge and twist the top off, taking a hefty swig as I drag myself to my door. More banging echoes throughout my condo, and I throw the door open. "Come to finish me off?"

"Fuck you." Kipley pushes past me, and I almost fall backwards. "Hannah!" he calls out. He aims his scathing anger back to me. "Where is she? Hannah!" he shouts again toward my bedroom.

"She isn't here." I walk back to my living room, needing to sit down.

"Bullshit. Hannah! Get the fuck out here now!" He doesn't take my word and storms down the hallway to my bedroom, shoving the door open and searching my room. A minute later, he comes out.

"Told you."

"Where is she?"

"How the hell should I know? I haven't seen her since you kicked my ass and told me to leave your family alone." I need to shut my anger down. I don't have the right to play the victim. I deserved what I got. "Just call her phone. I'm sure she'll answer for you."

"You don't think we've done that? Her phone's off."

I fall onto my couch, grunting in pain. "And you think she came here? After I sexually assaulted her and all?"

"You motherfucker."

I launch myself up, ignoring the stabbing in my side and the nausea, and get in his face. But when I stand there, face to face with my best friend, I stand down. "Yeah. I am a motherfucker." My chest sinks, and I wait for him to strike.

Silence washes over us for a moment until he speaks. "Why, man? Why my *sister*?" There's so much hurt and betrayal in his tone, it feels like he's beating me all over again. I'd actually take another blow if it took away the betrayal in his eyes. Instead, I stare back at twenty-four years of friendship. The first kid to be-friend me in kindergarten by sharing his bag of Doritos. My first sleepover where his mom made me my first peanut butter and jelly sandwich and allowed us to cook s'mores in the house and watch *The Karate Kid* over and over. The boy who stood by me when my father threatened to kick my ass for taking lunch money when I hadn't eaten in almost two days. The guy who spent endless nights helping me study my way through my first batch of law school after I chose to let go of a pipe dream. A friend who stood by me through thick and thin, never questioning me or my decisions.

Feeling defeated all over again, I throw myself back on my couch, using my hands to cup my wounded face. "Why your sis-ter?" I ask. Images of her pouty lips when she's frustrated and the passion in her eyes that can set a room on fire filter through my mind. "Because as much as I tried to stay away, I couldn't. I fought it. I knew she was off limits. But her spark for life and enigmatic spirit found its way into my heart."

The floodgates of truth crack, and I start pouring out con-fessions in waves. "I treaded lightly with her. She wasn't just a girl.

She was special. She suddenly became this bright color in my dull world. A warmth that fed my soul and made me feel something I'm not sure I've ever felt before." I pull my eyes from my hands to find his, hoping he understands. "She made me feel complete in a way I've never felt before. What it truly meant to be so consumed by someone, it almost hurt. And eventually, I stopped fighting it. I craved her light. Her warmth. The embrace of someone who truly saw me for me. She did that for me." I have to break contact. It hurts too much to express how much I love her. I never actually got the chance to tell her, and now I've lost her. "I fell in love with her," I whisper, not sure whether I'm saying it to him or myself.

"Shit," Kipley cusses, and without looking up, I feel the cushion next to me sink as he takes a seat. "You've got it bad."

A pathetic chuckle filters up my throat. I finally open my eyes to glance at him. "You have no idea."

We sit quiet for another minute, until he breaks the silence. "Why didn't you tell me?"

"So you could kick my ass sooner?"

He nods. "True." There's another round of silence. "Damn… so you're really in love with my little sister?"

"I am." Fuck, I am. I love her. But it's too late. I fucked everything up. I shouldn't have lost my temper with her at the office. Made her feel like I lost trust in her. In us. If she'd just waited for me and we could have talked it out, maybe we could have avoided all this mess.

"Shit." Kipley swipes his hand down his face. "Wasn't expecting this." Yeah, neither was I, but for some reason, the world decided I needed something good in my life and granted me her. "Say I decide to not kill you for touching my little sister, my next question is—"

"Hannah didn't submit that harassment complaint. That, I'm sure of."

"But why would—?"

"Hannah didn't submit it. Ask her yourself. Yeah, we had a

fight. I was angry about the case. Fuck, I blamed my slip up on my distraction with her." I shake my head, wishing away the horrible accusations I made. The disappointment and hurt on her face when I suggested we take a pause. "I fucking hurt her, but she would never do that. I know she lov—she just wouldn't."

"This is all fucked up, man. If she didn't…"

"Someone is setting me up. Ask her yourself. She'll tell you the same thing."

"She never showed up at work today. Never came home last night. My parents are beside themselves with worry. It's why I came banging your door down. To get her to at least call home."

A wave of unease hits me, and I sit up straighter. "What do you mean she didn't come home? Weren't you with her?"

"She yelled at me for being a shitty friend and ran after you. By the time I calmed down and left the bar, her car was there, but she wasn't. I assumed she left with you. Then Dad called me today, concerned, and here I am."

A sinking feeling tightens my soured stomach—and it's not from the excessive booze or wounds. "I—she didn't leave with me." With everything that happened, I forgot about our call. She'd gone to see Clara Hill. Panic begins to flood my system.

"Dude, you don't look so good. What's going on? What do you know?" There's an edge to Kipley's tone.

I replay our conversation. "She'd gone to see a witness."

"And that's bad because…?"

My voice shakes. A thickness in my throat makes it difficult to breathe. "The witness—the case—we were fighting about—she pulled out—"

"Okay, you're starting to freak me out. You're not making any sense. What does this have to do with Hannah?"

I stumble as I stand, a ripple of dizziness smacking me in the face, causing me to trip.

"Whoa, slow down, man." Kipley steadies me, but I slap his hand away. My eyes are frantic, searching for my phone. I spot it on the floor and practically dive for it, dialing Hannah's number. It instantly goes to voicemail. "Come on…" I hang up and dial again, but it doesn't even give me the satisfaction of a single ring before her voicemail picks up.

"Levi, you're starting to scare me. What the fuck? Is Hannah in danger? Do you think something happened to her?" This time, Kipley's voice is strained. I wish I could alleviate his worry, but I can't. Kipley's phone breaks our stare down, and he snatches it from his back pocket. I pray it's Hannah telling him she's fine. "Hey, Dad." Fuck. "Yeah, she's not here. I know…she's not this careless…sure." He pulls his phone away to speak to me. "He still hasn't heard from her. She's still on my parents' phone plan, so he's called the cell company to locate her. Everything will be fine."

We both wait, holding our breath for Jim to come back on the line. I don't realize my hands are trembling. "What'd he say?" he starts back up, and I stay super close, needing to hear him say she's all right. "I'm headed there now." He hangs up and faces me, confusion setting in. "Her phone pinged at Jake's bar."

"What? Why—?"

"I don't know. Let's go."

CHAPTER TWENTY-FIVE

Hannah

There's an entire orchestra playing in my head. Not the good kind either. *So much banging and pounding.* I groan, turning to my side, hoping to block out the bright light coming from my window. Something restraining my arms stops me, and I groan louder, tugging at my hands, a sharpness around my wrists causing me to wince. What in the heck? I open my eyes, the light sending a zap of agony to my brain. Fighting through the pain, I force my vision to focus on my surroundings and lift my head. My hands are bound by thick rope and tied around a headboard.

"Oh my god," I gasp, tugging at the restraints, groaning at the tear of skin around my wrists. Terror ignites in my chest. Fear overwhelms my body. Ignoring the ripping of my flesh, I begin to tug harder. "Help!" I call out, the sound of my voice etched with panic. How did I get here? How long have I been like this? My head is too foggy to grab any memories or reasoning. My chest starts to pound, stealing the air from my lungs. "Help!" I yell again.

"Don't bother. No one can hear you." I'm suddenly paralyzed by the familiar voice. My head veers to the side, causing more dizziness to slice through me. "Oh my god, Braydon, what's going on? Help untie me please." He doesn't make an effort to move. A chill skates over my aching skin. My throat swells. "Braydon, untie me."

A slow smile spreads across his face, filling me with dread. I pull at my restraints, grasping for any hint of a memory. "Braydon, this isn't funny, untie me!" I force my voice to sound stern, but he can hear the shiver in my tone. My body shudders with dread at the way his predatory eyes stare at me, almost as if he's staring right through me.

How did I get here?

Think, Hannah, think!

Dammit!

I can't even recall what day it is. My lower lip begins to quiver. "Braydon, why are you doing this?" How long have I been here? Does anyone know I'm missing? "I thought we were friends?" My comment agitates him. He starts pacing, and that's when I see the shiny metal in his hand. "Braydon…" I beg, the last of my cool evaporating. I tug harder on my shackles, kicking my feet to free them from their ties. When his focus lands on me, his eyes are wild. I don't have time to register his quick movements. My shrill scream is deafening as he jumps toward me, his arms raising and thrusting down, the large knife slicing mere inches from my side.

"Oh, come on. You know I wouldn't hurt you." He yanks the knife out of the mattress. "Unlike him. *He* left you there, upset. Turned his back on you. I would have never done that to you." What is he talking about? Who left me?

Jake's. Kipley and Levi fighting. He ran out, and I followed. I was standing by my car. Braydon—

"Ahhh…she's starting to remember. I watched what he did to you. He should have never treated you that way. The things he did to you at work. The disrespect. You should be cherished, not taken advantage of in an office like some *whore*." He whirls around and starts pacing again, taking the knife and stabbing at the air.

I need to catch my breath. Calm the rapid beats of my heart and find a way to rationalize with him, which is hard because I'm seconds away from hyperventilating. "I'm sure if you untie me, we can talk about—"

He waves his knife around, his eyes manic. "And have you run away from me? Not a chance." He walks over to the dresser, leaning forward to observe the framed photos. My body jolts when his hand shoots forward, swiping the frames to the ground. It's in that moment I take note of the people in those photos. My stomach threatens to expel everything boiling inside it. More observing around the room confirms my grave assumption. I'm in Clara Hill's home.

"Bray—ayden…" My voice shakes. "Why are we in Clara's bedroom? Where's Clara?"

He stands straighter, pivots on his heel, and walks toward the bed. His dilated pupils narrow into crinkled slits, and he bends down. The hairs on my arms stand as his eyes close and he inhales a big breath, smelling me. He quickly pulls back, shaking his head as if he just took a hit of his favorite drug. "You know why," he says, averting his eyes from mine, tracing the lining of my shirt. "You should have let it be, Hannah."

I can't decipher his cryptic words. Why am I here? Where is Clara! How did I not notice this side of him? Never once did I recognize any red flags. Holy shit, Braydon is a psychopath. *Calm down, Hannah.* I need to focus. Rerouting my tactics, I take in a deep breath. "Listen. I agree. Thank you for noticing. I honestly never knew you felt this way about me. I—I wish I'd known."

His eyes, carrying a mixture of shock and anger, pierce into mine, searching for truth or lies. "You *do* like me?"

I nod furiously. "Yes! Of course! How could I not? That's why I spent so much time with you. I thought it was *you* who didn't like me."

His lips crest into a hopeful smile, then curl down. "Is that why you turned to *him?*"

Levi.

"Yeah. Yes! I was so hurt, I only pretended to like him because I wanted to make you…um…jealous. How immature of me." I pray he eats the lies I'm feeding him. He starts rocking back and forth on his heel, tapping the knife against his thigh. A lackluster smile appears, and hope surges inside my belly. "Please untie me. If you say you really like me and I like you, we can talk this out. I never thought you would feel this way about me. I've dreamed…hoped…"

The words burn my throat like acid. I push away my real thoughts, expelling a deep breath, and conjure up fake tears. "I can't believe you did all this for me. Please, I need you to just hold me. Tell me we can have a future and see where this can go."

The muscles in his face tighten, then transform into a toothy smile. He waves the knife in the air. "I knew you would see this the same way." He points the knife in my direction. "You're not gonna run or anything, right? If I untie you?"

"No! Of course not. I just want to be near you." *Please bite. Please bite.* He contemplates my words, then nods eagerly and steps toward me. "Once everything settles down, we can get a place. I'll have so much money, I can give you whatever you want. More than *he* could." He bends forward, taking the knife and slicing through the ropes, releasing my hands. Pain radiates up my arms from being captive in that position for so long, and I groan. "There's this great spot we can go eat. I've been wanting to take you there." He moves down to cut my legs free. "You can meet my dad. He's going to love you." Once my legs are unbound, I sit up, but not too fast to alarm him. He's showing no signs of hesitancy and helps me to stand. When our eyes meet, his are filled with optimism as he wraps his arms around me, bringing me in for a hug. I return the embrace, feeling him relax around me.

When he becomes too lax, I lift my knee and shove it as hard as I can into his balls. He howls, his arms twitching and releasing me. I turn on my heels and run, making it down the hallway before I hear his angry voice.

"Hannah!" Braydon yells, but I don't stop. I race through the house until I make a quick right into the living room I visited sometime earlier. I'm halfway through the room, only mere feet away from the front door, when his hands latch around my neck and he barrels into me, throwing me to the ground. I scream in horror and pain. Both consume me when his knife slices into my side.

CHAPTER TWENTY-SIX

Levi

We pull up to Jake's, and Kipley's Tahoe is barely in park before we both jump out. The second I see her, I'm going to pull her into my arms and hold her until my uneasiness settles. Then I'm going to throttle her for giving everyone such a scare. On the quiet drive over here, I took the time to reflect on the last couple weeks, wishing I'd handled things differently, ashamed I ever suggested we keep our feelings for one another private. I should have been honest from the get-go with the case. I know better than anyone how resilient Hannah is. She would have stepped up and helped solve the problem with the strange occurrences. If anyone would have been able to, it would have been her.

Once I make sure she's okay, I need to confess everything. How I feel. Where my intentions lie. I need her to know I fucking love her with every fiber of my being.

We enter through the front, and the smell of stale beer smacks me in the face, twisting my stomach. "Lunch doesn't start 'til noon," the bartender calls out as he wipes down the bar.

My eyes trail down the long bar in search of her. "Not here to eat. Looking for someone," Kip says, his eyes skating around the freestanding pub tables.

"Unless it's me, I can't help you. I'm the only one here. Betty gets in at one."

His words don't register at first. They can't because that means she's not here. Time slows as my eyes scale the bar, refusing to believe she isn't. *Just look harder. She's here. He just hasn't noticed her yet.* But who wouldn't notice Hannah Matthews?

"Yeah, that can't be. My sister's phone was pinged here. She's here."

"No one's been here since close of yesterday. Sorry, buddy. Maybe she left her phone here. Let me go check the lost and found." He walks off into the backroom, and Kipley and I stand there frozen.

"Kip—"

"Don't go there. There's got to be an explanation for all this. Hannah's not irresponsible like this."

"*Exactly.* This is not like Hannah. Something's wrong. Listen, the case, the witness she went to visit—"

"Sorry, no phones. Check the parking lots. Sometimes people drop them getting in their cars or taxis."

Her car. Kipley said it was left here. We both push past the exit and spot her car in the back of the lot. I hit the ground in a sprint with Kip right beside me. When I get to her car, I halt, realizing I'm holding my breath. I stall as Kip leans forward and pulls on the handle. It's unlocked.

My chest constricts. Hannah would never leave her car unlocked.

Kip opens the door and leans in, then pops back out. "Nothing looks stolen or out of place." His cell rings, and he withdraws it from his back pocket. "Dad…yeah, she's not here. Hasn't been. Not sure. We're at her car right now."

It's then I spot it.

I bend down, extending my hand to reach behind her front tire. When I stand with her phone in my grip, my stomach bottoms out and I struggle against throwing up. "Call the police," I whisper, refusing to believe what I'm asking. My mind is spinning, and I can't keep up with all the tell-tale signs I should have seen from the moment she went unaccounted for.

"*Someone got to Clara Hill.*"

"*She has to have been threatened. There's no other explanation. We can't let this happen. She has to testify.*"

"*I went to see Clara Hill. I got her testimony. The Millers did get to her. Threatened her son. I told her we'd protect her.*"

"*Hannah! That puts you in fucking danger!*"

"We need to call the fucking police!" I roar, finally finding my voice, reliving the conversation we had. If Clara was being threatened, Hannah going to see her put her right in harm's way. I grip tightly at my hair, dread crushing my chest. "We need...shit...we need..." I can't breathe.

Someone got to Clara Hill.

Someone got to Clara Hill.

"They fucking did something to her. He fucking has her!" I grab at my chest, my lungs feeling as if they're filling with cement, the gravity of the situation choking me. "Kip, your dad. The case...they got to her..."

CHAPTER TWENTY-SEVEN

Hannah

"**N**o, no, no…" Braydon jumps off me, but I'm paralyzed on the floor. Fire shoots from my side, blinding whiteness in my vision at the pain exploding in my side. "No, no, no, NO!" he yells, losing his mind.

"Braydon, call 9-1-1," I cry out. I'm afraid to move. My ribs spasm with every breath, and I'm not sure if the knife is still jammed in my back. "Braydon, please, you have to call for help."

"No, I can't!" He begins pacing around me. "Fuck, why did you run! You said you weren't going to run!"

"Braydon, please. I'm hurt really bad." I start to cry. I can't assess how severe the cut is, but it hurts. I twist my head over my shoulder to assess my wound and see blood. "Braydon, if you don't get me to a hospital, I could die." This sends him into a complete panic.

"No, you'll be fine. I'll just call my dad. He'll fix everything. He always does."

The wound in my side throbs. "Unless your dad is a doctor, we need a hospital." *Oh my god, I'm going to die here.* I can't stop the dreadful sobs. I've tried to stay strong long enough.

"No, don't cry. It will all be okay, I promise."

"How!" I yell, regretting the force, wincing in pain. "You stabbed me. Don't let me die here."

He's suddenly on the floor, kneeling next to me. "You won't.

I'll fix this and we'll be together." He rips his phone from his pocket and dials a number. A deep voice sounds on the other end. "Dad? I fucked up…"

Levi

My lips are moving a mile a minute, trying to explain my theory. I doubt I'm even making sense. It takes Kip's rough grip to stop my tirade. "Man, you have to calm down. I don't understand what you're saying. Who's Clara? Why would she hurt my sister?"

Jim pulls up and jumps out of his car, rushing over to us. "Any news?"

Kipley shakes his head, his eyes creased. "No, we're still waiting on the police to arrive."

"Where's Hannah's phone? Give it to me."

"It's dead," I say, handing it over. Jim doesn't say another word and stalks back over to his vehicle to plug her phone into his charger.

The cop finally arrives. He takes his time climbing out of his car, and I explode. "What took you so fucking long?" I get in his face, but Kipley sticks his hand out and pulls me back. "Is this how fast you move with every missing person call?"

The officer doesn't appreciate my tone, taking a stiff stance in front of me. "Sir, I'm gonna need you to calm down—"

"Calm down? I'm not going to calm down! My girlfriend is missing."

The sun is hotter than usual for July. "Why does it have to be so hot?" I gripe, smoothing my frizzy hair down. I spent all morning trying to make it look nice because Kipley was having his friends over to swim in our pool. Too bad five seconds outside and it's back to resembling Einstein on his worst day. My feet skip from side to side, debating

on going over there. Mom bought me a new tinted Chapstick, and I want to show it off. It makes me look older, like the girls Kipley hangs out with. Ben tosses his shirt to the side and jumps in while Chase pushes my brother in. Laughter fills the backyard, and I can almost feel the burst of coolness on my skin as the water spreads and they disappear underneath.

The moment my eyes drift away from the water to him, an inferno of heat blasts through me. I feel like I'm on fire watching as his smile burns into my memory. His stance is casual and laid back as he lifts his shirt over his head, exposing his tan, muscular stomach. I swallow, my throat dry, as he tosses his shirt onto the lawn chair and takes an impressive dive into the pool.

I skip across the lawn, throwing my pink towel on the chair next to his shirt, and make myself comfortable. It's my pool too. Kip waves at me, and I wave back, ignoring the noises Chase makes at me. I adjust my chair and press my sunglasses up my nose, pretending to read a magazine. My young mind wanders, and I imagine I'm in the pool, laughing along with them. I can't reach the bottom, so Levi comes and scoops me up, carrying me in his arms as we float in the water. His laughter is meant for me, and his eyes stare into mine, silently telling me he knows we're soulmates and he can't wait to marry me one day.

"Hannah, you need sunblock. You're starting to burn." I don't realize I'd dozed off until Levi's large frame blocks the sun as he leans over me. "Here, give me your sunblock. I'll get your back." His willingness creates a tornado of butterflies in my belly. I hand him the bottle and turn to offer him my back.

"You're burning up," he says, his hands feeling like fire against my skin. "You're burning up, Hannah," he says again, and I groan under his tortured touch. His hands start to sizzle against my skin, and I howl out in pain.

"Jesus, there you are! You passed out on me for a minute."

It hurts.

Everything hurts.

The faint memory of that day at the pool evaporates into the back of my mind as reality settles in. Levi's hands disappear, Braydon's in their place. He presses his hand to the side of my ribs, and I scream out in pain.

"I know it hurts. My dad is on his way. I had to put a bandage on to help stop the bleeding, and you passed out on me. We can't have you dying. I won't let you."

My eyes fill with dread as tears pour over. My lower lip quivers with doubt. "Braydon, I need more than your dad. I need a hospital." The fact that I'm still alive gives me some hope that he didn't puncture anything major, but the severe dizziness confirms I'm losing a lot of blood. I can't gauge how much longer I can fight this. "Please, call 9-1—"

"No! I told you I can't do that." He becomes agitated, pressing too hard on my wound. I yelp, blinded by the pain. "Shit!" he eases up and falls back against the couch, sitting on the floor next to me. His hands rub over his face, smearing my blood down his cheek. "This is all *his* fault. I should have convinced you to leave with me sooner. Not allowed *him* to get in your head. Then you wouldn't be hurt. *He* wouldn't have hurt you."

He's still talking about Levi. "Levi didn't do this to me, Braydon, you did. If you want to make it up to me, help me. Call someone."

His head shakes back and forth furiously. "No. I told you. I can't. I've gotten this far, I won't ruin everything I've worked for. You'll be fine. Just…be patient." He kicks his legs out to stand. Pacing the room, my eyes catch something or someone lying between the living room and kitchen. My heart sinks at the familiar floral dress I saw Clara in some time earlier.

"Oh my god, Braydon. What have you done? Is…is…did you kill Clara?"

Braydon stalls, his back to me as he stares off at Clara's lifeless body. "You should have never come here, Hannah. Everything was set in place. She was handled. But you had to stick your nose in it and couldn't let it go. The case was closed. Dead in the water. You should have let it be!" The last of his words are hissed in a raised, angry tone.

He rears his leg back and thrusts forward, kicking Clara's body. I scream, the movement tearing at my wound. My stomach clenches. Before I can expel the sourness burning inside my stomach, I lose consciousness again.

Levi

I eat up the ground beneath my feet from pacing back and forth. We have zero leads. The cops don't know shit and are fucking useless. They just keep asking us the same damn questions, as if we took her. The douchebag cop who first arrived keeps threatening to arrest me if I don't calm down, so I've pulled myself away to try to do just that. I explained as best as possible my theory about the case and how it links with Hannah's disappearance. Since Crete is out of their jurisdiction, they put in a call to the local law enforcement department over there requesting a wellness visit for Clara Hill. That was over an hour ago. And still nothing.

I gaze over at Kip, who's beside himself with worry. The severity of this is starting to set in for us all. Jim has been on his phone calling in every favor he has, pleading with anyone who can offer him assistance in finding his little girl. It's impossible, even at a time like this not to admire his endless love for his daughter. The way he's always held her to such a high standard.

"And that's why, when I grow up, I'm going to become the first woman President of the United States of America." Mr. Matthews claps his hands, loud and proud, as Kip's little sister jumps off the coffee table. She walks past me, and I swear the little kid winks at me.

"Isn't she truly something?" Mr. Matthews says, watching his daughter bow in front of Kip, then skip off into the kitchen. Something is right. A little wild, if you ask me. "Only seven years old and already

destined for great things. She's already reading my old law school text-books. Cheryl gives me slack for letting her. Says she should be reading books written for her age range. Barbies and all, but she's an old soul this one. Already wants to debate law cases with me." His hand falls to his chest as he chuckles. "She's such a spirited child. I can't wait to see what she becomes. She's gonna make one man very happy one day."

I was fifteen at the time of that memory. Didn't put a second thought past his words letting me know his daughter was something special. Spending a lot of time with Jim growing up, I listened to him talk about Hannah often. How honored he was to be her dad. How her wanting to follow in his footsteps made him so proud. From awards, recognitions, Dean's list to scholar-ships—she hit all the marks. She was, as he always said, making a strong path for herself. It was in those small chats I would dig for any memory of Hannah, ones of her not trying to annoy us or make a scene. She was always scurried away by Kip or chased away by Chase. There was never a moment that crossed my mind that one day she truly would be magnificent. In all facets. As I stand, watching the worry in his eyes, I wonder what my young, fifteen-year-old self would say if he knew years later, it would be me pining over his magnificent daughter, hoping she chooses to make me a happy man.

He's listening to whoever is on the other line when I notice something distract him. He leans into his open vehicle and stands straight again, Hannah's phone in his hand. Her battery must have enough juice to turn back on. Curious as to what leads her phone will offer us, I trek closer. I'm two feet away when the color on Jim's face pales.

"What? What is it?"

Jim tears his searing gaze from her phone to meet mine. "My daugh—why does—someone sent her photos of Braydon and—he…he's standing in what seems to be a family photo with Benjamin Miller."

CHAPTER TWENTY-EIGHT

Hannah

"**W**hat the hell have you done?"

I'm jolted awake by yelling. My head is like a hundred-pound bowling ball as I try to lift my eyes toward the commotion. "I asked you to take care of this quietly. This is NOT quietly."

Braydon comes into view. "It was an accident—"

The man strikes his large hand across Braydon's cheek, snapping his head sideways. "An accident? An *accident?* There's a woman lying lifeless over there and this one's bleeding to death. I see no accident, son." The man's large frame adjusts until he's in my line of sight.

Confusion followed by recognition sets in. Disorientation washes over me at the disbelief. My voice shakes with incredulity as I say his name. "Benjamin Miller." It's not a question. It's a statement. Because I know that face. I never doubted if I ever came eye to eye with this man, his would shine like the Devil's. Evil comes in many forms, one being Benjamin Miller.

"Dad, she needs help. I need you to help her."

"Don't you dare touch me, you monster!" I spit out, using most of my energy.

Benjamin eyes me with contempt for a quick moment before he speaks. "Don't worry. I don't plan on it." He cocks his head back to his son. "Clean this up. Burn the house down for all I care.

Make it look like an accident. Two ladies catching up over tea when a glitch in the stove causes the house to blow up in flames."

Braydon's horrified expression mirrors mine. "What? No, Dad. I won't. Not with her in it. She's coming with me," he pleads with this father. "Please, just help her. I'll make sure this doesn't fall on us. Without that bitch over there, we're as good as free anyhow. I've done everything you've asked."

What has Braydon done?

The scary manic expression he holds in his gaze says it all. Levi's suspicions have been right all along. The person threatening Clara has been Braydon. His hands are just as dirty as his father's.

I'm going to be sick.

My stomach convulses, sending a throbbing spasm to spiral down my side. "You…" I choke out, "you're the one who messed with all the files."

Something inside him shuts down. Gone is the Braydon who cares, in its wake a blank stare. "I did what had to be done."

"Had to be done? Allowing people to die?"

He takes a menacing step toward me, his shoulders trembling in unexpected anger. "I protected my future. Miller Industries will one day be all mine, and your father and his company tried to take that away from me. So yes, I did what had to be done."

The missing files.

Changes in log-in information.

"It was you. You changed all the information in the system. Deleted the testimonies." How did he get away without anyone putting two and two together he was Benjamin Miller's son? "Why? For what? You haven't helped your future, you've killed it. A law school degree? You won't ever practice unless it's from a jail cell!"

Braydon starts to laugh, and his father joins in. "What law degree?"

My eyes pop wider, my head bobbing back and forth between father and son. "I don't understand?"

Braydon starts first, filling in the blanks. "No law degree, just a genius at hacking a system. It was simple. All I had to do was hack into Matthews and Associates server and create my profile. Make it appear like *Braydon Connor* went through the interviewing process and was set to start. No one even batted an eye on my first day."

"How were you able to complete your cases? You knew what you were talking about—"

Braydon, or whoever he is, shrugs with ease. "Before you came along, I'd been sleeping with Christine on my team. Seems all it takes to have someone else do your workload is a cheap dinner and sex." He realizes what he confesses and leaps at me, bending down on one knee, pressing his face within inches of mine. "But understand, this was before you came along. I was supposed to set you up. But I couldn't. You were just so perfect. So, I changed routes and set *him* up."

My foggy head can't comprehend the insanity he's feeding me. I can't grasp what he's confessing. Panic resonates deep in my chest, and I start to hyperventilate. My heart thumps like a steel drum, my pulse throbbing in my ears. I attempt to scream, but only end up choking on my own breath. Pain shoots from my side, and I howl in anguish. Whatever sort of bandage Braydon put there dislodges from my wound, and I feel the open air saturate the cut, blood dripping down my side.

I need to calm down or my own primal fear will kill me before this injury will. A few staggered breaths, and I turn my focus on Braydon. "Listen…" I cough. "Just let me go. Please. I know you don't want to hurt me—"

"You foolish girl. How do you think this ends? My son falling for your sweet, innocent girl act and you living to see tomorrow?" He throws his head back, a sadistic laugh barreling up his throat. "My son may be smart in some aspects, but when it comes to women, not so much. He has a tendency to let his weak little heart overrun his logic. As much as I find it cute, you're not going anywhere." He turns to his son. "Now, say your goodbyes and finish what you started. I'm too close to being done with this nonsense." Without another word, he walks to the kitchen, stepping over Clara as if she's nothing, and exits out the back door. I search for a reassuring sign in Braydon's eyes, but they suddenly seem void of emotion. As if something in him snaps, he turns a switch. He nods to himself, no longer acknowledging me, and starts to move around the house, knocking things over, searching for something.

"Braydon, wha—what are you doing?"

He doesn't bother answering me and walks through the kitchen, leaving out the same door as his father. The second I hear the backdoor slam against its hinges, it's fight or flight. If I don't try to move now, I'm as good as dead. My adrenaline kicks into overdrive, and I fight through the pain. Pushing my limp body off the ground, I jam my foot into the carpet and stand in a sprinting formation, only to lose my breath. I fall sideways into the couch, a guttural sound I don't recognize as my own vibrating my eardrums.

I can't do this. I can't do this. I'm going to die here.

Blackness surrounds me, and I'm close to passing out. *You're a fighter, Hannah. Push through it.* Time ticks in slow motion, and images of my family come into view. I swear I see Kipley in the distance, hear Levi begging me not to give up. I see my mother's face smiling at me, and my dad's proud smile giving me the fuel I need. Hope blooms inside me. With another rough intake of breath, I get myself on two feet, pushing through the pain. Each foot is like lead as I force my legs to move. Three feet, two feet, one—

Rough hands wrap around my neck, fingers lacing in my hair. Braydon's grip is vicious as he wrenches me back. My scream is wild with desperation as my body slams into the coffee table. The collision knocks the air out of my lungs. The stabbing in my side blinds me. I blink away the blackness, fearing I'm about to pass out. If I do, I'm dead.

"Braydon...you don't have to do this..." I cry. Warmth soaks my cheek, and I fear I'm bleeding from where my head hit the corner of the table. I'm scared. I don't want to die, but I'm drained of all hope this is going to end any other way. My tears of despair spill over and soak my face, the saltiness mixing with blood from my wounds. I want to urge myself to continue to fight, but my body is too broken. Braydon continues to walk around the living room. It's not until I smell the fumes, I realize what he's doing.

"No...no, no, no... please, God no!" My vocal chords burn as I begin to sob. The retched stench of gasoline fills the room. Braydon's holding a gas can, soaking the furniture.

He's going to set the house on fire.

I'm going to burn to death.

"Hannah, understand. I wouldn't choose this for you. But it's not going to work out. And if I can't have you, I'm certainly not going to let him." He tosses the gas can, followed by the cruel sound of a lighter flickering. "Plus, now you know too much."

CHAPTER TWENTY-NINE

Levi

It takes pointing out someone is a killer to get anyone to take us seriously. Officer Douchebag gets on his radio, calling into the station. I hear the muffled words of missing girl, possible murder, out of jurisdiction. Regardless of my fight to stay positive, my mind is at war, battling away the negative thoughts. She's been missing since last night. She's in the hands of a killer. She could already be dead.

This is my fault.

I should have done more to push my theories. Gone to Jim when I first had an inkling of uncertainty about Braydon. Or should I use his real name, Connor Miller—Benjamin Miller's son. A *criminal's* son, placed in Matthews and Associates to sabotage our case. Jim takes call after call from the office, HR, legal, searching for how this could have happened. How did Braydon—*Connor*—find a job inside the law firm?

It takes a simple Google search to learn he's no more than a high school dropout, still being cradled under his daddy's wing. The prodigal son notorious for doing his father's dirty work. Furthermore, an FBI agent shows up and informs us Miller Industries has been under investigation for years, way before the Crete incident. It's a shock his botched project even made it off the production floor before being shut down by the feds.

Anger simmers through my veins. This could have been

avoided. People didn't have to die if certain *people* had been doing their jobs. My mind takes another dark turn as Connor's comment from the bathroom the other night comes to par.

"Once you're out of the way, I'm taking your place. Get a taste of the sweet Hannah Matthews."

His comment is the match that sets fire to the gasoline that's been poured over my patience and emotions.

"Why the fuck hasn't anyone gotten to Clara Hill's house? It's been almost two fucking hours!" I snap at the closest officer near to me. A detective steps up to me, holding a pad of paper. He introduces himself as Detective Shaw. "It seems her phone is or has been disconnected. We're working on getting a local officer to make a wellness call, but it's not that easy when the town is small staffed. The only working officer out there right now is on a traffic call. Once he's done—"

"Fuck this." I give him my back and storm toward Kipley's Tahoe.

"Levi, where're you going?" Kip calls from behind me.

"I'm not waiting. I'm going to Clara's."

"Levi, wait—" He grabs for my shoulder, but I throw his hand off me, whipping around. I can no longer hide the horror in my eyes when I stare at my best friend, fearing the worst has happened to his little sister and it's all my fault.

"I can't wait. I need to do something. She came after me…I should have known she would. She would have never allowed me to leave the bar like that. And I *know* that! If I would have just waited, we could have talked it out. I could have at least taken her home. Sent her back—"

"Jesus man, stop!" Kipley wraps his hands around my shoulders and shakes me. "This is *not* your fault. This is that little psycho fucker's fault. And we don't even know that's what happened. Have faith, man."

I want to have faith. I want to bask in the idea that she's safe somewhere being the Hannah we all know, reckless and annoying.

That she'll pop out wherever, her hair in disarray, her face flushed with understanding that she's in trouble.

"Kip—"

"I get it. She's my sister. I love her too. Let's go. I'm driving." I stare at Kip for a quick second, then nod, slamming back on my heel as we both race to his car.

"Where you boys going?" Jim calls from a few feet away, pulling his phone from his ear.

"Clara Hill's. If they won't do something, we're going to," I say. Jim takes in my words. Strong with devotion. I hold his gaze long enough for him to understand. I would do anything for his daughter. He nods once, and I take that as his approval.

The forty-five-minute drive is quiet. There's nothing to say that will eliminate the miles between us and Hannah or make the drive go by faster. *God, please be there and be safe.* The silence only encourages my mind to stir up more memories.

"Hey, Levi?"

Hannah calls my name. I'm half asleep with her naked and snuggled up next to me. She rests on my chest while I play with her wild hair. "Yeah, babe?"

"When we were kids...well, when I was a kid I guess, since you were always an adult to me, did you ever...ever...notice me?"

Her body stiffens. I give her credit for her bold question. I'm sure she feels the gentle rumbling of my chest. "Never mind, stupid question. I was terribly—"

"Remember your junior year? You wanted to go to the dance so bad, but you weren't asked?" Her body deflates against mine. A deep breath fans over my chest. "Okay, not what I thought you would bring up. Don't remind me what a loser—"

"I was home visiting from law school and Kip and I had made plans to head down south to catch that NFL game. Tickets cost me a fortune. I had to get two credit cards to pay for them."

"But I thought you guys didn't end up going to the game. It was rained out or something?"

I pull my fingers through her hair, loving the way her chestnut locks fall against her bare back in waves. "It wasn't."

Hannah lifts her head, her eyes finding mine. "I don't understand..."

"I may not be a Matthews, but I always felt at home there. When I got back, I came straight to your house. It was my sanctuary too. I never said it, but I got homesick a lot when I was away at law school. I missed family poker night and your mom's meatloaf. Missed the chaos of your home and...well, other things." She keeps eye contact with me the whole time I babble, but there's that twinkle, wanting me to get to the point. "Anywho...when I walked down the hallway to surprise Kip, I passed your bedroom. The door was slightly open, and I heard you crying. I didn't want to impose, but it still didn't stop me from standing by your door longer than appropriate listening to you cry and wishing beyond anything I could make it better."

She grunts, her head falling back onto my chest. "God, how embarrassing. I think I cried so much, my eyes looked like two bee stings. And you and Kipley were forced to endure my presence all night and hang out with me since you guys didn't go to the game."

I lock my fingers back into her hair, brushing it away and teasing the lining of her neck. "Our team won twenty-seven to seven that night."

That grabs her attention. Her head arches up at me. "What do you...I thought..."

"Kipley told me why you were so upset. You deserved to go to that dance as much as any girl in your school. And for some reason, seeing you so upset did something to me. I hated it. I almost went and beat up every single loser in your school for not thinking to ask you."

"What are you saying? You guys didn't go to the game 'cause I was upset?"

"I wanted to go to that game. God, did I. But not as much as I wanted to replace those tears with laughter." I love the way her eyes shine, wide like an owl. It makes me chuckle.

"Why are you telling me this now?"

"*Because you asked if I ever noticed you when we were younger. And the answer is, in some strange way, I guess I did. It's funny how we view things at certain ages and when we get older, those views start to change. Shift in a way. I can't say I saw you the way I see you now, but I saw you. I saw how resilient you were. Tough skin, soft heart. Maybe I should've noticed the shit everyone put you through more. But what I saw from afar was a girl in an iron suit, without fear, ready to take on the world. You let everything roll off you and went on your way. I saw you as a girl who purposely took the hard road because you wanted to prove to everyone you could do it. Which you did. I mean, you did claim your spot as the first lady president at age seven.*"

Her body shakes with laughter. She tries to be smooth about it, but I see her swipe away a stray tear. She's on the move, her body straddling mine, and I love every bit of it. Of her. "Thank you," is all she says, leaning forward and pressing her warm lips to mine. "Thank you for noticing me."

She doesn't say anything more. She's fighting not to show the emotion brewing inside her. I change the subject, giving her the pass she desperately wants. "How about we order that pizza I promised you before I confess too much and give you too big of an ego?"

She slaps my chest, but grants me the ultimate reward: more of her sweet mouth.

My heart constricts, wanting her to be here now so I can confess every single time I've noticed her. Wanted her. The moment I began to love her. Why didn't I tell her then? I knew I was in love with her. And now...what if she'll never know?

I bury my thoughts and stare out the window, noticing the signs for Crete. Damn, how long was I in my head?

"We're here. It says Clara's house is down this road."

I sit up straighter, ready to fly out of the car as soon as her house comes into view. My heart starts to beat in loud thumps with each second that passes. Kipley pulls into the driveway of a rundown ranch, and we both rip at our seatbelts and bolt out of the car.

My feet pound against the gravel as I run up to the house. My hand forms into a fist, and I pound with force on the front door. I lean to the side to peer through the open blinds and choke on my own breath. A real-life nightmare plays out in front of my eyes, the hairs on my neck bristling in horror.

My eyes crash into Braydon's as he stands there holding a lit lighter. Seconds feel like years before he finally breaks contact and tosses the lighter in the air, making contact with the drapes. A burst of flames explode up the wall.

Something inside me breaks, and a thunderous rumble expels up my throat as I throw my body into the door. I ignore the punishing snap in my shoulder as I rear back and throw myself into the locked door again, the wood splintering. Kipley takes quick notice of the smoke and rushes to help me and we both plow though, snapping it off its hinges.

Braydon flinches at our intrusion, then sticks his heel into the carpet and takes off toward the back of the house. "Levi, wait!" Kip calls out for me, but I ignore him, along with the smell of burning wood and smoke. I sprint after Braydon, my adrenaline taking over. He makes it into the kitchen, stumbling over something, giving me the chance to reach him. I leap at him, wrapping my hand around his ankle as we both plummet to the kitchen floor. I grunt in pain, feeling another jolt to my shoulder, but push it away.

"Get off me—"

I climb up his body, my knee crushing him in the stomach as I rear my hand back and pummel my fist into his face. "You motherfucker! Where the fuck is she!" Again, I smash my fist into his face. "Where the fuck is she!" I howl, losing my mind. The crackle of burning wood echoes around us. Black smoke billows across the kitchen, filling my lungs. I cough, rear my clenched hand back, and slam into his face again. "Where's Hannah, you asshole?"

An explosion sounds around us, and I duck, the light fixture falling from the ceiling. I struggle to focus, my eyes starting to burn.

"Oh my god. LEVI!" Kipley yells. The anguish etched in his voice causes my next swing to pause midair. "LEVI!!! Fuck, fuck, fuck, HANNAH!"

A sickening feeling washes over me, and I stare down at him, terrified of what I see. "What the fuck have you done?" The words feel surreal leaving my mouth. The flames become brighter, roaring around us, the heat of the beast threatening to burn my clothes to my skin.

Braydon doesn't answer me. When his lips curl into a sickening smile, I wrap my hands around his neck and squeeze, slamming his head against the old laminate floor. "What have you done!" I scream, the smoke burning my throat.

His eyes are as dark as the smoke. "I made sure you can't have her either."

My heart stops. My conscious submerges in fear. I'm frozen, staring down at him, needing him to take those words back.

Two hands grab at my shoulders and thrust me back. "We have to get out of here. The house is seconds away from collapsing."

"Not before he tells me where Hannah—"

"She's here. I found her," he chokes out, his voice dripping with grief. My heart sinks to the bottom of my soul as Braydon becomes an afterthought. I release him, climbing to my feet, needing to get to Hannah.

"Fuck," Kip howls, trying to fight through the maze of flames. Orange and red engulf the entire floor, and I struggle to see in front of me. Another loud crack, and Kip dives to the side to avoid being singed to death by falling debris.

"You okay?" I call out, coughing with each tattered breath I take. A large enflamed beam separates us, the magnitude of the heat and smoke forcing me to cover my eyes, as I cough.

"I can't get to her! You have to get to her!" he cries out, pointing to the left. I follow his finger, searching to the location where he's pointing. The smoke is so thick, I can't—

"No..."

Paralyzing fear strikes me, almost taking me to my knees. Laying lifeless on the floor, mere inches from the burning couch, is Hannah. My muscles cramp. I can't move, consumed by the fear of her... not being alive. Kip's booming voice breaks me from my stupor. I throw myself through the blaze, falling at her still body. There's no disguising my panic when I see blood. Without worry I may be hurting her, I lift her in my arms, and rear back around. There's no clear way to the door, but if I don't make a run for it, we both die. "Hold on, baby. I'm getting you out of here." I tuck her limp body to my chest and run. I can barely see through the thick smoke as Kip throws himself through the door, making it outside. A fiery ball of fire explodes behind me, igniting a blast of sparks to shoot at my back. My teeth grind, ignoring the searing pain. A series of hissing gushes around me. I hurl myself through the flame coated doorway, and another blast of heat hits me as I dive toward the lawn. My body cradles Hannah as I hit the ground. Sirens break through the hissing sound. The front window explodes, and we take cover, Kipley hovering over us as another barrier for his sister.

Time speeds up, and Kipley rips his sister from my arms. "Hannah..." He lays her on the ground, calling her name, but she doesn't respond. "Hannah, please wake up. Fuck, she's bleeding. Where is she bleeding from?" Kipley is on the verge of breaking. His hands are frantic, searching her body for wounds. "Hannah, please! Hannah!" His voice cracks, splintering my heart in two. *She can't be.* I refuse to pull my eyes away from her, waiting for any flicker, twitch, any kind of sign.

Sirens become louder, signaling they're close. The lights of a firetruck bounce off the roaring flames of Clara Hill's home. I lean forward and press my ear against her mouth to see if she's breathing.

"Here. She's bleeding here," Kip cries. I watch in horror as he pulls her torn, bloody shirt up to reveal a nasty slash in her side. "Jesus, no." He shakes his head uncontrollably, "Hannah, wake up! Hannah!"

I rip my charred shirt off, pressing it against her open wound. She groans.

"She's alive. Oh, thank God!" I hold my hand to her side while Kip crawls up, putting his face close to hers. "Hannah, can you hear me?" She doesn't respond. *Come on, give us something.* "Hannah, we're here. Help is here, you're going to be okay." Kipley's voice is shaking, evident doubt in his tone. Without the glare from the flames, her skin is pale. I grip her hand in mine, so she knows I'm here. Her skin is clammy.

Her lips open just a sliver, and she releases another groan. "Hey, don't try to talk. We're here." Kip tries to comfort her, while her eyes work to open. God, I want to see those beautiful almond eyes.

I squeeze her hand and lean forward, pressing my lips close to her ear. "Fight, Hannah. Fight for me." I need her to make it through this. It's faint, but it's there. She squeezes my hand back, her lips fighting to talk. "Cl—Cl—" She coughs, unable to finish.

We're suddenly surrounded, two men in medical jumpsuits kneeling next to us. "I'm going to need you to move aside so we can work on her." They wait, but neither of us move. "Sir, she needs medical help—"

Hannah's body starts to seize. Gargling sounds erupt up her throat, and her eyes flicker. "Oh my god, what's happening!"

"She's going into cardiac arrest—move!"

CHAPTER THIRTY

Levi

Beep. Beep. Beep.

The sounds of helplessness while a machine works to help the person I love to breathe. *Stab wound to her side. Severe blood loss. Smoke inhalation to her lungs. Concussion.*

Swoosh. Swoosh. Swoosh.

The sounds of powerlessness as her air ventilator goes up and down. All I want to do is fix her, but I can't.

Her heart stopped twice. *Twice.* I didn't know this until someone came to my own hospital room to inform me.

Beep. Beep. Beep.

I tear my swollen eyes away from her to watch the monitor, her heart rate slowing. I hold my breath until it picks back up and levels out. The alarm has gone off twice now, sending nurses and doctors in a panic. *Twice.* This is the first time I've been alone with her since they brought her in three days ago.

The first two I spent in my own hospital bed being treated for severe burns to my back and smoke inhalation. When I was finally able to walk, it took half the floor nurses to hold me down before they gave up and allowed me to walk down to Hannah's room, with no shame my ass was hanging out of the small-as-shit gown the entire time.

We're now on day three of waiting for her to wake up. I've graduated into a pair of scrubs instead of the lousy gown, and they brought in a more comfortable chair for me since I refuse to leave her side. Morning turns to afternoon by the time Stacey finally convinces Kip to go back to his own room, since he was also admitted for smoke inhalation, and take a shower, and Jim finally convinces Cheryl to get something to eat in the cafeteria.

Cheryl fainted twice while begging her daughter to come to. *Twice*. She couldn't bear to see her little girl with tubes down her throat, so beaten and pale. This was not the Hannah we all knew and loved.

"Jesus," I choke out, covering my face with my hands. No matter how many times I wash them, I still see her blood. I want to stay strong for her, for when she wakes up, but every time I tell myself to pull it together, I crumble into more pieces than before. My chest heaves up and down as my torment eats away at me. "I'm so sorry," I cry, needing to confess so much to her. "I'm sorry for being such a coward and not believing you. Not trusting you. For not telling you I love you. I need you to wake up so I can tell you that. Please come back to me." I feel trapped in my own nightmare, a life that may not involve her. She may not wake up. A pain ignites inside my chest, and a sob escapes my throat. A knock on the door has me sucking in my breath and wiping at my face. "Yeah?" I cock my head to see Detective Shaw standing in the doorway. "What do you want?" I snap, turning back to Hannah.

He doesn't ask to be invited in before entering the room and standing on the other side of her. "Surprised to see you out of bed. Read your hospital chart—"

"I said, what do you want?"

He nods, getting to the point of his visit. "I thought you should know forensics came back. The body was indeed Clara Hill."

I shake my head, the pit in my stomach weighing heavily at what I already concluded. Hannah's strangled words when she was lying there. She was trying to tell us Clara was still in the house. "Do you know if she was…"

"Still alive? Unfortunately, we can't answer that. Unless Miss Matthews can give us more details, we won't ever know."

"And her son?" I ask, guilt washing over me. Her poor son.

"He was notified a couple hours ago. The facility is doing their best to keep him calm. Now that we know, we can proceed with future action—"

I shove my chair out from under me, and it skids halfway across the room. "You can *proceed* now? Why didn't you *proceed* when you first got wind of Miller Industries? Huh?" I stop, my lungs straining, and I cough. "Pointless lives lost because you didn't do your job! And where is Benjamin Miller now? His son? Have you found his son?"

There's no hiding the slip in composure, guilt riding in his tone. "I understand you're upset—"

"I'm more than goddamn upset! I'm fucking furious! I'm a wreck! My girlfriend is lying in a hospital bed fighting for her life and I feel useless to her." I cover my mouth, another round of barking coughs.

"And I'm sorry it's come to this. Sometimes cases aren't followed through as they should be. I won't make an excuse for why Benjamin Miller has gotten away with what he did, but I will promise to make sure he doesn't ever again and goes away for a long time."

My heart pounds. In and out, like an emotional volcano is about to erupt in my chest. "And Connor?"

Goddammit.

"I'm sorry. Still nothing. We have our best men out searching for him. His picture is splattered all over the news and he's on a no-fly list. He can't get too far—"

"Hey, Poindexter, why don't you beat it? Go do your job or something, yeah?" We both turn to see Chase walking in holding two coffees. Shock, yet relief washes over me at a familiar face. Detective Shaw nods and heads to the door. "I'll keep you posted," he says before walking out.

"Hey, you didn't have to come all—"

"And support two of my closest friends? Not a chance. I'm here for you, man." He pats me on the back, and I wince. "Oh shit, sorry." He hands me a coffee, and I readjust, sitting as close to Hannah's bed as possible in hopes she can sense me by her. Chase follows suit, taking up the extra seat on her other side. "How's she doin'?" he asks. Lost is his sarcastic tone, in its place genuine concern.

"Better, but not as good as the doctors had hoped. They expected her to wake up by now, but you know, trauma can cause people to stay under until they're mentally healed and able to come back to us," I say, the same words I continue to repeat and repeat and repeat. She's healing. She'll come back to us when she's ready.

Silence takes over for some time before the beeping sound becomes too much and Chase breaks the quiet. "You okay, man?"

I take some time to digest that question. When I lift my eyes to meet his, my answer is honest. "No. I'm not."

Fear is like a disease. It shows no mercy and spreads like a wildfire to the mind, body, heart. It creates a dark mass, eradicating any hope to flee from this nightmare. Weariness crashes into me like a tidal wave, and my shoulders slump.

"So, little Hannah Matthews, huh?" The question breaks my thoughts. He's trying to change the subject. Find an open window to lighten the mood. A crest of a smile breaches my face thinking about all the happiness she's brought into my life. "Yeah, dick. And she's not little anymore."

"Yeah, got that at Kip's wedding. Are her boobs real, because she sure filled out that—*ouch!*" he yelps when I toss a cup at him. "I'm kidding. I just wanted to make you smile. Shit, you look like hell. Should you even be out of bed?" I'm fine. I'm right where I need to be. With her. "Dude, when she wakes up, she's going to be greatly disappointed. Have you showered? Eaten? If I was a chick, I'd definitely be a little pissed to wake up to the sore eyes of you."

I stare at him, realizing he's right. I haven't done any of the above. I've convinced everyone else to eat, shower, take some time, but I refuse to take my own advice. Because if she wakes up and I'm not here...

"I mean, I find you quite attractive in those hospital scrubs, but for real, go find a water fountain and bathe in it or some shit. Even better, have your special nurse give you a sponge bath. I'll sit here with her."

"And if she wakes up and sees you? I believe she'd rather see my piece of shit self." We both laugh, and Chase shrugs, agreeing.

"Either way, take care of yourself. Walk down the hallway and back. Move your legs. You're not helping her by not taking care of yourself. She's gonna need you when—and I do say *when*—she wakes up."

I can't fight the tears at his words. I'm sure I look like a pussy, but I can't stop them. "Thanks, brother."

"None needed. Like you said. Brothers." I get up, not saying anything else, and he gives me a reassuring nod. I face the door, urging my feet to walk out of the room. I'm two steps out when I almost turn around, but Chase is right. I need to be strong for Hannah when she wakes up.

I allow my legs to drift down the quiet hallway. The lights are dimmed low, so it must be night. I've lost track of time since I've been here. My head is so jumbled, I beg my psyche to dislodge from the negative thoughts. Trying to search deep within my memory for something positive, a strange memory tucked away deep in my mind, becomes visible, as if it were just yesterday.

We stumble in the house, no doubt reeking like booze. "Dude, hurry while my mom's distracted." Kip sprints down the hallway into his room, but the raised voices have me slowing, then stopping. I bust out laughing at the argument, almost getting us caught. We're well over an hour late and smell like two kids who haven't been at the movies all night.

"Dude, let's go!" Kip grabs at my shirt and drags me back into his

room. "*Shit, that was close. Good thing Pops is out of town. You think Stacey's really gonna call me?*"

"*Huh?*" I ask, leaning against his doorframe as Hannah stomps down the hallway. I take it she didn't win that argument.

"*Stacey, do you think she'll really call? I don't know, man. I really dig her.*"

I cross my arms over my chest as Hannah lifts her head, still mumbling to herself, grabbing her attention. Her face lights up like it's the fourth of July and she smiles. "*Hey, Levi.*"

"*Hannah,*" I return.

"*Watcha guys doing? Can I hang?*"

I chuckle at her wanna-be-an-old-kid lingo. I swear she eavesdrops on Kip's phone calls and takes notes. I heard her tell her dad to slow his roll the other day.

"*I don't think that's a good idea, Hannah. Shouldn't you be getting ready for bed? It's kinda late for you.*"

Her smile fades, along with the sparkle in her eyes. They still shine, but shit, for a whole other reason. Her hands fly to her hips, her chin stiff and lifting to the sky. "*For your information, Levi, I'm almost a woman.*"

That gets a snort out of me. "*Aren't you, like, eight?*"

If she sticks her chin up any higher, she's going to fall backwards. "*Yes, I am. Thanks for noticing. And soon, I will go through the proper channels of becoming a woman, which means I am perfectly capable of staying up late.*"

This kid. I shake my head, my crooked smile partially Boons Farm related. "*Oh yeah? Proper channels? What exactly is that? You mean like puberty?*"

Her cheeks explode in crimson. "*No, when I become a woman. When a woman grows breasts, they become women.*"

I can't help it. I bellow out in laughter. "*Well, how about this, when you grow breasts, ask me again, and I'll say yes.*"

Kip jumps off his bed, sticking his head out, wondering who I'm talking to. "*Oh, hey, Han. If Mom asks, we've been home for an hour, cool?*" he says, then shuts the bedroom door on her.

"Jesus, I thought you'd *never* leave that room."

The hair on my skin stands on end, pulling me out of my memory. I slow my step and pause. With caution, I pivot to face him. "How'd you get in here?" He looks like shit. He's dressed in a pair of scrubs, the tag hanging from his waistline stolen or fake. His face has seen better days. There's no doubt from his two black eyes I broke his nose.

He coughs violently into his hand. "As easy as I got into your company and became a stellar first year lawyer."

Fury overwhelms me. He shouldn't be here. He should be in a jail cell—or even better, dead. I take a menacing step toward him, my hands beginning to tremble with rage. "You're fucking dead."

His malevolent laugh will forever haunt me. "I don't think so. You'd think after everything, you'd figure out I'm the one who laughs last. Unlike you, who won't be walking away from this."

I take another step when he waves his hand around and I see the object he's holding. "You think you're going to *shoot* me in a hospital and walk away? You're a lot dumber than I thought."

I stare him in the eye, waiting for his next move. He's casual in his stance, uncaring we're in an open hallway and anyone could walk out and catch him. "Tsk, tsk, lover-boy. Are those going to be your last words? You know, I thought you were an okay guy at first. But then you had to get in my way. I always planned on destroying your life somehow. It actually became a little game for me. But then Hannah had to put a wrench in my plans. Definitely didn't see her coming. Tell me, since you stole the chance from me, how did it feel to have her naked and open wide while you fucked her?"

"You son of a—"

"I'm not done! Answer me. How was it? Fucking such an angel. Did she scream your name? Moan like a wild whore?" I take another step, and his arm straightens out, pointing the gun directly at my chest. "She deserved better than that. Treating her like trash, fucking her in your *office*? You didn't deserve her. *I* did.

She was mine!" His hand shakes, and I jerk to the side, tugging at my bandages in fear of the gun going off and shooting me.

I witnessed him starting to unfold the night in the bathroom, but seeing him now…he's completely unhinged. There's no doubt he would shoot me and then attempt to hurt Hannah all over again. I need to distract him so I can get close enough to take him down. Even if he shoots me, I'll be able to tackle him, which will alert someone. He won't get near her ever again.

I throw my head back and laugh. I search for all my energy and bellow out a deep howl. When my eyes return to his, he stares back in confusion. "You really think she—" I laugh harder. "Wow, that's good. You actually think Hannah would ever be with you after figuring out what a fucking psycho you are?" I slap my knee, fighting the tinge of pain from my burns. "You're a joke, man. And yeah…she screamed *real* loud for me. The feeling of her lips locked around my cock, like a sweet angel…damn, it felt like heaven." I pause and watch as the seed I plant in his mind sets fire, the inferno of fury blazing in his eyes. His arm stiffens, and his finger tightens around the trigger.

"Shut up."

"Why?" I taunt. "I thought you wanted to know. Man, did we get a good laugh about you. How stupid you were to think she would ever like you. How embarrassing for you, right?"

"Shut the fuck up! You don't know what you're talking about. She told me. She told me we could be together, but my dad put a stop to it. If it wasn't for him, we'd be together."

I take a step closer, my humorous mask falling, revealing my true anger. My hands shake with fury knowing he's the reason Hannah's fighting for her life in that bed. "Really? If it wasn't for your *dad*, she wouldn't be lying in a hospital bed fighting for her fucking life."

"It was an accident. You—you did this!" he yells, and I only hope his loud voice alerts a nurse close by. "She shouldn't have tried to run. She promised me she wasn't going to run!" He squeezes his eyes shut, and my impulse kicks in as I dive for the gun. His eyes reopen just as I lunge at him and take him down. His legs kick out, and he falls backwards. My fist rears back and thrusts into his face, busting open my scabbed knuckles and reopening the slice on his lip from my previous hit.

Unlike the other times, he fights back. His knee surges forward, crushing into my balls, and I grunt, jerking just enough for him to flip me and crawl away. Before I can recover, his foot jams into my back, splitting open my fresh wounds. I growl out, white dots shooting through my vision. "Fuck!" I blink away the tears caused from the pain and reach for his ankle, pulling him toward me. He trips, a loud crack as his chin smacks against the hard tile echoing down the hall. He becomes limp, and I use the opportunity to take a breather, making the mistake of allowing my aching body a second to rest. That's when he surges forward, clenching his fingers around his gun. He points it directly at me. "You should have let me just shoot you in the chest. At least she would have been able to say goodbye. Now I'm going to shoot you in the face and love every second of watching that pretty smile splatter around this bullet." I stare at his hand, watching his finger press down on the trigger. I wait for the bullet, when someone surges out of nowhere and tackles Braydon. The gun goes off, the bullet whizzing so close to my face, it snips my earlobe, knocking me over before lodging into the wall behind me.

I lift my head to see Chase on top of Braydon, who's knocked out by the attack. "Fuck, that was awesome. I knew I should have joined football. I would have whooped your ass, Dent."

Jesus Christ, how is he making jokes at a time like this? When it all hits me that I almost just died, I can't do anything but join in and laugh. I laugh so hard, tears start falling down my cheeks and I have to hold my chest in fear of damaging more skin on my back.

"Man…this guy has issues," Chase pants, climbing off him,

then taking his foot and slamming into his ribs to make sure he's truly down. "Now, if you're done cock fighting over the girl, I came out to tell you she's awake."

She's awake.

Hannah's awake.

I urge my legs to stand, still grabbing at my ear as it gushes blood.

"Shit, you may want to do something about that before—"

I don't hear anything else. As I stand, a mixture of pain and dizziness take me out by my knees, and I pass out.

CHAPTER THIRTY-ONE

Hannah

My throat burns. My vision is blurred, and I can't focus on my surroundings. I hear sounds, but they're unfamiliar. I work harder to blink away the confusion, a bright light peeking through the fog.

"Oh shit. Go figure you'd wake up and have to see me first. Be right back." The shadow in my vision disappears. My heart beats fast, and a buzzing starts to rattle in my brain. Where am I? Panic sets in, and I raise my hands, grabbing at the intrusion in my mouth.

Another shadow blocks my light. "Relax, Hannah. I'm Doctor Wilson. You have a tube in to help you breathe." A tube? Why do I have a tube in to breathe? Beeping sounds pulsate my eardrums, and I fight once more to remove the barrier. "Shhh…all right. Relax, and we can get it out."

I continue to blink as colors and shapes become more prominent. A man in a white lab coat stands over me. "Wh—?"

I attempt to speak, but can't. Tears burn my eyes in frustration. Where am I?

"Hannah, do you know where you are?" I shake my head furiously, wincing at the pain coming from my head and side. "Take it easy. You're in Crete General Hospital. You were involved in an accident." *Accident?* Oh my god. Is everyone okay? I'm still fighting through the heavy slumber, trying to search for recollection.

Everything is slow moving. I become agitated at the detachment of my memory. "It's understandable. In situations of major trauma, the mind tends to protect the psyche."

Trauma? My mind carousels in circles, but I can't seem to grasp anything. Does anyone know I'm here? A loud boom in the distance has the doctor unnerved. He leaves my bedside to see what the commotion is about. When he returns, his face is drained of color. He shuts the door, hitting a button. Lights begin to flare. A warning light? Emergency light? I stare back at him, silently begging him to tell me what's happening.

"Everything is going to be fine. No one will get into this room, okay?"

My monitors are going berserk. He rushes over to check my stats and presses a few buttons, thankfully getting them to stop. "I hate to do this, but I can't have you in distress." He takes a needle to my IV bag and injects something. My eyes widen in despair, once again staring at him for answers, but before I can hear his response, I fall into the abyss of blackness.

"And did she say anything? Does she remember anything?" My eyes begin to flicker at the sound of my mom's voice. I hope it's not a dream. I miss my mom. I can't remember the last time I saw her.

"And how was he allowed access to this floor? We were told there was surveillance." *Dad!* His voice sounds angry. Am I in trouble?

"No one knows at this point. Just that he was able to get on the floor with an employee keycard. The officer couldn't give me much detail, but from what I gather, he came in through the employee cafeteria dressed in nurse scrubs. No one suspected a thing."

I want to know who they're talking about. I blink rapidly, opening and closing my eyes, allowing the streaks of bright light to penetrate my sensitive sight. "Mom?" I croak, my voice hoarse.

My mother's eyes whip to mine, a gasp leaving her sullen lips. She comes to my side, her warm hands embracing mine. "Oh, baby, you're awake." Tears rush down her face as she spreads motherly kisses over my cheeks and forehead. When she pulls back, my dad takes her place. "Hey there, kiddo. Welcome back."

"Dad," I cry, my emotions getting the best of me. Swallowing hard, I try to work my vocal chords. "Why am I here?"

My mother's sudden cry has my eyes wide, needing my dad to tell me.

"Kiddo, do you remember anything?"

My heart starts up again, racing in a frantic search for answers. "No, please. Tell me. You're all scaring me."

Dad grabs my hand and sits next to me. "Honey. You were taken…" He stalls, swallowing hard. "Braydon Connor kidnapped you."

My eyes open to their fullest. Dad's mouth remains in a grim line as he goes on. "He…held you captive at Clara Hill's home. We're unsure what happened, but you were injured. You have a stab wound in your side—thirty-seven stitches—a pretty bad gash in your head, and a concussion. You suffered some smoke damage from the fire—"

"What? Fire—what fire?"

Mom starts to sob quietly in the corner. "Hannah…Braydon set the house on fire. With you and Clara in it."

Clara.

Flowered dress.

Lifeless.

Clara.

Just as easily as I forgot, all too soon the scenery before me changes. I'm back in Clara Hill's house. The pain. The smoke. Braydon. "Braydon." His name falls off my tongue, wrapping around my neck as if the word alone is suffocating me. I clutch at my chest, struggling to breathe, the panic inside me closing off my airways.

"Baby, calm down. It's all over. He can't hurt you now. You're safe."

But he can. And he is. I begin reliving my own nightmare, feeling the knife stab through my flesh all over again. The fear. The fire. Clara. "He...he killed Clara," I cry out, grabbing for my neck. The images wrap around me like a noose, and I fight to inhale.

"Hannah, calm down." He turns to the doctor. "Do something dammit! She's having a panic attack!"

The doctor leans over to my IV, inserting a needle inside the tube. I watch as my father stares at me in torment before my eyes fall shut.

"How long has she been out?"

"Almost three hours. You really should be resting. The doctor said he doesn't want you up and straining your lungs."

"I'm not leaving her side, Mom."

Mom and Kipley.

I miss Kipley. I hope I didn't miss the baby being born. Fighting once again, I force my eyelids past the brightness of the light and find my brother.

"Kipley." I can't find my own voice. It's so hoarse, and my throat burns when I speak.

"Hey, there she is." He leans down, placing a kiss on my forehead. "Glad to see you're awake."

He reaches for my hand, and I squeeze back. "The baby?"

"The baby's good. Stacey's having pregnancy munchies, so she ran down to the cafeteria."

What day is it? How long have I been here?

"You haven't had the baby yet?" I ask. Why does he seem confused? Did something happen to the baby? His eyes search out my mom's for guidance before claiming back my attention.

"No, Han. We still have a ways to go. Do you know what day it is?"

"Kipley!" My mom smacks him, as if his question is inappropriate.

I try to search for any memory of what day it should be. "I... um...I'm not really sure. It was a Monday when I went to see Clara. But I can't recall after I went to Jake's—I went to Jake's and you guys fought—oh my god, you and Levi fought—"

Bits of memory slice through my brain, and I begin to cry. "I'm sorry. I'm so sorry," I repeat, a hurricane of emotions drowning me. Violent waves of tears blind me as I gasp for air with each retched sob.

Kipley is in the bed with me, his arms cradling me. His own tears mix with mine as he silently weeps alongside me. "Oh, Hannah, you have nothing to be sorry for. I owe you the apology. Please, please stop crying." My sobs settle into desolate whimpers, and I allow my brother to comfort me until the energy takes its toll and I fall asleep in his arms.

I'm walking around a house. It's unfamiliar to me. I search for anything that will help me understand why I'm here. My feet paddle along the worn carpet, and I look down to see I'm wearing a floral dress. *Why is this dress so familiar?* A sinking feeling takes root in my belly, and I turn the corner, only to find myself back in the same room. Disoriented, I turn around to find my way out, but no matter which way I take, I end up back in the same room. Unease begins to crawl up my spine and I work harder to find a way out, only to end up in the same place as I started.

"Where am I? Somebody help me!" I call out, my voice echoing off the walls. Confusion takes flight in my mind. I begin spinning, trying to find a new way out. Faster and faster, I spin, with no way to stop. "Somebody help me!" I call out again. Two hands grab me, halting me in place. The face of a monster appears in my vision, and I hear the flicker of a lighter. "If I can't have you, nobody can."

I wake up screaming just as he sets me on fire.

CHAPTER THIRTY-TWO

Levi

"Take the pain meds, idiot."

I swat at the nurse standing next to Kipley. "No. How long have I been out?"

He shakes his head in frustration. "I don't know, a little over twenty-four hours."

Fuck. I need to get to her. Be with her. "Hannah…"

"She's okay. She's been in and out."

I'm lying on my stomach due to the brand-new patchwork on my back. "Help me up. I need to go see her—"

"You *need* to take the goddamn pain meds and rest. You re-opened half the scab wounds on your back. That shit has to hurt. Not to mention the damn chunk missing from your ear." It does. Like a bitch. But nothing hurts as much as the unknown with her. If he won't help me, I'll get to her on my own. "Oh hell. Stubborn jock." As I twist around to a sitting position, he grabs at my hand and helps as I slide my legs off the bed. My back is as stiff as a board, the bandages making it difficult to bend in any which way but straight. With every groan, Kipley threatens to put me back in bed, and I threaten to kick his ass if he even tries.

When I'm finally standing, I need a minute to catch my breath. "You sure this is a good idea? You look like shit."

My hands reach out, using his shoulders for support. "I need to see her. I need to see for myself she's okay." He stares at me with understanding and nods. He guides me to the door before stopping and facing me.

"You should know…she didn't remember anything at first. It took her some time, and she took it hard. She's been in and out, mainly due to the doc putting her back under. She's lost it a few times and it's been pretty fucking scary." His confession pierces my heart, splitting open all my fears and searing all my hopes. My biggest hope is she's a fighter. My worst fear is this will break her spirit. The unstoppable, ironclad Hannah Matthews who doesn't let anyone get through her armor. "Hey…it's going to be okay. She'll get through this."

I want to collapse and lose myself in the darkness of my own thoughts. What if she can't look at me after this? I heard some of the report. The tirade *Connor* went on about me taking her from him. I did this. He repeated it over and over once he came to. What if she believes that and there's no longer room in her heart to forgive me? What if she only sees the horror of her journey when she sees me? "I need to fucking see her, man," I beg my best friend. The only one who would understand.

Nothing else is spoken between us as he helps me down the hallway, past the seven rooms that separate us. We reach her room, and he gives me a moment to catch my breath and gather myself.

My heart beats heavily, and the fear of rejection threatens to take me to my knees. I inhale a deep breath and allow Kip to knock on her door. No one says anything, and I'm thankful when her parents excuse themselves, claiming a strong need for coffee. Kip settles me in the chair by her bedside and tells me he's going to find Stacey to give me a moment.

It's not until everyone leaves that I bring my eyes to her. She's asleep. Her hair is matted by the thin bandage around her head. A small chuckle leaves my lips imagining her making some snarky comment about the bandage being made of steel to keep her wild hair in place.

Once the laugher subsides, the tears come. I fight to stay strong, but I can't. Seeing her lay here, so broken, and being unable to help her kills me. I sit by her side and grab her hand, spreading kisses across her fragile skin. I inhale a breath for strength and start babbling.

"It was the year Kip and I graduated from college. Your parents threw us a huge graduation party. You showed up in this insanely obnoxious, sparkly dress. Chase kept fucking with you until you ended up changing into a skirt and tank top. For a slip of a second, I thought you looked stunning in it."

I take a deep breath and continue. "You asked me if I ever noticed you. Your eighteenth birthday family dinner. Your mom made you your favorite cake, which was still *The Little Mermaid* with vanilla cake and strawberry filling. You had been so embarrassed, and I heard you argue with your mom that it made you look childish. Later that night, I busted you on your computer Googling when boobs developed because you had yet to blossom. The blush in your cheeks was so fucking adorable. I noticed you."

My eyes drift up to her face. "Kip's wedding, I told myself I didn't notice you. But I did. I studied the curve of your neck and the shape of your heart-shaped lips. Fuck, I shocked my own damn self. To be honest, if I had put more thought into that night, I may have even figured out it was you while we were in the closet. The way you fit perfectly in my arms, against me, your lips…their shape was like a perfect puzzle piece against my own."

I stop to wipe at my tears.

"I've had so much fucking loss. So many people in my life have let me down. But then came you. This perfect little spitfire girl who's actually been there my whole life. And you, without a doubt, showed me how it felt to feel alive. You reached parts of me I never knew were shut off. And that was the problem," I choke on my words. "I didn't expect you. I didn't know…"

I have to stop to catch my breath, my lungs still healing. "I never knew what this felt like. Us. True love. I'm sorry it took me so long to figure it out." My head rests on her bedside, hiding my weakness as the tears fall. "Please give me another chance, because I haven't even begun to show you how much I truly notice you. *See* you." Another wracked sob breaks my chest in half. "For Christ's sake, I knew it was you who took my hoodie. I caught you dancing with it one night in your room. I could have watched you all night, the smile on my face as you talked to it. After that, I knew I'd never ask for it back or ask who took it. Because I knew...I knew it was in good hands. So, you see? It's taken me too fucking long to realize it, but I've always noticed you. And now, I don't ever want to stop. Please...please come back to me and give me another—"

"Levi?"

My head whips up, seeking out her slate blue eyes. Her voice sounds pained. "Do you need something?" I pounce up from my chair. "Anything. Just tell me. I'll go grab—"

Her hand squeezes mine, her eyes locking on me. "No, please don't leave me."

I nod, sitting back down. "Of course. I'll never leave you again." Her eyes search for something in mine, and it sets fire to the torch of nerves inside me. "What do you need? Whatever it is, I'll get—"

"You. I just need you." Her voice is filled with such emotion, it steals my breath. "Where have you been?" It's then her voice cracks and her own tears begin to fall.

"Oh, Han, I've been here. I've been trying to get to you." I'm brought back into the shadows of my guilt. I should have gotten to her sooner. If I would have listened...

Her lips quiver. "I know you don't want this anymore, but I don't want to be alone." She clamps her eyes shut, fighting the tears that still manage to escape through her thick lashes. I squeeze harder, needing her to know, feel, see.

"Hannah Constance Matthews..."

Her eyes, still weak, manage to widen. "You know my middle name?"

This causes a much-needed smile to form. "Kip and I came home one night from a party and you and your mom were in the kitchen in a heated argument. You hated your middle name and insisted your mom submit a change of name to the county records. She wouldn't, and you swore the day you became of age, you were going to change it. Hannah *Constance* Matthews, if I remember."

"How…I was like eight. How do you—?"

"Because I notice everything about you. I just needed reminding." I reach forward, not giving away the shooting pain in my back, and brush a wild strand of hair behind her ear. "I wish I could take back so many things. Starting when you were seven. But I'll start with what I said at the office that day. I should have never…god, I feel like I have a lot of sentences that are going to start with I should have never…"

I feel like I'm fucking this up before I even get started. "I should have never let you believe I wanted out. I panicked. And I took the coward way out. It wasn't about you. It was about your dad and his disappointment in me—"

"Levi—"

"No, let me finish, okay? I spent the first few years of my life without understanding or feeling what love meant. What it felt like. I met a boy who shared a pack of chips with me and my world changed. I was welcomed into a home full of warmth and happiness. It was clean and safe. From there, I spent the coming years building this life with a family I pretended was my own. Those years with your dad were the most important years of my life. He gave me something I didn't even realize I needed: love. He loved me as his own." Her tears cause me to break. I lift my hand to wipe at her cheek.

"That day, the disappointment in your father's eyes broke me. I had virtually let down the only father figure I've known, whether I caused it or not. The way his contempt ate at me, it killed me. In return, I said things I didn't mean."

"I would have never made those errors."

The fact that she still sees the need to defend her actions guts me. "I know. I would have made a mistake before you. And I did. I didn't trust you." She opens her mouth to argue, but I stop her. "I did so much wrong with you, Hannah. I shouldn't have done what I did with you in that supply closet." Her eyes dull at my comment. "Our firsts should have been something better than that. You deserve better than that." Hannah begins to speak, but her coughing interrupts. I reach forward to grab her water, helping her with the straw. "Just rest, you don't need to—"

"No, it's my turn to talk." And this is where she breaks my heart. I hold her hand, memorizing the feel of her soft skin underneath mine, preparing for this to be the last time she may allow me to touch her. "I do," she starts, and the first crack slices through my heart. "And so do you. I stole a piece of you that night. I was selfish and uncaring to your feelings. The consequences. I didn't think past a lifelong fantasy. But what I won't do is apologize for it. You may not have realized it, but you gave me something that night in the closet. You allowed me to finally feel alive. To finally understand what it felt like to just let go and feel." She pulls her hand back to swipe at a loose tear. "I may have grown up in a house filled with love, a loving family, loving brother, but the love I've felt since that night, it's...it's made me feel more alive than I could have ever imagined. I may have loved you from afar my whole life, but loving you up close has been like nothing I could have ever imagined."

She reaches out to catch the tears trailing down my face, her thumb brushing against my cheek. "I can't seem to understand... grasp what happened. My mind fights me at every turn. But what I do know is I fought. I remember fighting. I didn't want our argument to be the last we had with each other. I remember wanting to fight for that." Her chest constricts, and I worry this is too much for her. "I don't remember why I stopped fighting. I couldn't get free. I couldn't stop him—"

"Stop. You did what you had to do. You survived. That's all

that fucking matters." I need her to hear my words and have them blanket her doubt. "Han, you did fight. You never stopped."

"Yeah but look what he did to you. You're hurt." Her fingers graze against the bandage around my ear. "He was here. He tried to—" Her throat constricts, a sob breaking through her lips.

My heart shatters in two. After the hell she's been through, her concern is for me. I let her hand go. Ignoring the restriction of my back, I climb onto the bed and cradle her into my side. "I would do everything again a million times over if it meant you were safe. If it meant you would forgive me. If it meant you were able to walk away from this still being that strong, ironclad future president I love more than my own life."

Her body stiffens in my arms, and her head whips up, knocking my chin. We both groan, and she tries to scurry away from me. "I don't think so," I say, squeezing her closer.

"No, wait." She pushes again, and I let her up. "What did you just say?" Her eyes are an ocean of hope, and I gaze into them, losing myself to the depths of possibilities. Fear of the unknown. I'm anxious and afraid at once, worried about choosing the wrong words to express this solid mass inside me that lives and grows and feeds off her every smile, laugh, grunt. My heart beats in a drum-like fashion to her song, the melody of chords paving the way to limitless possibilities.

I adjust our position so her back is against the shitty hospital bed while I hover over her as best I can without pulling out her IV. I inhale a deep breath for strength, praying she understands, feels what I feel. I open my mouth, but I worry the words won't come out right. She won't feel the gravity of my promise.

The backs of my knuckles skate against her cheek, the feel of her offering me strength. "If someone would have asked me ten years ago what the biggest rush in life was, hands down, I'd answer football. There was nothing that could have possibly compared to it. Nothing that set fire to my soul like the intensity and passion of the game. That rush I felt while crushing my cleats against the turf. The way I dominated that field like a hawk flying yard for yard until I crossed over that touchdown line? God, I can still taste it. But one day, that rush took a new course, and I found a whole new high: law. I wasn't beating my body up like football. Getting high off each tackle. But power comes in many forms. The day I hung up my jersey and helmet for a suit and a voice, it was like no rush I've truly ever felt before. Helping people. Saving lives. That took its spot. Fighting in a courtroom for someone who can't fight for themselves. *That's a fucking rush.*"

I stop and extend my tongue, wetting my bottom lip. Understanding casts over her eyes, giving me the fuel I need to continue. "If someone would have asked me four months ago, the answers may have stayed the same, or I would have stumbled over them because I'd begun to question what truly drives me. Ask me three months ago, and I would have probably socked someone because my head and heart were at war and I couldn't answer it. Fought myself to understand what that feeling inside me was. It was a rush all right, more powerful than a game or a court case, because I didn't know how to win it. Ask me a month ago, three weeks, today? And I would tell you this force has dug its way so deep into my soul, it's blinded me along the way. It was this un-stoppable force that turned my life upside down. A rush so in-tense, I'm not sure I deserve it. But it's inside me, and I want to fight to fucking keep it."

Her tears cause pause. I stop to place my lips against hers. "I'm probably fucking this up." Her head shakes back and forth, and I release a breath of relief. "Hannah, I've lived, but I've never truly loved until you. Everything in life has been so surface level. And then you. My wild, mouthy, sexy, intelligent—shit, I can go on—little anchor sucked me into the depths of your world, and I can't get enough of it. I love you. Maybe I always have."

Doubt pierces through me at the tears pouring down her cheeks. Her eyes may be closed, but the creases slice through my hope of—

"Levi Dent." Her eyes reopen. The sun cascades against her angelic face, and I want to kiss away her sadness. Her own doubts and reservations. Her hand raises to cup my cheek, and I can't help but lean into her warm touch. "From age seven to...what day is it?"

Confused, I scramble to answer. "Um...Friday. I think it's a Friday." Shit, I don't even know. Time has blended too damn much being in this place.

"From the age of seven to today, Friday, it's always been you. You're *my* rush. My passion. I've been in love with you my whole life. But even after everything, doubt eats at me, scared you...this is just a dream."

"It's not. I swear it."

"I know. I've pinched myself enough times to know." God, she's amazing, making jokes even while lying in a hospital bed. "My feelings have never changed. And they probably never will. You've been this entity in my world, and I think you're always meant to be there. But I will always doubt that the way I tricked you altered something in our path. I can't stop wondering if I hadn't been deceitful, would we be here? Well...not *here*. But us?"

She doubts. Fuck.

"Levi, what happens in another year when someone asks what drives you? My biggest fear is it won't be me."

I don't give her a chance to say another word. "Let me make things clearer for you. In a year, if someone asks me what my current rush is, I hope to tell them my wedding day." Her subtle intake of breath fuels me. "Each year for ten after that, I hope to say our children, because I want to have a fuck ton of kids with you. And in fifty years, if I don't keel over from giving you so much amazing sex, I'm going to respond with the peaceful life I've built with my loving wife, the mother of my children and my saving grace. Because one day, a long time ago, while she laid in a shitty bed, being romanced by the love of her life, she agreed to take a life journey with me, and then we got a good laugh because her man bawled like a baby for being so thankful—"

Any remaining words are cut short when she lifts her head and claims my lips, the saltiness of our tears blending together. I'm no-where near done trying to convince her how much I love her, but I won't ever say no to her lips. Her hands, still weak, find strength in the clutches of my hair as she presses her mouth harder against mine. God, I can spend a lifetime kissing this mouth.

"I love you, Levi."

"Fuck, I love you so damn much." Kiss after kiss, we can't keep up with one another, our unbreakable connection a silent promise and vow of our love. She's like an addiction, and I won't ever be done getting my fix. A weak moan falls from her palpable lips and steals my breath. I swirl my tongue with hers, getting lost in this moment, memorizing it. Her love is my salvation, and I will spend eternity showing her how worthy I am of it.

Our kiss starts out innocent, but quickly sparks the inferno of desire always thriving inside me for her. I don't think I'll ever be able to explain the fireworks that explode in my chest with every touch. I ache to remove all things between us and sink inside her, bask in her warmth—

"Seriously? Aren't you two like super injured? Does the little guy even work right now?" We pull apart, my eyes transfixed on her swollen lips. I feel drunk off her. A shy grin covers her face. We both shift our focus to Chase standing in the doorway with Kipley and Stacey next to him. Kip slaps Chase in the chest and pushes him aside to enter the room.

"Dude, injured or not, get the fuck off my sister. At least wait 'til you're both cleared and I'm not around for round two of kicking your ass for violating my sister."

"Kip," Hannah complains, a sexy as fuck flush spreading across her cheeks.

"Seriously…fuckin' chicks, man. First it was Kip, crying like a pussy when he asked Stace to marry him. Now you."

This time, it's Stacey's turn to whack him in the chest. "My pro-posal was beautiful."

"Well, pussies are beautif—ouch! Jesus!" He grabs for his chest.

"Nurse!" he yells, sticking his head out the door. "Where's that hot nurse who was in here earlier? I need her to help lick my wounds, amongst other things—okay, shit, put your weapon down." Stacey eyes him, until he throws his hands up in surrender and sits.

I laugh and roll off the bed, wincing as I straighten out. I stretch my neck to peek over my shoulder. Blood seeps from a few bandages. Shit. Unlike Hannah's apparent hot nurse, mine was a behemoth man pretending to be a woman. Shivers run down my spine at the thought of her impending anger.

"Hey, you okay?" Hannah grabs my hand.

I bring it to my lips, pressing a kiss to her delicate skin. "Never better."

"Minus the bleeding. Big Bertha's gonna kick your ass for that. She specifically told you not to move." Chase shakes his head. Hannah's eyes grow wide, worry cascading across her beautiful blues. I could kick his ass for that.

I kiss her hand once more. "It's fine. I'm fine."

"No, you're not. Have you *seen* Big Berth—"

"*Shut up*, Chase," both Kip and Stacey chime in.

I bend down to kiss Hannah's lips when a deep voice resonates around the room. "There you are, young man." I pause and look to the right, as does everyone else.

"*Whoa.*" The word is spoken in unison by all.

"Fucking told you all," Chase says, crossing his legs.

"Look what you've done. Now we have to undress you and re-patch you." She comes at me, and I won't lie when I say I shudder a little bit. Stacey's mouth hangs open while Kip laughs at me. Glad that fucker finds this funny. "You come with me this instant. Don't make me tie you to the bed."

Kip loses it, busting out laughing, while Stacey finally gives in and chokes out a giggle. Bertha comes at me, and I wave my white flag before she takes matters into her own hands and tries to carry me back. "Okay, okay. I'm going." I turn to Hannah, gifting her my most charming smile. "We're not done here."

CHAPTER THIRTY-THREE

Hannah

One week later...

I'm anxious. There's chaos in my room. Kipley, Mom, Dad, and my nurse all crowd the small space, but my focus won't pull away from the door.

Where is he?

Doubt eats away at me, nipping at all the spoken promises. Was this all a dream? *He's not coming back.* My fingertips are tender from biting my nails, the taste of blood on my tongue as I chew through my cuticles. I rip them from the thin line of my lips. My hands are jittery, so I tug on the clothes my mom brought me to wear home. I swipe my clammy palms down my favorite pair of yoga pants, but they feel rough and loose around my hips. The doctor said I'll gain weight back in no time, but I'm not worried about being too thin—"too frail" as my mother whispered to my dad—I'm afraid of him not coming back.

After a week of being in the hospital, Levi was released yesterday. He said he'd be back for me, but he hasn't come back. Swipe after swipe, I brush my hands down my yoga pants to distract myself, but the looming fear doesn't dissipate. My shirt is suddenly too heavy against my ribcage. I pull it away from my chest, needing my lungs to expand. I'm having trouble breathing.

He's not coming back.

"Honey, relax." Mom pats my shoulder, mistaking the

pounding of my heart for nerves about being released today. I don't correct her.

"I am relaxed," I lie. I'm far from it. My mind flickers back to the last week. The in-depth conversations we've had. The confessions of love and promises. He wants a future. He wants kids. He wants me. *Then why isn't he here?* Maybe he fed me the words I wanted to hear to help me heal. Cushion the guilt that's tearing him up inside. Even after I vowed he wasn't to blame and told him I didn't hold him responsible for anything that happened. Maybe he…maybe he…

"Baby girl, you're all set. They just need to go over your follow-up care and we can get you home." I want to scream that I don't care about my follow-up care, the importance of taking it slow and starting a regiment with a counselor about working out my traumatic experience—I just want *him*. I stare up at the clock. It's a few minutes after ten in the morning. It's been fourteen hours since he left. Enough time to reconsider. He's realizing he made a mistake.

He's not coming—

"Sorry I'm late." Levi hustles through the door. As if I was the only one in the room, his eyes find mine, locking us in an intimate visual embrace. My cheeks flush with shame. All his honesty, and I doubted him. He eats up the distance between us as I capture my lower lip between my teeth, biting down in hopes it reroutes my emotions and keeps my tears at bay. He pulls me into his arms, and I immediately find comfort in his presence and snuggle my face into his chest. He smells freshly showered.

"Hey," he says as his lips press into my hairline.

"Hey."

"Why the sullen face?" he asks.

I press my head further into his shirt, regret causing my lip to quiver at my failed trust in him. "I thought…"

"That you couldn't wait for me to come rescue you from this god awful hospital and whisk you away to a romantic island only to feed you Savino's pizza and sex you up 'til you can't feel your legs?"

My cheeks explode with color, forgetting the room full of family. Thankfully, he says it so softy, it's only heard by my ears. "Yeah, something like that," I lie, ashamed at my lack of judgement. I should have never doubted him.

He pulls us apart, exposing the emotions clear as day across my face. "I'm sorry I'm late."

"I… I thought you weren't coming back," I confess.

He leans forward, pressing a reassuring kiss to my forehead. "I'm sorry I worried you, but, babe…" he pulls back, needing me to see the sincerity in his eyes, "I'm never leaving." He waits for his words to resonate before continuing. "I just had to take care of something, and it took me longer than I expected."

"You kids about ready? I'm pretty sure this place is going to start charging us for using the oxygen in here soon." My dad breaks up our moment, and we pull away. "Everything all set, son?" he addresses Levi. Confused, my eyes bounce back and forth between them.

"What is all set?" I ask.

Levi nods and faces me. "If you're okay, I'm going to take you home. But before I do, I have a surprise for you." I gaze back to my dad for any insight. He smiles back. My mother appears on the verge of tears, but the happy kind. *What is he up to?* "Of course, if you're tired or not ready, we can just—"

"No. I'm okay."

"You sure?"

"Yes. Sure. A lot sure. Super sure." Levi laughs, grabbing for me, his strong arms cradling me into his chest as he places a kiss to my head without any reservations of my parents watching.

The butterflies that resurface in my belly begin to swarm. A shyness washes over me realizing we're on full display for my family. Going from a secret to fully exposed couple has to have been a lot to digest. Especially for my parents.

Kipley coughs into his hand, reminding me he's still in the room. "Okay, let's get this party started. I'm ready to get home and make my wife cook me a real meal. If I have to eat another hospital meal, my intestines—"

"Okay, we're good, honey." Stacey tugs at his arm, shutting him up.

A nurse shows up with a wheelchair, insisting it's hospital policy for me to be wheeled out. Levi takes control, insisting boyfriend duties. Levi's car is parked up front. My mom hands over my bag of things I've collected since my stay. Dad gives me a kiss goodbye and tells me he loves me, followed by my brother and Stacey. Before too long, it's only the two of us on our way back home.

"Are you going to tell me what this surprise is?" I ask.

His eyes leave the road to look at me, a slight curve at the corner of his mouth. The anticipation has me jittery in my seat. He waits a few short seconds, which feel like forever before he answers. "No."

"Oh! Come on! I hate surprises."

"I know. And that's what makes this all the more exciting." He returns his sight to the road, seeming pleased with himself for torturing me. I don't push further, and he doesn't say another word. His hand slides across the center console, engulfing mine under his strong hold. We stay connected the entire forty-five-minute drive home. It's not until we're pulling up to his place that my curiosity piques.

"What are we doing here?"

He doesn't answer me right away. We pull into the underground lot and park in his designated spot. Shutting the car off, he opens his door.

"Quick stop," he says, then climbs out, hurrying over to my side to assist me out. "Take it easy. I've got you."

"I'm fine."

"And I still want to baby you, so let me." He holds my hand as

I climb out, working hard to hide the small wave of dizziness. As much as I argue I'm completely recovered, the concussion keeps setting me back. Not to mention the thirty-seven stitches in my side that itch like hell when they rub against my shirt. We walk as he guides me to the elevator and the front door of his condo. He has to let my hand go to dig for his keys, and when he unlocks the door, he steps aside. "After you."

I step through the threshold and head to the couch for a much-needed break after the short walk from the car. It's not until I'm halfway through his condo I notice it.

A frame sitting on the end table by his couch that wasn't there before. It's a picture of us.

A throw blanket resting across the cushion, along with throw pillows. *Girly* throw pills. My eyes take flight, soaring around his place at the sudden explosion of life. Colorful paintings. Sports memorabilia mixed with an old boyband poster from my room at home. *What in the...?* A pile of books on the coffee table, the dust jackets familiar because they're some of my favorites. I open my mouth, then close it again. Like a fish out of water, I gasp for the words to form the questions. But they don't come.

"Come with me." He takes my shaky hand and guides me down the hallway. I don't remember my feet moving, but it's then we're in his room. He brings us to his closet and opens the door, positioning me so I'm able to get a front row view of half of it full of...

"Are those my clothes?"

I don't comprehend how long I stand there in shock before whipping around to face him. His hands are shoved in his pockets, his eyes gleaming with the same uncertainty mine did earlier. "I told you before. I'm never leaving you."

"But...what...?"

"Hannah..." He takes a step closer to me. His hands stay in his pockets, the tips of our shoes our only connection. "I've fought hard for the things I wanted in life—football, my career, to be a part of a family—but none of it will compare to how hard I'm willing to fight to make sure you know and never doubt my love for you. You don't need anyone taking care of you. You've always been so tough. An angel behind your warrior suit. I saw the doubt in your eyes today, and it almost brought me to my knees. If your family wasn't standing there, I'd have shaken you silly until you understood what truly has me consumed with such possessiveness. I want to hide you from the world and keep you for myself. Even though your father and brother would probably try to kill me right on the spot, I was ready. Because like I said, I'm ready to fight. For you. For your trust. Your kindness. Your *love*. I want to slaughter all your doubts. Kiss away all your fears. And I'm realizing I'm a very selfish man. While I should be allowing you to heal, giving you space to figure out what you want, I can't stop putting my own needs first. And that's making sure you know every single day my intentions with you."

My heart thumps in heavy beats. I hang onto his every word, watching his eyes flare with hope, worry, determination, fear.

"I can't imagine spending one day waking up and you not being next to me. The sound of your breathing that brings me to life. I took all your stuff and moved it in here. I want you here. I want us to be an us. And I want to take care of you, help you heal. Band-Aid all your fears with my obsession with you."

At that, I can't help but laugh. "You're obsessed with me?"

"I am. It's becoming a problem. I might as well get a tattoo on my forehead that says WWHD. Because any direction I take, I want to know what you would do. You're all that matters to me, and I want to never stop putting that smile I crave on your face."

My eyes shine, a tingling sensation spreading along my entire body. "I don't really think you need to get a tattoo to show me. I love you too. I would follow you too, wherever."

Relief settles in his upcurved smile, happiness dancing in his eyes. There's a nervous energy surrounding him, and I smile wider, enjoying this version of him. "So, this still doesn't explain my clothes, and I have to ask…how did you find my—your hoodie? I had that thing pretty securely hidden."

My knees wobble, and Levi panics, mistaking my cause of dizziness on my injury. His hands thrust out of his pockets to steady me, being mindful of my wound. The thing is, it has absolutely nothing to do with my injury. There's so much beauty in the depths of his eyes, it's too easy not to get lost in how handsome he is. But I've always been consumed by all things Levi Dent. His smile is like oxygen for me. It's a vital part of my being. It's no longer a childish fantasy to know exactly how wonderful his hands feel, the taste of his lips, the way his heartbeat speeds up every time we kiss. There's one thing he and I have in common: I would spend my entire life fighting to be the one who puts that smile on his face.

"You okay? Do you need to sit down? Shit, this is probably too much for you. I shouldn't force this. I can take you—"

"Yes."

His eyes widen in shock as if he misheard me. "Yes?"

"Yes. My answer is yes. I'm not sure what you're really asking, but my answer is yes."

Understanding sets in, and he realizes he never even got to the point. "Wow, don't even wait to hear the punishment you're being sentenced to before agreeing and jumping in blindly to damnation."

"Well, looks like I'm a sucker for sanction." I chuckle. "From what I gather, you like me, a lot—"

"Already wrong, I love you."

I nod, my teasing smirk on full display. "You love me. Good to know we're on the same page." He nods, stealing a quick kiss. I continue. "But the girl pillows and band posters tell me you have some deep-rooted fantasy about becoming a teenage girl."

"So close." He steals another kiss.

"And the closet tells me this is your retribution for the stolen hoodie. I steal something of yours, you steal everything of mine?"

"God, you're so sexy when you're right." His mouth is so luscious, I lose focus on our conversation and bathe in the ripeness of his lips. "There's one thing you missed, though."

"Hmmm?" My eyes fall closed as he rains a path of kisses down my neck.

"I'm hoping for you to live with me in my teenage girl pad, wearing only my hoodie, since that's what I deserve after being away from it for so long, and let me cherish, spoil, and devour you." He pulls away, his playful smile now drawn back. "I know this is a lot. You've been through hell, and it's going to take some time to heal. It may not be easy, but I want to be the warrior for once. Let me be your warrior. Play the damsel. Let me show you I can protect you and will never let anything like this happen again."

"Levi, I told you, this wasn't—"

"And as much as I fight to believe that, it might take me some time. But what I want you to understand is no matter what, it won't ever happen again." He leans forward, brushing his lips to mine, sealing his case with a silent vow. "I love you, Hannah Constance Matthews."

I can't fight the smirk on my lips and pull away. "I love you too, Levi...wait, I don't know your middle name." I'm amazed there's something I *don't* know about him.

"Maybe if you let me do that little thing with my tongue when you're feeling better, I'll tell you."

His spoken vow shoots a blast of excitement though every nerve ending, setting a spark of fuel to my own obsession. "I'm feeling better." I'm embarrassed how hoarse my voice sounds.

"How much better?" His tone is deep, like a wolf teasing his prey.

"So much. Actually, maybe too much. *Ouch, please.* I need you to take care of me like you said. I have this pain..." His eyes shoot to mine, on alert. "Where, where do you hurt?"

Crimson skates across my cheeks. I take my hand and point downward, between my thighs. "Here. It hurts here."

The musical sounds that erupt from his throat is what fairy-tales are made out of. His laughter bellows throughout his bed-room, and I can't help but follow. "Well, I did make a lot of prom-ises, none of which I plan on retracting. So, if that's what I have to do to prove to my woman she's the reason for my being, then so damn be it."

He's done talking.

Another giggle bursts from my lips when he grabs my hand and guides me toward his bed. "Lay down, my little queen. I'm about to feast like a king."

CHAPTER THIRTY-FOUR

Levi

Three months later…

"**N**O! Please NO!"

Hannah's screams jolt me awake. I turn to her, her body flailing. "Hannah, wake up. It's only a dream." Just like the others, my voice goes unheard.

"NO!" she screams, her voice etched in such pain. I know exactly what her nightmare is about. It's the same one she's been having since the incident. Connor Miller is setting her on fire.

I grip her in my arms, her skin hot and clammy. She's sweat through her shirt. "Hannah, wake up. Baby, you're safe." Her eyes start to flutter open, confusion masking her face. Her eyes become wide with terror, her nightmare following her into conscious. "It's okay, babe, you're safe. You're in our bed. Feel the sheets. Take a deep breath. Smell the clean air. There's no smoke."

Hannah went too long claiming she was fine after the incident before her nightmares gave her away. She could no longer hide her secret fears that Connor would come for her, even though the fucker was locked up. Her nightmares were always the same. She was stuck in a house, and Connor was setting her on fire. Her therapist suggested cooling sheets. Sounded silly, but the specialized bamboo material would help cool her body while she slept, and in cases like this, it would take away some of her fear. She would wake up and grasp the sheets, feeling the coolness under her terror filled grip. At first, I thought it was bullshit, but they've helped.

The other savior was the air diffuser. In the beginning, it felt like forever to get her to snap out of it. She would scream and howl as if she was burning, and it fucking killed me. When we tried out the diffuser, the first nightmare after that, I got her to take deep breaths. This would allow her to smell the lavender from the diffuser and not the smoke stuck in her subconscious mind.

Overall, the nightmares became fewer and farther between. Until now. The trial. Today, Connor Miller takes the stand. I wish beyond anything I could make it all go away. Jim wouldn't let her near the case anymore. His main priority was shielding his daughter from anymore distress caused by the Miller family. The trial was postponed. Seems Hannah has a friend in the judicial system on our side, and got the trial delayed until I was released from the hospital and well enough for the fight of my life. And when that day finally came, Matthews and Associates went full force. It didn't take much before Benjamin Miller was arrested. Everything happened fast and intense. Not only were we ready to take down Miller Industries for what they did, we were going to take down his son for what he did to Hannah.

Putting Hannah's case together was and will be one of the hardest things I've ever done…next to watching her lay in the hospital bed. Connor was a sick fuck. He gave his statement that day to the police, a full confession of his intentions, the kidnapping of Hannah, the murder of Clara Hill. But once his father got wind, he lawyered him up and they fought tooth and nail, claiming his confession was under duress and ultimately getting it thrown out.

Four days of trial against Miller Industries, and we gave it all we got. But it wasn't us who truly won that case. It was the testimonies of the victims who lived that day. Clara Hill may have been the only one strong enough to stand up to Miller Industries in the beginning, but her death gave those too scared to come forward the strength to tell their stories.

"*Can you please state your name for the record.*"

"*Phillip Hensley, sir.*" A middle-aged man, wearing a worn suit and boots sits up straighter on the stand.

"*And Mr. Hensley, can you please state for the record your line of work with Miller Industries?*"

There's an excruciating amount of pain that radiates from his tired eyes at the mention of Miller Industries. "*I was hired as the construction manager. Benjamin Miller had approached me at my home to work on the upcoming job site.*"

"*And what did he offer you?*"

Phillip takes a gander at the jury, then back to me. "*He offered to double my salary. I'd been at the paper mill for over thirty years. But my wife...Virginia...she had cancer. We were struggling to pay for treatments. She was a fighter, but without more money, we were going to have to stop her chemo.*"

I take a breath, allowing him the same opportunity. "*Was there anything else?*"

He nods. "*Yes. He offered us treatment. He said he knew doctors who could help my Virginia. If I left the mill and took the job, he would get us the income we needed. Virginia would get better.*" His voice cracks, right along with my heart knowing how this story ends.

"*What happened when you took the job?*" He adjusts himself in his seat, feeling the discomfort as Benjamin Miller sits at the defense table staring him down. "*It's okay. Go on...*"

"*Production started. People got right to work. Men were distributed to specific jobs, some of which never had experience in job labor.*" He takes a moment. "*I did what I was hired to do: watch over the construction, and make sure men were working fast and diligently. Mr. Miller had offered me a bonus if the job was completed before the expected timeframe.*"

"*And what was that?*" I ask.

"*Six months. Which all seemed impossible. This building he was fixin' to build, it was massive, and he had nowhere near the amount of manpower needed to complete it in such a time.*"

I walk around my table, toward the jury. "And did you ever express your concerns about this to Mr. Miller?"

His expression morphs into anguish. "No. I was too worried about losing my job. You see, Mr. Miller was a powerful man. He didn't take lightly to anyone questioning him. I tried to speak up in the beginning simply about the safety of some of the men in the pit. That night, I received a call that our payment had not been received for insurance. I'd gotten the hint right away. I was to do my job." He pauses, torment almost taking his breath. "I just kept thinking of my Virginia. I thought if I just kept my business to myself, the building would be up in no time and my wife would be better. We'd take the extra money and go on a trip. We'd never been outside Crete."

I let the jury take a moment to digest his statement before continuing. "Mr. Hensley, where were you the day of the explosion?" The jurors sit straighter, their ears pinging at my question.

A storm of emotions shifts through his eyes, a current of pain he'll forever bear. "I was at the front of the site. There was some sort of hold up that morning. Clifford Winters and one of Benjamin's watchdogs were arguing. Clifford came from the pit saying it smelled off. He'd also been at the mill with me and was familiar with gases. Told the man they needed to send someone to check it out. The man threatened Clifford's job if he didn't get back to work. Clifford refused, and they started to get physical. Before any fists were swung, the floor shook beneath us, and then the ground exploded."

Phillip pauses, and I take two steps closer to the stand, giving him my silent support. "And then what happened?"

He swallows, struggling to find the words to explain the travesty he lived through. "The explosion knocked us three off our footing. When I lifted myself off the ground, my eyes were struck with horror. A ball of flames shooting from the center of the site. The screaming. So much screaming. Like a whistle in the wind, carrying the shrieking voices of men everywhere. Clifford was up and running toward the disaster. I screamed for him not to get closer, but he didn't listen. His sons...his two sons were down there." Phillip's voice breaks, his hand going to his mouth to hide the choked sob.

"Mr. Hensley, can you tell the jury what you saw next?"

Tears fall down his frail cheeks, his hand wiping at his scarred face, third degree burns forever etched in his skin. "I ran too. I got close enough until the flames were too much. So many bodies. Men on fire running in all directions. Men succumbing to the flames and collapsing to their death. Samuel, my best…my best friend since grade school, he pulled himself from the rubble. He was burned, flames covered his back. I threw my shirt off and tried to put out the flames, but it was no use."

"Did Samuel survive?"

"No. He died in front of me that day."

"Thank you. I know that was hard to relive." I shift toward the jury. "Lives, thirty-four of them to be exact, died along with Samuel Gunner that day. Eleven men. Twenty-four, barely eighteen years of age. Children. All hired illegally under the hands of Benjamin Miller. A suicide mission to benefit his pocketbook." I adjust my body and point to Benjamin Miller. "The man who sits in front of us knew the risks of breaking ground, the risk of disturbing uninhabitable land. What would have happened if that building had been fully developed? How many other innocent lives would have been lost if something, say a simple shift in the earth, triggered that natural gas? Should we ask the businessman who only cared about the dollar signs? A ruthless entrepreneur who not only walked away without a care, but tried to cover up his wrongdoings with blackmail, taking more lives."

I take a short pause to let those words settle in, then turn to Phillip. "Mr. Hensley, after the incident, what came of your healthcare?"

A lifetime of sorrow weighs heavily on his shoulders, a sadness ripping through the courtroom and felt by all. "It all but stopped. My Virginia is with God now."

"No further questions, your honor."

"Can you state your name for the record?"

"Sherman Wilson."

I face the jury. "Sherman Wilson, forty-two years old. Married to Bethany Wilson for twenty-five years. He's a father to thirteen-year-old daughter, Sylvie, who was diagnosed with severe autism spectrum disorder at three, and seven-year-old, Becca, diagnosed at age two with high functioning Asperger's. You all can imagine the journey these two parents have endured raising two amazing, unique children on a labor man's salary." I pause for a moment before bringing my focus to Sherman. "Mr. Wilson, can you tell the jury where you were the day of the explosion?"

The burly man stretches his neck to make eye contact with Benjamin Miller. The two men battle in a stare down. Anger. Loss. Regret. They shine in Sherman's eyes as he recalls that day. "I was on site. I was in the pit breaking up a dispute between some of the veteran crew and the kids."

"By kids, do you mean the younger laborers?"

"Yes, sir. Kids. They were barely legal to work on a site like that. Just the day before, a kid lost control of the skid-steer loader, sending a man to the hospital. Drilled into the wrong area and hit a crewman, slicing his leg right off." There's an intake of breath from the jury as Sherman builds them a gruesome mental picture.

"I can't imagine. From your experience, did the crew lack experience?"

"Damn right they did. They were kids. They shouldn't have been there. No experience causes lots of accidents. For everyone onboard."

The defense stands. "Your honor, he's belaboring the point here."

Judge Foster eyes me. "Mr. Dent, let's get to the point of your question."

I nod. "Mr. Wilson, the day of the accident, Jason Stone was operating the drill rig that caused the accident, correct?"

"That's right."

I turn to the jury. "Jason Stone, age seventeen, employed by Miller Industries. Never worked a day in construction in his young life. He had no background or knowledge of the trade. Before being hired on by Benjamin Miller with the promise of a prosperous future,

Jason Stone had just graduated high school. He held a 4.0 GPA and would be the first of his family to attend college in the fall. His passion was football and science. He donated his time to the local charities and pet adoption center in town." I bring my attention back to the witness. "Mr. Wilson, can you describe the morning for the jury?"

"I had just come up the freight elevator from the pit minutes before the explosion. Like I said, everyone was heated over the experience barrier. They wanted something done."

"And what was that?" I ask.

"Pull them kids off the site. No money was worth the safety of the crew. The accident with the skid and Hank rattled us all. Even the young ones were spooked. But it seemed everyone in some sort of way had been roped in by Miller Industries. They just wanted to get the job done and collect what they were promised."

I take a step closer to Sherman. "Were you promised anything?"

He struggles to hide the guilt. "You see, it ain't easy trying to raise two girls who need so much. Sylvie—"

"Objection. The counsel is misleading the witness testimony. This has no bearing on the case at hand."

"Overruled. Mr. Wilson, answer the question."

Sherman nods, inhaling a hollow breath. "He offered to increase my pay. Pay off medical bills we were drowning in. He told Bethany they planned on putting a daycare in the lower level of the building and she would be able to find work. She would be able to bring the girls there for free."

I turn on my heel and head back to the table to grab the blueprints Jim hands me. "At this time, I would like to submit exhibit one as evidence." *I hold the blueprint up for the jury.* "I show you today the blueprints submitted to city hall by Miller Industries. You have all been given a copy of the layout. Please note the first-floor zoning layout." *I shift to hold eye contact with Sherman.* "There is no projected plan for a daycare of any sort."

Sherman breaks eye contact with me, his chin dipping as his eyes close. The jurors share in the gutting of betrayal by Benjamin Miller.

"Mr. Sherman, I only have two more questions, then I will let you get back to your family. Can you state for the jury the injuries you sustained the day of the accident?"

The question summons memories. Sherman's throat bobs, choking down the painful recollection of that day. "I was about twenty yards from the pit when it exploded. The pressure shot me forward, and I slammed into the digging trencher. The blades ripped right through my leg and arm, damaging my nerve endings where I no longer have use of most of my right side. I have third degree burns down ninety percent of my back. I'm lucky to even be alive."

I take a moment to allow them to process his life changing injuries before addressing the jury. "A man who got up every single day to support his family, his children who need him, now fights every day just to get out of bed. He is no longer able to support the needs of his children's health, nor pay the necessities of a home, food, and care. That day took everything from this family. A fake promise from a man only seeing dollar signs for his own benefit." I take a deep breath and speak to Sherman. "Where are your children now?"

Sherman stares at me, his eyes filling with sadness and pain. "In a state facility." Betrayed and heartbroken, he slumps in his chair. "We had to forfeit parental rights because we didn't have the means to take care of them."

"No further questions, your honor."

There's a round of audible gasps and shock as our last witness takes the stand. No doubt because it's hard to see. Even I struggle to hide the guilt and remorse for what he's endured.

"Can you please state your name for the record?"

He brings a device up to his trachea, his prosthetic voice helping him speak. "Caleb Johns."

"Caleb, can you tell the jury how old you are?"

"I'm sixteen, sir." This shocks the jury, with a noticeable intake of breath coming from their section.

"*Wow, sixteen. You have your whole life ahead of you still.*"

A flash of anger etches behind his deformities. "*What future? He took that away from me.*" *He viciously points to Benjamin Miller.*

"*And in the eyes of the judicial system, we're here to see your pain and suffering be compensated. It may not take back what you sustained that day, but it will offer you some guidance for your future. Please, would you describe your experience the day of the accident?*"

No one can prepare for the horrific scenes Caleb is about to describe. "*I was late for work that morning. My mom...she's... she was pregnant and wasn't feeling well. It's just us, so I didn't want to leave her all alone. When I got to work, I snuck in behind the site trailers. Mr. Miller had eyes everywhere and I couldn't afford to get fired with a little brother or sister on the way.*" *He pauses, the tube in his neck helping him take a breath.* "*I was scheduled to work the rig that morning. I watched some videos the night before to make sure I knew exactly how to operate it. Since I was late, they threw Jason on it. I'd just made it to the machine and was flagging him down so we could switch. He shouldn't have been up there. If I hadn't been late, he wouldn't have—*"

Caleb starts coughing, and I reach for the glass of water on my table and offer it to him. He attempts a sip, but it doesn't mask the horrified sob that erupts from his chest. "*I distracted him. When he turned to look at me, he must have hit a lever. The crane holding a beam released, sky-falling straight into the pit. A cloud of red, yellow, and orange burst up from the center, the echoes of screams and cries with it. The flames ripped through the site. I was blown backwards into a pile of dirt. I was able to get up, but the fire was so intense, my skin started to burn. My first thought was to get to Jason, but when my eyes focused where I last saw him, the only thing I saw was flames. The entire rig was on fire, he was still inside.*"

Caleb stops, putting his finger up, silently asking for a moment. "*Everything went up in flames. Every two seconds, it felt like an explosion went off. The fire took no pity, consuming every crew member in that pit. No one down there had a chance of surviving. The ones who* did were trying to save others or save themselves. But it was no use. I fought like hell to get up, even though I knew my leg was broken. There was movement off to the side, and I needed to help whoever was there."

"Were you able to get to that person?"

His eyes tear up and what's left of his lower lip quivers. "It was Kellen Winters. He was missing his two legs. Half his face was blown off. His eyes...they were vacant. He...I wasn't able to save him. I couldn't save anyone." A guttural sob ruptures from his chest, and I watch as horror washes over the faces of the twelve jurors.

"Caleb, would you like to take a minute?" I ask.

He shakes his head, wiping at his face. "No. I want to finish." With his inhaler for assistance, he takes a deep breath. "Before I could do anything else, shards of debris shot through the air in all directions. A shard of glass struck me in my left eye, and three shattered into my face. The foundation started to collapse, and I thought I was as good as dead. I managed to drag myself far enough to where I avoided being crushed by a burning beam. I almost made it to the gates when I was struck in the back with flying debris. I tripped and landed on a burning body, the flames taking ninety-percent of my skin off."

Caleb's face is unrecognizable. His skin was charred down to his bones, unable to be rebuilt, even after multiple skin grafts. He will forever hold the burden of that day every time he looks in the mirror. "Caleb, did your mother give you a sister or a brother?"

His face transforms into a blank void. "My mother gave birth two months early. The stress of the accident was too much for her. The baby was in distress. She had a girl. They both died during childbirth."

Seven witnesses testified. Seven horrified victims who relived that day, the loss and the struggle.

In the end, Benjamin Miller was found guilty of thirty-five counts of first-degree murder. Twelve counts of attempted murder. Not to mention, violation of environmental law, corporate fraud, antitrust violations, and bribery. Benjamin Miller won't step foot on free land ever again. We were happy with the victory, each family being rewarded a substantial amount in damages. It won't bring back their loved ones, but it will help their future and to rebuild.

Today's trial is to bring forth all the horrible things Connor did and sentence him for his crimes in the Miller lawsuit, as well as his wrongdoings with Hannah and Clara Hill. It fucking guts me thinking about how she'll have to stand on trial and relive her time in Clara Hill's home for the jury. Jim was out of his mind when she suggested it. He wanted her nowhere near him. We would win the case without her testimony and send Connor to jail for a very long time, there was no doubt about that. But of course, the little warrior wanted to take the stand. She said telling her story would help her move on.

Fuck that.

Even I fought it. Night after night, leading up to this day, going to bed angry. Her body quietly crying next to me and me giving in, cradling her in my arms, needing her to understand why I couldn't put her on that stand. In return, she would shift and face me, the shadow in her eyes that have refused to go away since the incident telling me this was why she needed to.

"Hannah, deep breaths. You're safe, baby. No one's going to hurt you." I wait for her eyes to focus and take in her surroundings. Her fingers clench the sheets in a death grip, and the faint scent of lavender begins to replace the smell of smoke.

"Levi." The pain in her voice when she says my name kills me every time. It makes me want to call this whole fucking thing off. Tie her to the bed until the trial is over and take the punishment of her anger later. How can I put her through this?

"I'm here, baby."

"Make it stop. Make it go away." She starts to sob.

I know exactly what she wants. I'm a fucking bastard for not finding another way to soothe her. Hold her until her worries fade back into the depths of her tortured mind. But this is what she wants. This is how she ropes herself around the reality of what's real and what's not.

I throw the blankets off her, ridding us of any unneeded heat, and climb on top of her. Lifting her soaked night shirt over her head, I discard it on the floor and take my lips to her skin, blowing against her balmy flesh. She's restless under my touch, so I work faster down her stomach, my breath feathering along her skin while my lips splay kiss after kiss until I'm pulling back her tiny shorts and spreading her legs wide.

"Please, Levi. Please." I shouldn't want this. Not like this, but goddammit, I'm hard as stone, loving the way her pink lips glisten as I spread them. A better man would say no and hold her until her terrors subside, but she creates this savage in me. I snuggle in between her quivering thighs and inhale her scent. My tongue slides out, and I make contact with her warm pussy. "Yes." Her moan is like fuel for me. I swipe up her center, licking at her wetness. She's so beautiful like this. Needy, aching, and swollen for me. Her thighs clench around my head, and I watch as goosebumps line her skin.

"You're so beautiful like this. Like fucking heaven." I swipe at her again, loving the way her body buckles with each assault. I spread her wider, using my greedy tongue to push inside her, needing to taste all of her. I fuck her with my tongue, loving all the sounds she fights to hold back.

"Levi," she moans my name again, and I work her harder.

"That's right. Say my name. Know whose tongue is fucking you. Owning you. Beg for more, and maybe I'll grant you my finger." God, I'm a fucking bastard. But my girl knows what she needs, and I know exactly how to give it to her.

"Levi, please. I need you. I need all of you." I wonder if she understands what that statement does to me. If I was standing, she would have brought me to my knees. Because she has no idea how much I truly need her. I give her exactly what she wants, pushing a thick finger inside. I pump in and out, still using my tongue to tease her clit. When I push two fingers inside her, her hips begin to buckle. "Oh yes, yes..." she hits her peak, and I use a third finger while she rides out her orgasm.

I lap at her juices until I can't take another second of not being inside her. I pull out and stand, kicking off my briefs, then find my way back to her. Her frenzied eyes, shining with undeniable lust, love, and need, mirror mine. When I drive inside her, it's like a needle being pushed into my vein. She's my fucking drug, and I'm so goddamn addicted.

We make love, we fuck, we struggle to breathe, until she moans my name, squeezing around me, soaking me with her release. I buckle once more, needing the deepest depths of her cunt, until I expand and fall over, mixing my orgasm with hers.

We lay quiet, catching our breaths, savoring in the aftermath. When my heartrate seems to level out, I lift up, wanting to assess her reaction. As I hoped, her eyes are shining with contentment. Gone is the fear. "You're absolutely intoxicating." I press a gentle kiss to her lips. Her breathing becomes staggered, and I worry she's about to lose it.

"I love you," she says, and it cracks my heart open.

"I love you too. Are you okay?" I have to ask. I need to measure what she's feeling.

She swallows, as if pushing away emotion. "You remember how you tell me all the time I'm your drug and you're addicted?" I nod. I'm not shy about telling her exactly what she is to me. "Well...I know I've never said it, but for me, you're like my medicine—being with you, it...heals me." It's my turn to choke down my emotions. "It's super corny. But it's the truth."

I want to spend my entire day, year, lifetime telling her what she means to me. But I let the silence of our breathing, the beating of our hearts, respond for us. Time passes too fast, stealing our moment. I know we can no longer pretend. It's time.

"Are you ready for today?" I hold her gaze, needing to see every emotion that passes through her eyes.

"I am. I want to move on. Be done. I want him to realize he was wrong for what he did. And accept that he won't. I'm prepared that it will be hard. But I'm ready."

My strong little warrior.

"All right. Let's get today over with."

We get up and prepare to sit in a courtroom, face to face with Connor Miller for the last time.

Justin West, our top resident lawyer who's been lead on the case, stands, addressing Connor. "Mr. Miller, please state for the record your full name."

"Connor Braydon Miller."

My palms are clammy. I fight the urge to pull at my neckline, my collar all of a sudden too tight. A million times I've been in this courtroom, but never has it been defending someone I love. I fought hard to be the one to take Connor down. It had to be me. I needed to be the one staring in his eyes when I took away his freedom. Even Jim had his moments of needing revenge. But there were too many conflicts of interest and his defense team shut it down. We are lucky enough to even be sitting at the counsel table. "And, Mr. Miller, please state for the jury your relationship with Benjamin Miller and Miller Industries."

Connor's disturbing smile sets an unease inside me. I worry what it's doing to Hannah. *Stay focused.* "He's my father. And that's his company. One day to be mine."

He's fucking demented. Miller Industries is already being shut down and disbanded as we speak. By the time Braydon gets out of prison, which our firm plans to fight tooth and nail to be never, he won't have anything. "So, you're also aware of the charges against Miller Industries. Thirty-five counts of first-degree murder. Twelve counts of attempted murder. Not to mention, violation of environmental law, corporate fraud, antitrust violations, bribery. Did I miss anything?" Justin begins.

Connor smiles at the jury and responds, but Justin cuts him off. "Oh, wait. I forgot obstruction of justice, racketeering, tax fraud. Mr. Connor, let me rephrase my question, what criminal offense didn't Miller Industries get prosecuted for?"

Connor's shit smile falters, but not before slapping the mask of the devil back on his face and aiming his evilness at me. "Maybe sexual assault. The things I got to do to one of my fellow female coworkers is probably frowned—"

"*You motherfucker!*" Kip's thunderous voice booms through the courtroom. Judge Foster slams down his gavel as Stacey stands, trying to get him to sit back down.

Connor laughs and starts licking his lips, enticing another round of expletives from Kip. "I'll fucking—"

"Order!" Judge Foster slams his gavel again. "Order! Sir, if you do not contain yourself, I will have you removed from this courtroom!"

I fight not to turn around. I can't bear what I'll see on Hannah's face. I need to stay focused. I hear Jim, who's also seated at the counsel table, shift, demanding in his fatherly tone for Kipley to shut it down. Before the trial, the family had a sit down. It was embedded in every single family member if they couldn't handle what they may hear, they should not be in the courtroom. Kipley lasted all of five damn minutes.

"Mr. West, please continue."

Stay focused. He has this. It's killing me not being up there. Justin continues. "Mr. Miller, what is your relationship with Matthews and Associates?"

Connor shrugs, keeping his cool. "I was hired as a first-year law associate."

"You were hired or you scammed your way into—"

"Objection!" their defense team calls out. "Leading. He answered the question."

Justin waves it off. "I'll rephrase. What level of expertise would you consider yourself in information security hacking—"

"Objection. Hearsay. My client has never—"

"He has a full confession on record," Justin points out, knowing it can't stand up in court.

"That was thrown out. It has no standing in this case."

Judge Foster slams on his gavel. "Mr. West, please get to the question."

"Mr. Connor, how long would it take to hack into a company system?" Before his lawyer has a chance to object, Connor replies.

"Under five minutes."

Got you. I mark that up as a point for us as the defense huffs, taking the floor.

"Mr. Miller, what was your relationship with Hannah Matthews?" the defense begins.

The hair on the back of my neck stands up. The defense attorney makes his way across the room and stands next to the jury, awaiting Connor's reply.

"She was my girlfriend."

"That's bullshit!" Kip goes off again, and the judge loses his patience.

"Security, I want that young man removed from my courtroom." Neither Jim nor I move to look behind us.

"All right. I'm going. Get your fucking hands off me." A few quick moments, and the door to the courtroom slams shut.

"Continue."

"Mr. Miller, how long were you and Miss Matthews intimate?"

"Quickly after she started. She became very interested in me and my side of the business. We spent a lot of time together. Before I knew it, she was throwing herself at—"

"Objection!" I fly out of my seat. "Relevancy. This doesn't have anything to do with—"

Jim grabs my bicep and tugs me back down.

"Mr. Dent, you are not the head counsel in this trial. I suggest you mind your place, or you, too, will be removed. Continue, counsel," Judge Foster reprehends me, and I sit, trying to slow my breathing.

"As I was saying, their relationship has everything to do with it, your honor. It's important the jury understands the persuasive relationship they had and how Miss Matthews conjured up the whole plan to—"

"Watch it," I growl back, shooting back up, slamming my hands on the table.

Judge Foster slams his gavel down. "Mr. Dent," he warns. Jim grabs my hand, and I sit back down.

The defense, wearing a snarky smile, continues. "Mr. Miller, can you explain the first time Miss Matthews approached you about the Miller case?"

Connor sits a bit straighter, his facial expression morphing into a sad puppy dog. "The first time she approached me was at lunch. It was the first time she asked me out."

Fucking liar. The first time they went to lunch. It was him.

"And can you tell the jury what you two talked about?"

He turns to the jury. "She asked me to help her destroy files for the Miller case."

"Can you please state your name for the record?"

"Hannah Constance Matthews." Hannah's focus is directly on the defense as she replies, and I find solace in knowing the middle name is meant for me. A silent understanding telling me she's okay.

The defense rounds his table and strolls over to the jury. "And, Miss Matthews, can you tell the jury your relationship to Matthews and Associates?"

Her smile is kind and genuine when her eyes find her father's. "It's my dad's law firm. He built it from the ground up."

"And you were employed there only because your daddy own—"

"Objection. Badgering."

The defense attorney puts his hand out before the judge speaks. "I'll rephrase. You were also an employee, correct?"

"I was. I was hired as a paralegal. I don't have my actual law degree yet, so I wasn't able to—"

"Thank you, Miss Matthews. Being a paralegal, would that give you access to confidential files? Security access to private files, let's say?"

Hannah nods. "Yes, it was part of my job to type and file everything my boss worked on."

"So, it's possible if you were working on a case, let's say Miller Industries, you could tamper with files if you wanted to?"

Hannah keeps her composure when responding. "I could. But I—"

"And let's say if you were upset over something, maybe rejected advances, you could see yourself tampering—"

"Objection!" Justin throws his hand in the air. "Leading!"

That son of a bitch. I'm fuming. How dare he turn this around, making Hannah look like the bad guy. Even Jim beside me is buzzing with fury.

Judge Foster speaks. "Sustained. Get to the question, counsel."

"Miss Matthews, did you make sexual advances toward Mr. Miller in order to coerce him to kill Clara Hill?"

"And then what did you do when Mrs. Hill opened the door?"

Connor's defense team is working relentlessly to suggest Hannah killed Clara Hill. They're holding a convincing testimony, which is making me sick to my stomach. Until Connor takes the stand and blows their case out of the water.

"When she attempted to shut the door on me, I kicked it open and took a bat to her head."

There's an audible reaction from the jury. Even his lawyer's eyes pop at the wreckage of their now impending case. Connor sits on the stand with ease, his delusional mind uncomprehensive of his confession. He seems proud of his actions.

"What did you do then? Was Clara still conscious when you entered her home after assaulting—"

"Objection!"

"On what grounds? He claimed fault right on this stand." The defense team concedes. They smell the loss right then and there as we all witness his mental haze as if he's reliving that day and enjoying it.

"Sustained. Continue, counsel." Judge Foster pushes us to go on.

Justin nods. "What did you do once you entered the home?"

With no sense of mercy in his voice, he answers. "She begged me not to kill her. Cried for her son, what's his name again? Not that it matters..."

"And then what happened?" Justin asks.

Detail after horrifyingly sick detail. "She reached out for me, grabbing my leg. Got blood all over my pants, so I hit her again."

The hairs on my arms stand at his chilling response. His tone is void of emotion. "Did you kill her then—"

"Objection! Hearsay!" His defense wears a desperate expression, pleading with him to shut it down.

"I'll rephrase. Was Clara still alive after you hit her again?"

"Yeah, until I took the rosery beads she had wrapped around her finger and choked her with them."

"Miss Matthews, how are you holding up?" Justin asks the question I'm desperately needing to hear the answer to.

"I'm doing as well as can be expected."

He walks around the table, giving her his undivided attention. "Miss Matthews, it has to be hard to hear the allegations presented against you, a victim in all this, being put on the stand as an accused."

Hannah nods. "Lies hurt anyone on the other end of their sharpness. But I'm here today to tell the truth and let the jury decide."

My strong girl.

"And the judicial system was built on fairness. Today, we will prove that. Hannah, do you think you can replay some of your time held captive in Clara Hill's home—"

"Objection. Hearsay."

"Sustained."

"I can." She inhales a deep breath and begins. "I woke up tied to a bed, later to realize I was in Clara Hill's home…"

She goes over her experience, and my stomach threatens to expel my coffee, the only thing I've been able to get down today. I listen because I need to feel the reaction of the jury, but I wish I could shut my mind off. "…then I was able to run, but he caught me shortly after. That's when he stabbed me with the knife…" The next few minutes are in vivid detail. Out of the corner of my eye, I catch a sobbing Cheryl leave the courtroom.

"Did he try to help you after you begged?"

"No, he said he couldn't. His father was going to fix it all."

"His father being?"

"Benjamin Miller." She explains in further detail her short interaction with Benjamin, and I have to force myself to stay calm and not go find him in his jail cell and wrap my hands around his beady neck when she confesses the son of a bitch told his son to set her on fire. "And then what happened?" Justin questions, and Hannah breaks, a small sob escaping her beautiful lips. "Please, Miss Matthews, take your time. Do you need a break?"

God, I want to get up and wrap my arms around her. Why did I agree to this? I should have never put her through this.

"No, I'm okay." She wipes away a stray tear before answering. "Braydon…or Connor, disappeared out the back. I was bleeding so bad, I could barely stay conscious, let alone run for my life. But I knew if I didn't try to escape, I was going to die." She weeps softly, then pauses to take a moment to compose herself. "When I finally found the strength, I got up and made my way to the door, but it was too late. He returned and threw me into the table, I believe. I hit my head hard and started going in and out of consciousness.

I remember waking up and smelling the gasoline. He was soaking the house. I begged and pleaded with him, but he wouldn't stop. He said I knew too much. The last thing I remember is the flick of his lighter."

"The defense rests, your honor."

I'm tired. Jim's tired. Our whole damn team is tired. It's been seven hours of going back and forth, jugular for jugular. The defense has finished their closing arguments. The rest of Connor's testimonies have me in a state of sickness and rage.

"*She coerced me to delete the files. She hated Mr. Dent for turning her down, so she wanted to get revenge.*"

Connor was the one on trial, but those wolves fed her to the jury like she was at fault.

"*She was in love with me. We were going to have a future until he ruined it.*"

The defense fought hard to make Hannah out to be the monster.

"*A lover scorned, out for revenge. What better way than with the privilege of daddy's company? Sink her claws into a properly raised boy, deprived of love, and enjoying the attention of this attractive, promiscuous girl.*"

"*No evidence shows Connor set the fire. Who's to say Miss Matthews didn't set it and her self-inflicted injuries refrained her from fleeing the house? Connor was still in the house. He wanted to help Hannah, but was brutally attacked before he was able to do so.*"

"*He ran out of fear. And when he came to see if Hannah was okay at the hospital, he knew he had to sneak in or they wouldn't let him see with his own eyes. That's when he was brutally attacked for the second time.*"

It only took their own witness to alter her back into the person she was: the victim.

"*Clara got what was coming to her.*"

"I thought I killed her, sure as hell didn't expect her to show up in court today..."

The jury wraps up, and we're notified of the quick verdict. We've been summoned back into the courtroom for deliberation. Everyone is silent as we make our way from the cafeteria, Hannah tucked to my side. She's been quiet since the break. It's driving me mad not to drill her on what's going on in her head, but now isn't the time. I stall while Jim and Cheryl, then Kip and Stacey, enter the courtroom. Blocking the entrance, I turn around, needing just a bit of reassurance.

"You sure you want to sit in on this?"

She nods, unable to hide the tiredness in her eyes. "I'm fine."

She's not. I sense it in the way her shoulders slightly slump. "Listen, we're all running on a low battery here, but soon it will be over, and I'm going to take you home. Run us a bath. Then, if you ask nicely, we can watch all my old high school football games since I know you love them so much." That earns the smile I've been craving all day.

"I'll accept your offer, but only if I get to wear nothing but your hoodie. It's kinda a thing for me when I super fan over you. Amongst other things I do." Resilient. Sexy. Mine.

"Deal," I reply as Jim calls for us to take our seats.

I escort Hannah down the center and stop at the aisle directly behind my seat as the jurors make their way back to their own. I've had wins under my belt in the courtroom, and I've had losses. Today is not about winning or losing, because I know how this unfolds. It's about justice, and for all the innocent lives lost. It's about Hannah finding peace and allowing everyone affected to move on.

Benjamin Miller used his son as a pawn to do his dirty bidding. He may have been a victim too in some way, but he chose his path. He chose, on his own, to kidnap Hannah and torment her. He chose to go against the law when he walked into that hospital determined to finish what he started.

Before I take my own seat, something or someone grabs my attention. My eyes focus and lock on Gregory Hill seated in a wheelchair at the back of the courtroom. A sudden onset of guilt shoots through me at the thought of him having to hear Connor's testimony about his mother. Our eyes lock, and we share a silent moment.

"All rise," the bailiff calls, and Judge Foster enters the courtroom. "You may be seated." I break our contact and stand alongside Jim. Judge Foster takes his seat. "I have been notified the jury has reached a verdict." He peers at the row of jurors.

"We have, your honor." A woman sitting at the end stands, handing the bailiff a thick piece of paper. He walks it over to the judge, who takes it and reads the ruling. "Proceed with your findings."

Silence lingers in the air as the woman unfolds a piece of paper holding Connor Miller's fate. My eyes flicker to the defense table, Connor's expression cool and collected. He's so lost in his head, he thinks he's getting away with this. My head buzzes with anticipation while we wait, the woman taking her damn time. I see cases all the time. Her expression. Fuck no. *He's actually going to get away with this.* My lips form a rigid grimace as hers open and begin to speak.

"We the jury, find the defendant guilty of the charge of kidnapping, attempted murder, and murder in the first degree. Guilty of conspiracy to commit fraud, including false claims of identity, corporate fraud, and bribery."

My heart stops for a moment when the first round of *guilty* praises my ears. Shit, I actually thought...

My fist clenches tight. I turn to Jim as we embrace. I slap him on the back and reach over, heartily shaking Justin's hand. "Good work."

Justin nods. "Thank you, Mr. Dent. Coming from you, that's quite a compliment."

I heave a sigh of relief, finally feeling the weight of this nightmare start to dissipate. We can finally put this behind us and move on. There's so damn much I want to do with Hannah, experience with her. She needs time to heal, but one day, I'll put a ring on her finger and make her completely mine. The only thing I want now is to get her home and naked. The thought of having her all to myself stirs a need in me so strong, I may throw her over my shoulder and run out of here.

A deafening uproar of chaos breaks out.

A gunshot blasts through the courtroom.

My heart seizes as the world around me slows. Like molasses, I fight my body to shift toward Hannah. Our eyes collide like magnets, and I hold her stare as time speeds up. I jump into action, throwing my body over the barrier between us and tackle her to the ground. My hands are quick, brushing up and down her quivering body. The courtroom erupts into panic, screaming wails coming from the front of the room. I pull up, searching her raw, tear-filled eyes.

"I'm fine. It wasn't me."

Thank Christ. I pull her off the ground, my attention to the back of the courtroom where two officers restrain Gregory Hill to his wheelchair. My eyes wide, I cock my head to the defense table. Connor Miller lays across the table, a bullet lodged between his dead eyes.

CHAPTER THIRTY-FIVE

Levi

Two weeks later...

"Stop! I swear to God, I'll give you another whooping if you throw me in!" Hannah squeals, dodging Chase's attempt to toss her in the pool.

"For the record, I hardly call that a whooping. You're a little girl. I'm a man," Chase argues, attempting another lunge and missing.

Kipley, who's sitting next to me outside on the lounge chair of his parents' pool, laughs, shaking his head. "Chase really has a death wish today I see."

If he gets my girl in that water, he's as good as dead. "You'd think he'd learn his lesson, since he's still limping from their last go-around." We both bust out laughing. The day had finally come for Hannah to get her revenge on Chase and the years of torment he's bestowed on her. Ever since Hannah, in her amazing, fierce way, put Chase in his place, their relationship has been quite entertaining. Him still trying to poke. Her always getting the upper hand—or upper cut, as the case may be.

We watch as Hannah jumps over a float, her smile radiating as bright as the summer day. Her cheeks are already flushed from the heat, and I shake my head, knowing how horrible she is about putting on enough sun block. She runs past Ben, bends down to pick up a noodle, and twists around. "Told you not to mess with me anymore. And for the last time, I'm not little." Then she whacks Chase in the face.

"*Ouch*." We both wince as Chase stumbles and loses his balance, falling into the pool.

Her vibrant laughter echoes across the pool, filling my soul with promise. Her hands grab at her belly, unashamed of the white scar that illuminates in the sun as she barrels over, fat tears racing down her sun-kissed cheeks. I love seeing her happy and carefree again.

Chase pops back up from under the water and whips his head around like a wet dog, throwing his hair out of his face. "Jesus, woman!"

Hannah's eyes shine with triumph. With her hands on her hips, she continues in short gasps of unstoppable giggles. Her eyes finally search out mine, and she steals my breath.

"How's she doin'?"

Kip's voice grabs my attention, and I unwillingly pull my eyes away from hers. I had imagined many different scenarios on how Kip would learn about Hannah and I. Each one resulted in him kicking my ass, but they all ended with uncertainty of where it would leave our friendship. Kip's not just my best friend, he's my brother, my family. And even though it did end with him cleaning the floor with me, what followed was nothing I could fathom.

It was shortly after Hannah had been released from the hospital. We'd been keeping a low profile, mainly because I was too obsessed with monitoring her every emotion. I needed her to know I was there for her. Kip had come by asking to speak to me privately. After swearing to Hannah I'd be alive when she got back, she left and let us be. That's when he handed me the worn, rolled up piece of paper, throwing me back to when we were twelve.

"*Do you think my dad will come for me here?*"

Kip kicks off his muddy shoes and tosses his jacket on the makeshift hook of their tree house. "No way. No one knows about this place. Plus, if he shows up, Pops will tell him to get lost."

I wish that was true. "I never want to go home. I hate him."

Kip lights the candle, bringing a dim glow into the small fort, and hands me a Hostess Twinkie from the stash of junk food he keeps hidden up here. "Maybe you don't. Mom and Pops love you just as much as Han and I. We can ask them to adopt you. You can share my room. I have plenty of clothes."

He makes it all sound so easy. So promising. But I know he'll come for me. Needing a punching bag or a servant to fetch his addictions. He won't let me be happy. "Hey, don't worry. He's not going to hurt you anymore. You're family, and we don't let family down."

"I'm not your real family."

He pauses for a second in thought, then grabs a notebook off the desk and sits crisscross in front of me. "You are to me. You'll always be my brother. Whether we share the same parents or not." He opens the notebook and begins writing.

"What are you doing?" I lean forward, trying to read his words, but he doesn't reply until he's done. Lifting his head, he hands it to me. "What is this?"

"It's a legal document between us. No matter what, this letter states we are brothers. Through thick and thin, we will always be there for each other." He grabs it from me, draws out two lines, and signs his name to one. "Sign." I fill the other line with my scribbled name. "Now, we seal our bond with blood."

"What!"

"Yeah! I saw it in a movie. Here." He unsnaps the safety pin from his backpack and pierces the top of his finger, drawing a drop of blood. "Just like this." He presses his finger onto the paper, placing a red fingerprint next to his signature. "Now, your turn."

I take the safety pin and prick my finger, squeezing until a drop of blood surfaces. I take the piece of paper and press my finger next to my name.

"There. No one can ever tell us we're not brothers. No matter what, as long as we have this seal of blood, we are. We will always be there for each other. Promise?" *I fight to hide the emotions surfacing.*

No one has ever cared about me like this. I suck in a deep breath and nod, unable to find my voice. "Cool! Let's look at the comic—"

"Boys!"

"Crap. Dinner's ready. Race you. Last one to finish their Twinkie has to sit next to my sister at dinner."

I couldn't believe he kept it. A makeshift document swearing us as brothers. He told me he meant what he said that day. Through thick and thin. The lies hurt. But knowing his sister was with someone who would do anything to protect her, he wouldn't want it any other way. When Hannah returned, she found us on the couch like any other day watching sports, talking stats. She never questioned anything or pointed out how my eyes were red-rimmed, and didn't press on the emotional moment between her brother and I.

Bringing my thoughts back to the present, my gaze returns to Hannah, her happiness the center of my world. She laughs at something Ben says, sticking her tongue out at Chase. I finally answer him. "She's good. Better. Happy. I'm not sure her battle is over, but she's a fighter. And I'll be right next to her the whole way, helping slay her demons."

We sit in silence for a bit before he speaks again. "Heard Pop offered you partner."

I nod. "He did."

A few seconds pass. "Heard you also turned it down."

I nod again. "I did." I can't take my eyes off my girl. A slow, mischievous smile spreads across her face as Ben says something, then throws himself out of his chair and dives into the pool after Chase. "I would love nothing more than to work side by side with your dad, but the long hours…it's not where I need to focus my time right now. She needs me. I need her. My decision was an easy one. It was the right one."

Jim's response made it even easier.

"I'm sad to know you're turning it down, but I've never been prouder of you, son."

His response shocks me. He's coached me for the position since the day I decided to become a lawyer, and then when the time comes, I turn it down. "You're not disappointed?"

Jim laughs, surprising me even more. "Disappointed? Well, of course I am. You're the best. This firm would thrive with you in the seat. But I'm more thankful to call you my son. A man who'll take my place one day as the most important man in my daughter's life. I entrust you to keep her safe. And knowing that's where your heart is, I couldn't be prouder of you. You've always been a son to me. You don't have to share the same blood as my children to be just as significant. You've been a part of this family since the day Kipley brought you home. And I have a feeling one day you'll make my little girl one happy bride. Be her strength. Her comfort. Help guide her just as I would, because she is miraculous and the most extraordinary thing in my life."

The Matthews family was hitting me left and right with such love, it was hard to keep my emotions in check. Even Cheryl got me one day, cornering me with hugs and tears, thanking me. But she didn't need to thank me. I'd give my life for her daughter's—always.

Hannah skips around the pool, stopping in front of us, her cute little body shielding us from the high sun. "What are you two up to, looking so serious?"

Kip snorts. "We're on the edge of our seats, waiting to see if Chase makes it out of that pool alive."

Hannah shrugs her shoulders. "I don't have it in me right now to make his life hell. Not sure about Ben, though. Chase told him his new girlfriend looks like his mom. Didn't take well to that." She looks at me and winks. "I'm going to go to the bathroom real quick. If Ben doesn't drown him, maybe I'll make an attempt to finish the job." With that, she walks off toward the house before disappearing inside.

"Dude...can you not look at my sister like that when I'm around?"

That gets a good laugh out of me. I shake my head. "Sorry, no can do. Better get used to it."

A gush of water shoots from the pool as Chase jumps out, shaking off in front of us. "Dude, you two look like a bunch of girls. What, are you two pussy-whipped jerk-offs sharing recipes and shit? Get in the water. Let's play a game of volleyball."

Kipley gets up and dives into the pool.

"I'm gonna grab some beers. Anyone want anything?"

"Yeah, grab the tequila. Losers drink. Wait...winners drink. Just grab the booze. And hurry. We gotta get Kip drunk before his mom-wife shows up and puts the kibosh on all the fun—*shit*, I swear women make you all violent." Even I hold my stomach feeling that hit Chase just took from Kip as I laugh it off and head inside to search for my girl.

CHAPTER THIRTY-SIX

Hannah

"Shoot," I grumble, leaning closer to the mirror, pressing my fingers to my rosy cheeks. I swear, no matter how much lotion I apply, the sun always wins. I assess the rest of me, noticing my chest is beet red, along with my thighs. My eyes scan down my stomach. Twisting to my side, I take in my red shoulders. When I scan down my back, I notice my two-inch scar, the sun accentuating the whiteness of the faint stitches.

You know too much.

You know too much.

I shake my head, ripping my eyes away from the permanent scar, and wash my hands, wishing I could as easily wash away the memory. I'm better. I'm getting better. He can't hurt me anymore. Physically at least. Some days, I still feel as if he's stabbing me all over again in my mind.

I found closure during the trial, but it also left me with new demons, one being uncertainty. How had I been so naive? Were they right? *Had* I been leading Braydon…*Connor* on? They painted me to be this awful person. And maybe I was. I hold the weight of Clara's death on my shoulders. A secret I can't share. My family…Levi…they'll try to convince me it's not my fault, but it is. She would still be alive if I hadn't been so eager to prove my credibility. I lie to my family and Levi once a week. My counseling sessions take as long as they do because I secretly visit

Clara's grave. I make sure she knows what an impact she's made on her town. I tell her how sorry I am she's not here with us and keep her updated on her son, even though I'm lying. His life is forever ruined. Not only will he never be able to walk again, he will spend the next few years in a juvenile center until he's old enough to be transferred to an adult facility. After what he's been through, he doesn't deserve that life, but he accepted his fate the second he entered the courtroom with a manmade weapon, untraceable by metal detectors, with intent to kill Connor Miller.

Levi has changed my life in so many ways, I've started to lose count. His dedication is something I don't or may never know how to truly thank him for. This can't be easy. My nightmares aren't easy. A lot of my worry stems from him giving up on me. How is someone as messed up as me what anyone signs up for? But for some reason and blessings above, he loves me. His heart is so big, I don't know how to repay his affection. But it's something I need. Crave. It was the truth when I confessed he was my medicine. Every single day that goes by, I feel better, smile a little more, and feel closer to being my old self. I'm grateful to him.

My therapist says stuff like this takes time. It's been four months. I wish my scars would fade along with the memories. Levi says it's a war wound that shows how strong I am. Sometimes I wish I could tell him how weak I really am. Times when he's at work and I cry, worry, panic. But in every low moment, there's a high. Levi's selfless love. My family. The baby who's about to arrive soon. Connor took something from me that day. He stole a part of that carefree piece of me, and I hate him for that. But I'll grow to be a stronger person. That, I promise everyone.

In the meantime, I'm finding me again. I've decided not to go back to work at Matthews and Associates. Connor tainted that dream for me. Maybe that will change. But for now, I've set bigger aspirations for myself. I applied to law school. I want to be able to fight for victims like me who need a voice. Stacey's kept me busy helping with baby shower planning, and I'm loving every minute of it, even though I have to stomach Rebecca.

I dry my hands and leave the bathroom, passing my old room. I still can't believe Levi and I *live* together. One of my many childhood fantasies was us playing house in a cute pink house with a picket fence made of candy canes and flowers blooming cotton candy. Our nights would consist of us on our swing, made to fit only us and we would swing back and forth as we ate our sugared flowers. Geez, my poor little self would just die over in sugar heaven to know where her older self would end up. No cotton candy flowers, but the dessert Levi serves is way better.

For old time's sake, I take a peek in my room. Laughing at some of the missing items on the wall, one being my old-school boy band poster Levi stole, which still hangs up in his place—*our place*. I tried telling him he could take it down, but he refused. He was so passionate about keeping it up, it was actually too cute. So, it stayed. It wasn't until Chase took a shot at it that I finally put my foot down, defending the poster *and* my man.

"Jesus, dude, tell me I've walked into the wrong place."

"No can do, man. Chicks dig boy band posters. You should take a tip out of my book for once." I hear Levi as he pops open the fridge, *two beer bottles clanking together. Levi's having the boys over for guys' night. I'm running late to meet with Stacey, and I bet he thinks I'm already gone since he's being typical Chase, running his mouth.*

"Dude, I'm about to put a missing sign for your balls on a milk carton."

"I think it's kinda cute. Levi gets to stare at his competition," Kipley says, knowing how much I was in love with them as a kid.

Chase's laugh is obnoxious, bouncing off the walls, and I think I hear a back slap. *"Oh, she brought her masturbation poster over. Wow, didn't know you weren't doing it for—shit!"*

"Mention one more time anything about my sister and that shit, and I'll punch you harder."

"Jesus, I wasn't saying it as a bad thing. Wouldn't mind watching

little Hannah—fuck! What's gotten into you two! Violence is not the answer, man!"

I grab my purse and leave the bedroom. When I round the corner, Chase's eyes bug out at the sight of me. "Oh shit."

"Yeah, oh shit is right." The room gets silent as I sashay right up to Chase, his mouth slowly dropping open.

"Hey, uh…Han. Didn't realize you were here. Great seeing you. New shirt? Lovely color." Kipley chokes out a laugh, while Levi tries to hide his smirk. They all knew this moment was coming. "For real, why the crazy eye? Please don't kill me. Levi, help, man."

"No way. You're on your own here," Levi says, putting his hands up. His smirk makes it hard to keep a straight face.

"For real? You're going to let her…wait, what are you going to do to me? Jesus, you scare me. Don't hurt me." He covers his face just as I make it to him.

"Chase, I've spent half my life taking your shit. Not. Any. More." With each word, I jab him in the chest. With each flinch comes another burst of laughter from my brother. "Today, it stops." I hit him with another jab. "No more Hannah Banana." Jab. "No more calling me little." Jab. "No more poking fun at anything I wear, eat, enjoy—and that includes my boy band poster. I know for a fact you went to that concert with Tricia Beckett in college where you screamed like a little girl, singing every single lyric."

His mouth hits the ground. "How did you—?"

"Guess it pays to be annoying and nosey. Should I mention the shirt you—"

"Okay, you win!"

"Good!" I smile. "Now, if you behave, I'll keep that little tidbit to myself. Amongst all the other things my little ears have heard over the years." A snicker falls off Levi's lips, and I can't contain my own humor. But then I do something that surprises everyone. I reach out and hug him. Chase becomes deathly still in my embrace. A few moments pass, and he relaxes, putting his arms around me, returning the gesture. "Thank you for saving him," I whisper, resting my head against his chest.

That's when he hugs me tighter. "*Nah, I was just doing my broth-erly duty. I think it's you who truly saved him.*"

I smile at the memory. Chase's and my relationship took a complete turn that day. He still pokes fun, and I still threaten, but there's a new understanding between us—appreciation and respect.

I walk over to my dresser, opening the second drawer. Behind some old nightgowns, I stretch my hand and reach for the hidden notebook. Sentiment hits me as I open the worn cover, flipping through years of my childhood doodles. Man, did I master the heart shape at a young age. *Hannah Constance Dent*—

"Hope you're not thinking about moving back in here and leaving me."

My hands fly up, slamming the notebook closed. I twist to see Levi standing in the doorway, leaning against the frame. "Shit, sorry, I didn't mean to scare you."

"Oh no, you didn't…just caught me off guard." He pushes off the wall and enters my room. Panic shoots through me, and I'm not sure what to do with the notebook. "I was just…." Ugh, I know I'm caught. "I was just looking at my old notebook of 'I love Levi' drawings." He comes up behind me, wrapping his arm around my waist, and leans his head over my shoulder.

"Well, come on, show me." His warm breath skates against my ear. I take a large breath, pushing down the embarrassment. Closing my eyes, I flip the page open. I keep them shut, unsure which page it opens to, knowing every single one is a bit overkill on the crush status. "Wow. You really nailed the whole heart thing. Is that us kissing?"

Gah! I shut it and turn in his arms. "This was a long time ago. I was a kid."

"So, what are you saying? You don't double heart me now?" Ugh…why didn't I throw this away?

"Yes…I mean, no. I mean…yes! I still double heart you. Probably add another heart. It's just embarrassing, okay?"

His lips curl into a smile that melts me. "I think we look cute kissing. And if you care to know, I double heart you too." I feel his smile when his lips touch mine, basking in the softness of his mouth as he takes his time kissing me and parting my mouth so our tongues can dance in a slow rhythm against one another. This is the moment I live for. The reason why I fight. Why I refuse to give into the dark path Connor Miller tried to send me down. When our breathing becomes labored, he pulls away, his eyes mirroring mine. Happy. Content. Perfect.

"Come on. Let's go whip Chase's ass in volleyball so we can leave. You've been torturing me in this bathing suit. I really need to take you home and get you out of it."

I take his hand, and we walk side by side through the house, until he's opening the sliding glass door for me. As we exit into the backyard, I spot Stacey.

"Hey!" I boast, excited to see her. Levi releases my hand, and I reach out and give her a hug, trying to work around her growing belly. "How are you and my little niece or nephew feeling?" I pull away.

"Today's a good day. No sickness or food cravings, so Kip's happy. He gets to chill without running all over town. There's this diamond in the rough Chinese place across town. It's become a staple in my and the baby's appetite—"

"Get *out*! I didn't know you were going to be here!" That voice. My eyes roll so far in the back of my head, I hope Levi is still standing behind me to catch them. I let Stacey go, and turn back, seeing Rebecca licking her lips at my man. "It's been *too* long." She goes in for a hug, and I've never loved Levi more when he dodges it.

"Oh hell no." He jumps to the side.

Her eyes widen in confusion, then they lock on me. "Oh, you two are *still* a thing? Wow, thought that was just the whole pity thing."

Okay. That's it!

I take a step, ready to pummel her, when Stacey reaches for my shoulder, stopping me. "Actually, Han. I got this." Stacey moves me to her side and takes center stage. "You know what, Rebecca? I've had enough of you and your tacky insults to my sister. Hannah is the nicest, most considerate person I've ever known. And Levi here is one lucky man to have her. And if you cannot show an ounce of respect, then you need to leave."

Rebecca may look shocked. No one's sure since her face is filled with so much Botox, it's stuck in the same position. "Stace, are you serious? It was just a joke. I mean, come on, no one thought they would last—"

"That's it!" Stacey's raised voice makes us all jump. "I've had enough! I've put up with your stuck-up attitude, your rude comments about every single person you come in contact with, and I've even sucked it up and allowed you to take part in my shower, which for the record, I do *not* need my lips done for..."

"No she didn't," Kip hisses.

"...but I'm done. I won't stand here another second and listen to you say another hurtful thing about my family."

Rebecca clicks her tongue, stunned at the way Stacey's talking to her. "Oh em gee, Stace. What's your problem? It was just a suggestion. You're seriously not going to take her side over mine, are you?"

"Yes," four male voices reply for her. She gasps, her mouth hanging open, staring down each and every guy. Flipping her hair, she goes back to addressing Stacey. "Girl, it's fine. Let's get out of here. I'm actually seeing this great guy who owns an Italian place down the way, Bill's Pub. We can—"

"Did you just say *Bill's*?" Stacey's eyes pop wide open.

"She just said Bill's," Kipley confirms.

"I knew there was a reason why I never liked your plastic ass," Chase chimes in.

"Get out."

"What?" Rebecca deadpans.

"I knew I was finally done with you the second you dared walk into my family's home and insult my sister for the last time. But you just confirmed it the second you mentioned Bill's. Everyone knows Savino's is the best. Get. Out."

Rebecca struggles, but manages to compose herself enough to whip around and storm off.

"Don't let the door hit you in the ass on the way out!" Ben yells.

We all stare, until we hear the swift slam of the front door. "Well, I think that went well." Stacey is the first to speak. A little shell-shocked myself, I turn and stare at her, making sure she's okay.

"I'm sorry, you didn't have to—"

"I did. I should have done that a long time ago." She eliminates the few feet separating us and brings me into her arms. Being difficult with the basketball in her belly, I lean forward, wrapping my arms around her. "I'm sorry for never sticking up for you in the past. I'm a horrible sister-in-law. I hope you can forgive me."

I squeeze her tighter. "You don't owe me anything, but thank you."

We stay like that for some time before Chase, being Chase, ruins the moment. "This would be a lot cooler if you two didn't have your tops on—*shit!*"

EPILOGUE

Hannah
Two months later…

Go, go, go…

I'm running so fast, I'm about to trip over my own two feet. The weather today is fierce as the angry rain pours down in thick drops, pelleting my face. The wind adding to the ferocity flips my umbrella inside out. I jump over a puddle as I wrestle with the wires, snapping it back in place.

When I was a kid, I loved the rain. I would sit outside during storms every chance I got and look up at the millions of raindrops, trying to count them as they cascaded from the sky. My mother would chase after me, dragging me into the house, claiming I would get sick being so careless. One time, she threatened to ground me until I was well into my eighties if I went back outside, so I locked myself in my room and opened my bedroom window, sticking my head out as far as I could to catch the raindrops on my tongue. Of course, I stuck out a smidge too far and fell out of my window. Thankfully, I landed on the awning, leaving less of a drop before I bounced off, but still managed to break my arm.

Every time it rains, I think of that memory. How distraught my mom was. My brother's "You never listen" gripes. The book I found lying on my bed one day a few weeks later, since I was indeed grounded 'til eternity and stuck in the house. A book. *Fun*

Rain Facts for Kids. I didn't know why it was there or who put it there, but I sat down, and before I knew it, I had consumed the entire two hundred pages. I spent the next two days walking around my house telling everyone simple rain facts. *Did you know rain has a smell? The wettest place in the world is a state in India. Did you know raindrops don't actually fall in the shape of a teardrop?* Everyone wanted to murder me.

But that's not what I remember the most. It was one day when Kip and Levi came home from school, racing past everyone to go do what they did in their top-secret treehouse. It happened so fast, I may have been the only one to hear it, but as Levi passed me, he leaned in and said, "Did you know not all raindrops that fall from the sky reach the ground?" And just as fast, he was gone.

My world stopped. Time didn't tick for eons as I allowed his question to sink in.

It was him.

He gave me the book.

It's crazy how the past takes flight in your mind and a different vision appears as life takes a different course. Simple memories, like the book, remind me how life can be funny sometimes. I may have loved Levi Dent my whole life, but in a strange way, I think he loved me too. There was a shift in the universe the day Levi walked through our door. As if he was always meant to be with us. Be a part of our family. Be a part of my heart.

I continue to fight the rain as the thunder above rumbles across the sky, lightening illuminating the thick, dark clouds. I finally reach our building and toss my broken umbrella into the trash, finding cover inside the lobby. With each step, I soak the floor, sprinting to the elevators.

My heart beats like a heavy drum against the envelope inside my jacket pocket. With each floor that passes, worry sinks in. Uncertainty. The unknown. When it stops on our floor and opens, I take off running down the hallway until my key is pressing inside the lock and practically fall inside.

"Levi!" I shout his name. I struggle to peel off my jacket soaked to my skin. Tugging at my arms, I become free, pulling the envelope from the pocket. "Levi?" I call again, shoving my soaking wet hair out of my face. *Where is he? He should be home.* He said he was going to be home. I called him and told him I had something very important to talk about. But he said so did he.

Breathe, Hannah.

I'm in such a frenzy, I slip on something on the floor, thinking it's just the water dripping off me. "Shoot." I balance myself. When I look down, I realize it's not water. "*Shoot.*" My eyes slowly lift up, following the trail of rose pedals, until my eyes find two feet. I gaze up and up, until they connect with Levi, who's leaning against the wall.

"Did you know not all raindrops are made of water?" he speaks first.

My heart stops. The way he casually rests against the wall, his strong arms crossed over his built chest, the way his hair has grown out some, brushed back in perfect, full dark waves. A hurricane of emotions strike me. I'm not sure if it's the extra weight of water threatening to tip me over or the way his eyes pull me in.

"Did you know in a single minute, a billion tons of rain can fall to the Earth?" I reply with another fact, unsure what else to do or say. Neither of us move. We simply stand there, our hearts resonating for one another. The silence becomes too much for me, so I'm the first to speak. "I got my letter."

He still doesn't move, and it worries me. "And what did it say?"

I begin to chew on my lower lip. Afraid. Excited. My answer will be a game changer for us, and I'm not sure which way he's going to play. "I got accepted." The words are shaky off my tongue. I wait for his response. Not showing his cards, he slowly pushes off the wall and walks toward me. Each step causes a vibration down my body. I love this man with everything I have to give, and if he doesn't want this…

When he reaches me, I'm dizzy from holding my breath. The scent of his cologne offers me the safety net I need, but he doesn't touch me. He's so close, I bask in the warmth from his body, aching for his arms to comfort me. Answer me. Too much time passes. His silence becomes suffocating. His eyes lock me in this possessive hold, and another wave of dizziness hits me. The intensity of his stare worries me. "Please say something." There's anxiety in my soft tone, but still, he doesn't ease my worry. His cool detachment has me in a sheer panic. His hand lifts and brushes against my cheek. In a slow manner, he bends down. "Oh sweet Jesus, what are you…?"

"I told you, wherever you go, I go." He reaches for my hand. "I've wanted so much in life. But nothing compares to how much I want you. How it feels to be so addicted to you, I know I'll never get enough. I love you. But there's no way to truly explain how deep that love runs. So, I'll say this again and again, until those worried eyes fade away. Where you go, I go." He stops to retrieve something in his pocket. Pulling it out, my eyes take note, my face not wide enough for how big my smile is. "I know you're still not ready. We have so much more to take on before I make you Mrs. Dent, but for now, I want to make you a promise. This is it. This is us. Only us. My life starts and ends with you. So, what happens next, we do it together. Understand?"

Tears rain down my face as I stare into the eyes of a man put on this universe for me. To love me. To make me whole. His eyes shine with promise, and as I search into the windows of his soul, I see our future. The one even my seven-year-old self couldn't have dreamed of. "So, you're really willing to pack up and move? Leave everyone we love just so I can go to law school?"

"I'd leave it all in a heartbeat, as long as I have you."

"Your job? My dad—"

"I'll land a job anywhere we go. I'm resilient. Your father taught me how to be that."

"What about the condo?"

"We'll rent it, sell it, or leave it open for when we come home to visit."

Oh my god, my heart is racing. These talks. We've had them a million times. They all seemed much easier when it was just talks. But this is real. I can't tell if I'm starting to sweat from nerves or if it's being soaked from the rain. "Are you sure?"

"I have never been more sure. Lead the way."

A fresh round of tears soak my cheeks. I can't fight the sob that erupts from my throat. Levi stands, bringing me into his arms and holding me close as I release a storm of emotions. Fear, relief…it all comes pouring out. Once my crying subsides, I pull away and focus again on the item in his hand. "Why do you have your high school championship ring?" I ask, hoping beyond hope he doesn't say what I think he's going to say.

Too bad the grin he wears confirms he is. Humor swims in his gaze. "I read once that a girl, long, long ago, had this fantasy that her one-day dreamboat boyfriend, who sounded really hot, would take his fancy football ring, offer it to her as a promise ring for their future, and they would ride off into the sunset on his ten speed."

Why did I not throw that damn notebook away!?

"This does not sound familiar whatsoever."

"Hmmm…." He pulls away just enough to reach for my hand and slide his football ring onto my index finger. "Are you sure? How about the part where they live happily ever after in her brother's tree house and her mom makes them peanut butter sandwiches so they have more time to talk and—"

"Oh, enough of this. That notebook needs to die."

Levi's laughter brings life to my heart. I can't help but smile as I roll my eyes. "Never." He plants his lips against mine and offers me a kiss that has nothing on my childhood imagination.

When we finally break apart, he keeps his arms secured around me. "You know, there's a page in there about your high school jacket," I say, lifting up my finger to admire his high school class ring.

"Oh, I know. The flowers are a path to our bedroom where it's laying out for you to wear—with nothing else. I'm thinking a little high school role-playing is in order."

"You have a deal. But only if your high school tapes are playing in the background. You know how I get a little freaky when you shout plays." His smile nearly knocks the wind out of me, just like all things Levi Dent.

"Together, babe, there is nothing we can't achieve." And with that double meaning, I'm up over his shoulder, being carried down the hallway to my very own happily ever after.

THE END

MORE FROM
J.D. HOLLYFIELD

Love Not Included Series
Life in a Rut, Love not Included
Life Next Door
My So Called Life
Life as We Know It

Standalones
Faking It
Love Broken
Sundays are for Hangovers
Conheartists
Lake Redstone

Paranormal/Fantasy
Sinful Instincts
Unlocking Adeline

#HotCom Series
Passing Peter Parker
Creed's Expectations
Exquisite Taste

2 Lovers Series
Text 2 Lovers
Hate 2 Lovers
Thieves 2 Lovers

Four Father Series
Blackstone

Four Sons Series
Hayden

ABOUT THE AUTHOR

J.D. Hollyfield is a creative designer by day and superhero by night. When she's not cooking, event planning, or spending time with her family, she's relaxing with her nose stuck in a book. With her love for romance, and her head full of book boyfriends, she was inspired to test her creative abilities and bring her own stories to life. Living in the Midwest, she's currently at work on blowing the minds of readers, with the additions of her new books and series, along with her charm, humor and HEA's.

J.D. Hollyfield dabbles in all genres, from romantic comedy, contemporary romance, historical romance, paranormal romance, fantasy and erotica! Want to know more! Follow her on all platforms!

Keep up to date on all things J.D. Hollyfield

Twitter: twitter.com/jdhollyfield

Author Page: authorjdhollyfield.com

Fan Page: www.facebook.com/authorjdhollyfield

Instagram: www.intsagram.com/authorjdhollyfield

Goodreads: www.goodreads.com/author/show/8127239.J_D_Hollyfield

Amazon: www.amazon.com/J.D.-Hollyfield/e/B00JF6U2NA

BookBub: www.bookbub.com/profile/j-d-hollyfield

ACKNOWLEDGEMENTS

It's not easy having to drink all the wine in the world and sit in front of a computer writing your heart out, drinking your liver off and crying like a buffoon because part of the job is being one with your characters. You truly are amazing and probably the prettiest person in all the land. Keep doing what you're doing.

Thanks to my husband who supports me, but also thinks I should spend less time on the computer and more time doing my own laundry.

Thanks for nothing to my toddler who made this book take forever to finish because he's so damn needy. Momma loves you.

Thanks to all my eyes and ears. Having a squad who has your back is the utmost important when creating a masterpiece. From betas, to proofers, to PA's to my dog, Jackson, who just gets me when I don't get myself, thank you. This success is not a solo mission. It comes with an entourage of awesome people who got my back. So, shout out to Amy Wiater, Ashley Cestra, Jenny Hanson, Amber Higbie, Gina Behrends, Molly Wittman, Melissa Shipe, Cindy Camp, Kristi Webster, Ella Stewart and anyone who I may have forgotten! I appreciate you all!

Thank you to Monica Black at Word Nerd Editing for helping bring this story to where it needed to be.

Thank you to All By Design for creating my amazing cover. A cover is the first representation of a story and she nailed it.

Thank you to my awesome reader group, Club JD. All your constant support for what I do warms my heart. I appreciate all the time you take in helping my stories come to life within this community.

Big thanks for Stacey at Champagne Formats for always making my stories look so amazing!

And most importantly every single reader and blogger! THANK YOU for all that you do. For supporting me, reading my stories, spreading the word. It's because of you that I get to continue in this business. And for that I am forever grateful.

Cheers. This big glass of wine is for you.

Made in the USA
Monee, IL
08 June 2020

32830903R00189